Say Hello
to Goodbye

SAY HELLO TO GOODBYE

sumaiyaahmedwrites@gmail.com

ISBN: 978-1-7397246-1-0

Cover Design by: Ashley Quick & Murphy Rae @ashley.ranae.art + @murphyrae_
Interior Formatting: Grandeur Luxe Shoppe

FIRST EDITION

To the ones who have the strength to walk from something that no longer serves them, even when it feels like it will break them: the universe will bring you back something so much more beautiful and dreamy. Every ending comes with a fresh start, full of possibilities and chances to make your life everything you want it to be.

Playlist

'tis the damn season – Taylor Swift

it's time to go – Taylor Swift

Say Hello to Goodbye – Shontelle

Never Getting Over You – Colbie Caillat

The Way I Loved You – Selena Gomez

Don't Wanna Be Torn – Hannah Montana

Cry – Kelly Clarkson

Last Kiss – Taylor Swift

Fix A Heart – Demi Lovato

Starts With Goodbye – Carrie Underwood

The One That Got Away – Katy Perry

This Town – Niall Horan

La Cura – Franco Battialo

O Holy Night – Mariah Carey

Last Christmas – Cascada

Silent Night – Taylor Swift

All I Want For Christmas is You – Mariah Carey

Santa Tell Me – Ariana Grande

It's Beginning to Look A Lot Like Christmas – Michael Buble

Baby It's Cold Outside – Idina Menzel + Michael Bublé

Dear Reader,

Thank you for picking up Say Hello to Goodbye – for picking up this Christmassy, wintery romance with the cutest fluff and the deepest angst. It's sweet, it's witty, it's emotional.

While Say Hello to Goodbye is a light-hearted, Christmas romance novella, with lots of hot chocolate, and the best movies to watch on those cold nights, it also does deal with themes of mental health.

Sabah is just stepping into the role of becoming a woman, and still navigating her life when everything feels scary and daunting. I hope you enjoy reading about the journey Sabah goes on this Christmas, all the movies, the songs, making delicious food and the sweetest romance.

Sumaiya Ahmed

xo

"We don't like change, we fear it. But we can't stop it from coming. We either adapt to change, or we get left behind. It hurts to grow. Anybody who tells you it doesn't is lying. But here's the truth: sometimes, the more things change, the more they stay the same. And sometimes, oh, sometimes, change is good. Sometimes, change is *everything*."

— *Grey's Anatomy, Meredith Grey*

PROLOGUE

Ten months ago

9th February 2020

SHE HAD LEFT BEFORE SHE FINALLY SPOKE THE words out loud. Before she told him she didn't want to be with him anymore. Enough was enough, and by the time she plucked up the courage to finally walk away, Sabah had reached her limit and realised she couldn't keep forgiving. She was giving everything she had, pouring out all of her love and her trust and her dreams until she was left empty, with nothing but slow boiling resentment.

As she stood in the doorway to the bathroom, her fingers playing with the hem of her t-shirt, she found herself, once again, wondering whether she was doing the right thing. But it was too late to take it back.

She said it. She told him she'd had enough. She told him she didn't want to be with him anymore. She told him she was too tired. She told him he was draining her. She told him she couldn't do this and she didn't want to keep trying. She didn't want to keep fighting for something that she didn't see a future in anymore. She didn't want to keep holding onto someone she was starting to hate more than she loved.

But she still loved him.

"Then why are you leaving me?"

His voice pierced her like a knife, a sharp twist in her heart, pulsing through her, hot and fiery. Sabah gasped softly, her head tilting back as she lifted her head to look up at him. He was so tall, more than a foot and two inches taller than her, and she always had to crane her neck to meet his eyes. She gripped the soft cotton material of her t-shirt in the palm of her hand, her nails leaving crescent moon indents in the soft skin, swallowing, trying to form the words strangling her throat.

She'd rehearsed everything she wanted to say in her head for the past three days, but the words had been coming to her for more than a month now. Each time she thought she was strong enough to walk away, to leave the first boy she ever loved, to realise that everyone else had been right from the very start, she sank into the comfort of familiarity, of love, of fear. She was scared. She didn't want to lose him. She loved him. But she was tired of putting up with his shit. She needed to put herself first.

"I told you," Sabah said, hating how her voice wavered. Her heart thundered in her chest and she swore that he could hear it. "I just can't do this anymore and I don't want to. I've had enough and I'm exhausted trying to give you every part of me. I need my own life that's not just you, all the time, every day."

"We've been happy." His eyes glistened with tears, a tremble to his words. His voice was quieter than she had ever heard it. "Haven't we?"

"I haven't been," she whispered. "Not for a long time."

CHAPTER ONE

Now

5th December 2020

PIZZA SOLVED EVERYTHING.

When it seemed like everything was going to fall to pieces and shatter like shards of glittering glass, Sabah turned to pizza for comfort. The soft, melted cheese, the tomato or barbecue base, the toppings always changing from pepperoni to chicken and mushrooms, with a whole load of veg and chillies, always, always satisfied her and kept her feeling whole when she was trying not to fall apart, the seams tearing and only being held together by a single thread. Having a stuffed crust, with thick and melted garlic cheese, was the crème de la crème of crusts. Over the last ten months, Sabah had probably eaten pizza once every two weeks, drowning her heartbreak in the hot pie dripping with the cheese pulling into a long stretch, tomato sauce seasoned with chilli flakes, pepper and smoked paprika, the toppings varying from veggie supreme to meat feast, to margherita, her eyes glued to her laptop screen as she watched *Friends* or *Modern Family* for the umpteenth time.

She had spent the last few months running from job to job, not even writing them all down on her CV because she knew how flaky it all looked. But she needed a change. Three months ago, she started going back to college, doing an intensive course in Health and Social Care. If she managed to get into uni, maybe she would choose to study Children's Nursing. At least she would be helping other people, even if she couldn't help herself. At least then her mum would finally be proud of her and her little brothers wouldn't be ashamed to call her their older sister, and maybe then Naveda wouldn't sigh every time she asked "how's it going at this job?", only to hear "I left there, I've got a new job at *this* place." Sabah didn't know what it was, but she kept getting bored and she couldn't stay in one place, do one thing anymore, without feeling the need to run, to leave, itching at her.

It was some kind of miracle that she had stuck to going to Lakeview Community College, the local college and sixth form that Sabrina had attended, built near the secondary school she'd also gone to. Sabah hadn't applied there, intentionally wanting a connection to Sabrina—in fact, she hadn't even *realised* it was the same place until she saw a picture of Sultana under the 'Class of

2019', above the 'Class of 2020', having achieved some of the best results at the entire school. The air had punched out of Sabah's lungs as she stared, like she couldn't breathe, and feeling the ache of missing her friend and cousin.

In some ways, it didn't make sense that the students who had left the sixth form in 2019 were still being celebrated . . . but maybe since they'd gone onto the noble and draining path of medicine; it was something to be proud of. Now on a Saturday afternoon, as Sabah stood outside the entry way to *Fairly Odd Pizzas*, a place she hadn't even been in since everything ended with Jake, she wondered whether this was a good idea.

Everything had exploded and burned to ash. Nothing could be rebuilt after the cruel words were thrown like darts of fire, carelessly and painfully.

She watched, through the glass door, the winter sun gleaming and bouncing off the glass, as Grayson walked over to a table and placed a wooden serving plate with a fifteen-inch pizza down at the centre, a smile on his face. He spoke a little to the couple sitting there, near to the large arching windows slanting the sunlight through into the pizzeria. Sabah took in a sharp breath and slowly pushed open the door, her eyes flicking from Grayson to the group of people she always had seen sitting there. They were laughing about something, the guy with the dark buzz cut and a diamond earring in his left lobe animatedly saying something to the boy with the long brown hair pulled into a bun at the back of his head, a shadow of stubble shadowing his jaw, a smile curving his mouth into something like sunshine. Beside him, the girl that Sabah always had seen with them sat, one of her legs pulled up to her chest, flipping through a copy of *Ugly Love*. Opposite her was a blonde boy, all gorgeous and light, his piercing blue eyes glancing over at Sabah as she stood there, in the doorway, her heart hammering and breath quickening, her fingers shaking so she shoved them into the pockets of her light pink teddy coat. She watched him as he turned his head to the girl sitting beside him, writing something in a notepad.

She watched as the girl looked at him, then followed his gaze, her eyes meeting Sabah's.

A smile spread across her face and she jumped up, grabbing her coat—Sabah noticed it was the same coat she was wearing and bit back a laugh—and bag, stuffing her notepad and pencil case into it.

"Hey, you," Sabrina said when she reached Sabah, her dark eyes glimmering with warmth. Her hair was a brighter shade of golden blonde, honeyed highlights blended through the strands, falling around her shoulders like a waterfall of sunshine.

"Hi," Sabah responded. Then, she looked at the pale pink teddy jacket over Sabrina's arm and her fingers brushed against the hem of her own jacket. "We match."

Sabrina looked at her coat and laughed, "Great minds think alike."

"How are you?"

"I'm, uh," wrinkling her nose, Sabrina shrugged, adjusting the straps of her black Prada tote bag. "Good. I've got so much work for uni to do and it's killing me. How about you? Should we go sit?"

she gestured towards one of the tables and Sabah glanced around, noticing the table they always sat at, over by the far right side, a red and white checked runner spread across the centre.

"Let's," Sabah smiled.

Sabah pulled out a wooden chair and sat down, unzipping her coat as she did and pulled her arms out of it. She raised her eyes to Sabrina as she tucked her fringe behind her ear, her lips a glossy pink, a sharp wing liner defining her eyes, outlined with kohl on her waterline. "So," she started. "How is the doctorate going?"

"Mm," Sabrina said, pulling her hair over one shoulder, twisting the ends around one finger. "Stressful. I've got two exams next month, and in May, and it's making me want to jump off a bridge."

"Don't do that," Sabah said, a smile quirking her lips up. "You need to live to be a doctor."

"Ugh," Sabrina replied. "Don't. Anyway, tell me how you're doing. What are you doing now anyways?"

"Well," she paused, taking in a breath. She glanced up at Grayson who stood behind the counter with Roberto and Katherine. He looked back at her and flashed a smile, which she hesitantly responded to with one of her own. Beneath the table, her fingers tapped against her tights-covered knee. "I'm fine, I guess. I broke up with Jake in February, I switched jobs like a million times in the last ten months and I started doing an access course in Health and Social Care in September."

Sabrina arched her eyebrows, all thick and perfectly shaped without her ever having to touch them. Sabah was envious. "I heard about the break up," she began slowly. "I'm sorry about that. Do you want to talk about it?" When Sabah shook her head, Sabrina nodded, and continued. "That's a lot of job changes," a small laugh escaped her mouth. "But are you happy at the one you're in now?"

Sabah shrugged, "I mean, it's good money and I guess I kind of like working in a bookstore, though I can't remember the last time I even picked up a book that wasn't for studying purposes."

"God, I relate to that so much," Sabrina sighed, quickly glancing at Grayson when he came over to their table. "I miss reading for pleasure," she said to Sabah.

"It's nice to see the two of you together," Grayson commented lightly, looking away from Sabrina to Sabah. She smiled tightly. "It's been forever."

"Seems that way," Sabah murmured. "Um, how are you doing? Congratulations on the wedding."

"Thank you," Grayson beamed. "I'm good thanks, Sabah. You alright? I was sad to see you couldn't come."

"I'm fine," she nodded. "And, um, yeah, I had work." She did, but she could've easily gotten out of it. But she hadn't spoken to Sabrina for months by that point so it would've been very awkward for her to go to Juniper and Grayson's wedding.

"Well, you should come to our anniversary party next summer," he says, arching an eyebrow. "Anyway, what can I get you two?"

"Just some water, please," Sabrina said, then glanced at Sabah. "What do you want?"

"Um, water as well, and maybe a mug of coffee please."

"Two sugars, caramel syrup, a dash of oat milk and double cream, right?" Sabah nodded. "Great, I'll be back soon." With a parting smile, Grayson walked away, disappearing behind a swinging door that said **KITCHEN**.

A minute later, he came back with two tall glasses, filled to the brim with water and ice floating on the top.

"Thanks, Gray," Sabrina shot him a smile, then turned her attention to Sabah. "It's good you're back to studying. How's it going?"

"Fine, I think, I mean I'm acing all of the assignments. There's an exam in February and March, I think, but I'm confident about them. But anyway, how are you? How's everything? Your hair is so much blonder now!"

Sabrina let out a laugh and took a sip of her water, keeping her eyes on Sabah's face. "I'm glad it's going well—what are your plans for after? And," she ran a hand over her loose waves. "Everything is good, I'm busy all the time which is both exhausting and everything I need. I feel like I'm finally making it, you know?"

"Must be nice to feel like that," Sabah said.

The silence that fell over them was heavy, the weight bearing down on her shoulders as she looked away from Sabrina, finding herself glancing back at the group that always occupied the table halfway between the pizza counter and the gelato display, a burst of laughter from the blonde guy and the guy with buzz-cut making her realise she couldn't even *remember* the last time her laugh was belly-deep and loud. She sat there, continuing to watch them, before her eyes drifted to the boy with the bun to find him already looking at her. His hazel eyes burned into her coffee-brown eyes, and she barely noticed as Grayson put her mug of creamy, sugary coffee down in front of her.

She stared at him, her eyes roaming over his face, taking in the sharp jaw-line that was coated with a dark stubble, the fitted hunter green jumper clinging to his shoulders and biceps, the sleeves pushed up to his elbows. She took in the tattoos snaking over his arms, a flash of heat rippling through her and settling in the pit of her stomach, pooling between her legs as she stared, before glancing back at his face. A small smirk tugged on his lips as he winked at her. A blush stained her cheeks and she looked away from him, her heartbeat rising in tempo.

"Sabrina," Sabah's voice was quiet, her breath a gentle exhale, as she knew she needed to address the awkward air stifling her. "I, um, I know it's been a long while since we last spoke and things between us even before weren't all that great. We both said things in the heat of the moment." She briefly glanced up to meet her cousin's eyes, seeing her already watching her. Their eyes met, coffee-brown on light brown, a myriad of emotions coiling around Sabah's heart. Maybe the breakup would've been easier to cope with if she'd had Sabrina by her side. God, she'd been right about everything. "Maybe we meant it, at the time, but the fact is that I miss you. We both fucked up. You were my best friend and you were sorry. What happened way back then was shitty, and it took me a while to get over it, but I am. You were going through your own issues and yeah, you shouldn't have flirted with him or sent those pictures when you knew I liked him, but you felt guilty, all the time, and that was what mattered. You were right about him. Veda was right about him. And I just . . ." she blew out a sigh. "I miss you and need you in my life again."

There was a lull in the air, only broken by the soft crooning of Mariah Carey singing *All I Want For Christmas*. Sabah kept her eyes on Sabrina, seeing the emotion splaying out on her face, the biting of her lower lip and the sigh that caved her shoulders beneath the ivory cable-knit jumper she wore.

"I miss you, too, Sabah. It's about time we both move on from the past."

Night fell as Sabah still sat in *Fairly Odd Pizzas*, a hand clasped around the handle of her third mug of coffee, scrolling through Twitter. Sabrina had left about an hour ago, needing to write a research paper and revise for her exam in January, promising to meet up for dinner or something in the coming week. Sabah stayed behind, reluctant to go home just yet—she knew if she did, she would come face to face with everything that reminded her of Jake. She probably needed to toss out all of her clothes, more because of the memories attached to them than the fact they were just a little snug on her now.

She sighed.

The pain had eased a little as the weeks wore on, but there were some days when she wished he was a better man, someone who realised what he had before she walked away. She could've loved him for a life time. But she knew she deserved better. So much better.

She lifted the mug of coffee to her mouth and took a slow sip, before lowering it back to the table, swallowing. She felt the stirrings of a headache beginning to form in her temples and sighed again, her phone clattering on the wooden table as she dropped it, rubbing her palm over her forehead.

"Are you okay?" a deep voice questioned, tugging back the chair across from her.

Sabah winced and then looked up at the person who sat in front of her, his elbows on the table and fingers clasped together beneath his chin. The hazel eyes staring at her flickered with a hint of concern and she slowly nodded. "Headache," she muttered, wondering what he was doing sitting there.

"Do you want a painkiller?"

"Sure."

He smiled slightly, then stood up, heading back to the table he'd been sitting at. Sabah couldn't bring herself to watch him, instead lowered her head onto her arm, closing her eyes.

"Here you are," the boy said. She held a hand out and he placed two white familiar capsules in the palm of her hand.

Throwing them into her mouth, Sabah sat up a little straighter to wash it down with the coffee, grimacing a little at the bitter taste of the Paracetamol. "Thanks," Sabah mumbled. "Appreciate it."

"No worries. You looked like you were about to die."

Sabah lifted an eyebrow in silent question, stifling the urge to tell him that she kind of *wanted* to die.

"I'm Ezra Carmichael," he continued, sitting back down in front of her. "What's your name?"

"Sabah." She stared at him, glancing at his smiling mouth. His lips looked so full and kissable. A smattering of freckles dotted his nose and cheeks, a pink glow to his face. His eyebrows were thick and straight, with a gentle tapering at the ends, set over large hazel eyes that had flecks of amber and gold around the pupil, lashes long and brushing the bottom of his brows. So unfair. His cheekbones were sharp and defined, set over a strong, chiselled jaw-line. He looked like how she thought Cupid might look.

"A picture would last longer," Ezra smirked, his voice teasing.

"Shut the fuck up," Sabah replied.

"Someone's in a bad mood."

"You don't say? I've got a bloody headache."

"Maybe stop drinking so much coffee?" Ezra suggested, tilting his head as he looked at her. A lock of hair fell over his eye and Sabah's heart fluttered. She squeezed her legs together, trying to ignore the thrum of lust unfurling in her.

"Maybe suck my dick," she said pleasantly, narrowing her eyes.

"Saucy. Maybe you should suck mine instead."

"I would, if there was anything to suck."

Her words were met with a brief silence and then a bark of laughter, Ezra's eyes brightened to a lighter green. "I'm more than happy to show you what I'm packing."

"Not interested," Sabah lied. He was hot. And he knew it. And she didn't like it. "Go away."

"I think," Ezra's smirk turned into a winning smile that made Sabah glare at him. "We're going to be great friends."

"I think not."

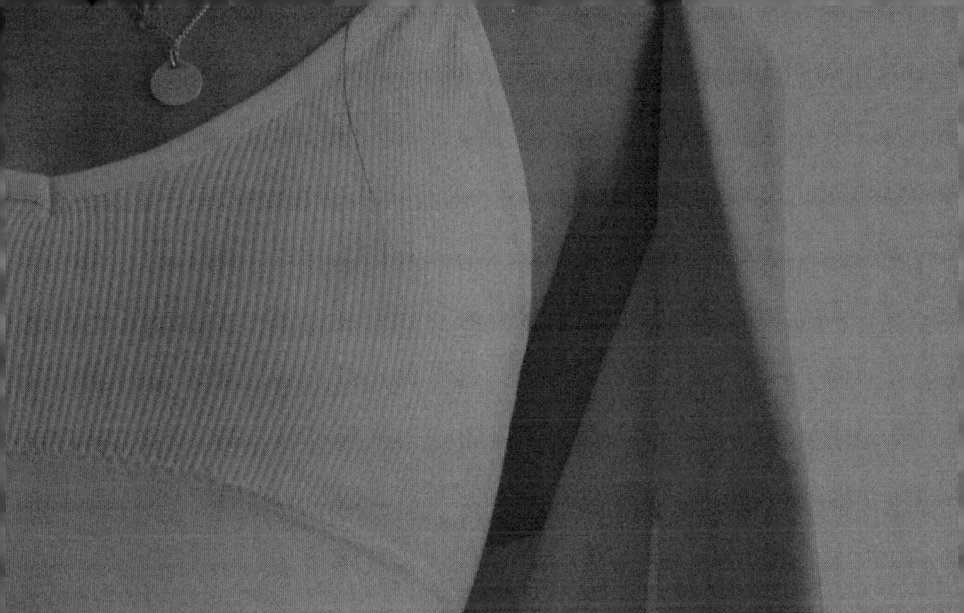

CHAPTER TWO

SABAH WAS DRESSED IN A BLACK TEDDY COAT, an oversized sage green knit cardigan, a fluffy sage crop top, and a pair of faded blue mom jeans and Converses, her hair up in a high ponytail, when she swept through the doors of *Fairly Odd Pizzas* a week later, gritting her teeth and telling herself that this was a *bad* idea. A terrible idea. Granted, she thought he was insanely gorgeous and she hadn't been able to stop thinking about his stupid smile the entire week, and they'd been talking every day since *last* Saturday when they *finally* spoke after years of seeing each other in the same place, but he was annoying and she was tired.

Her eyes went to Ezra straight away, as he sat at his usual table with Ashton, a plastic plate in front of him, with a slice of margherita pizza placed over a red and white checked wax paper. He had another slice in his hand, his lips shiny with oil, taking a large bite of it, when he caught sight of Sabah. She took slow, measured steps toward him, her eyes narrowed and a darker shade of brown.

"Seriously?" she demanded. "Pizza at ten o'clock in the morning? Who does that?"

"Obviously me," he drawled, looking her up and down. "You look good."

"Shut up, Ezra."

"Wake up on the wrong side of the bed this morning, did you?"

Pulling out the chair beside Ashton, Sabah sat down, glaring daggers at Ezra as he rolled up the pizza slice in his hand and stuffed it into his mouth. "What's wrong with you?"

"It's good pizza," Ezra defended. "And I'm supporting my buddy's family's business."

"Still," Sabah rolled her eyes. "It's not even lunch yet."

"Try it." Ezra pushed the plastic plate toward her, the corner of the wax paper coiling over the edge and brushing the wooden tabletop. "It's good."

"I've had, like, all the pizzas here before, idiot."

"Don't call me an idiot, you dickrocket," he snapped, before a smile appeared on his face and Sabah felt a slew of emotions rushing through her like a riptide. She grimaced. "Eat the pizza."

"Bro," Ashton sighed, standing up. "She doesn't have to eat it. Sabah's got a point—it's really fucking early."

"She should eat the pizza," Ezra said. "It's really good."

"Okay, *Joey*," Sabah rolled her eyes again. Keeping her eyes trained on his face, she lifted the margherita slice and took a massive bite. She almost moaned, having forgotten just how delicious *Fairly Odd Pizzas* was. "Okay," she conceded, swallowing her bite. "Yeah, it's good."

"Nothing beats pizza for breakfast."

"Sleeping in does," Sabah pointed out, pushing back the slice of pizza to Ezra who grinned and took a bite. "But somebody was adamant at meeting at fucking *ten* A.M."

"Chin up, buttercup," Ezra grinned. "We're going to Winter Wonderland."

"What?"

"We're going to Winter Wonderland," he repeated, still smiling.

The rumbling of feelings she couldn't decipher awoke in her from a slumber, twisting and coiling around her heart and lungs and she could only stare at him, feeling bewildered and lost, wondering how this guy she barely even know, found annoying and had only been talking to for a very brief period could be taking her to Winter Wonderland, when her ex boyfriend never did. A wave of emotion came over her and she sucked in a deep breath, nodding. "Right. Okay."

His eyebrows arched, "everything okay? I just thought it would be something nice and their churros are amazing so, you know, thought it would be great for us to go there. Plus, you know, get some Pokémon toys."

"You're annoying," Sabah said flatly, looking at his mouth when his smile wavered a little.

"Don't act like you don't like it."

"I don't," she said, shifting in her seat when he folded his arms over his chest, his eyes on her face. She crossed her arms, leaning on the tabletop, and stared back at him.

"Hmm, whatever you say," Ezra smiled. His damn smile.

"When are we going?" Sabah asked. "Also, why? We're not even friends like that."

"True," Ezra acquiesced. "But this is a chance to build that friendship and solidify our relationship."

"We don't have one."

He rolled his eyes. "That's literally my point."

"Whatever."

After they headed out of the little restaurant-slash-ice-cream-parlour, the snow drifted down as they caught the bus to Hyde Park, Sabah found herself glancing at Ezra and wondering how this was even happening. She didn't know why she agreed to meet him this morning—maybe it was because she had nothing else to do with her time (she'd already finished the two thousand word essay on childhood attachment types and the impact on adolescence), or maybe it was because she wanted to get out of the house, where all she ever did was argue with her mum.

When she moved back in with her mum and her little brothers, Nadim and Sadiq, back into her bedroom with candyfloss pink walls and lilac drapes, posters of One Direction blue-tacked to the wall and long beaded necklaces strung around the mirror on her dressing table, she told herself she would to try to mend the rift in the relationship she had with her mum.

But that was easier said than done.

Especially when her mum constantly threw the end of her relationship with Jake in her face, asking if it was worth it to move in with the boy who ruined her prospects in life and took her away from her family, a smug smile on her face and disappointment in her eyes, sighing and looking at her brothers, telling them not to end up like her. *It wasn't worth it*, Sabah wanted to say, none of it was. She thought that the love she experienced with him would've been worth the pain, that maybe the good memories they shared would've been enough to make her feel like the demise of their love was worth all the heartache, that maybe the laughter was worth it all in the end—because wasn't it better to have loved and lost, than to not have loved at all?

They had been together for almost two years and it was both the worst and the best time of her life, full of smiles and nights spent wondering whether she would ever be enough, whether the screaming fights would ever end. Even when she moved in with him in 2019, she spent nights laying in the bed beside him, staring at the ceiling, as the car headlights cast their lights through the parting in the beige drapes, shadows dancing across the edges, wanting sleep to take her under. She'd lie awake until the sun peeked through the curtains, dancing on the edge of her lashes and breaking the little sleep she got. She didn't know how to end it until she finally did, breaking her own heart, as well as his.

She stared out of the window, feeling the heat of Ezra's body sitting beside her, his leg pressing against hers, sending jolts of want coursing through her veins like liquid fire, burning away the remnants of guilt and not wanting to get into anything else with anyone else. This sudden, almost unwanted and unbidden, desire for him (being *so* physically attracted to him, it hurt), made her confused and frustrated, smouldering like a blazing inferno. A red flush coated her cheeks when she turned to look at him, seeing his gaze already on her, a crooked smile dancing on his lips.

Sabah dropped her gaze to his mouth, licking her lower lip. She wanted to kiss him. Goddammit. Damn him for being so hot.

Her nails dug into her hands when she coiled them into fists, his fresh wintery smell assaulting her nose and making her want to press hot, open-mouthed kisses to his neck and down his chest, lower and lower.

"You're blushing," Ezra said, his voice husky and amused. "And staring at my mouth." His lips curved into a bright smile.

She met his eyes, her eyes dark, her nostrils flaring and lips parted. "It's cold," she said, frost cutting through her voice. His grin widened.

"Very cold," he agreed. "But that doesn't explain why you're looking at my lips like you want to kiss me."

"Keep dreaming," Sabah snapped coldly. "I don't. You're not my type."

But he was tall and had dark hair, light eyes and sleeve tattoos. So he *definitely* was her type.

She just didn't want him to know that. He was annoying.

"You're not my type either," Ezra retorted, laughing, as he pressed the red STOP button.

Sabah snorted. "What, gorgeous and charming isn't your type?"

"Emotionally unavailable isn't."

"You asked me out."

"I didn't," Ezra responded, glancing at her sideways as they left the bus, their arms brushing together as they walked, waiting at the pavement for the traffic light to turn red and the crosswalk light to turn green. "Not in a date way, anyway. I'm not into you like that."

"Sure you're not."

"Do you want me to be?"

Yes. "No," Sabah laughed. "I don't care whether you are or aren't. I don't have the time for relationships right now."

"What do you do anyway?" Ezra asked, his hand on her elbow as they crossed the road to head into the park. *GET YOUR TICKETS READY* said a billboard, with the Winter Wonderland logo and a picture of a Ferris wheel blazing on it. The wind was bitterly cold, making her shiver and pull up the zip of her teddy coat. She glanced up at the sky briefly as the snow began to fall heavier, whistling around them. Everything was covered in glittering white; the bare branches glistened with snowflakes, the grass completely covered in a blanket of snow. Sabah followed the footprints in front of her, stepping onto them so she didn't slip and drag Ezra down with her. Which she would. If she went down, she wasn't going alone.

"I'm a student," she said to him, moving his hand from her elbow to lace her fingers with his as leverage. She didn't notice the cold so much when she felt the warmth of his hand curled around hers. "I'm doing an access course in Health and Social Care, and hoping to do paediatric nursing at uni next year. And I work. What about you?"

He looked at her, the smile she'd come to recognise as flirty on his face, snow dotted across his dark brown hair, soft and silky, and clinging to the ends of his lashes. "That's amazing," he praised. "An impressive career goal. You seem stubborn and determined enough to achieve whatever you want."

Sabah let out a quiet laugh at that. If only he knew.

"I graduated last year," he told her, their fingers still entwined as they reached the queue. There were only three people in front of them and the security was quickly checking the tickets and bags. "In History. Now I'm a receptionist at the local GP." He snorted. "Nothing related to the subject I went into fifty grand debt for."

"Why don't you," Sabah shifted, turning her head to look at him as he got his phone out to show the tickets to the security guard. "Go into law or teaching or something? Do a Postgrad course?"

"Maybe," Ezra replied, as they entered Winter Wonderland. "I need the money for the time being though. Once I've saved up enough, and can afford to cut down my hours at work, I might."

"Where do you live?"

"Meadowbrook."

"Where's that?"

"About forty minutes to an hour from London," Ezra said, his eyes gazing at the stalls, landing on a shooting game. His eyes glittered excitedly, his breath coming out in a light mist, dissipating into the air. "Let's do that one," he pointed at the stall.

Sabah followed his gaze, then shrugged. "Okay."

"How much is it to play this?" he asked the man standing behind the counter, in front of the plush toys lining the shelves. Sabah's eyes landed on a purple unicorn with a white mane and paws, and a glittery purple horn.

"A fiver for ten shots. You have to knock down five of the bars to win a prize," the man replied.

After paying, Ezra took hold of the rifle. Sabah kept her eyes on the little silver bars he had to knock down and winced when he missed the first one. Seven tries later, he managed to shoot down four bars. He missed the next one and on his final shot, it bounced off the holder. Sabah's eyes went to the man when he walked towards it and flicked it down, clearly taking pity on them.

"Which one do you want?" he asked Ezra, the hint of a smile on his face.

Ezra turned to Sabah and lifted his eyebrows.

She shrugged. "The purple unicorn."

Five minutes later, Ezra won her a giant penguin with specks of glitter on the black fur. Sabah felt light, as she stuffed the unicorn into the pocket of her jacket and held the penguin by the small black satin-hook on the top of its head, waiting in line at the churros stand.

"Thank you," she said to Ezra who simply winked.

"I'm gonna win you more. We're nowhere near done."

Sabah felt a flutter of desire, mixing with her need to punch him in the face because he irritated the hell out of her, as she gazed at Ezra. He was looking at her with a soft smile on his face, and a warm look in his gold-flecked hazel eyes. She looked up at him, thinking he was so different from Jake. He was so much nicer. Kinder. Gentler. She hated to compare, didn't know why she was, but he made her feel different. He annoyed the hell out of her but she liked talking to him.

He paid for their order and handed her the cone holding the chocolate and cinnamon covered churros, holding his own. They continued walking; breathing in the cold December air, eating the decadent chocolatey churros, eyes glimmering with excitement at all the stalls.

"I'm going to go for that one next," he said, pointing at a ring toss game.

"You won't win," Sabah deadpanned. "It's literally impossible. The bottle necks are too small."

"Have faith, young skywalker."

"Shut up, idiot."

Ezra's eyes locked onto her face, a teasing glint in his eyes. "Make me."

Sabah's heart stuttered, staring at him as the snow fell around him like a canvas of pure art, a picture perfect snapshot. He bit the end of a chocolate covered churro, a smear of chocolate on the corner of his mouth. She looked at it, wanting nothing more than to lick it away and taste the chocolate on his tongue. "Uh," she said, then cleared her throat. She looked back at his eyes, then back to his lips. He was standing closer to her, close enough for her to tiptoe and press her mouth to his in a soft, sensual kiss. "Shut up."

His low laugh sounded like music to her ears, all wine-smooth and light magic. She really wanted to punch him in the face.

The sky darkened to a deep shade of indigo, scattered with faint stars, snow still falling like the heavens had opened up and decided to pour out every dream of a white Christmas. London looked like a scene straight out of a Hallmark movie as Sabah and Ezra caught the bus, arms aching from carrying two giant pandas, the glittery penguin, baby Yoda, Charmander, a humungous fluffy unicorn ball with purple wings, that Ezra was holding, gripping onto the golden horn, and a huge stuffed cat that was black and white, with a light brown patch on one eye while the other had a black patch, and pink ears and nose. Sabah called it Fat Louise, a nod to *The Princess Diaries* and the adorable Fat Louis.

By the time they got onto the bus, stumbling to the back, Sabah knew her arms would feel like she did an intense workout the next day.

"Everyone's staring at us because of you," she whispered to Ezra, who grinned.

As they'd walked out of Winter Wonderland, a few people had commented on the number of toys they'd won. The security guard told them they smashed it. A cute old couple smiled at them and said they did well. A woman told them she was jealous of the purple unicorn ball. Some man in a lorry driving past beeped at them and shouted *great job*, laughter tumbling in the air.

The whole time, Sabah's face burned red, but she couldn't keep the smile off her face.

"Don't blame them," Ezra murmured, leaning close to Sabah. His breath rustled her black hair, the front layers falling over her eyes. "We're pretty good looking."

Sabah rolled her eyes. *This boy*. "You're so annoying."

CHAPTER THREE

THE SKY WAS A GLORIOUS SHADE OF PURPLES AND blues, the wind cold, but the hairdressers anything but. It was warm with the heating on, soft music playing overhead, as Sabah sat in front of the mirror, a black long jacket from the salon on beneath the cape, *Foster London* patched on in white cursive lettering. She stared at her reflection as Christie blow-dried her hair. It was the Monday after she'd gone to Winter Wonderland with Ezra, and she was meeting Sabrina later at some café she said had to-die for red velvet brownies, feeling apprehension twist in her gut. She felt unsettled and anxious, desperate to erase the last two years of her life.

Her once jet-black hair had been dyed with a blush pink and ash blonde balayage, cut to her bra-strap line instead of reaching her waist and her front layers had been chopped to resemble a 90's curtain fringe. She looked good.

"What do you think?" Christie asked, after spritzing frizz-control and hair-shine oil to Sabah's hair and brushing out the loose curls.

"It's different," Sabah murmured. And it was. All she needed now was a whole new wardrobe and bedroom décor, and she would be free of any and all reminders of Jake. "I love it."

She kind of felt like the Tumblr grunge aesthetic personified: she needed to add the all black outfit with a rock band t-shirt, with a dark plaid skirt and fishnet tights. The urge to giggle rose in her chest, but she stamped it down as she stood up, following Christie to take pictures. Shaking her hair out, Sabah faced the plain white wall as Christie snapped a few shots of her glossy and silky-smooth hair, wishing she knew how to style it to make it look as good. A small part of her wondered what Ezra would think of this new look, but she stashed it away, locking in a deep box in the back of her mind.

"It's pretty low maintenance and will look good, even when your hair gets longer," Christie told her as she shrugged into her black teddy coat, a black woolly scarf around her neck. "But make sure to use treatments in your hair. Olaplex four and five are amazing to keep your hair feeling healthy and strong."

Sabah nodded, making a mental note. "Thank you. I'll come back if I want any changes or whatever. You did an amazing job."

As she headed over to the reception to pay, a gorgeous blue Greyhound puppy brushed against her legs. She glanced down, taking in the big brown eyes and her heart melted. "Oh, my gosh, hi," she cooed, bending down to stroke the pup's head and ears.

"You're so gorgeous! Where'd you come from?"

"He's mine," Christie laughed. "He's just a baby so I bring him to work with me."

"Aw, how old is he?" Sabah asked, still petting him. He sat down, tail thumping and cocking his head as he stared curiously at Sabah. She smiled.

"Four months."

"What a little cutie," she beamed, wishing she had one of her own. Maybe when she had her own place one day.

After paying for her new hairdo and internally wincing at the price, Sabah got on the bus to get to Mile End station, where she took the Central line to Bond Street. Once there, walking like she was on a catwalk, she made her way to the café Sabrina had told her about, *Coffee & Dash*, eager to grab a cup of coffee and sit down with a brownie.

Her phone buzzed with an incoming call as she walked down Bond Street, past all the shops and department stores. She took it out of her caramel-brown satchel, swiping to answer the call from Sabrina and adjusted her Airpods

"How far are you?" Sabrina asked in lieu of a *hello*.

Sabah rolled her eyes at a couple of slow walkers in front of her, annoyed at the leisurely pace they walking at, and hurried around them. "About one minute," she said, glancing down at her phone. "It's just a straight walk from where I am now."

"Cool. I'm already here."

"You're *early*?" Sabah gasped. "Oh my god, that's crazy. I . . . oh, wow, Sabrina, there are some pigs flying. Holy shit."

"Shut up," Sabrina said, her laugh loud. "I'm not *always* late."

"If you say so."

"Oh my god, just get here already. Speaking of, I ordered you a red velvet brownie. What coffee do you want?"

"Um, a caramel latte with a shot of espresso and caramel syrup, and whipped cream, obviously."

"Obviously." Sabrina's voice was amused. "I'll see you in a bit."

"Yeah, yeah, see you."

The air was freezing, snowfall flurrying to the ground like angel tears, as Sabah and Sabrina held hands, sprinting down the streets of Great Portland Street to get to *Fairly Odd Pizzas*, and warm up their shivering bodies. In the late evening, the coldness seeped through the many layers Sabah wore, sinking beneath the black oversized hoodie, long-sleeved t-shirt and bra she wore, paired with leggings under her joggers and two socks and Nike trainers. As she ran, hand-in-hand with her cousin, laughter spilling from their mouths, Sabah wondered whether this was going to be a memory locked in her mind, cutting through every bitter moment like a knife and filling it with warmth. Some memories were like priceless wine, only getting better with age.

She found herself glancing at Sabrina, her blonde hair blowing in the wind, snow drifting around her face, her golden-brown skin gleaming beneath the orange glow of the streetlights and car headlights, lips shining pink with the *Glossier* cherry lip balm they both had. In the months that passed since she'd spoken to Sabrina, she found herself floating, hollow, thinking that maybe things wouldn't be so hard if she'd had some friends, if she'd stayed in touch with the girls she'd gone to school with. She should've. But she didn't. Jake was the only person in her life. She barely spoke to her mum and her brothers. Veda was busy all the time.

She'd been alone and empty.

In the aftermath of walking away from Jake, Sabah found herself wishing she had a friend she could cry to, one that would cuss him out and they could drink and toast to new starts without shitty boyfriends, maybe even get a celebratory cake to mark the end of a fiery disaster. She still missed him, hated herself for doing so, wishing it didn't sometimes still feel like a punch in the gut whenever she thought of him, came across all the things that reminded her of him. She wasn't as sad as the first month, but she was still fucked in the head, spending some late nights sliding down her wall and crying, crestfallen and gasping for air. How could it go from thinking she'd spend the rest of her life with him, to never wanting to see him again?

She'd walked away and it was the best decision she made, but she wished it didn't end the way it did. It ended so painfully, her heart breaking with every word and every step she took away from him. She left a part of herself behind when she closed his door behind her and took a cab back to her mum's. She was still not whole and wasn't sure she ever would be. But she was still trying. She was trying to keep going on, trying to rebuild everything she'd left crumbling and falling around her like debris, trying to move on with her life. Trying.

In this moment as they reached *Fairly Odd Pizzas*, spying the gold awning and the wide arching glass windows and the double doors, the lights inside a soft glow streaming out into the night sky, running in the early December night, feet pounding against the snow-covered pavement, footfalls muffled by the thick blanket of white, her heartbeat a staccato in her chest, rising in crescendo, Sabah found herself thinking about hazel eyes and annoying smiles, a blush heating her cheeks up. She stumbled, gripping tighter onto Sabrina, her feet skidding against the snow and crashed down. She dragged Sabrina to the cold ground with her. A gasp escaped her mouth, her hands gripping the cold snow, her arms and legs soaking wet. Her hands had taken the brunt of the fall, cushioned by the snow, the wet cold sinking into the teddy coat and wetting her clothes.

"Oh, my god," Sabrina said, half sprawled across Sabah. "What the fuck was that?"

"I tripped," Sabah offered.

"No shit. Did you have to take me with you?"

"If I fall, you fall with me."

"How romantic," Sabrina snorted. "I'm all wet now."

"I bet you are," Sabah winked. "I can't help my sexiness."

"Should we smooch?"

"Isn't that incest?" Ezra called out. Sabah glanced up from the cold floor, spying him leaning against the open doorway of *Fairly Odd Pizzas*, his arms crossed over his chest, a wide grin on his face and a Santa hat on his head.

"Oh, fuck," Sabah muttered. "Of course he *had* to be there to witness that."

Sabrina let out a laugh, her eyes crinkling at the corners. The soft light shone across her face, her mouth turning into a smile, dimples carving into her cheeks. "Tui tareh bala fasni?"

"What?" Sabah shrieked, when Sabrina got to her feet, almost falling again in the process. "Oh my god, no," she continued, still half laying on the snow. She was cold. "I *don't*." Sabrina's eyebrow lifted, a smirk on her lips at Sabah's insistence that she didn't like Ezra. "He's annoying," she hissed, as she grabbed Sabrina's hand to climb to her feet. A grimace spread across her face. The snow had found its way into her trainers and now both of her socks were wet.

"Mhm, sure you don't," Sabrina nodded. "I believe you."

"Shut up, man."

"When you're done flirting with your cousin," Ezra interjected. Sabah could *hear* the smile in his voice. "It would be great if you could both come in."

"Bite me," Sabah said, turning to face him. His face was amused, his hazel eyes dark as the light glimmered behind him, strands of fairylights strung up around the ceiling of the restaurant. The Santa hat he wore was a little crooked, his brown hair loose and hanging around his face, just brushing the tops of his shoulders. She felt heat blazing through her as she looked at him, taking in the stubble dusted across his face. He was still smiling, looking at her like he wanted to kiss her, and she stood there, staring at him, watching as his gaze went from her to Sabrina.

"Your cousin's really cold."

"She *can* be a bitch," Sabrina agreed. "It runs in the family."

"I couldn't tell," Ezra smirked. Sabah sighed.

Inside *Fairly Odd Pizzas*, Sabah sat down beside Sabrina. The other girl at the table, who Sabrina had introduced as Kira, Ashton's girlfriend, had obsidian black hair twisted into a Dutch braid, a giant white puffer jacket hanging on the back of her chair, was sat next to Ezra, drinking an iced salted caramel latte. Her eyes were on Ashton, watching him with a loving look splayed out on her face, as he talked to a few other customers scattered around the tables.

"You're free later this evening, right?" Ezra asked suddenly, looking up from his phone and into Sabah's eyes. She swallowed, trying to dampen the excitement flooding her.

"Yes?" she replied cautiously, arching an eyebrow. "Why?"

"Good. We're doing something later." He looked back down at his phone and typed something. "I'll be back in two hours or something, my sister wants pizza so I'm going to drop that off then meet you here."

"What makes you think I even want to do anything with you tonight?"

He smirked, glancing at her quickly. His gaze dropped to her mouth for a few seconds before meeting her eyes. "We both know you're into me."

She scoffed. "Well, that's a pile of shit."

"Is it? Is it, really?"

"Yes."

"Sabrina," Ezra said, his face serious. "Does your cousin have feelings for me?"

Sabrina looked at him, raising her eyebrows, then looked at Sabah who narrowed her eyes, her mouth twisting into a scowl. She crossed her arms over her chest when Sabrina grinned and shrugged. "Keep me out of it," she laughed. "But I think you two have a little, uh, what's the word . . ." she trailed off.

"*Chemistry*," Kira finished for her, smirking. She looked at Sabah, her eyes the darkest shade of brown, almost a fathomless pool. "You two totally need to bang."

"I agree," Ezra exclaimed, pointing at Kira. "*Thank you.*"

"You lot are dumb," Sabah sighed. "We're just . . ." she wrinkled her nose, "friends."

"So you admit we're friends?" Ezra smirked, looking at her, leaning in. His hair swept forward, framing his face. Sabah's fingers itched to brush it back from his face, to see if his hair was as soft as she imagined.

"Obviously," Sabah stared at him. "I wouldn't just spend my time with anyone."

The grin spreading across his face warmed her from the inside, a flicker of attraction unfurling in her stomach. She wanted to see that smile every day. She swallowed, watching him as his eyes went back to her mouth. She licked her lips, wondering what it would be like to go on a date with him. To kiss him. To hold him. To wrap her legs around his waist.

"Ezra," Roberto called, interrupting the dirty thoughts circling around Sabah's head. She was blushing, still staring at him when he glanced over at Ashton's stepdad. "Your pizza's ready."

"Wonderful," Ezra beamed. His smile lit up his entire face. He grabbed the box Roberto put in a large paper bag, holding it as he glanced at Kira. "You staying til Ashton finishes?"

"Yeah, gonna go to his tonight."

"Cool, I'll see you later. Sabrina," he glanced at her. "It's always a pleasure." Sabrina laughed, blowing him a kiss. "And you," he turned his attention to Sabah, smirking when he met her eyes. He totally knew she'd been staring at him the whole time. She flushed. "I'll be back by nine and we'll head out."

"Whatever," she replied, trying, and failing, not to smile. She watched as he pressed a kiss to Kira's cheek then Sabrina's. She clenched her hands; a feeling of jealousy she had no right to feel sliced her in half.

Thirty minutes later, Sabah was spooning up the last of her strawberry gelato topped over a hot fudge brownie, ignoring the fact that all she'd eaten today were literally just brownies, washed down with coffees. She was listening to Sabrina and Kira talk about some Comic Con event and costume ideas. Having no idea what that even was, Sabah was staring unseeingly at the gelato bar, thinking about what Ezra had planned for them later that night. She didn't want to go home after.

"Bubbles, can I stay at yours later tonight?" she asked, when there was a lapse in the conversation.

Sabrina glanced at her, "of course. Everything okay at home?"

Sabah shrugged. "Same old. I'm a disappointment, so that's always just . . . thrown in my face, and the boys don't even talk to me. I just don't want to go home tonight."

"Fair enough. I don't know what it is with Asian parents and their expectations," Sabrina sighed. She pulled her hair over one shoulder, using her index finger to pick up a brownie crumb from her pale pink bowl. "Like, it's so toxic and unhealthy. It's exhausting."

"You can say that again," Kira said. "My parents were so disappointed when I kept working at *Mabel's Designs* after graduating. Dad wanted me to do a GDL after I graduated, but he didn't get that studying law would be literally what kills me."

"Your job pays well anyway," Sabrina said. "It's not as if it's minimum wage. And you're on your way to be assistant manager, so what's the big deal?"

"*Exactly*," Kira said. "And I get fashion experience working there and get to meet Mabel like every week and help out with photo shoots, so it's got its perks."

"What did you do at uni?" Sabah asked.

"English Literature. You're not at uni yet, are you?"

Sabah shook her head. "I'm hoping to go to uni next year for paediatric nursing."

"Damn," Kira whistled. "Good luck. The hours will be exhausting."

"I like keeping busy," Sabah mumbled. "No time to think."

"I feel you on that," Sabrina sighed. "I'm still working at *Sainsbury's* on the weekends just to shut my mind off everything. I'm always heartbroken."

"This time was kind of your own fault though," Sabah said slowly, unsure if her words were a welcome comment or if she'd shatter the fragile friendship they were working on rebuilding, her eyes on Sabrina's face. "You should've had the conversation."

"Too little, too late," Sabrina smiled wryly. "All I can do now is stew over the fact that I lost the best man I ever found."

"He was one of a kind," Sabah agreed. "I still have him on Instagram."

"I deactivated my Insta last year," Sabrina said. "After seeing him post a story with some woman. I just didn't want to see that. So I deactivated."

"I don't understand why you didn't just remove him from it," Kira said, frowning, unscrewing the lid to her water bottle. "Instead of deactivating, I mean."

"Social media is toxic," Sabrina said. "I kept comparing myself to other women, especially the models on there. I feel a lot better now though, since I've not used it in months."

Sabah silently agreed. Just that morning, she wished she had the same sharp cheekbones as the women she saw on her home feed, the models perfect and skinny with the pretty faces and small waists.

Her cheeks were too chubby, making her look like she had a baby face. She still looked she belonged in secondary school. She wished she had bigger boobs and a slimmer, more symmetrical face, with the perfect eyebrows Sabrina and her sister, Sultana, had. "I feel like that, too," she said finally. "I wish I had their perfect bodies. Even on Twitter as well, all the girls are just so gorgeous. And I see people saying how Bangladeshi girls are so gorgeous and have this amazing natural beauty, like even on Eid day as well, and I'm just like . . . am I one of the only people that the beauty skipped? I don't have that same prettiness."

"I feel that," Sabrina said. "But also, are you stupid? You're one of the most gorgeous people I know and your ass is perfect."

"Seriously," Kira said, nodding. "It's so big and round. Looks so perky. What do you do?"

"Eat," Sabah shrugged. "I just eat a ton of shit."

"And it all goes to your ass?" Kira asked.

"Sadly, yeah. I wish it went to my chest as well, but no." Sabah looked down at her chest, frowning. "They're so tiny."

"You're such a bitch, I'm jealous," Kira sighed. "If I eat recklessly, it all just goes to my face and waist."

"Same, and my stomach," Sabrina laughed. "It's why I no longer have a flat stomach. Honestly, I look a little pregnant."

"No, you don't," Sabah rolled her eyes, taking a swig from the water bottle next to her bowl. "Your waist is small and you've got the perfect hourglass figure."

"Not with the same tiny stomach I had," she pouted. "But I

can't even bring myself to give a shit. Like, I still go running twice a week, if that, but that's about the extent of my exercising now."

"It doesn't even matter, or it shouldn't," Kira said. "Like, I'm totally jealous you can eat the way you do and still have a tiny frame and just have the gains go to your butt, but at the same time its like, beauty standards are forever changing. And really, who gives a shit? We're going to be in our bodies for the rest of our lives. The least we can do is fall in love with ourselves and our bodies, and love it. And take care of it."

"Taking care of it should include some form of exercise, I think," Sabrina said. "It's why I try to run whenever I can."

"I walk most places, if I can," Sabah shrugged. "I should probably do some workouts at home, but I just can't be asked. It's so boring."

"Find something you enjoy doing, or change up the ones you do," Kira suggested.

"It's all boring."

Sabrina laughed, "That's true. I was doing some strength-training exercises some weeks ago and stopped after ten minutes because I got so bored. I don't get how people find enjoyment in it. It's like doing maths." She looked down at her phone when it lit up with a notification, then turned it over, face-down, on the table. "Anyway, Sabah," she lifted her eyebrows. "What's going on with you and Ezra?"

Throwing a quick, cautious look at Kira, Sabah shrugged.

Kira smirked. "Don't worry," she said, a glint in her eyes. "I won't tell him anything."

"I don't know what you mean," Sabah shrugged. "There's nothing going on with us."

"Is that why you were eye-fucking him?" Sabrina cackled, smiling at Roberto when he put down a steaming mug of hot chocolate. Kira burst out laughing.

"*I was not*," Sabah spluttered indignantly. "Oh my god, how could you even say that?"

A playful smirk was on Sabrina's lips. "You definitely were. Personally, I think you two are very well suited."

"I agree," Kira said. "I've known him all my life and he's one hundred percent got a thing for you."

"I just got out of a relationship," Sabah said, playing with her spoon, her eyes on the small drops of ice cream. "I mean, in February so it's been a while. But yeah, I don't know. He's annoying anyway."

"He likes you."

She doubted it. Because even if he did, and a part of her hoped that he did—he was insanely hot—she wasn't sure if she was even ready to jump into another relationship. Not yet.

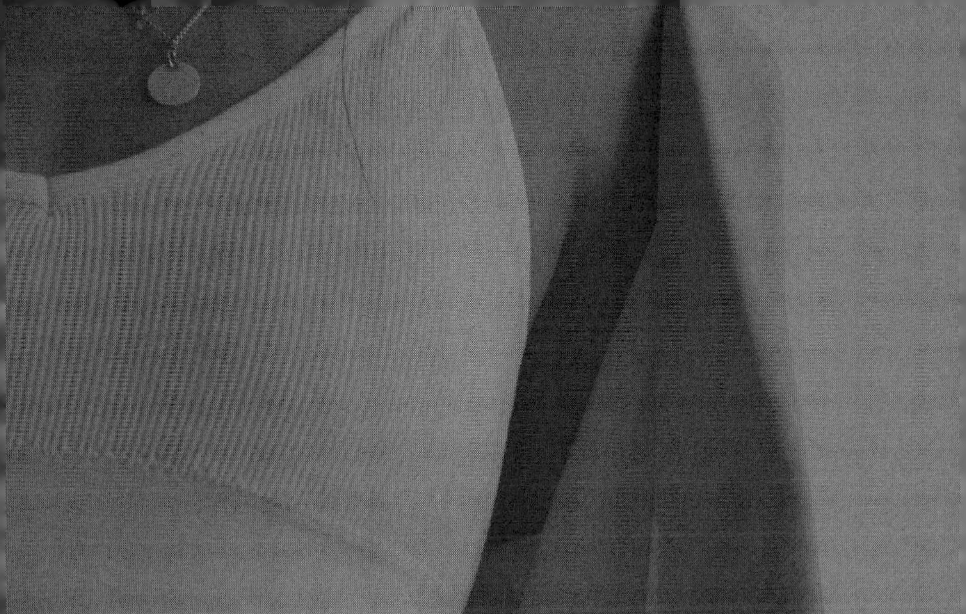

CHAPTER FOUR

21st December 2020

SABAH DIDN'T KNOW WHY SHE LOVED WORKING in *One More Page*, but she did. There was something alluring about being surrounded by shelves upon shelves of books, and piles of the current bestsellers sorted by genre displayed on six different tables throughout the store. It was dark out, the navy blue sky dotted with faint stars and barely-there clouds. The moon was luminous in its light, a crescent curve casting a soft glow in the cold night. The earth was still covered in fresh snow. This entire week's forecast was the same as it had been for the past two and a half: snow, snow, snow.

At the start of her shift, Sabah had done laps around the entire store, making sure all the books were in the right shelves and taking notes of any that weren't in stock and ones they needed to order, while her colleague, Avery, manned the checkout counter, and their supervisor, Sydney, sat in her office, going over the details of an indie author's launch party in the new year. Earlier, a girl had come in asking for a copy of *Stupid Cupid* by Carina Khan, and after failing to find it on the shelf it was *supposed* to be in, Sabah found it nestled in the fantasy YA section. Now, she was wrapped in a large black ribbed knit cardigan, over a cable-knit red jumper, leaning against the checkout counter, flipping through a copy of *Stupid Cupid*. She wasn't typically into rom-com books but found herself soon realising just why Carina Khan had quickly risen to the number one spot on the bestsellers list with her debut novel.

She was more than halfway through, after spending the last two shifts reading it whenever it got a little quiet, in love with the way the relationship between Brooke and Zayn was developing. It made her wish that a man like Zayn existed.

It would be so *nice* to have someone who was so caring and reassuring and patient.

Dog-earing a page, Sabah lifted her eyes to the glass doors, car headlights and the street lights bright in the panoramic view, when the bell dinged softly and the doors slid open. Ezra stood there, snow-speckled and grinning, a Santa hat sitting crookedly on his wild brown hair. He was holding a box of pizza. She raised an eyebrow as she looked at him, hating how her pulse jumped and her breath caught in her throat when she met his eyes.

For the entire two and a half weeks they'd begun talking, there hadn't been a day that went past where a part of her didn't want to launch into his arms and kiss him with all the pent-up desire and feelings she had swirling in her like a storm. It had just gone five-thirty and Sabah finished work at six P.M., so it wasn't surprising that Ezra had come to the shop to pick her up. But it *was* surprising that he was early.

When she had work on the weekends, he'd meet her at *One More Page*, snowflakes clinging to the ends of his hair, dusted across him like specs of glitter, *always* with that bloody Santa hat that he wore—and he *still* hadn't explained why—or sometimes, they'd meet at *Fairly Odd Pizzas* and have the best coffee before sweeping out to go on another winter wonderland-esque adventure. But as Ezra approached her with a warm smile and a bag swinging in his gloved hand, the warm smell of the pizza making her stomach rumble, Sabah wondered what all of this even *meant*.

He flirted with her unabashedly and, okay, *sometimes* she flirted back, but the truth was . . . well, she didn't even know what the truth was. She liked him. A *bit*. Even though she wanted to punch him sometimes, she wanted to kiss him just as bad, and sometimes when she caught him watching at her with this tender look in his gaze and a soft smile on his lips, she hoped it meant that maybe, hopefully, he liked her too. But even with this slow hope tenderising her heart, Sabah didn't want to be in a relationship. She didn't want to be with anyone.

She needed this time to heal, and even though moving on with somebody new would help her properly let go of everything, and time wasn't in her favour—because god, how could she meet someone when her life wasn't on track and she was on the road to mend all the wounds caused from the knives thrown into her back?—which meant that she would have to be patient and keep him as a friend. And nothing more. Because the thing was, even her little crush aside, Ezra was *fun* to be around. He helped her step out of her comfort zone and he was a part of that change she was making.

And it felt good.

Six days ago, Sabah had bundled up all of her clothes into black bin bags, along with her half-full bottle of Paco Rabanne *Olympea*, and hauled them down to the local charity shop, with her brothers' help. Then, while blasting early 2000s songs, she painted her bedroom white and let the freezing snowy air in, and spent a few nights sleeping on the sofa downstairs as her bedroom dried. She kept the lilac curtains up and she knew there was no way in hell her mum would've let her sell her bed or wardrobe, but it didn't matter. It wasn't like Jake had ever seen her bedroom. Everything Jake had touched, had seen, had liked, was gone.

It felt like a new start, like everything was beginning to change with her, the first step to the rest of her life. And it hurt. It yanked and twisted her heart as she said goodbye to her life before, finally standing in the doorway to her bedroom after sticking up Polaroid pictures of her with Sabrina, Veda and Reina (from their second sleepover, the night after she got a nose piercing and three butterflies tattooed on the inside of her left wrist), on a cute notice board, draped with fairylights and tickets from when she went bowling with

Ezra. On the desk beneath it, she had a large oval mirror and it had a stack of books Sabrina had recommended, and a framed photo of her with Veda at her graduation from law school. On the wall above her bed, she had one of Daniel's paintings: it was the kind of house she wanted one day with a tree-lined driveway and a white picket fence, snow drifting down and covering the roof and driveway and branches in pure, glistening white. It looked like a perfect Christmas card.

Sabah sighed quietly, her shoulders caving beneath the layers of knit sweaters, and tilted her head, glancing at Ezra when he came up to the checkout counter, still smiling. Those damn dimples winked at her. Her own lips turned up at the corners, finding the lifeboat coming towards her in the murky depths threatening to drown her and reaching her hands toward it, kicking her legs with all her might. And trying to just keep swimming.

"Hey, you," Ezra said, leaning one arm on the counter, his fingers drumming against it, in time to *Baby, It's Cold Outside.*

"Hi, there." Her voice was soft, a musical lilt seeping through and, behind the cash register, Sabah clenched her hands into fists, keeping her face impassive, with a barely-there smile. "What's the plan for tonight?"

"Well, I did want us to maybe sit on the steps of Trafalgar Square—"

"And freeze to death?"

"Don't interrupt me," Ezra narrowed his eyes, a twinkle in them. "As I was saying, I wanted us to do that, but it is—" he nodded at her, "—way too cold for that. So I was thinking, maybe we could just eat in here, since you're the only one here anyway. We can just flip the sign to closed, turn off some of the lights. And it's warm in here."

She stared at him for a moment, then shrugged, "why not?"

Avery and Sydney had clocked out at five on the dot, as it was Sabah's turn to close tonight, so she was alone for the remainder of her shift. She enjoyed the solitude, playing her heartbreak playlist on Spotify on a constant loop and finding new books to read, before she was interrupted by a gaggle of customers. Today, though, what with it being the week of Christmas and whatnot, Sabah settled on all the festive songs.

Baby, It's Cold Outside came to an end, and Cascada's version of *Last Christmas* came on.

Thirty five minutes later, Sabah had changed the pink door sign to **CLOSED** emblazoned with gold cursive and turned off the lights near the front of the store so nobody could see in. She positioned two chairs from the staff room near the checkout counter, the back of hers touching one end while Ezra sat on his chair, opposite her, shelves of books behind him. He was still wearing his stupid hat, making Sabah sigh, but she decided against questioning it. He was weird, that much she knew.

They used a little footstool as the table for the pizza box, the delicious aroma wafting out and assaulting all her senses as she picked up an extra cheesy, spicy chicken tikka slice, folding it in half and taking a bite. It was still a little warm and tasted so. Damn. Good. She let out a moan of appreciation, closing her eyes.

"God, Ezra, this is so fucking *good*," she groaned, taking another large bite.

"I love it when you moan my name," he smirked, starting on his third slice. "It's so sexy."

Ignoring the flare of heat flushing her russet brown skin, Sabah simply rolled her eyes at him. She finished off her slice and grabbed the margherita slice, looking at him. "How long did you take off work again?"

"Two weeks. Two beautifully long weeks."

"I'd love a holiday from work," Sabah sighed. "But I need the money."

"Do you want to stay in London for uni?"

"I have to; I can't afford to move out."

"You could probably get a maximum of eight thousand from SFE, I think," Ezra said, his eyebrows pulling together as he thought about it. Sabah watched him, her eyes taking in his perfectly chiselled face. He was so undeniably hot, it made her angry. "Yeah, it's about that much," he continued, looking at her. He smiled. She blushed.

"I guess. But yeah, no, I'd rather stay in London, and I've already got this job here. And I actually love it at *One More Page*."

"It is pleasantly nice here," Ezra agreed. "I've not read a good book in a while, but coming here often is making me want to pick one up."

"I know, right? I've been reading whenever I can during my shifts. Anyway, I don't really want to talk about work," she laughed. "Doing over thirty hours and going to college at the same time is *not* fun."

His smile made her stomach do a somersault. There was a heat in his eyes that made her want to say, *hey wanna get out of here? Maybe we could find a nearby pub that's open in this snow and hook up in the bathroom, maybe I could get on my knees for you, maybe we could kiss and I could find out if your lips are really as soft as I imagine?* But instead, she dropped her gaze and tore a large chunk off the pizza slice and chewed slowly. She swallowed and licked the tomato sauce from the corner of her mouth, realising just how much she loved plain cheese and tomato pizza. "I need a coffee," Sabah mumbled, quickly glancing up at him. "Like, so bad."

"Is there coffee in the staff room?"

"Yeah, there is, but I'm way too comfortable to move right now." She'd pulled her legs up beneath her and was sitting cross-legged on the wide velvet chair, her trainers kicked off on the deep red, gold and indigo blue patterned carpet.

Ezra swallowed his bite of pizza and brushed the crumbs off his hands, wiping them on his dark blue jeans. Standing up, he adjusted the pizza box on the foot stool and threw a smile at Sabah. "I'll make us some. Where are all the mugs kept?"

"Top cupboard on the left, above the coffee machine," Sabah smiled. "My mug's the Phil Dunphy one."

"Ah, a fellow *Modern Family* fan, I see," he grinned as he headed toward the staff room and ducking inside, leaving Sabah to finish off her second helping of the chicken tikka pizza.

The speakers connected to her Spotify were playing *Santa Tell*

Me and Sabah quietly hummed along, quickly reaching for another margherita slice and hoping the coffee Ezra was making would be done soon. She didn't know why, but something about him—about the boy who reminded her so much of seductively handsome male leads from Regency era romance novels, kind of like Alistair Caulfield, and gorgeous boy-next-door love interests with a heart of gold and sunshine-flecked eyes and starshine smiles—made her want to do whatever it took to burn down every painful thing ripping her apart at the seams and use that fire to scorch a path for herself leading to everything bright and sparkling. She wanted to prove to herself that she was healing and was doing perfectly fine, even when she wasn't ready to fall in love again.

She did, however, want to feel his skin against hers, and the thought sent a lightning bolt through her chest.

Letting out a shuddering breath, Sabah finished her last slice and closed the now empty box and moved it to the floor. She squirted a few drops of the citrus and jasmine scented hand sanitizer, which had its designated spot behind the register, onto her hands and rubbed them together, inhaling the lovely fruity smell. Settling back down on the chair, Sabah glanced up just as Ezra came around a corner, out of the staff room, with two steaming hot mugs of coffee, topped with whipped cream.

"One extra hot coffee with half double cream and half oat milk, with lots of caramel syrup and topped with whipped cream and cinnamon," he grinned, passing her the mug.

"You're a fucking angel," Sabah said, unable to stop the huge smile gracing her face. "Thank you."

"Mm, I've been told," Ezra said, lifting the mug to his mouth and taking a slow sip, keeping his warm gaze trained on Sabah's face. She felt her cheeks flushing, thinking there were stars twinkling in his eyes for a bit, before realising it was just the reflection of the fairylights strung up around the entirety of the bookstore. His smile was like a gently simmering heat uncoiling from her belly, sweeping lower and lower. She suddenly wished she had something stronger to drink. "You know, I was thinking, if the snow isn't too bad tomorrow, maybe we should go to the Natural History Museum? And then grab dinner and drinks or something."

"I forgot you have a thing for dinosaurs."

His laugh was like fireworks exploding, all bright and beautiful and making her hold her breath in anticipation, savouring the sound and the way it made her feel. Every tight knot in her chest fell apart. "I did have loads of dinosaur toys growing up. I was obsessed with them. Every birthday, when my parents asked me what I wanted to do, I'd ask to go the museum."

"Oh my god, I know who you are," Sabah snorted, biting back the urge to giggle all girlish and love-struck. She took a large mouthful of her caramel-drenched coffee, using her index finger to wipe away the dot of whipped cream on her nose. When she put her finger in her mouth to lick away the cream, she noticed Ezra's eyes searing into her, focusing on the way she sucked on her finger. She felt her lips tug into a small smirk, and gave her finger a little suck before pulling it out of her mouth and gave another little lick.

"You're Ross fucking Geller," Sabah finished, her voice hoarse.

Ezra's bark of laughter was sudden, and Sabah felt herself laugh in response, totally picturing him playing with a bunch of dinosaurs. "I mean, I'm no paleontologist, but I'm not ashamed to admit that my love of those beautiful beasts definitely rivalled his."

"Please tell me you still have them?"

"I do," he nodded, grinning. "I mean, some are up in the attic, but I've got a couple small ones in my room still.I use them as bookends."

It was Sabah's turn to laugh. She pictured his bedroom, the bookshelves lined with books and dinosaurs. "God, I've got to see these."

"Maybe you can." Ezra cleared his throat, glancing away from her. Sabah untucked her fringe from behind her ears, shielding her face so he didn't see the furious blush turning her face pink. Ezra lifted the mug of coffee back up to his mouth, "so what was that book you were reading anyway?" Ezra asked, licking his lips, wiping away the whipped cream.

Sabah's heart stuttered as she met his gaze. "It's a romance novel that came out this year, by this Bengali author, and it's just so damn cute and wholesome. I mean, I'm not gonna lie, I wasn't a hundred percent sure I would be into it because I've never really *read* romance books like that since I was a kid, but I really do."

"How come? What's it about?"

Sabah huffed out a laugh, "really? You want to know about some cute little rom-com book I'm reading?"

"Yeah, why not?" Ezra replied, leaning forward to look at her and putting his mug down on the foot stool. Using his left hand, he took the Santa hat off and put it down on his lap. Sabah watched as he pulled his hands through his hair, ruffling up the silky loose waves. He quickly pulled it up into a bun on the back of his head, tying it with a thin black hair band.

Forcing down the slew of dirty thoughts circling her mind, Sabah arched an eyebrow. "Well, okay then. It's basically about this girl, Brooke, who's an English student at some university and meets a guy, Zayn, and he's a History student. They meet at a library while waiting at the printer and kinda just have this instant connection, and they go out on a date that same night. It's kind of insta-love which is an annoying trope but I'm really enjoying it so far, anyway. At the moment, there's some conflict getting in the way of Brooke telling him she loves him, which is obviously typical, because she's terrified of opening up like that because of how her last relationship crashed and burned and her ex is kinda messaging her again as well. And," Sabah laughed, her heart fluttering in her chest like a hummingbird at the soft look in Ezra's eyes. "Well, this Zayn guy is Pakistani so—"

"Is this a fan fiction or something? About Zayn Malik?"

"Oh my god, no. Zayn *is* a name, you know. It's a super common South Asian name."

"Oh, right," Ezra muttered, splotches of pink appearing on his cheeks. "Go on."

"Right, anyway, so he's Pakistani so his family don't know about Brooke which I guess adds to the conflict or is a subplot or whatever, and his dad's also in the hospital, which makes him a little distant and that scares her a bit too, and she's all in this freak out. And he's obviously anxious about it."

"Bloody hell, it sounds very dramatic."

"Yeah, I guess it is. But it's super cute and I love their love and how kind and communicative Zayn is, except right now because he's so scared. I just," Sabah took a sip of her coffee, closing her eyes briefly. "God, this is good coffee, Ezra. Anyway, um," she blushed, "I kind of wish men like that existed."

"You mean fictional men written by women?" Ezra asked, a hint of a smile lifting his mouth up.

"Yeah."

"Fictional characters are that for a reason," Ezra said. "They're perfect and don't have any flaws, they've got everything going for them. It's a bit unrealistic to pin all your expectations of men on the portrayal of someone that doesn't even exist."

"Maybe so," Sabah shrugged again, taking another large mouthful of the coffee and whipped cream. "But I can still dream about finding a man that does all the lovey-dovey, romantic grand gestures and declares his undying love for me in ways that makes me never have to doubt his fucking loyalty. I can still want a man who isn't toxic and horrible, and wants to hold my hand in front of his friends and doesn't make me feel like I'll never measure up. Maybe that's asking for the bare minimum, but I also know I'll never find someone like that." Sabah's sigh was loud in the lull of the music, Elvis Presley crooning about blue Christmases, and she looked away from Ezra, shifting on her seat. It squeaked a little beneath her weight. "But anyway, I can still have these expectations. It's not like I ever plan to, you know," Sabah looked at Ezra. "Fall in love or get into a relationship again, so I'll never face that crushing disappointment."

"Why not?" Ezra's voice was gentle, caressing her skin like a velvety blanket, wrapping around her like a welcoming hug after a long and exhausting day. His eyes were warm and light.

"What's the point?" Sabah asked softly, picking at an imaginary hangnail on her thumb. "It always ends. It's fine to read about it, or watch it, it's fine to want that kind of happily ever after love, but the reality of it is that it doesn't exist. I mean, I can want a man like the Duke of Hastings, but I know a man like that doesn't exist so it isn't all that heartbreaking. It's easier to want something when I know it's not real, than to hope for a love that will end."

"I was in a long-term relationship a couple years ago," Ezra said after a moment. "She was from Nepal and I thought she was the love of my life. I thought I'd never move on from her." Swallowing audibly, Ezra brushed away a lock of hair from his eyes, meeting Sabah's gaze. There was something sad in his expression, a glimmer of heartbreak that tugged on Sabah's heartstrings.

It made her want to kiss away any fragment of pain enveloping him.

"But her parents would never have accepted it, so she broke up with me. For a while, I thought I'd never move on or get over her, or want to love anyone with that kind of depth or my entire heart again. But," he continued softly, "that's the beauty of love. You can't define all relationships on one experience, life's about continuing to push on and take that leap of faith. You have to heal from what ended and the person that broke you, you have to be able help yourself take one step at a time. And when you're ready, don't be afraid to put yourself out there and find love. You can't be afraid to let someone else in and bring in the light, because maybe they'll have the tools to help you fix your heart."

CHAPTER FIVE

THEY PASSED THE DIPLODOCUS SKELETON FOR THE fifth time as they walked out of the gift shop, a small fluffy panda and a soft and fluffy triceratops huddled together in the paper bag swinging in Ezra's hand. His other hand was curled around Sabah's, his fingers threaded through hers like a missing puzzle finally spotted together. Throwing one last glance at the dinosaur skeletons behind the glass cabinets and plaques with historical records, Sabah followed Ezra as they left the museum, gentle snowfall cascading around them and glittering against the darkness of Ezra's parka coat and Sabah's pale pink teddy coat.

"Where do you want to eat?" Ezra asked as they walked toward South Kensington station, following the imprinted footsteps in the snow. Sabah clutched his hand tighter as her knee-high boot clad foot slid against a sheet of frost, a gasp escaping her mouth. The tight grip of Ezra's hand on hers kept her from falling.

The sky outside was a quickly darkening lavender with streaks of rose pink and gold threaded through like ribbons, the air had the winter smell, all cold and frosty. All around them, heavy snow fell in heaps of frozen flakes catching the light of the passing cars and glowing yellow streetlamps, landing like fat, cold droplets on Sabah's cheeks and dancing over her eyes. She ducked her head to slightly shield her face from the onslaught of the freezing cold snowfall.

"Uh," she said, once she gathered her wits and ignored the feeling of *comfort* sweeping her up in a warm glow. "I'm feeling a burrito and beer."

He glanced at the side of her face, and when Sabah looked at him, she saw the dimples winking at her as his smile widened. "Your wish is my command, m'lady."

She rolled her eyes, biting back the urge to smile. He really was starting to grow on her and she wasn't sure whether it was a bad thing anymore.

"This really hits the spot," Sabah groaned in pleasure, taking another bite of the chicken, rice, beans, salsa and cheese stuffed burrito, her fingers denting the foil it was wrapped in. Some of the sauce dripped down onto the tissue she had laid out over the table, but she ignored it as she continued to tuck in. Opposite her, Ezra was almost finished, some of the red salsa smeared at the corner of his mouth. "You've got a bit of sauce there," she gestured to his mouth. When he lifted his hand to wipe it, Sabah shook his head. "No, it's still . . . wait, let me," the smile on her face was full of heat. Placing her burrito down onto the tissue, Sabah leaned forward and ran her thumb over the corner of Ezra's mouth, her gaze locked onto his. Her thumb ran across his full bottom lip, caressing it longer than necessary, before sliding back to where the salsa had been.

She swiped her finger over the stain again and pulled it back, taking it into her mouth and sucking away the salsa sauce. Ezra stared at her as she did, his eyes darkening to a deeper hazel, and she hid a smirk as she glanced back at his mouth. "All gone," she breathed, her voice all throaty and tinged with unsolicited desire.

"Thank you," Ezra murmured, capturing her gaze, a flare of lust flickering across his eyes. His face was warm and open, making Sabah inhale slowly before she dropped her gaze and picked her burrito back up again.

She bit into it, tasting the explosion of the grilled chicken combined with the rich tomato rice and black beans, her cravings sated. She looked at the burrito clutched between both hands; a little sad that she was almost finished, but knowing there was no way she'd even be able to eat another one. She still wanted the beer though. "No worries," she said to Ezra, swallowing the chicken, black beans and rice. "Where do you want to grab the beer?"

"There's a pub here," Ezra answered, crumpling the foil and the wrapping paper and tossing it into the paper bag sitting at the end of the table. "Just across from here." They were currently upstairs, in the *Tortilla* at Leadenhall Market, overlooking the snow-covered cobbled streets below, the lights all bright gold and twinkling with fairylights strung across all the doorways of the shops, restaurants and pubs. Wreaths of green, red and gold hung over a couple doorways, specks of snow falling over the top. At the centre of the market stood a giant Christmas tree, lit up with sparkling fairylights and glittery baubles, gently swaying in the cold wind with a myriad of tinsels, from silver and gold, to red and green, the pine-needles covered with glistening layers of snowflakes, basking in the attention of all the passerby's and the queue of people lining up outside the local pub. "*The Lamb Tavern*."

"Want to go there?"

"Yeah, hurry up and finish your burrito."

"Don't tell me what to do, Ezra Carmichael."

He smirked wolfishly, his eyes glinting. "You seem like a girl who loves being told what to do."

Her exhale was flush with a simmering desire unfurling in her chest and slinking through her veins like liquid fire. But she knew she needed some liquid courage to get through this evening. To have the confidence to climb up her chest and help her say the words swirling around her mind, on the tip of her tongue. "You have no idea what I'm like," she said quietly, her voice husky and coated with a thick layer of temptation.

Ezra's quiet laugh was like a rumble of thunder, sending a strike of lightning straight through her and pooling a wet heat between her thighs.

A small part of her wanted to fight the attraction, to pull away from the need to grab his hand and pull him to her. She wanted to fight the desire making her want to catch his lips in a tantalising kiss, full of fiery heat and passion and the promise of so much more. She wanted to thread her fingers through his hair and toss that stupid Santa hat to the ground; she wanted to press her body against his in a searing make-out session.

Forty minutes later, they were sat in the dimly lit pub, the air permeated by the fragrance of perfumes, all the different alcohol concoctions, and the delicious aroma of all the food being cooked in the kitchen wafting as they were loaded onto plates and carried up the stairs leading into the dining room. Sabah was sitting at a table pushed up against the frosted window, strings of fairylights hanging over the glass pane, opposite Ezra, eyeing him over the tulip beer glass filled with Guinness. She swallowed the mouthful she'd taken, tasting the malty sweetness with a tinge of bitterness. It felt creamy and smooth on her tongue, the colour a dark ruby red in the glass, the foam all frothy and bubbly.

They were both on their third pint, people-watching and lapsing into a comfortable silence. The space surrounding them was heavy with the smell of food and beer, people's perfumes mingling in with everything and the slightest stench of BO slipping through. Sabah watched as a couple of people danced, spilling over each other, in the middle of a makeshift dance floor at the centre, half-blocking one of the doors letting out into the freezing night.

"You know," Sabah mused slowly. "I'm kind of glad that my work Christmas party was super low-key and at the bookstore. I don't think I could handle being surrounded by so many drunk people."

"Mine was just like this," Ezra laughed. "We went to the local pub last Friday and there were about three other parties going on at the same time. It was pretty wild."

"Yeah?" Sabah asked, arching an eyebrow. "You hook up with anyone?" A hot and angry hand clawed at her insides, scratching at her chest and stomach. She swallowed, biting her lip, when she recognised it as jealousy.

"Wouldn't you like to know?" Ezra smirked, his eyes sparkling. Sabah narrowed hers. He laughed. "No, I didn't."

"Good," she whispered, downing the rest of her Guinness. Then, louder, she glanced up at Ezra who was staring at her with an almost impressed look on his face, she said, "Sucks to be you, not getting laid and all."

"It's not so bad. But I mean, I do have my eye on this gorgeous girl and I guess I'm just waiting for her to make the move."

Sabah's heart stuttered in her chest, beating rapidly. A light sheen of sweat glossed her upper lip and she surreptitiously lifted a hand to wipe it away, twirling the pint glass in her hands. "I need something sweet now," she said, ignoring the way he was looking at her like she was something wonderful, ignoring the way her heart was thumping his name with every beat—*Ez-ra, Ez-ra, Ez-ra*—and ignoring the horniness creeping inside her like a smooth sailing boat. "I want something with chocolate. Maybe Nutella."

"Do you want to come over?" Ezra suggested, his voice low and rich and brimming with desire. There was no masking it. He wanted her. "I've got croissants and I've got Nutella."

Sabah met his eyes, "do you have butter, too?"

"I do." He poured back the rest of his beer into his mouth. Sabah watched his throat work as he swallowed the Guinness, wondering briefly what it would be like to have his mouth on her. "I've got the whole chocolate and croissant package, and toast, if you want that."

"Lead the way."

Ezra's place was a beautiful Victorian house with a tree-lined driveway, snow completely covering the roof, the edges lit up with bright and sparkling fairylights, the same as the ones sparkling in the windows. A huge green and red floral wreath, dotted with magnolias and glitter, hung on the dark blue front door. The snow had slowed as Sabah took Ezra's hand once they got out of the Uber, carefully following him up the pathway to his front door, marvelling at the bare branches glistening with snow flanking the large house. Around them, the snow had piled up high, and Sabah was glad for the leather boots she wore, the thermal tights working to keep her legs warm, as she slowly shuffled through it with the low-heels.

When he unlocked the door, the warmth was the first thing to hit her, followed by the scent of fresh mint and vanilla. Sabah glanced around the large hallway, taking in the archway leading into another extended foyer and the photograph-lined wall along the staircase, the cool grey painted walls and the deep, plush grey carpets.

She saw a red and gold garland twisted around the banister, as she walked deeper into the house, somehow managing to take her boots off without needing to sit down and pull them off with a loud grunt, and leaving them by the shoe-rack, following Ezra as he led her down the foyer and into a large kitchen. The kitchen was gorgeous and bright, with one wall entirely made of glass, looking out into the garden, with a herringbone patterned hardwood flooring, pale grey cupboards and cabinets and the biggest island she'd ever seen at the centre of the room catching the attention, while all the important necessities were stainless silver. The countertops were a taupe marble, the walls a bright white, fairylights strung around the ceiling, passing off a soft gold glow. There was a large table by the far right corner, a deep mahogany, in sharp contrast with the rest of the colour palette in the kitchen, with the chair frames the same mahogany but the linen covers were a pale grey. At the centre of the table, over the red and gold-edged table-runner, was an expensive looking crystal vase, spilling over with bright red flowers, large and trumpet shaped, paired with baby's breath and hollies.

Everything was so Christmassy and beautiful; Sabah wanted to capture it in her mind, save it for later. “Your house is gorgeous,” Sabah whispered, turning her head to look at Ezra, who had taken off his Santa hat and shrugged out of his coat. He hung it over the back of a chair, placed the hat down on the dining table and looked at her, grinning.

“Thank you. We had the kitchen remodelled last year. Mum decided it was time for a change after my dad left,” he paused, then turned his face toward the open doorway, where a burst of laughter reached them, along with the sound of a movie that Sabah recognised as *Elf*. “Elsa,” he called out, moving toward the doorway and shouting out “I’m home.”

There was a pause, where Sabah took her teddy coat off and hung it over Ezra’s on the chair, and she leaned against the table, looking out of the wide glass doors into the garden. Everything was covered in a brilliant white, the sky a deep violet, dotted with a few stars.

“You want just Nutella or will you have it in a croissant? Or do you want toast?” Ezra asked, as he opened a white door to a built-in pantry opposite the dining table. He took out a tin and held up a plain croissant. Sabah’s mouth watered as she debated between the croissants and Nutella, or toast with butter or Nutella. *Which was better?*

“I’ll have two croissants, please,” she said.

He nodded. “Grab me two plates and a knife, will you? They’re both on the drying rack.”

"Hey, *oh*—" Sabah glanced up, two ceramic white plates in her hand, paired with a butter knife, at the girl who looked remarkably like Ezra. Walking slowly over to him, she handed him the plates and knife and he took them from her, loading up four croissants onto a plate, before slicing into them and spreading a heavy layer of Nutella inside each. "Who're you?" the girl asked, glancing from Sabah, to Ezra. Beside her was a gorgeous blonde girl, chewing on her lower lip. They were both still stood in the doorway, watching as Sabah stood near the open pantry cupboard.

"Um," Sabah said, suddenly feeling a little shy. She didn't know why she hadn't expected his little sister to be home. Christmas was only a few days away, so of *course* she would be. "I'm Sabah, I'm a friend of Ezra's."

"Right," Elsa nodded, a slow smirk tugging on her face. "A friend. *Sabah*. I've heard a lot about you." Beside her, the blonde girl giggled.

"Shut *up*," Ezra sighed, putting the plate of croissants into the microwave for a few seconds and then putting the tin of the remaining croissants back into the pantry. He put the knife in his mouth, sucking away the chocolate. Sabah watched him. "Don't be weird."

"You're the one that's weird," Elsa replied. "This is Sailor, by the way," she put her hand on her friend's elbow. "My friend."

I gathered that, Sabah wanted to say. "Nice to meet you."

"When's mum back?" Ezra took out the plate of croissants after a few seconds and put two on the other plate, handing it to Sabah with a gentle smile. "It's Christmas Eve in two days."

"Tomorrow evening, I think," Elsa replied, coming a little further into the room, still eyeing Sabah curiously. "You guys smell like alcohol."

"We had some beer." Ezra shrugged and took a seat at the kitchen island, on the grey barstool with gold legs, his back to the wide glass windows. Sabah took a seat beside him and picked up a croissant, the Nutella all melted and perfect inside. A dollop of melted chocolate dropped onto her plate and she swiped it up with the croissant, taking a giant bite of it.

"So, are you going to stay for Christmas?" Elsa asked, her eyes on Sabah.

Feeling her cheeks heat up beneath the soft kitchen light, Sabah stuttered out a reply, "um, n-no, I'm, uh, not."

"That's a shame," Elsa beamed wider, her eyes glittering with mirth. "I'm sure Ezra would love for you to stay. Isn't that right, big brother?"

"Go away," Ezra mumbled around a large mouthful of chocolate pastry. "Finish your shitty Christmas film." Sabah sniggered, hiding her smile behind her hand as she chewed.

Sailor gasped. "Oh my god, take that back."

"*Elf* is shit," Ezra deadpanned. "I don't know how you guys can watch it without cringing."

"That's blasphemy," Elsa narrowed her eyes. "I renounce you as my blood."

"I don't care."

"He's got a point," Sabah interjected, watching the back-and-forth banter. "It's a crappy Christmas film and the second-hand embarrassment is *real*. It's unrealistic that he's that stupid. And Will Ferrell sucks. He's annoying and plays the same role in everything."

"I don't like you anymore." Elsa sniffed and turned on her heel, her fingers splaying over Sailor's forearm and stalking out of the kitchen. Sabah's laugh spluttered out as she heard them turn up the volume of *Elf* in what she assumed to be the living room.

"It's okay," Ezra told her when she looked at him, his eyes sparkling with stars. "I still like you."

"I'm so glad," Sabah fluttered her lashes. "That makes me feel *oh-so* good."

He smirked. "I could make you feel better, princess."

Tilting her head a little, her hair fell over her left shoulder, the sleeve of her oversized grey jumper pulled up a little, revealing her slim forearms and the three butterfly tattoos on her left wrist. "Is that a promise?"

"Most *definitely*, my sugar plum fairy princess."

Sabah burst out laughing, her hair feeling like silk against the nape of her neck and tumbling around her shoulders and back. "Is that a *Nutcracker* reference?"

His laugh was light. "Yeah, I mean, *Barbie and the Nutcracker* is a very underrated movie." His voice was serious but his eyes were lined with humour.

"*The Princess and the Pauper* would like to ask you to reconsider," Sabah teased. "But I do have to ask," she lifted an eyebrow, tearing off a chunk of her second croissant and plopping it into her mouth, "why am I a sugar plum fairy princess?"

"Your hair," Ezra murmured, turning to face her fully, his knees spread wide. He reached up a hand and stroked his fingers along her curtain fringe, touching the glossy candyfloss pink strands. "You look so beautiful." His voice was low and gentle, humming over her like a song she wanted to listen to for the rest of her life. "And I like your nose piercing, by the way. I don't think I ever told you."

Sabah swallowed. "You didn't," she whispered.

His legs were touching hers and something blossomed in Sabah's chest, a flutter of nerves and pure *feelings*. She looked at him beneath the light silver and gold glow of the fairylights, the gentle snow falling behind Ezra like a perfect winter backdrop, the air heavy with the smell of mint and vanilla. Sabah felt raw and open, her breath caught in her lungs, her stomach fluttering with butterflies. A spark of electricity flooded through her system as she met his gaze and, really slow, leaned forward, her hand reaching up to cup his jaw, feeling the beginnings of a beard shadowing his jaw and cheeks.

She stared into his eyes for a second, seeing them darkening with lust, a fire of anticipation swirling like a flame, before she bridged the gap separating them. She kissed him.

It was everything poetic and divine, full of fairytales and every over-the-top lyrical description Sabah could think of, as her fingers swept through Ezra's long soft hair. His lips were also really soft and supple against hers, feather-light and so gentle. He teased her with another light brush of his lips before deepening the kiss, nudging his tongue against hers with bold and sensuous strokes. It was a lusty, alcohol-soaked kiss, full of exploration and passion and ardent desire.

He tasted like chocolate croissants and the bittersweet Guinness. Sabah's fingers continued to tug on his thick and soft hair, curling her fingers into the chestnut brown waves. Her heartbeat pounded, thudding hard against her ribcage, so loud she thought he could hear it.

A gasp caught in her throat when his teeth slowly, teasingly, nipped at her lower lip. A little moan escaped her mouth and into his as he kissed with purpose, his hands sliding through her hair and down her spine, to the curve of her ass. He peppered open-mouthed kisses against her jaw and down the column of her neck, swiping his tongue in one long sweep along the pulse beating at her throat. She held back a whimper when he pressed a kiss against the shell of her ear, his breath hot and tantalising.

"Does the rest of you taste as good as your pretty mouth?" he whispered in her ear. She closed her eyes, her breath escaping in a sharp exhale, her fingers slipping to his wide shoulders and grasping the thick material of his jumper.

She tilted her chin up to capture his lips in another kiss, tracing nonsensical patterns as her hand slid down to his. She kissed him for a long moment, remembering to breathe through her nose, her tongue nudging his in a slow dance. Heat bloomed beneath her skin, his other hand reaching back up to hold the base of her neck gently, his fingers stroking her skin slowly. His touch felt like the lightest brush of silk. Sabah moaned into Ezra's mouth quietly, and held his hand tighter, squeezing for a second, before putting his hand on her thigh and sliding it up higher, between her legs.

His breath fanned over her face as she moved back slightly, just enough to look him straight in the eyes. "Why don't you find out?"

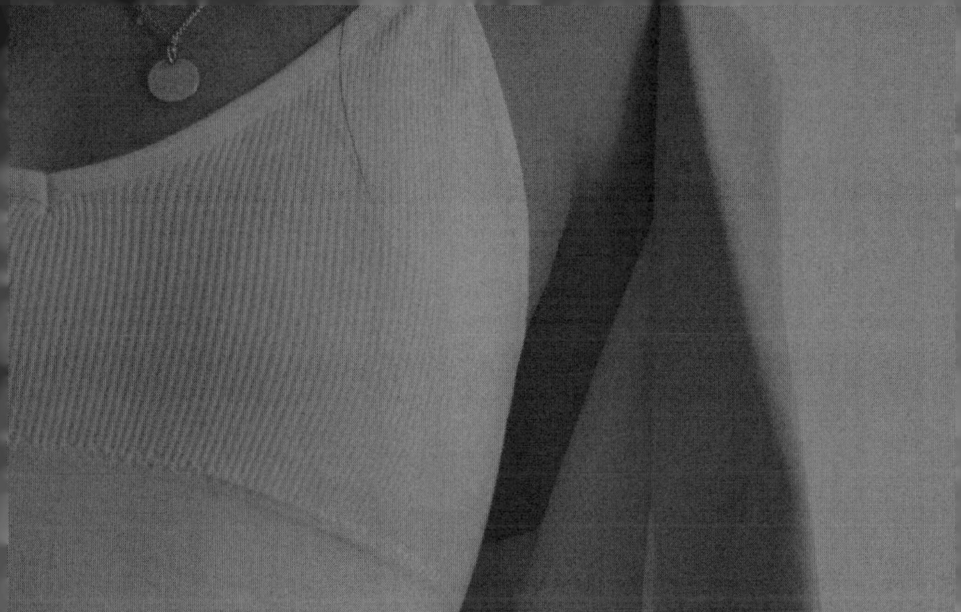

CHAPTER SIX

THE PALE SUNLIGHT SLANTED THROUGH THE light grey drapes, bouncing off the bright white snow sheathing the world outside in a dangerously cold canvas. The falling snow tumbled down heavily from the slate coloured sky, like a sunlit glitter of ballet choreographed by the whistling wind, layering the cobblestone ground in a thick layer of a sparkling wintry landscape. Feathered crystals frosted the windowpanes, while the weak gleam of the sun's glow rippled beneath Sabah's eyelids the next morning.

There was a faint headache creeping up around her temples and settling in the centre of her forehead, her mouth dry and throat parched. With a quiet groan and a careful stretching of her limbs, Sabah opened her eyes, squinting against the light pouring in through the parted curtains. She lifted a hand and covered her mouth as she yawned widely, sitting up to glance around the slightly unfamiliar room. She knew she was in Ezra's bedroom, alone, but she'd barely had a chance to look around the night before when they stumbled up the soft carpeted stairs, pausing every so often to press against the wall in a smouldering kiss, hands scraping beneath clothes and leaving behind a blazing trail.

Shoving away the heavy goose-down duvet encased in a soft cotton cover, Sabah swung her legs over the edge of the bed, staring down at her feet. The raspberry pink nail polish she had applied a few days ago was beginning to chip. As she sat there, the faintest of headaches scratching her eyeballs, snapshots of the night before swept through her mind like a montage, muddled with the gleaming red wine he'd brought up a little after two A.M., while she lay naked beneath his sheets, heart racing and trying to catch her breath after the way he'd had her legs hooked over his shoulders while she gripped the pillows, turning her face into it to muffle her moans. It had been a long time since she'd had sex, had felt comfortable enough to be so completely vulnerable and open, to express what she wanted. Somehow, the moment Ezra gently laid her down on his bed, he cracked the guards she'd had up and slowly brought down the walls—he made her feel safe.

They'd gone at it for six hours and Sabah could feel the soreness in her limbs and abdomen, the volume on his TV loud enough to stifle her moans, the sky outside a deep violet, the soft glow of the moon breaking through the falling snow. Running her hands through her hair, Sabah sighed and rose to her feet, sliding on the thick stripy dressing gown hanging on the back of the door, before slowly opening it and creeping out, footfalls muffled by the plush carpet, into the landing. She could hear quiet chatter and festive music downstairs, her heart tugging at the sounds, as she walked into the bathroom, the door wide open. There was a post-it note on the mirror that caught her attention as she washed her hands.

There are some spare toothbrushes in the cabinet (take your pick of the colours)! :) -Elsa xx

A smile slid across Sabah's face as she plucked the note off the mirror and crumpled it up before tossing it into the bin, near the toilet. Tucking her hair behind her ears, she opened the mirrored cabinet, to the right of the large circle-shaped wooden mirror at the centre of the wall, above the sink and wide marble counter. The bathroom was all natural and bright with wood aesthetics and a big bamboo laundry basket over by the built-in storage cabinet, the bath a large claw-foot tub against a white tiled marble wall.

Taking a purple electric toothbrush out of its packaging, Sabah spread a liberal amount of toothpaste on it and sat down on the edge of the bathtub. As she brushed her teeth, she thought about texting Veda and Sabrina, letting them know that she'd hammered the final nail in the coffin and had a hell of a time at the wake.

Getting laid was long overdue.

Ten minutes later, she was back in Ezra's bedroom and had tugged on a pair of his boxers, after spying the partially open drawer and deciding to throw them on instead of wearing yesterday's thong, as well as his t-shirt and socks. His shirt hit mid-thigh—she could get away with it being a dress, paired with a cute belt and tights and it would be a nice look. She swallowed back the giggle climbing in her throat and grabbed the dressing gown she'd thrown at the end of his bed, sliding into it and dropping her phone into the deep pocket. It was a little unfair how guys' clothes always had pockets, but finding an article of women's clothing that had pockets was like an Olympic sport. Glancing at the light pouring into the room between the gap in the curtains, Sabah pulled them back and grimaced at the sight. Everything outside was covered in knee-deep snow, a thick bed of brilliant white, with flakes still drifting.

"Shit," she breathed. There was no way she was going to be able to go home.

With a million thoughts buzzing through her mind and her stomach feeling jittery, Sabah slowly walked down the stairs, her fingers dancing over the garland coiled around the banister and her footfalls inaudible over Michael Bublé's *It's Beginning to Look a Lot Like Christmas*. She took note of the photographs lining the wall, various pictures depicting Ezra with his mum and Elsa, and another girl that was so clearly another sister. They all shared the same brown hair and hazel eyes, carbon copies of their mum, with the same warmth and huge smiles. But some of the pictures, she noted, held an aura of sadness within it, a kind of tightness around their eyes and forced smiles. She wondered what had happened, holding the photograph in her mind, as she headed into the kitchen where Elsa and Sailor were sitting at the table, eating cereal and Ezra was standing by the counter, flipping through a cookbook, a mug of what smelt like coffee in his hand.

"Well," Sabah said, her voice falling into the kitchen in the lulling of the music and the comforting silence, "looks like we're all stuck here for a while."

"Looks that way," Ezra smirked, meeting her gaze. "Morning, sleepyhead."

She rolled her eyes, fighting back the urge to smile and took a seat opposite Sailor at the dining table. "Morning, guys," she said to them, meeting Sailor's gaze as her lips kicked up a notch into a wide beam. Sabah found herself smiling back, unable to resist—that girl's smile was infectious.

"You know," Sailor began, glancing from Sabah to Ezra, her smile dipping into a smirk and eyes glinting with mischief. "Other than Elsa and I being here, being snowed in would be the cutest start to a Christmas rom-com for you two."

Ezra's laugh twinkled in the air, dancing over to Sabah and yanking away the hollowness of her chest and settling into her heart, making a home. Sabah grimaced and turned her head to watch him as he grabbed a pink Sleeping Beauty mug and placed it on the counter, near the kettle bubbling and steaming away. He put two spoonfuls of Nescafe coffee and sugar in the mug, before pouring in a dash of oat milk and vegan double cream, followed by a squirt of caramel syrup and the boiled water. As he stirred, he glanced up to meet Sabah's gaze. "Toast?" at her nod, he flashed a smile and took out four slices of brown bread from the bread bin and dropped them into the toaster.

Sabah felt her heart hiccup, her chest swelling with an emotion that she shoved down, out of reach, trying to shake away the hearts in her eyes as Ezra leaned against the counter, a wide beam on his face and a satisfied look in his eyes. His hair was dishevelled and falling over his eyes, his jaw-line sharp and angular, and his lips all rosy and pouty in the early morning as the sun poured through the windows and lit up the kitchen. When the toasts popped back up, Ezra grabbed them and put them onto two separate plates, before putting the oat milk and cream back into the fridge, and grabbing a tub of light butter and strawberry jam to spread over all the toast slices.

With the toasts liberally coated with butter and jam, Ezra brought over Sabah's plate and mug of coffee, before going back to get his own, and sitting down beside her. As she took a long and slow sip of the coffee, her palms taking in the warmth from the mug, Sabah found herself thinking about last night again, while Sailor started listing all the Christmas movies they need to watch today, starting with *The Santa Clause*. Staring out of the window at the piles of snow that was still rising, and still falling, Sabah thought about Ezra and the fuzzy feeling he gave her, the blossoming crush she knew would, inevitably, crush her—it was a burden anchoring her to a broken ship.

It was like she was underwater, trying not to drown, while she forced herself to remember the way they fell into this friendship, this kind of weird relationship where he made her, for the first time in months, laugh. She didn't want to lose that when whatever this whole thing was, sex and undeniable attraction, came to end in flames, because goddammit, she valued him so much. He meant so much to her and she couldn't lose that, lose him, when she was barely hanging on by a thread.

Sighing deeply, Sabah took another sip of the coffee and bit into her first slice of toast, bread crumbs scattering over the mahogany tabletop. Around her, the conversation continued on, and she felt a little like she was drifting out of her body, watching everything unfolding and whirling like a tornado, ripping apart everything she'd become comfortable with. A small, hopeful part of her wanted to risk the end, to tell Ezra that she wanted to try, but the saner part of her, the stronger part, was screaming to hold back, to tell him they could never have a repeat of the night before. It was a mistake. *One giant colossal mistake.*

She crunched down the toast, finishing it off, and reached for the other slice, startling as Elsa asked if she had any plans for the day.

If she hadn't been caught up in this blizzard and stuck at Ezra's, she would've had work from nine to five-thirty, followed by going home and shutting her bedroom door while she switched onto Netflix and watched her favourite episode of *Friends*, The One Where Everybody Finds Out, and grabbed her secret stash of popcorn and Aero from the bottom drawer of her dressing table. She would've probably reapplied the chipping nail polish in an attempt to make it *look* like she had her life on track and like she wasn't trying to push away anything that made her *feel.*

"Uh, no," Sabah said, brushing the crumbs off her hands onto the now empty plate. "I just need to call my manager to let her know I won't be in, but other than that," she shrugged, "no plans."

"I want a mug cake," Elsa declared, after slurping up the milk from the yellow and pink floral bowl. "A chocolate one."

"At eight in the morning?" Ezra lifted his eyebrows, stacking his plate on top of Sabah's and leaning back in his chair.

"You can't chat," Sabah pointed out to Ezra. "You had pizza at, like, ten, remember?"

"Yeah, but," Ezra narrowed his eyes at her, the ghost of a smile flitting across his face. "She's twelve."

"I'm *eighteen*."

Sabah continued sipping her coffee slowly, the caramel and sugary sweetness coating her tongue and sating her caffeine needs,

"Same thing, Els."

"It's so not," Sailor laughed. "I think you need to go back to primary school, Ezra. How did you even graduate?"

"With great difficulty," he sighed. "I just about got a first."

"At least you got a first, Mr Perfectionist," Elsa rolled her eyes. "*Anyway*, the point is, stop being a hypocrite."

"It's the older sibling syndrome."

"I can make you the mug cake," Sabah piped up in the world's most casual voice, ignoring the way butterflies erupted in her stomach, fluttering their wings a mile a second, as Ezra smiled that beatific smile. "If you want."

"Oh, will you? That would be brilliant," Elsa practically buzzed with excitement. "I'd do it, but I just can't be arsed to move."

Sabah laughed. "I've got fuck all to do today, so I'm more than happy to bake whatever your heart desires."

"The woman of my dreams," Ezra mumbled, swallowing his mouthful of coffee, his hazel eyes glimmering with a soft look that made Sabah blush. Damn him and his pretty eyes and pretty dimples and pretty fucking face.

After putting Elsa and Sailor's mug cakes into the microwave, Sabah made two more chocolate mug cakes for Ezra and herself, laden with extra Lindt chocolates and sprinkled with powdered sugar. She yawned and stretched, ignoring the heat in Ezra's gaze when he looked at her, blatantly checking her out. She looked away from him and busied herself with deftly working her hair into a fishtail braid, telling herself that everything was fine and they could go back to the very sexually frustrated friendship they'd had to begin with. Loads of people hooked up and stayed friends, so they could too. It was just one night of glorious passion and probably the best sex she'd had in a very long time. But it didn't mean that everything they had before it would have to end.

A dinging caused her to turn her attention the built-in microwave. When she took out the two chocolate mug cakes, walking around the kitchen island over to the table where Elsa and Sailor were sitting, both of them on their phones, Ezra put the remaining two mugs in the microwave and set the timer for one minute and thirty seconds.

"Do you guys want whipped cream with it?" Sabah asked the girls, playing with the ends of her braid.

"Nah, I'm good, thanks though," Sailor shot her a smile. "And thank you so much for making this. I appreciate you tons." She spooned up a heapful of the chocolate cake onto a teaspoon and blew on it before taking a bite, her eyes widening. Sabah found herself feeling a little envious of just how blue Sailor's eyes were, like a gorgeous bright cyan, with a darker sapphire around the outer edges. She was so fucking beautiful. "Oh my god, Sabs, can I call you that, by the way? This is freakin' amazing!"

"You can," Sabah laughed. "And thank you. It's just putting some ingredients together."

"Yeah, but mine never tastes this good," Elsa said, her mouth full. "Seriously. This is amazing. If you can do this with a mug cake, what can you do with an actual cake?"

"That's what I want to know, too," Sailor nodded. "Like, for real. I thought I could bake, but this is so good."

"Don't be modest, Sailor," Ezra interjected. "Your cupcakes and macaroons are to die for. Fairylights are gorgeous, and so are stars. You're both good at what you do and shouldn't compare."

"Comparison is the thief of happiness, or whatever that quote is." Sabah made to go to the microwave when it dinged but Ezra shook his head, making her sit back down. She looked at him as he grabbed the Sleeping Beauty mug for her and the Groot mug for himself, filled to the edge with a delicious scented chocolate cake that was all hot and gooey with melted chocolate inside.

"Thief of joy," Ezra said, sliding her mug to her at the table as he sat down.

"Right," she nodded. "Joy. And anyways, baking a cake and making a mug cake are totally different. I just follow instructions, but with mug cakes it's a little simpler and I've added my own little tweaks to it."

"What's your favourite thing to bake?" Elsa asked her, swallowing and loading another mouthful of cake into her mouth. "Besides cake."

"Brownies, for sure," she shovelled the hot chocolate cake into her mouth, almost burning her tongue in the process. "And cookies, I guess, or like a mix of the two, like with layers of it. God, that's just so good."

"You know what would be chaotically good and sickening?" Sailor leaned forward, a chocolate coated smile on her face. "Making a layer of cheesecake, cookies and brownies, and it would be the perfect dessert for Christmas."

"With the brownie at the bottom?" Elsa asked.

"No," Sailor shook her head. "We'll have the cheesecake as normal, but make extra of the, you know, filling and have it in between the brownie and cookie and then another layer on top, too. And each layer of it will be different, methinks."

"That sounds long."

"And so good. Sickening, but good," Sabah grinned, intrigued. "It'll be a lot of bowls, though."

"I'm not helping," Ezra said. "You lot can do that on your own."

"You're doing Christmas dinner anyway," Elsa pointed at him. "Speaking of, how are you doing the potatoes? Because I want it mashed but Sailor wants it crispy."

He sighed. Sabah bit back a smile.

"I'll help you?"

"It's okay," he smiled at her. She swooned inside. "As long as you guys do the dessert first, and stay the hell out of the kitchen, I'll be fine."

She shrugged, "if you say so, dude." After scraping up the last of her chocolate cake, Sabah turned her attention to her vibrating phone.

Mother Dearest at 09:34: *Where are you? Could've let me know you weren't going to be home, especially with this bloody weather. Are you with Jake?*

Mother Dearest at 09:36: *For goodness sake, Sabah, this is getting ridiculous. How many times are you going to make the same mistake?*

Gritting her teeth, Sabah quickly tapped out a reply.

Sabah at 09:35: *i'm not with jake, i'm with another mate and staying here til this blizzard blows over. In meadowbrook.*

Feeling annoyance flickering through her, Sabah locked her phone and put it face down on the table. She didn't want to let anything, or anyone, ruin this semi stress-free blissful few days snowed in with the guy she was kind of, sort of, maybe crushing on, a little, and his sister and her best friend.

It was a few days away from her life, away from the constant doom and gloom of the rainy clouds hanging over her head, and she wanted to savour every moment. She wanted to be able to hold onto the lingering looks and the feather-light touches between her and Ezra, feel close to him without being terrified of losing it all, before everything got crapped on. But already, she was feeling the low, morose sense of foreboding crawling towards her.

She had no idea what would happen when she told him that they couldn't have a repeat of the night before. She didn't know how to, and a part of her didn't even *want* to. She *liked* it. She *wanted* it to happen again. *Even if it petrified her.*

Later that night, as the sky was speckled with shades of lavender and violet, darkening to a deep blue, dotted with the faintest stars. The snow had only stopped falling about an hour ago, as Sabah put the lasagne into the oven. She'd got the recipe off Sabrina, adding the Bengali twist to one of her favourite meals, and paired it with garlic sautéed vegetables and extra cheesy garlic bread. Ezra had brought out a bottle of Tesco's Finest Montepulciano D'abruzzo and poured them into four wine glasses, as they sat and ate in the living room, watching *The Santa Clause* and discussing the possibility of Santa being real.

"But how do we know he's not, though?" Sailor asked. "Anything could be real. Like, even vampires and witches."

"This isn't about paranormal creatures," Ezra said, pointing the wine bottle at her, before refilling his glass and Sabah's. "It's about Santa and you're doing a poor job at selling his realness, Sailor Moon. He's based on a person, right, Saint Nicholas or whoever, and it's one of those urban myth—"

"But how do we know though? It could all be real, based on things that have been seen thousands of years ago. It's the same as our dreams. How do we know they're not real when we see them?"

"We don't know—"

"Exactly!" Sailor exclaimed, turning her attention back to the TV briefly. "Like I said, anything could be real. It would be magic concealing Santa and the North Pole from us, more because as we grow up we stop believing in magic and the excitement of Christmas and everything. We just stop believing and that stops us from seeing."

"Okay, Peter Pan," Ezra snorted. His fingers grazed Sabah's thigh and she shivered slightly, feeling the warmth of his body heat radiating against her, remembering how it felt to have his fingers running down her body. "You can't convince me. Santa's not real, let's just leave it that."

"You suck," Sailor said, throwing a soggy pea at him. It fell on a sofa cushion and he flicked it away, where it disappeared out of sight.

"Oh my god, what did you do that for?" Elsa groaned. "Now we're probably going to squish it into the carpet."

"Hoover tomorrow, then," he shrugged, sipping his wine. Sabah leaned against him, watching as the new Santa rode away on his jingling sleigh.

"On Christmas Eve?"

"Yep."

"You do it."

"Nope." Ezra's smile was dripping with sweetness, a teasing note belying his words. Sabah glanced at his side profile, taking in the overgrown stubble that was turning into a dark shadowed beard, making him look wild and dangerously sexy, like some kind of rock star with a heart of gold when he flashed that dimpled grin. It ripped something open in her, bleeding and saccharine, coloured in rose pinks and crimson reds, spilling into her chest with the kind of familiar bloom she was trying not to feel.

It was kind of pointless though, as she sat there, sandwiched between him and his sister, the dressing gown she stole tugged tautly over her bottom and thighs, where she draped it to cover her legs. The same feeling from that morning swooped her under its blanket, wrapping around her in a suffocating embrace as she slowly breathed in and out, trying to calm the nerves battling inside her. They were just friends, for god's sake, so she didn't get why she felt flustered whenever she caught his eye or when his hand brushed against her thigh, or when he put his hand on her knee like he was doing now.

She sat up a little straighter, keeping her eyes focused on the screen as Sailor grabbed the remote and scrolled down Disney+ to find another movie.

"*The Nutcracker and the Four Realms* okay?" Sailor asked as she pressed play.

"Even if we disagree, are you going to listen?" Ezra asked, stroking slow circles on Sabah's knee with his thumb, his other fingers gently squeezing her thigh. His hand slowly trailed a little higher and she swallowed. She shifted on the sofa and cracked her knuckles, not looking at him because she knew if she did, her eyes would betray every emotion she was burying.

"No, not really," Sailor replied.

This was going to be a long night.

CHAPTER SEVEN

SABAH SAT CURLED ON THE LARGE NAVY VELVET armchair, the edges gold-stitched, amongst a collision of brightly coloured cushions—(okay, there were three, but they *were* super bright and clashed with the chair and were some of the only bright colours in Ezra's room: red, yellow and gold)—reading a book on the Kindle app she'd downloaded on her phone, feet covered with a pair of Elsa's fuzzy socks and her upper body drowning in one of his hoodies (a grey Nike one that she was planning on stealing).

She was safe from the harsh cold of the blizzard outside, the snow on the ground etching higher overnight, breathing in the warm scent of cinnamon and chocolate, the brownies and cookies she'd helped Sailor make earlier still spreading their magical aroma throughout the entire house. With the flurry of snow going on outside, a promise of a gorgeous and bright white Christmas, Sailor had then shooed Sabah and Elsa away from the kitchen as she made the three different cheesecake fillings—chocolate, lemon, and cream cheese mixed with crushed Oreos.

While Elsa had settled in the living room to watch *The Princess Switch*, Sabah had slinked upstairs to read *Tweet Cute*, trying her best not to stare at Ezra as he sat on the gaming chair facing his TV, playing *Fortnite* and chatting on the headset to some of his mates. Even as she read, her gaze kept drifting to him, unable to focus on Jack talking to his dad about his relationship with his mum—she kept rereading the same line: "I fell in love with your mom within a minute of meeting her. Nothing in the world was gonna stop it."

It was only when Ezra took off his headset, clicked off the game and put on *Friends*—The One With the Ride-Along—that she was able to stop staring at him with heart eyes, a blush staining her cheeks with a pink glow, reminiscing their kisses. But that was only because, with his attention undisturbed, Sabah wanted to appear indifferent. It helped when he disappeared to have a shower and she was left alone, with the magic of Emma Lord's words and her thoughts about Ezra with his stupid smile and his stupid dimples and his stupid freckles she wanted to trace with her fingertips and his stupid abs and his stupid arms that held her up as he plunged into her.

"No," Sabah said out loud, as she kept losing focus and found her pulse threading with desire and her thoughts swimming with Ezra and the way it felt to be kissed by him. "We are not fucking doing this. Bad idea."

The door creaked open and she jumped, her heart pounding in her chest. Her phone went flying, landing on the floor by the bed.

"Talking to yourself is the first sign of madness." Ezra's smile was teasing, his eyes a light amber in the brightness of the early December morning.

Sabah ignored him and instead, went to pick up her phone. She held her breath as she checked it over for any cracks, knowing she wouldn't be able to replace it without making a massive dent in her bank balance. "Have a good shower?" she asked, perching on the bed, leaning against the headboard. She watched him as he came around to the side of the bed she was sitting at, leaning to open the top drawer of the bedside table.

"I did," Ezra said absently, taking out a tub of *The Body Shop*'s coconut body butter. "It was very pleasant."

"Good." Sabah swallowed, her gaze sweeping over his bare chest, the strong muscles defined and carved as if they were made of stone. He had a perfect v-line, cutting down to strong thighs and a big— Sabah shook her head, tearing her eyes away from his towel-wrapped waist, glancing up at his face and the smirk tilting his lips up.

Ezra looked at her and lifted an eyebrow as he unscrewed the tub, dropping it down with a clatter on the bedside table. Sabah tried to keep her face blank as she met his eyes, clenching her hands, knowing he was slowly rubbing that delicious coconut scented body butter all over his chest, arms and neck. She didn't want to feel the heat of desire slashing through her like a cut, she didn't want to feel that flash of emotion sinking into her stomach and uncoiling in her veins. She didn't want her heart to stutter and thud with an echo of his name, or think about him, or remember the feeling of his mouth. Remember how tenderly he kissed her. How gentle his hands were on her face as they slipped down her entire body, caressing her like she was a delicate thing. "Do my back for me, please?"

She sucked in a breath, her coffee-brown eyes slipping down his body and poring over all the hard lines and sharp angles, before rising back up and meeting his eyes, deepening with a look she recognised. "Sure," Sabah exhaled. She stood, taking some of that coconut body butter and warming it on her palm, rubbing her hands together. Slowly, as she stood behind him, taking in the sharp planes of his shoulder blades and the strong back muscles, the dimple on his lower back, Sabah gently ran both her hands over the backs of his shoulders. Sweeping her hands down, she smoothed the body butter all over his back, massaging it in, watching her fingers moving over his muscles. He had freckles scattered over the tops of his shoulders, spread like faint stars. Three white stretch marks graced the middle of his back, indented into the skin and tapering like claw marks.

His skin was unbearably soft. He shivered slightly, making Sabah pause, her hands resting over his lower back, right above the towel covering the curve of his butt.

"You good?"

"Yeah." Ezra cleared his throat. Sabah watched the muscles in his bicep shift as he lifted a hand, running it over his damp hair. "It feels nice. You have magic hands."

Releasing a quiet breath that was full of unspoken desire, Sabah rubbed some more of the cream into his shoulders, working her way down his arms. She felt the heat from his body rippling into her, a racing thunderstorm splitting across the caverns of her pounding chest. She quickly moved around to his front, keeping her gaze on her hands. Desire slid all across her body, singeing her fingertips as they danced across his collarbones and swept over his neck. She lightly rubbed the body butter from her fingers against his throat, the Adam's apple bobbing as he swallowed, the bristly hairs on his jaw scraping across her knuckles.

Ezra's hands slowly slid around her waist, pulling her flush against him, her hands curved around the nape of his neck. Lifting her eyes to meet his, Sabah's eyes darkened to deeper brown, all dilated pupils and lust, her breaths coming in short gasps when he squeezed her sides.

She raised her chin slightly, her mouth hovering close to his when he leaned down, his Roman nose brushing against the side of hers, their breaths mingling together. She could taste the mint from his mouthwash, smell the passion flower shampoo, the coconut scented cream across his skin.

A ripple of want yanked her under its tidal wave and she tiptoed, slanting her mouth over his in a soft kiss. His mouth danced a little smile as he kissed her back straight away, playfully nipping her pouty bottom lip with a sharp scrape of his teeth. His body was hard and soft at the same time, unyielding against her hands pressing over his pecs. She could feel his heart thumping beneath her hand, a steady beat that soothed any nervousness she might've felt—it was calming and thrilling all at once.

This kiss was like everything she'd been feeling since their first time melting together, exploding like burning hot and bright fireworks, a kaleidoscope of colours bursting as his mouth moved against hers. His hand slid up from her waist to her neck, cupping the name of her neck, beneath her hair, strands slipping through his fingers, as his other hand pulled her even closer to him. Sabah moaned into his mouth, and he kissed her slower, longer, deeper, his tongue brushing against hers, once, twice, thrice, in a teasing dance that made her ache for more. She twisted her fingers around the quickly drying strands of his chestnut brown hair, all silky in her hands, arching her body as she pressed herself against the hard planes of his body. She felt a flare of irritation at all the layers between them.

Ezra backed them up until the backs of Sabah's knees hit the edge of his upholstered bed and she sank onto the duvet, her legs quickly wrapping around his waist. She felt him hard against her, in between her legs, somehow the towel having fallen away in their movement. She ground her hips against him, a gasp escaping her lips as he bit her lower lip. She moved her hands down, feeling his muscles rippling and flexing under her palms as she caressed his back, moving lower until she cupped the firm globes of his butt. She squeezed them, her nails digging into his skin, as they continued kissing, a little rougher and harder.

A moan rasped out of him, tearing through her defences like a flame. His mouth trailed open-mouthed kisses of fire against the corner of her mouth, her jaw, peppering her neck with kisses and the light grazing of his teeth. His tongue licked down her neck and collarbone, sucking on the skin, fingers slipping beneath the hem of the hoodie she wore and branding her skin. She melted right then, putty in his hands, arching her back and grinding her hips against his bare body, aching for more than he was giving right then.

The warmth of his skin seared into her as her breaths escaped quickly, her chest rising and falling beneath the thick grey hoodie, her breasts lightly misted with sweat. Sparks of heat landed and burned her everywhere his hands were trailing across both rough and gentle, fingers scraping against her stomach and climbing higher.

Ezra shifted back slightly, pulling Sabah up with him to yank his hoodie off her. She stared at him, giving him those fuck me eyes, as his own, in that moment, were a dark shade of hazel, pouring over her body with a look that made her blush. She was only wearing fuzzy socks and a pair of his boxers. Sliding the *Deadpool* boxers off her body, Ezra tossed it over the bed, keeping his eyes trained on Sabah's face as he kissed her again.

She pulled him down on top of her again, feeling him pressing against her centre, right in between her slick thighs. Their mouths were warm and gentle against each other, in a kiss that could've melted the snowfall outside his window. Sabah moaned, her toes curling, when Ezra pressed his mouth to the side of her neck again, licking and kissing the skin there, leaving behind red marks that would turn into love bites. She wound her fingers through his hair as he dropped kisses all over her, sliding lower until he reached the valley between her breasts, licking away the light sheen of sweat coating her skin. She swallowed, her breath audible in the quiet lull between them, as his mouth closed over the dark peak of her left nipple.

His mouth on her was wet and hot, his other hand circling her right breast and squeezing before slipping down the length of her body, fingers dancing over her waist. She shivered at the contact, eyes closing and a sigh escaping, a breathless giggle dancing on the edge of her tongue when his knuckles brushed over her stomach. Her laugh turned into a moan when his thumb found her clit and his index finger slipped inside her.

This was nothing like their first time, their kisses and sex beer-soaked and quick. He was taking his time: his mouth licked a blazing trail across her breasts to suck her right nipple, his finger sliding in and out of her, his thumb rubbing her clit in quick and gentle circles. Her gasps and moans were loud, her hands clutching the cotton duvet cover beneath her. Sabah opened her eyes to meet Ezra's, when he lifted his head from her chest, finding him watching her with desire painted all over his face, a small smile that speared through her heart like Zeus's lightning bolt.

She stared into his eyes as his fingers worked faster, every sensation in her body rising to the highest point, her hips lifting off the bed. She was so close, tingles sparkling through her entire body down to the tips of her toes, as he slid another finger inside and his thumb continued working in circles.

"*Ezra*," Sabah gasped, moaning, the orgasm rolling through her like a crashing wave, spreading a warm heat and a gloss of sweat over her body. She shuddered as he pulled his fingers out, spreading her wetness over her folds, continuing to rub her clit for a few seconds longer. She bucked her legs, arching her back again as another orgasm swept through her. "Oh my *god*."

A low chuckle reverberated in his chest as he leaned down to kiss her again, his breath hot and undoing everything that held her together. She stroked his body lightly, before grasping hold of him, hard and almost silky in her hands. She pumped him, once, twice, continuing to kiss him.

Ezra's moan was quiet in her mouth, colliding into her like a tsunami, making her legs fall open wider and wrap around his waist.

"I need to be inside you," Ezra breathed against her mouth, tasting a little like the cinnamony hot chocolate she'd had earlier. A delighted thrill seeped into her bones as she nodded, watching as he reached over into the top drawer of his bedside table. Once he found the condom and tore it open, he quickly rolled it down.

Sabah lifted her legs over his shoulders, her eyes looking into his as he rubbed himself against her. He used a hand to position himself directly at her entrance before sinking in. He leaned down a little to kiss her, keeping his hands on her legs to hold them in place. Ezra's name swept out of Sabah's mouth like magic as he kept kissing her. They shifted together as he lowered himself and her legs slid down to wrap around his hips again, their hands entertained. Sabah murmured his name again like a prayer, pulses of blissful pleasure sweeping through her as he moved in and out, his thrusts becoming faster and deeper. She was enamoured with him in this moment, full of him and a third orgasmic bliss, oblivious to the cascading snow outside, flurries of snowflakes dancing down to the nearly two feet of snow.

Sabah bit his lower lip, her mouth moving sloppily against his bearded jaw and his neck, as he pounded into her faster. He moaned, his breath hot against her ear, making her shiver and gasp, slipping her hands out of his and raking her nails down his back. With a groan and a whisper of her name, Ezra shuddered and clutched her tighter. She locked her legs around him. He pressed a kiss to her damp forehead.

For a few seconds, they stayed like that, in a post-coital daze, coming down from that high. Sabah lay beneath him, feeling his heavy weight on her, her hands sliding up and down his back like before. She stared up at the ceiling, realising she'd broken the promise of it happening only that one time, but she couldn't bring herself to regret it. After all, he had magic hands and a magic fucking—

"You want to go make some lunch?"

Sabah blinked at him, startled out of the drifting of her thoughts. "Uh," she said. "Yes."

His smile, as he moved off her and sat up, was so utterly Ezra that it melted her heart.

The absence of his body on hers was an anchor that weighed her down. A feeling she couldn't name gripped her heart as she laid there, watching him as he disposed of the condom, tossing it into the bin full of nothing but wrappers and crumpled receipts.

Twenty minutes later, Ezra had a saucepan full of Tesco's spinach farfalle boiling in lightly salted water and a large frying pan with caramelised onions, red peppers and mince, seasoned with salt and pepper, curry powder, Cajun and some chilli flakes. On the kitchen island, there was a bowl of grated cheese, four light blue ceramic pasta plates, forks, and wine glasses, with an open bottle of red that Sabah had already poured into her glass.

She was sat on the chair, watching Ezra as he stirred the mince, onions and peppers with a wooden spoon, Italian music playing on the speakers. He was dancing as he worked, making Sabah smile slightly, her chin resting on her closed fist, a wine glass in her other hand, halfway to her mouth. When he looked at her with a grin splitting wide and a bright glimmer in his eyes, Sabah knew what he wanted. A laugh burst through her chest and out of her mouth.

"No," Sabah laughed. "I don't dance."

"Everybody dances," Ezra replied, coming around the island to put his hand on her shoulder, sliding down her arm. He plucked the wine glass out of her hand and put it on the table, then grabbed her hand, pulling her off the stool. "Dance with me, bella ragazza."

She expected herself to say no again, but it was overpowered by the curiosity cutting through the doubts circling her mind. She smiled at him, letting him guide her to the centre of the hardwood flooring. She followed his lead as they fell into step with the music, letting it steer their movements. Ezra's hand was clutched around

Sabah's, his fingers threaded laced with hers, while his other hand was circled around her waist. She could feel his touch through the grey hoodie she wore, her legs encased in a spare pair of Elsa's black leggings. Some small part of her was annoyed at having to wear other people's clothes for the past few days. Her right hand was on his shoulder, weaving into his thick locks, twirling them around her fingers.

"What song is this?" Sabah asked, tipping her head up to look into Ezra's eyes. The dark lashes framing his eyes cast a crescent shadow over his cheekbones, his eyebrows dark and straight. His mouth lifted into a crooked smile, dimples denting his cheeks.

"*La Cura* by Franco Battiato," he said quietly. His breath skimmed the top of her head, her baby hairs gently blowing. "It's one of my favourites. My parents used to listen to it all the time, until—" he sighed. "Until he cheated on her and left us for his whore."

"Did she know your dad was married?"

"Yeah." Ezra's laugh was sharp. "She knew. My parents had known her for years. I went to school with her daughter, Analiese, and we dated in school until year ten."

"What a pretentious name," Sabah smirked. Her fingers curled beneath his hair, stroking the nape of his neck. Touching him sent sparks of euphoria through her, an almost serene sense of calm that rocked with her in a gentle sway as they danced.

His smiling response was like a trickle of honeyed comfort as he twirled her around twice before dipping her gently, his mouth inches from hers. Her fingers splayed out across the expanse of his shoulders, creasing into the fabric of his soft beige jumper, her other hand on his elbow. His left hand was on the top of her back, while his right arm was around her waist, his hand holding and supporting her weight as if he could do this for the rest of his life. The way he was looking at her made Sabah blush, her thoughts clouded by him, him, him, as she stared into his eyes.

As he held her in that position, her gaze drifted to his parted lips before meeting his eyes again. A smile twitched on her lips when she noticed him looking at her mouth for a few seconds too long. His gaze held a look of *something* that sent an ache through her, as the soft baritone of Franco Battiato filled the kitchen.

Her chest blossomed with flowers, bursting to life in the cold winter as he slowly lifted her back. His hands were still around her, still holding her close to him. Sabah slowly breathed in and out, dropping her eyes to his jumper. She stroked her hands over the material, trying to calm her racing heart as the dance ended.

"Y-you should check on the mince," Sabah bit out, stepping back. Her voice felt loud in the silent kitchen, the song having come to a close She looked up at him from beneath her lashes. "It might burn."

"You two are so freakin' adorable," Elsa's voice came from the kitchen doorway, dipping in between the start of another song. "I can't even."

Sabah felt her cheeks burning as she spun around to face Elsa and Sailor, standing near the door, wide grins on their faces. Elsa had her hands clasped against her chest, eyes glittering. "You guys saw that?"

"Oh yeah," Sailor smirked. "I was hoping for a big, sweeping kiss, so I'm a little disappointed."

"Gross," Elsa said, wrinkling her nose. "I don't want to see my brother kissing someone. Ew."

"It's *romantic*."

"Still yucky, in my opinion."

"Dinner's going to be ready in a minute," Ezra interrupted their discussion, rolling his eyes, and throwing an amused smile at Sabah. She felt her own mouth curving up into a grin, her cheeks still flushed. "So you can just wait here."

"We're going to eat in the living room," Elsa said, coming into the kitchen. "We want to watch the second *Princess Switch*. Want to join?"

"No," Ezra replied flatly. "I do not."

"Same," Sabah mumbled, taking the boiled pasta and draining it in the sink, while Ezra opened a jar of Homepride creamy tomato pasta sauce. She put the saucepan back on the hob and watched Ezra spoon the mince, onion and peppers into the pasta, followed by the sauce. He handed it to Sabah and she filled it with a dash of water, sloshing it around to clean up the sauce on the sides of the jar. She stood next to him and poured it into the saucepan as he stirred everything together, and throwing in the grated cheese. She set the glass jar on the countertop, watching him as he continued mixing the pasta, the creamy sauce coating the food and the wooden spoon. It looked damn good. When it was cold outside, creamy pasta was heaven.

Everyone loaded up their plates, filled their wine glasses to the brim and parted ways: Elsa and Sailor headed into the living room, the *ta-dum* of Netflix reaching Sabah's and Ezra's ears as they sat at the kitchen table. Ezra had lowered the music volume, so it was just a soft background noise, along with *The Princess Switch: Switched Again* drifting through from the living room.

Sabah lifted a large forkful of the creamy, cheesy pasta and mince, diced pepper in the mix, and took a bite. She groaned at the taste, "this is so good, Ezra. Well done."

He laughed. "I aim to please."

"Oh, you *definitely* do." Sabah punctuated her words with a wink and a flirty smile, a little shocked at her brazenness. She'd never been so . . . forward-ish.

The grey, gold and beige accents of the room fit like a puzzle piece, brimming with light and opening up the space. She lifted an eyebrow when Ezra beamed, keeping her face neutral to stop a smile spilling over her mouth.

"Your cries of pleasure were proof enough of my abilities."

"You need some work," Sabah smirked around a mouthful of wine, using the glass to hide her blush. She tucked her hair behind her ear, glinting with four rows of sparkling pink studs from *Lovisa*.

"I'm more than happy to keep practicing." His voice fell into her like poetry, weaving its way through her soul like an incantation, burying beneath her rib cage like hidden treasure.

Sabah glanced up at him. He ate some more pasta, swallowed

the bite, and then washed it down with a deep sip of the ruby red wine. The pale sunlight cracked through the windows, the rays bouncing off the glass and reflecting on the table's surface. The snow outside made everything bright and incandescent, the snowflakes crystallised against the window panes—it was straight out of a glittery Christmas card, all white and silver, bare branches glistening with snowfall.

She took another long sip of deep red wine before putting the glass back down on the table, rolling her lips into her mouth as she sopped up some more sauce and mince onto her fork. She took a bite, chewing slowly, before taking another big forkful into her mouth. "This is so not Italian," Sabah said after a moment, swallowing. "Can't believe you're betraying your heritage like this, Carmichael."

"Shut up," Ezra laughed. "Blame your cousin for this anyway. At a dinner party a few months back, she made the most delicious pasta I ever had and I've been using a variation of her recipe ever since."

"Bengali twists to classic dishes are her specialty." Sabah felt a sliver of jealousy snake through her at having missed out on so much of Sabrina's life, of nights spent with her and Veda, because she chose some guy instead, ignoring every rule that said to never pick a guy over a girlfriend.

But at the time, she was still so angry.

"Speaking of Sabrina," Ezra said, refilling his wine. Sabah pushed her glass towards him and smiled when he filled it to the brim. "What happened between the two of you? One day, I saw the two of you together all the time at *Fairly Odd Pizzas*, and then the next, you were like strangers or something."

"We still talked occasionally," Sabah mumbled. "We had to. We were family and my sister lives with her. But um," she sighed, feeling her gut twist at the memories, the sharp ache of betrayal. "When I first met my ex, Jake, online, I told Sabrina about him. She messaged him telling him she heard a lot about me and all that, and then, I don't know, I guess they started talking and flirting. She knew I really liked him. It had only been a couple days at that time, but I did. Anyways," Sabah took another mouthful of her warm pasta. She swallowed. "He was talking to me a little less when talking to her and then told me they were flirting and had sexted and she sent him some nudes—"

"*What?*"

Looking up at his sharp tone, she found Ezra staring at her, slack-jawed, eyes icy. His fingers tightened around the fork he was holding. He blew out a sigh, shaking his head, his hair swaying with the movement. A thick strand fell over his left eye that he impatiently brushed away with his hand, dragging his fingers through his hair and holding it there, for a moment.

"Um, yeah, so," Sabah continued, her voice a little softer, keeping her gaze on Ezra's face. She felt a flash of heat sting her cheeks as he stared at her, straight into her eyes, as if he was trying to peer into her soul. "I was like she'd never do something like that, but he sent me a screenshot of their chat and I just, I don't know, I felt sick and so angry. I was so upset. I mean, Sabrina was my best friend, you know, and I know that's weird, because she's basically my cousin and three years older than me."

"It's not weird," Ezra said softly. "And that is a very shitty thing to do. I'm sorry she did that."

Sabah shrugged. "After that, I confronted her about it, because I knew she would never tell me. I hate that it was him who did. She apologised, but it didn't mean anything because it was just . . . she only said sorry because she got caught, you know? So I kinda stopped speaking to her for a bit, and everyone told me to cut them both off. But I couldn't really blame him as we barely knew each other. But I could blame her. I didn't speak to her for ages, until I did, and we talked everything out. The thing is, even after she apologised, she continued talking to him for a few weeks. And then I think she blocked him, I'm not sure. But she didn't like the fact that me and him were together."

"Why not?"

"I'm not sure. She kinda just hated him, I guess. I mean he had a ton of issues and wanted me around him all the time. He didn't like that I was forgave her and started talking to her again, or that I moved in with her. So I ended up staying at his all the time anyway, even though I was paying so much in rent. And for some time, Sabrina told me that he was just going to fuck me over and he was trying to isolate me, but I told her to stay out of it. I told her about all the fights we used to have, like all the time." She paused, dropping her gaze to the fingers holding the stem of the wine glass. She lifted it to her mouth and gulped down a third of the glass without pausing for breath. Letting out a little sigh, she wiped the back of her hand over her mouth, feeling the wine slosh down in her stomach.

"And then what happened?" Ezra's eyes poured into hers from across the table, the light from outside brightening his eyes.

"I moved in with him some time later and everything between us just imploded. It got so toxic, so fast. I was with him all the time, constantly, and I barely spoke to anyone. My mum was so angry at me because I was with him," Sabah laughed, "she didn't approve of him. We both worked during the week but I'd have to have dinner ready for him, and do whatever I could to make him happy. I found out he was flirting with some other girls online and when I tried to confront him about it, he just said that it meant nothing and that he loved me. But it kept happening. And every time, we'd fight and I'd cry and he'd tell me he love me. But then when we'd fight again, he would tell me that these other girls were prettier than me and it didn't matter what he did, because I would never leave him."

"He said that to you?" Ezra asked, voice hard.

She nodded. "He did. We'd have our good days and I thought they'd outweigh the bad. Towards the end, we talked about our relationship and tried to work on it but the same issues kept creeping back. He kept talking to other girls and I kept feeling like I wasn't enough. I was giving him everything I had while he just kept taking and taking and making me feel even more insecure. So I finally ended it and it was the most difficult thing I'd ever done."

"It was brave." His words were soft, wrapping her in a hug. "He sounds like a total dick. I'm sorry you had to deal with that manipulation and abuse. Nothing he did was your fault."

"I guess, but I wasn't completely blameless either. I was a bitch at times, too. We both used to say shit to each other, but I never would've done to him what he did to me."

Scraping up the last of her pasta, Sabah shovelled it into her mouth and used her index finger to wipe up the remaining sauce on her plate. She sucked the sauce off her finger and wiped it on the hem of Ezra's hoodie, before taking a small sip of the wine.

"And that says a lot," Ezra said."You owned up to it and he didn't, he just threw your love in your face and that's just awful. You shouldn't have had to deal with that, or what Sabrina put you through either. I'm glad you're both in a better place now."

"Yeah, you know that day when you and I spoke for the first time?" When he nodded, she continued, "that was the first time in ages Sabrina and I started talking again, like properly. We put everything behind us and yeah, it's been good. I missed her. And I know she feels really bad."

"She should," Ezra laughed. "I still can't believe that about her, I'm so disappointed." He stood up, taking his plate to the stove. "You want more?"

"No thanks." He nodded at her reply and dished up some more pasta on his plate before coming back to the table.

"What about you?" Sabah questioned, taking another gulp of her wine. "What's your whole messy history with your ex?"

"We were together from year thirteen up to our second year of uni," Ezra looked down at his plate. He moved some of the pasta and mince around. The song in the background added a sad soundtrack to his words. "I fell head over heels in love with her and I thought I was going to marry her. She broke up with me right at the start of our summer break, saying that she didn't want to be with me anymore because her parents would never be okay with it."

"Didn't she know that before you two even got together?"

"She did, but I guess she never thought about it. She wasn't even going to try to fight for us and it just . . ." he sighed. "Hurt, a lot. Like I wasn't enough for her to even try."

"It has nothing to do with you," Sabah said, reaching her hand out. Ezra stretched his hand out, twining his fingers with hers. "At all. That's all on her. She's the one that wasted your time and took those years from you, leading you on, knowing that she wasn't going to make the effort to put you first. There's no point getting into an interracial or interfaith relationship if, at the end of it, you're not going to fight for it. Relationships are hard enough as it is. She accepted you when you first got together but when it came down to it, she just walked away like that?" Sabah shook her head, annoyed. "God. What a bitch."

Ezra huffed out a laugh, "she's not really a bitch. Just, I guess, reliant on her parents and didn't want to walk away from her culture."

"Bitch," Sabah muttered again. She took another sip of her wine. "I hate her."

"I hate your ex, too."

A small smile lit up Sabah's face. "All that shit," she waved her hand around, "is why the idea of falling in love again or getting into a relationship terrifies me. I mean, how do you get over that?"

There was a pause as her words settled between them. Ezra looked outside, the snow falling like a scene straight out of a fairytale. "I thought the same after my dad left. It ripped everything apart and my mum didn't leave her room for weeks. My older sister, Eva, had to come back from America to help us out, to help mum try to heal. That, and then the whole thing with Aanchal, really changed the way I viewed love and relationships. I was so fucking bitter about everything. I stopped talking to my dad, I actually still don't speak to him—I didn't go to the wedding either." He paused, rotating the wine glass in his hands. "But after mum was able to let go, after we all sat down together for the first time after my dad blew up our family, I realised that I can't let his actions affect the rest of my life. And then when everything happened with Aanchal, I was sad, sure, but it didn't make me stop believing in love. If I keep letting every bad thing impact me, if I let it change the way I view the world, I'm just going to be miserable. And I don't want to be a sad sack of balls forever."

"You're so wise," Sabah said, tilting her head as she looked at him.

She tucked his words away, repeating them in her mind, keeping them safe for later. She wanted to believe him; she wanted to feel the way he did. But the thought of lowering her guard, the thought of falling in love again, trusting someone and letting them in, made her want to run screaming in the opposite direction. Having deliciously hot sex was one thing, but catching feelings and letting them see all your weaknesses was another. But maybe if she fell, maybe if she jumped off that cliff, Ezra would be there to catch her.

CHAPTER EIGHT

AT SOME POINT THAT NIGHT, RAIN BEGAN TO shower down from the night sky in a torrential downpour, pattering against the frosted windows. The silver icicles of rain dripped down the frosted glass like teardrops, a constant angry tap-tap-tapping. It was as if the heavens had opened up and the world was being drenched in a sluice of tears. The ground was still covered in over a foot of snow that was turning to slowly turning to slush, but the temperature was still below zero on the night before Christmas.

The heat from the bathroom was fogging up the windows and mirrors, a combination of the radiator having been on all day and the steaming hot bubble bath. A foot away from the bath was a ladder shelf, carefully positioned to face them, with Ezra's laptop balancing on the top shelf, playing an episode of *Modern Family*.

The scent of the lavender bath oil, some mermaid bath bomb and the marshmallow scented bubble bath all floated through the air, as Sabah sat in between Ezra's legs, her back pressed against his chest, his arms circled around her body. Her head was tipped back, resting on his shoulder, eyes closed, as she felt herself unwinding and melting into the warmth and relaxation of the bath oils, bubbles and bath bomb, all perfectly concocted for a relaxing evening.

His breath was warm on her cheek, his fingers tracing nonsensical patterns on her forearms.

"This must be what heaven is like," Sabah said, voice barely above a whisper. She didn't want to break the spell they were under. Maybe this was part of some kind of domesticated bliss, but being here, in his arms, having a deliciously hot bubble bath while watching her favourite show, kind of felt like it was meant to be. Some small part of her wanted to keep doing this . . . weird happily-ever-after type of thing, to keep holding onto this feeling of happiness before it slipped away from her. They were in this cute, happy little bubble and it was everything she needed. She needed this to be a good memory, to keep every part of it close to her like a closely guarded secret, buried in the chambers of her heart.

Ezra was like the smooth dances of light on a warm carpet, the sunlight glossing over it like a lazy afterthought on a quiet Sunday afternoon after a delicious roast dinner. He was cuddling together on the sofa, watching a repeat of *Friends*, something familiar and welcoming, still laughing at the jokes even after watching it a million times, rubbing his hands over your bare legs like it was habit.

He was coming home after a long day and sitting at the kitchen table, eating the food that brought you comfort, listening to your stories and your laughter with a soft, saccharine smile, his eyes a thousand different shades of browns and greens and golds, all swirling together.

Sabah pressed herself closer to Ezra, shifting in the bath. The water and bubbles rippled with her movement, a cloud of sparkling bubbles slipping down her breast. Her nipple peeked through like the chocolate at the bottom of an ice cream cone, a pleasant surprise. She noticed Ezra's gaze dip to her tits before looking back up at her face, his pupils dilating and the hazel of his eyes darkening to a deeper gold-brown. She sat in the bathtub with her legs under her, facing him head-on, her hands resting on his thighs, covered with a mountain of bubbles with specs of glitter.

As Sabah leaned in closer to Ezra, her fingers inching up higher to the tops of his thighs, the tips of her fingers brushing his quickly hardening dick, she was half-listening to Phil tell Claire that he was going after Haley because she was his baby girl, not knowing Haley was standing there. Her eyes flickered to Ezra's mouth for a few seconds, wondering what it would mean if she just kissed him. If she just burned down every sensible thing that was screaming at her to stay cautious, because men are never just *nice*, and liking someone—not that she did, not that it was anything more than just a crush—was so dangerous. Having a crush meant being crushed and she couldn't let that happen. Never again.

His breath skimmed her lips as he leaned forward, his hands on her hips, fingers a little pruney. Her heart hiccupped in her chest as she brushed her lips over his, softly, teasingly. His sigh against her parted mouth was all it took: she slid one hand up his toned stomach, fingers stroking along the ridges of his abs and the curve of his chest, glossing over his rose pink nipple.

She felt his sharp collarbones—god, he even made collarbones look gorgeous—and drifted her hand up his throat, stroking the side of his neck with her hand as her fingers played with his hair, the ends damp and dripping with water. Her other hand lightly brushed against his dick before she palmed it, taking it in her hand. Neither of them broke the kiss, their tongues sweeping against each other as if they couldn't get enough.

It lit a fire in Sabah's stomach, one that rose higher and swept downwards at the same time, burning with the kind of need that made her melt into Ezra. She gripped him tighter and jerked him off, her breasts pushed against his chest, his moan in her mouth filling her with the aching need to give him more, take more, do more. She wanted more of this, more of him.

Fireworks exploded in her head, every touch magnified as their lips moved together in a marriage of excitement and arousal. He tasted like the wine they drank earlier, the chocolate truffles they shared with the girls, ones that his mum had saved for Christmas Day. His hands trailed up her body to squeeze her breasts, fingers pinching her nipples

She moaned into his mouth at the sudden pressure, pain and pleasure blurring together as one as she scraped her nails against his inner thighs. She bit his lower lip gently and tightly stroked him again, gasping as he lowered one hand to her ass and the other to her pussy, exploring her body with expert fingers.

Gasping lightly against his mouth, Sabah pulled back to look at his face, seeing his eyes closing, lids fluttering, as she continued working him. Her grip around his dick became sloppier as he applied pressure to her, his fingers moving in and out rapidly, his palm putting some weight against her clit and pelvis, intensifying every feeling.

"Ezra," she gasped, closing her eyes briefly as tingles spread through her body, feeling as if she was falling into a pool of liquid ecstasy. Her toes curled, sinking into the bubbles surrounding them in the tub, her fingers tightening around him. A gut-wrenching, earth-shattering explosion fizzed all around her, heat flaring over her skin like magic, like fairy dust. Sabah sighed his name again, against his mouth, as her hand drifted back up his chest, dragging her nails over his glistening skin.

Lifting her hips up with one arm and adjusting himself, Ezra slowly lowered her body back down, her pussy sheathing him in its wet heat. Sabah gasped in his mouth, her moan caught between them, as he filled her to the base with a groan.

His hands were tightly gripping her waist, moving her up and down on his dick, eliciting loud moans from her as he hit *just the right spot*. She grabbed his hair, yanking at the strands as she tightened her legs around him. She loved that he was taking control, slamming into her over and over with perfect control as he kept bouncing her, holding her with a hard grip, his fingers digging into her skin.

"You fuck me so good," Sabah whispered.

He pulled back a bit to gaze at her, eyes staring into hers, amusement flickering across his face.

Sabah bit her lip, sweat glossing her temples. She squeezed his shoulder as she shifted, moving her legs behind her so she was sat on her knees, taking control. A small smirk played on his lips as he stared at her, all stardust and moonlight, the soft glow of the lit bathroom dancing over his features. She leaned forward to kiss the fluttering pulse on his neck, kissing and sucking on his earlobe as she kept moving up and down, grinding against his pelvis. Her hips had their own rhythm as she rocked against him, squeezing and scratching at his body.

"God. You're so fucking tight," Ezra groaned, dragging his hand up the side of her body. She was thankful the heat of the bathroom hid her blush. He cupped and squeezed her breast in one hand, using the other to wrap around her throat gently. He didn't squeeze, just kept his hand there as he stared at her, mouth parted. A moan shuddered through him as her movements became faster and more erratic, bouncing down hard on him, milking his dick for everything, feeling him in every wild thrust. Her pulse beat like a drum, magic and lust and her heartbeat swirling all around her as she came again with another loud moan, his name falling out of her mouth again and again.

Sabah moaned, her cries swallowed in Ezra's mouth as he kissed her again, hard. She sank into the kiss, chest heaving, knowing that the peak was coming again, knowing that he was close to the edge. Their kiss was wet and unbound, soulful and consumed in a blazing fire. She continued bouncing on him, her hands feeling every muscle on his chest, sliding up his arms and shoulders, her movements slightly weaker and reckless.

Her veins were full of liquid gold and lust, pleasure unfurling in her stomach, sweeping all over her body until, with a guttural groan, Ezra moaned into her mouth. His body quaked, the tension unleashing and spilling inside her, releasing wave after wave of pleasure.

Their mouths separated, breaths mingling together. Sabah opened her eyes to watch him, seeing him fall apart, coming undone. He met her gaze through half-lidded eyes, glittering like the twinkling sky outside. Sabah moaned as he gave one last hard thrust, their bodies moving as one, even though he'd already cum, his fingers branding her skin.

His eyes burned into her as she remained straddling him, chest to chest.

The water had gone lukewarm, some of the bubbles spilling over the edge of the bathtub. On Netflix, *Modern Family* was still playing, Alex, Haley and Luke complaining about their parents scaring them with bad news as Claire and Phil sat, all contorted, in the hospital bed.

"Enjoy that?" Ezra asked, his fingers caressing Sabah's jaw. His thumb followed the outline of her bottom lip, poutier than her top lip. He lifted an eyebrow when she stayed silent for a beat too long.

"You didn't?"

"No, I did," Sabah replied, moving off him and shuffling backwards in the bath. The water moved with her, every ripple dancing beneath the lights. She leaned back enough that the cold metal of the taps sent a jolt through her. "It was fine."

"Just *fine*?"

She smirked, "what do you want me to say? That it was mind-blowingly exceptional?"

"That would be nice."

"But it would be a lie."

"Ouch," Ezra pouted, lifting his hands to rest over his heart, flinching back. "You sure know how to wound a guy."

"I was the one on top," Sabah pointed out, "so it's kind of—"

"True." He pushed his hair out of his face. "Maybe you need to work on your riding skills. I hear practice makes perfect."

"But nothing is perfect, idiot."

"That's not true," Ezra sighed. "I am. I'm perfect. You could reach that level if you tried hard enough."

Sabah snorted, feeling around beneath her to yank the plug. Finding it, she pulled it and listened to the rush of the water being sucked down the drain. "Whatever helps you sleep at night, Carmichael."

"Fucking you helps."

With a roll of her eyes, Sabah flicked some water at Ezra, who laughed, shaking his head. He stood up in the bath, all gloriously wet and naked, droplets of water snaking down his body. Sabah stared at him, watching as bubbles and water dripped down his body, trying to cling onto his fawn gold skin. As the water quickly swirled down the drain, the remnants of the bubbles still floating along the tub, Ezra turned on the shower, washing them away. Some of the water sprayed over Sabah as she sat in the bath, her knees pulled up to her chest, watching Ezra.

"Do you have, like, one of those scrubbing pads or anything?" Sabah asked after a moment, as he held the shower over his body, tipping his head back.

"Mhm, in the bottom cabinet, under the sink. What for?"

"To clean the bathtub? Since, you know, we just had a bath and fucked in it." She stood to take the shower head from him, holding it over her head and running her fingers through her ash blonde, pink and black strands.

"Oh right," Ezra muttered.

He got out of the bath as Sabah put the shower head back up in its holder. As she quickly washed her hair with some of Ezra's passion flower shampoo and conditioner, he got back into the tub and scrubbed it with washing up liquid, running the shower over it as he did so. Sabah watched the bubbles and water slide down the drain beneath her feet.

After she squeezed the water out of her hair and slid her feet into a pair of the bathroom flip flops, Sabah shrugged into Ezra's striped dressing gown, while he wrapped himself in his navy bathrobe that had been hanging over the bathroom door. He used a mustard yellow bath mat to soak up the water that had spilt onto the floor, dragging it around with his sandal-clad foot.

"I hate that colour," Sabah told him as they left the bathroom, stepping out of the flip flops, clutching Ezra's laptop under her arm. He laughed, flicking the light switch.

The pale glow of the moonlight fell across the landing, shadows of the bare tree branches tracing across the soft carpet. Tucking her hair behind her ear with one hand, Sabah's arm brushed Ezra's, a blush creeping across her face at the contact.

The sound of footsteps coming up the stairs made her pause, glancing at Elsa as she came up the steps, a mug clasped in one hand, her other hand trailing over the banister. She felt a flash of discomfort take hold of her, thinking *oh, shit*, at the sight of Ezra's younger sister catching them red handed.

"I hope you used protection," Elsa said, arching an eyebrow, as she reached the landing, looking between Ezra and Sabah. Humour lined her words, her lips twitching into a full blown smile. "Or not. I'd love a little niece or nephew."

Oh shit. Sabah glanced at Ezra, her eyes wide. She saw the panic reflected back at her in his expression, before he quickly masked it with a smile of his own.

"Mind your own business, Elsa," he replied coolly, guiding Sabah back to his room. "It's past your bedtime," he threw over his shoulder.

"We haven't had a bedtime in years, dickface," Elsa yelled at him as she headed down the hall and into her own room.

Sabah stood by the bedside, a whirlwind of panic-induced

thoughts rushing to the surface as Ezra sat down on the edge of the bed, looking at her. His face was concerned. Reaching out a hand, he grabbed Sabah's and tugged her down next to him.

"I'm not on the pill," Sabah said after a moment, pulling one leg under her, facing Ezra. Her voice was a little shaky, her heart thudding in her chest.

"Hopefully it'll get a little warmer in the next few days and the snow melts away," he murmured softly, squeezing her hand gently. "We have three days to get the morning after pill. It'll be fine." He paused. "Are you ovulating?"

She stared at him, "how the fuck—god," she shook her head. "I don't know, Ezra. I don't keep track of that. I'm not trying to, you know, conceive or anything."

Letting out a little laugh, Ezra let go of her hand and fell back onto the bed with a thump, staring up at the ceiling. "Right," he said. "Of course not."

The dim lighting from his lamp cast an almost romantic atmosphere in the room, the soft shadows flickering on the edge of her vision. Sabah moved to the middle of the bed, her fingers lightly brushing against the sleeve of Ezra's bathrobe, inching closer to his arm. She didn't know what to say as she sat there, listening to the ticking of his clock, the wind whistling outside. Everything around them was silent, as if to bask in the magnitude of their hasty decision.

"Do you want hot chocolate?" Ezra asked suddenly, breaking the silence.

"Um," Sabah said, swallowing. Her mouth felt dry. "Sure."

"Great." He jumped up and disappeared out the door, leaving it wide open. Sabah continued sitting on the bed, staring blankly at the TV opposite her.

Five minutes passed quickly and then Ezra was back, holding two mugs of hot chocolate. She took the Sleeping Beauty one from him, her lips barely quirking into a smile. He'd added more than a dozen little marshmallows, dotted all over the whipped cream.

"Thank you," she breathed, taking a large mouthful and almost burning her tongue. "Ouch."

"It's hot," Ezra said helpfully. She rolled her eyes at him. "Listen, Sabah, whatever happens, it'll be fine. It makes no sense to worry or freak out over something that hasn't even happened. Panicking will only take you out of the moment, you know? Nothing has happened yet and it's not like there's that many chances to actually even get pregnant. That whole thing they teach us at school, about there always being a fifty percent chance to get pregnant? That's bullshit. So it's fine and we're gonna deal with this."

"I know that," she stared into the whipped cream swirls. Plucking up a little pink marshmallow, she plopped it into her mouth. "I'm not freaking out. I'm chill." She ignored the disbelieving look he tossed her way. "Like you said, we'll get the morning after pill anyway. And," she shrugged. "It's all whatever."

"Exactly," Ezra lifted his mug of hot chocolate in a mock toast. "That's the spirit."

CHAPTER NINE

ON CHRISTMAS MORNING, THE SKY WAS BRIGHT blue and cloudless, the sun gleaming down on the soft snow-glistened earth and branches. Every rooftop in the cul-de-sac was covered in a heavy sheet of snow, the cars in the driveway frosted with ice, topped with a light layer of snow. The rain last night, with the combination of the warm sun this morning, had helped to melt away a couple inches of the snow, but it wasn't nearly enough. The house smelt like cinnamon and gingerbread, thanks to the cinnamon rolls Sailor had made at seven A.M., presenting them with a flourish when Sabah and Ezra stumbled downstairs, all sleepy eyed and dishevelled sex hair.

Elsa was sitting at the island, icing smeared around her mouth, her hands clasped around a mug of hot chocolate, topped with whipped cream, a gingerbread man floating half inside and a candy cane adding another festive sparkle to the drink. Sabah had bit back the amused smile, a pang of envy sinking in her stomach, as she realised that the Carmichaels went all out for Christmas. Every room was decorated with fairylights, the windows sparkling with the lights when night fell. She watched as Ezra and Elsa chatted to their mum on FaceTime during breakfast, passing it over to Sailor and then conferencing in their sister, Eva, who was five hours behind in some little town called Ivory Wells.

"This is Sabah," Ezra said to his mum, while taking a large bite of his cinnamon roll. She watched his Adam's apple bob as he swallowed, the muscles in his throat shifting with the movement, before flicking her gaze up to the few-days-old beard covering the bottom half of his face, his mouth that had some icing on the corner of his bottom lip.

For a few seconds, she stared, wanting to taste the sweetness on his tongue, arousal clutching her in a death grip. The sound of her name startled her out of the trance she'd fallen in, tearing her gaze away from Ezra's lips, and to the phone pointed in her direction, the faces she'd seen in so many photographs lining the hallway outside on the screen.

She blinked, remembering to smile and lifted a hand, that wasn't sticky with white glazing, in a half-hearted wave. "Hi," Sabah forced down the anxiety threading through her, trying to ignore the uncomfortable pricks of heat stabbing the back of her neck as her whole body warmed under the extra attention. "I'm Sabah."

"Hi honey," his mum, Raffaella, said, eyes crinkling at the corners when she smiled. She had laugh lines on her face, but other than that, she could've passed for being in her mid thirties.

"Hey Sabah," Eva smiled widely, large dimples appearing on both cheeks. "Wow, you're so pretty."

Feeling her cheeks burn with the compliment, she choked out a soft *thanks*. Her pulse quickened as her gaze darted to the open door leading to her escape, back up the stairs and in the safety of Ezra's bedroom. She needed to call her sister. She needed to call her cousin. "You're really gorgeous, as well," she managed to say, internally wincing. She didn't want Ezra's sister to think she was just returning the compliment in lieu of something better to say—she meant it. Eva was so beautiful, with a mass of dark curls down to her shoulders and hooded light brown eyes, framed by such long lashes. "I like the lipstick you're wearing."

"Oh, thanks," flashing a smile, Eva lifted a hand adorned with rings and pushed her fringe out of her eyes. "How are you finding it at our home? Mum mentioned you've been there a few days now?"

"Since the twenty-second," Ezra's mum said. "Isn't that right, hon?"

"Yep," Ezra replied, leaning in close to Sabah. She caught a whiff of his coconut body butter, the lavender from the bath oil still clinging to his skin. "It's been a wild couple of days."

"They fucked in the bathroom," Elsa called out, taking the candy cane she'd been sucking on out of her mouth. At the glare Ezra had on his face, she laughed. The smile on Sabah's face froze as she stilled, her heart thundering in her ears. She swallowed thickly, her mouth dry. She wanted the ground to swallow her whole, pretend like none of this had happened, or was happening. She'd never met Jake's family, even when they lived together. He always had her hide in the bedroom whenever someone came round to pick something up or drop something off—they knew of her existence but never bothered to ask to meet her, so she had no idea how to deal with this. And now his mum had found out they screwed in the bathroom and she was mortified.

"Era necesario?" Ezra hissed, still casting a withering glare at his little sister. Elsa shrugged, biting on the red and white striped candy cane, grinning. "Sei così fastidioso."

Some part of her picked up on his words, translating necesario to necessary, but she had no idea what else he'd said. But from his tone, the annoyance flitting across his face, Sabah could only assume that he was admonishing Elsa for what she'd said.

"Well," Ezra's mum began, laughter tingeing her voice. "I at least hope you two are practicing safe sex."

"I thought you wanted grandkids, mamma?" Elsa asked, her face a picture of innocence. Ezra groaned loudly, covering his face with his hand. Sailor burst out laughing, and even Eva sniggered. Sabah wanted to die.

"Elsa, smettila di inimicarsi tuo fratello," their mum sighed. "Sabah, darling, I hope my boy's treating you well? Are you eating enough?" Her brown eyes were warm through the pixels, the light behind her swathing in her a gentle glow. Sabah felt tears strangle her throat, a knot tightening in her chest as she sucked in a deep breath.

"Um, yeah," she said, looking from Ezra's mum to Eva, the phone shaking slightly in Ezra's hand as he shifted in his seat, the stool squeaking a little beneath his weight. "Ezra's, um . . ." she looked at him, taking in those wide hazel eyes that looked at her with such tenderness and a little guardedness that she understood, a shuttering feeling of fear at losing it all but wanting to risk it anyway, his lips curved into a smile setting her soul ablaze and filling the cavern of her chest with hope, watering the blooming flowers, their petals unfurling beneath the glow of his sunshine smile.

"Great," Sabah finished, flushing. "Yeah, he's great and his cooking's amazing. It's really a testament to you," she added quickly, ignoring the way her heart pounded in her chest at the realisation rolling over her, a rogue wave she couldn't ignore as it came to the surface.

When she'd finally been able to escape, telling everyone she had a call to make and taking the steps two at a time, shutting the bedroom door behind her with a firm click, Sabah exhaled loudly. She wanted to be that brave girl she had always been, ignore all the self-doubt and anxiety choking her and reducing her to a bumbling mess, stumbling over her words and burning red.

Everything she was trying not to feel suffocated her as she whipped her phone out with trembling hands, heading over to the window seat so she could stare down at the Christmas card-esque picture outside, the slowly melting snow a sight of pure magic and, like Sailor had said, a Christmas rom-com. It was something straight of some stupid Netflix movie, Sabah thought as she waited for Veda and Sabrina to answer the joint FaceTime call.

As she sat there, her knees pulled up to her chest and socked feet playing with the edge of a throw pillow, looking at the wintery scene, she contemplated making a break for it. She knew Ezra was right, that she couldn't be scared of love and relationships forever, but Jake . . . had been her first everything and she was the daughter of a man that had walked away from her family years ago. Her mum had raised four kids all by herself, doing whatever she could while on benefits and trying her best to give them everything they needed.

Sabah could remember nights her mum sat in the living room, pouring over bills and borrowing money from her aunts and uncle, crying to them on the phone. For years after, Sabah piled together as much as she could from all her part-time jobs, giving the money to her mum. Even when she'd left to live with Jake, she sent money every so often, both her and Naveda pooling their money together to chip in with the bills, and discussing whether they ought to buy the flat they grew up in one day.

"Hey, hey," Sabrina's voice chirped through, breaking the dark tunnelling of Sabah's thoughts, a semblance of light peeking into the cracked ice. Sabah jolted, tearing her gaze away from the tree-lined driveway, the house opposite his glinting with snow and fairylights emitting a faint glow in the bright morning. "Merry Christmas!" she squealed, a party hat on her head, the strings tied tightly under her jaw in a loopy ribbon.

"Merry Christmas, ya filthy animals," Veda crowed, answering the call a few seconds after Sabrina.

"Where are you guys?" Sabah asked, pulling her hair over one shoulder, adjusting one of the cushions behind her to keep her back from getting cold.

"I'm at mums," Veda said, "and Sabrina's at ours, throwing herself a pity Christmas party for one."

"Complete with a party hat?" Sabah laughed, feeling the anxiety easing, her shoulders relaxing.

"Yeah, why not? I mean, I'm happy and whole all on my lonesome, so I might as well make a day of it. It's not like our family celebrates Christmas anyway."

"I thought you would've done something with your siblings and the girls?"

"They're spending Christmas in Ireland," Sabrina pouted. "Well, Sultana's gone skiing with her friends."

"Jesus, how rich are they?"

"Extremely. But anyway, how is it going at a la casa Carmichael?"

"Yeah, you've been there, what, four days now?" Veda enquired, lifting a water bottle to her mouth. She squinted at the screen and reached over for something, disappearing from view. A few seconds later, she was back in view, wearing large glasses.

"Something like that, yeah," Sabah nodded. "Guys, it's like . . . there's something wrong."

"Oh?" Sabrina enquired, arching an eyebrow. "Do tell."

"I . . . think I might," wrinkling her nose, Sabah thought over the words she wanted to say, repeating them slowly. "I think," she began again, "I might like him."

"And what's the something wrong?" Veda asked.

"That. That's what's wrong. Me liking him."

"What? Why?"

Sabrina shifted, the phone shaking before she leaned back on her sofa, a wine glass filled with white wine in her other hand. "Yeah, why?"

"It's just that, with him, it's different to anything before and he makes me laugh. I feel happier and it's easy to talk to him, to settle into this, like, *thing*." Sabah groaned, putting her phone down against one of the cushions on the windowsill, showing an unflattering angle of herself to Veda and Sabrina. She quickly pulled her hair into two Dutch braids and continued, "He doesn't have any red flags, or anything I've noticed so far because obviously everybody has flaws and he's just so optimistic which is I guess annoying. I mean, he is annoying as fuck as it is."

Sabah breathed out a chuckle, coated with a light layer of fear amidst the light, tinkly laugh. "I'm scared though, because he's a great friend and I love talking to him and having him in my life. But I can tell he likes me and we've got this good thing going. But . . ." she sighed, crossing her legs beneath her and swapping her phone to her left hand. She tucked her hair behind her ear, pulling a face.

"I'm just too fucked up to be in a relationship right now so I don't know what to do, and maybe it's too soon? And maybe everything feels so perfect because we've been putting our best selves forward?

Like yeah, we've been together every day for the last couple days and seen each other loads over the last few weeks. But really, like, it's all just so . . . it's too much. I'm wildly attracted to him, I like him and I kinda don't want to, and I'm terrified of it burning and crashing. There's too much to lose with Ezra."

Sabrina frowned, playing with the ends of the ribbon on her hat before pulling at one end, letting the shiny and glittery party hat slide off her head. "Sabah, I'm gonna offer you some advice because I don't want you to go through the same thing I did and ruin what could be the best thing to happen to you." Sabah laughed shortly at that. "Listen, babe, you can't always judge the next relationship based on your previous one, not all people come from toxic experiences so every relationship is different, and so is the other person and the experiences they bring. So honestly, you just gotta go for it, and if you get hurt again, then you get hurt again—you have to pick yourself back up, knowing that you put in your all and you tried.

"You can't always go in a hole and be afraid to try with someone else, because life is about always trying even if you're scared, about learning from what you've been through and becoming a better person. In the last ten months, you should've learnt a lot about yourself as well." Sabrina paused to drink another glug of wine, pushing her fringe out of her eyes with her index finger. "And the mistakes you made, the things you shouldn't do in a relationship and you should now know what to do or what not to do, because sometimes relationships get toxic because of two people. A couple months ago, you couldn't have even imagined yourself sleeping with someone new, right? And now you've fallen for Ezra and that's something wonderful in itself, it's the next step to reclaiming ownership of your heart again."

"Jheez," Sabah muttered quietly. "Okay, Miss-I'm-Going-To-Be-A-Doctor." After a moment, she bit her lower lip. "I don't even know how to go about this. Everything with Jake was just, I don't know, it just happened and we didn't really talk about it, kind of just got into our relationship and this is so different from that already. I mean, god, Ezra is so different to him. I don't want to get hurt again, I mean I know it might happen anyway so it's why I don't want to tell him and then risk everything ending, because we all know relationships don't last forever. They always leave. Or you have to, for your own peace of mind."

"You can't run from relationships and love forever, Sabah," Veda said softly. "Jake was your first love and heartbreak, but it doesn't mean it'll be like that with Ezra. Don't go chasing toxicity as a way to fill some void in your heart and don't run away from your chance at happiness because you're scared."

"Not to mention, you guys have already seen each other naked, you've already had sex, so you can just say you want more out of it, that you want to be with him," Sabrina added. "I think you should talk to him. I mean, you already think he likes you, and he's my friend as well, so I know that he's a great guy. He's so kind and he's funny and he's great at communication. Sometimes it's worth taking the risk, you know? Maybe he's the right person and this is the right time. Maybe this is your chance for happily-ever-after."

"But what if it's not?"

"Then it's not," Sabrina said, delicately sipping at the wine. "And you've got us by your side."

"Exactly," Veda smiled. She lifted her glasses up the slope of her nose and added, "the thing is, hon, liking someone is terrifying but it's exciting, too. Don't make him the centre of everything this time, he should add to your life and your happiness, not *be* the cause of that happiness."

After hanging up with the girls and wallowing in the magnitude of her feelings for another two hours, away from the explosive familiarity of the Carmichael siblings plus their honorary sister, trying to make sense of her jumbled thoughts and emotions, all running together in a mess of *Ezra, Ezra, Ezra*, Sabah decided it was time to make an appearance downstairs.

An hour after finishing off the massive meal Ezra put together an hour ago, Ezra and Sabah were cuddling on one end of the massive sofa, a blanket thrown over their lap, while Sailor sat on the other end, one leg stretched out on the seat between her and Sabah, and Elsa was curled up on a cream boucle armchair. Sabah had helped him peel all the vegetables, swapping them out with the baby potatoes seasoned with smoked paprika, pepper and Cajun, while Ezra made sure the mashed potato was all smooth and creamy and cheesy. The Yorkshire Puddings were done five minutes before the chicken that Sabah loaded onto all four plates, with everyone getting two of the pastry Puddings each, followed by the honey glazed carrots and parsnips, a small handful of thyme grated and tossed over them, and Brussels sprouts with bacon, caramelised with butter and maple syrup, the two different kinds of potato, all covered with a ton of gravy. The entire meal passed by in inane conversation—Ezra and Elsa bickering over Christmas film choices (he wanted to watch *Die Hard* and she wanted to watch the *Grinch* animated movie that came out in 2018), and Sailor telling Sabah about loving kala jams since she first tried it when one of her and Elsa's friends, Jahanara, bought some for them after they finished year eleven.

When Elsa grabbed the remote to play *While You Were Sleeping*, Ezra pressed a kiss to Sabah's forehead and got up.

"Where are you going?" she pouted, grabbing his hand. Her thumb stroked the back of his fingers, feeling the light hairs on his knuckles.

"To get us brownie-cookie-cheesecake," Ezra grinned.

"Okay, hurry up then. Go, go, go." Sabah shooed him away, a smile glossing her lips. "I can't wait to try it, oh my god," she said to Sailor. "It's going to be so good."

"It better be. We didn't slave away for nothing," Sailor laughed. "God, I love baking. It's like one of the only things that give me joy in this world."

"What about me?" Elsa said, glancing over at Sailor with narrowed eyes.

Just then, Ezra came back into the living room, balancing four rose-printed dessert plates in his hands, loaded with thick slices of cheesecake-chocolate-cream-brownie-lemon-cream-cookie-crushed-Oreos-cream and little gold spoons.

"Oh, that looks so amazing," Sabah gasped in delight, taking her plate from him and immediately digging her spoon into the slice. She took a bite with all the layers of chaotic goodness and groaned. "Holy fuck."

"I'm in looooove," Sailor said. "God, we're *good*."

The sharp citrus lemon curd melted into the decadent chocolate and crushed Oreo biscuits, as Sabah tasted her second large bite, the silky smoothness of the creamy fillings soaking through the biscuit base, the rich chocolate brownie with milk and white chocolate chips mixed in and the white chocolate and raspberry cookie baked to perfection and nicely cool. Sailor had decorated the edge of the sweet invention with sliced strawberries and blueberries—the bitterness of the fruits offsetting the sweetness of all the chocolatey goodness—the tartness of the lemon flavoured cheesecake filling adding another layer of dreams. It wasn't as sickening as Sabah thought it would be as she spooned another bite into her mouth, closing her eyes as she tasted all the flavours working together.

"Honestly, I think if we had this cheesecake monstrosity yesterday, we would've found it super sickly and probably died," Elsa beamed around a large mouthful of cookie and cheesecake cream, the crushed Oreos peeking through.

"What a way to go," Sabah laughed. "When I die, I want it to be after eating a *massive* fuck off cheesecake."

"I'll bear that in mind," Ezra said wryly. "And I think everything marinating in the fridge for a day helped with the whole not being sickening thing."

"Definitely," Sailor nodded, scraping up the chocolate cream and crumbs from the plate. "I made a super chocolatey cheesecake once and it was horrible because of all the chocolate, it was so rich, but the next day was so much better."

As they watched Sandra Bullock on screen, Sabah glanced over at Ezra, the huge Christmas tree in her peripheral vision, sparkling and glinting in the dim lighting of the living room, the angel in a glittery pink dress with silver wings grazing the ceiling and wondered what it would be like to be sitting here with him, every day. She slowly lifted another spoon of brownie, covered in a delicious lemon curd flavoured cheesecake cream, to her mouth and savoured the way it melted against her tongue. She kept peeking at him, realising Sabrina and Naveda were right: she couldn't spend the rest of her life afraid of losing love, when she was too afraid to reach out to grab it. Most people spent their entire lives waiting and hoping for something great, something that was beautiful and extraordinary, a moment of realisation brimming with the kind of connection and love that was maybe a once-in-a-lifetime kind of thing.

And here she was, sat next to the guy that made her laugh and feel like she more than enough, who made her laugh even when he was annoying as hell, terrified of telling him she really, really, really, really, really liked him—even though he was her someone special. She was lucky enough to find that once-in-a-lifetime kind of moment, of everything glittering and special on Christmas Day, surrounded by a bright and sparkling Christmas tree draped with tinsel and sparkly glass baubles and warm fairylights, his family, delicious dessert and watching a cute rom-com. She wanted to keep holding onto this feeling, this moment where she was so damn happy she could cry.

She didn't want to let this go.

CHAPTER TEN

31st December 2020

FIREWORKS BURST IN A KALEIDOSCOPE OF bright colours, exploding in varying shades of pinks, reds, oranges, blues and greens, in the night sky, a black mirror glimmering with the faintest wisps of clouds being pulled by an invisible string. The delicious scent of barbecued chicken, beef burgers and kebabs permeated the air, floating into the kitchen through the opened door, as everyone milled around the cold winter garden and the doorway, laughter spilling into the night. Sabah watched from her spot near the radiator, the blazing heat weaving in through her strawberry red cable knit jumper and faded blue jeans, warming her body, as Isioma, Eleanor's girlfriend changed the song on her Spotify, connected to the Bluetooth speakers Ashton had brought over for the New Year's Eve party that Sabrina had decided to throw last minute with just close friends.

Early 2000's music played softly from the speakers, not quite loud enough to cover the sound of the fireworks the neighbours were setting off in their garden. Every time it exploded in the air, Sabah felt herself jump, her heart race. She gritted her teeth in annoyance, feeling like a jumpy kitten, surrounded by everyone who was connected in so many ways: Sabrina was friends with Ezra and all of his friends: Kira, Ashton, Carver and Wade, and Sabah was kind of dating Ezra. Even though it was only a small group of people, Sabah could feel herself feeling anxious and the butterflies swarming her stomach. She felt her fingers sinking into the soft brioche bun in her hands, the beef burger still unbitten, a dollop of mustard and mayo dripping onto the paper plate balancing on her lap, and wondered whether she could disappear upstairs without anyone noticing.

But just as she was planning her escape, Naveda met her gaze across the kitchen counter where she had loaded a couple kebabs onto a plate. Forcing a small smile on her face, Sabah raised her eyebrows and lifted the burger to her mouth, taking a large bite. It was spicy, juicy and married with her favourite topics: cheese, mustard, mayo, two pickles and some lettuce. Her sister smiled back at her before tearing off two sheets of kitchen tissues and placing some kebabs on them, making her way to where Sabah sat, still feeling the cold breeze sweeping in from the garden, but comforted by the heat of the radiator.

"Here, these kebabs are really good," Veda said, squatting down beside Sabah and putting the kebabs onto her plate. The steam and aroma rose up from the two kebabs, the large drop of mustard and mayo coating one end. "It's from some shop in Green Street, I think. Sabrina went the other day and brought these back."

"How nice," Sabah muttered, taking another large bite of the burger. "Did she get this from the same shop?" she covered her mouth as she chewed, glancing quickly at Sabrina as she came in through the door, holding two plates full of chicken pieces and beef burgers. Following her was Reina, arms laden with another two plates of more chicken and kebabs.

"Okay, guys, this is the last of it," Sabrina called out, her voice carrying over the music, in the lull of the fireworks. "Everything is here," she motioned to the countertop beside the cooker. "So take your pick of whatever. Just clean up after yourselves instead of being tramps."

Wade laughed, plucking up a couple chicken pieces onto his plate, waving his hand. "Ow, fuck, that's hot."

"No shit," Sabrina rolled her eyes, bumping him with her hip. "Do we need more buns or anything?"

"Nah, we're good," Rin replied. "There's four extra packets already open."

"Is there no dessert?" Sabah asked loudly, her cheeks burning pink as everyone glanced at her. She looked at Ezra, feeling the butterflies in her stomach fluttering as his light brown-gold eyes brightened.

"They're all in the dining room," Veda pointed through the archway leading into the open-plan dining and living room. "Cakes, biscuits and a bunch of other snacks are all there."

"Wait, why did we put them in there anyway?" Sabah queried, finishing off her burger when the conversations all resumed. She pretended not to notice as Ezra made his way over to her, plopping down beside her with a plate full of two burgers, four kebabs and three large chicken pieces and some coleslaw.

"I actually don't know," her sister shrugged. "The table's bigger for all those packets, I guess. And we needed the countertops for all the plates."

"Still can't believe Sabrina bought a whole barbecue grill. It's so . . . *grown up*."

Beside her, Ezra's leg pressed against hers, and the blush sweeping over Sabah's face made her glance down at the kebabs on her plate. She picked one up and bit into it, barely hearing Veda's reply, tasting all the flavours on her tongue, lost in the feel of Ezra's body, his leg flush against hers, his shoulder a gentle touch, next to her own. She could smell the coconut of his body butter, the scent of his shampoo, the *Toy Boy* Moschino perfume spritzed on his neck and black jumper.

She'd left his house the day after Boxing Day, taking the train to King's Cross and then swept through the front door with a cake from *Patisserie Valerie* in hand and an apology for her mother on her lips. That night, she sat down with her mum and spoke to her, perhaps for the first time in what seemed like forever, about everything, feeling her heart pounding with every word, her mouth dry and feeling anxiety slide through her veins and creep up her stomach and chest and twist around her throat. Every word escaped with difficulty, stuttered with a shaky cadence, unable to meet her mum's gaze, and instead, staring at the floral wallpaper decorating the living room.

Sabah told her everything she could about her relationship with Jake and how he'd made her feel, the inexcusable screaming fights that left her with a red-face and tear-stained cheeks, wishing she could find a way to stop everything from falling apart, wishing she could stop time for just a moment, just enough to sew back together all the fragments of her heart and fix the mess the two of them were making. She'd screamed back at him until her voice was hoarse and her throat hurt, hands clenched into fists and tears glossed her eyes, spilling over like a waterfall without an end. And it never ended.

Not until she'd finally convinced herself to walk away. "And it still hurts," she'd whispered to her mum that night, still unable to meet her gaze. "I know I should've listened to you, to Naveda, to Sabrina, to everyone who'd said that it was all too much, too soon, and that he wasn't good for me. But the thing is, amma . . ."

Finally looking up at her mum, her voice shaking, she said, "it's not that he wasn't a good person. He was. He is. Jake's a wonderful person but he just has his own demons and so do I. I'm still trying to fill this void from . . . from not having dad in my life, from constantly trying to measure up to everything that you and nani and Yara khala expect of me, to follow in Veda's footsteps. But we're not the same person and she's known what she's wanted her entire life and I don't know what I want, or what I even need. I mean, yeah, I know now I want to study children's nursing at uni once I've finished this course, I applied for it and it just depends on my grades now, but it's so hard.

"Trying to be someone I can't ever be, while feeling this immense loss and this heartbreak weighing on me, even though I know I did the right thing in walking away and that it was the best decision I could have ever made for myself and my future, is hard. I'm tired and I'm throwing myself into working and studying and striving for a better future because I don't have anything else. I know I disappoint you all the time and you're not proud of me, but I am trying. I'm trying."

"Sabah," her mum, Shabnaz, sighed. She ran a hand down her face, as if she was trying to wipe away some kind of emotion. "Yes, I was disappointed with you, honey, but you have to understand, it all comes from a place of worry. I'm glad you're talking to me now, but I wish you could've before. You shouldn't have even . . . you're too young to have gone through what you went through, too young to have even tried moving in with the lad. You haven't experienced life yet. First love isn't meant to last and that first heartbreak, what you're experiencing now? Sweetie," her mum leaned forward, sadness flickering in her eyes, frowning. "That will fade and it will get easier with time. Sometimes you have to go through the hardest moments to come out shining brighter, to come out stronger, to find something wonderful."

"But you didn't," Sabah said quietly. "You're still—"

"Honey, I didn't want to be with anybody else after your dad left.

Not because I didn't believe in love anymore, but because I needed to put you, Naveda, Nadim and Sadiq first. I needed to save enough to give you everything you needed. I don't want you to think love doesn't exist because your bastard father walked out, or because that Jake boy wasn't good enough for you, or because you've had your heart broken once. Love will find you when you least expect it."

Biting her lip, Sabah glanced away from her mother, images of Ezra flashing through her mind as she sat on the new dark chocolate brown sofa her mum had bought a few months ago. She knew she needed to tell him how she felt, she was already treading in dangerous waters, but the *danger* neon sign kept repeatedly flashing in her head whenever she tried to formulate the words '*I like you*'.

She didn't know why she felt so scared, so shaken, to profess her feelings—it wasn't like she was in love with him—even after speaking to both her sister and cousin about it. The whole thing was just a mess and it was all she could think of in the days that followed, leading up to the end of the year. But at last, the day before New Year's Eve, Sabah decided to text him.

Sabah at 21:17: *i like you*

She waited, staring at the time, heart in her throat, for his reply.

When it finally came, Sabah let out a squeak and shoved her duvet away from her where she was laying in bed, car headlights tracing across her ceiling as someone peeled away from her building, a loud shout slicing through the otherwise silent night.

Ezra at 21:34: *I like you too, Sabah :)*

Oh my god, she thought to herself, standing in the middle of her room, staring at his message. He was online and typing.

Ezra at 21:35: *I thought it was pretty clear lol… I think we should be exclusive? I mean, I want to date you, but I'm happy to go at whatever pace you need*

Sabah at 21:35: *same. but i also do want to take it slow – i'm not ready to be a 'girlfriend' just yet, but i do want us to be exclusive*

Sabah at 21:36: *lol this shit is scary*

Sabah at 21:36: *fuck does this mean i have to be like more open and shit? bc that's like . . . a little frightening tbh. ok*

Ezra at 21:37: *I mean, being open and communicative is a given, no? but yeah, I understand how it's scary. Like I said, your pace – you dictate how slow or how fast you want this to go and I'll wait for whatever you need. No pressure.*

Now, as she sat beside him on the floor, she hoped that this wouldn't crash and burn. The rippling anxiety that clawed at her mind was filling her with a kind of fear she hated—she was still so goddamn insecure, still so afraid, but being with him, being around Ezra, feeling him next to her, inhaling his familiar scent and seeing the way his eyes sparkled, made her feel like everything, new and fresh and full of beautiful promise, was going to be okay. That, just maybe, it could become *so much more.*

"Did I tell you that you look scrumptious tonight?" Ezra whispered to her, his breath sending a delightful shiver down her spine, tingles of bliss jolting through her as his lips grazed her ear. Sabah turned her head to look at him, a kebab halfway to her lips, pink with a Glossier cherry lip balm.

"You told me I look hot as hell, but scrumptious works too," Sabah replied, smirking. "I do love hearing how sexy I am."

"It's amazing your big head could fit through the door," he said wryly, fighting back a grin.

She shoved him, laughing. "Oi, you literally just told me how *scrumptious* I am."

"It won't hurt you to be a tad bit humble."

"What's the point in being humble when I look this good?"

"Is Sabah being vain again?" Sabrina asked, sitting on the floor on Sabah's other side, stretching her legs out in front of her. Veda had disappeared through the archway with Eleanor, though their laughter was loud enough to fill their absence in the kitchen.

"When am I not?" Sabah said around a bite of the lamb kebab. "But also, you're one to talk."

"Do you blame me? Being sexy just runs in the family."

"Think it might've skipped a few people though. Have you seen Taibah?" Sabrina burst out laughing at that, finishing off her burger in three large bites. "Seriously. I mean, I know she's family, but c'mon, man."

"That's so rude, Sabs, oh my god. But *also*, how is her kid so cute when she looks like that?"

"An act of God."

"You two are so mean," Ezra muttered, demolishing a chicken breast, looking from Sabah to Sabrina, shaking his head. "You wouldn't like it if someone spoke about you like that. It's really unkind."

"It would be a lie if someone spoke about us like that though," Sabrina said, pointing a kebab in Ezra's direction. "We're hot. And she's just not. Also, she's our cousin, so we're allowed to say that."

"That reminds me of that song," Sabah interjected. "You know, the one from *Camp Rock*?"

Ezra rolled his eyes, mumbling something under his breath. He turned his attention to Carver and Wade, in the middle of some kind of discussion about Triple H and The Undertaker, their voices cutting through the song. Kira closed the garden door, leaning against it as she talked to Isioma, her gaze briefly meeting Sabah's, a small smile dancing on her lips. Sabah smiled back, before glancing back at her cousin.

"Seriously. What was that song?"

"It's by that really snobby girl, right? I know what you're talking about. It goes like *you think you're hot but I'm sorry you're not*, right?"

"Yes!" Sabah exclaimed. "That one. Maybe that is what it's called."

A burst of laughter interrupted whatever Sabrina was about to say, making the both of them look over at Wade and Carver, as they shoved each other, laughing before Carver tripped, nearly falling backwards. He caught his balance, fingers grasping against the fridge handle, an easy smile on his face as he righted himself. Sabah watched as they both continued talking, Ezra gracefully rising to his feet and falling into the conversation. She couldn't tear her eyes away from him, at the slope of his nose, the curve of his cheek, the dark beard covering his jaw and carving out his cut-glass cheekbones, the deep dimples always so visible whenever he smiled.

She kept staring at him, snapshots of their moments together flipping through her head like a slideshow, the fireworks still exploding outside and the music adding a soundtrack to all the feelings and the memories bubbling inside her, spilling over like candied syrup. She felt soft and luminous when he turned his head to glance over at her, crushing up the paper plate in his hands. He had a gentle look in his eyes and a sweet smile on his face as their eyes met, everything else falling away.

In this moment, it was just them and all her fears and anxieties about drowning in the wake of his leaving faded into the background. She couldn't let her insecurities get in the way of her chance at happiness. He didn't give her any reason to doubt him and the way he was looking at her made her feel *safe* and warm and fuzzy inside.

She liked him and he liked her. And right now, that was what mattered.

EPILOGUE

Two months later

27th February 2021

THE UNTHINKABLE WAS HAPPENING.

Sabah's entire world: shattering and falling around her, glittering shards of glass reflecting back the last few weeks—the last two months—as she stood in front of the mirror, now surrounded by this moment and the impending future it brought with it. Beside her, Sabrina was perching against the countertop, arms crossed over her chest, gnawing at her bottom lip, a worried frown marring her otherwise flawless face. The soft glow of the bathroom lights overhead cast an almost sepia glow over both of them, capturing this very moment in a frozen snapshot. Reality was suspended in time, with the rain pounding against the stained-glass windows of the bathroom in *Fairly Odd Pizzas*.

January had come and gone, and with it, Sabah had fallen a little deeper for Ezra, lost in the stars swirling in his eyes, the way he made her feel safe, the feel of his arms around her. When the snow melted away and the weakened sun rose higher and glowed a little bit brighter in the dull grey sky, rain pouring down in sheets of cold droplets, coupled with a biting breeze, Sabah found herself dropping her defences, little by little. The fear of getting hurt again, the terror that came with falling for someone new, was still paramount, but she was trying her damn hardest to not be so scared. To look through the thorns and breathe in the fresh scent of rain on the air, because at the end of every thunderstorm, the sun still shone and the birds still sung.

Outside the bathroom, Sabah knew her real life was waiting to slap her in the face. When she stepped out of the safety of the bathroom, she would be forced to deal with the consequences of every decision she made in the last two months.

The words were tying into knots in her throat, unable to escape her lips as she stared down at the stick, the two pink lines causing her stomach to somersault, her chest rising and falling as she tried to take in deep breaths. The floral air freshener assaulted her nose, nausea climbing up into her mouth as that one word kept flashing in her head, like a broken neon sign. The overhead music was too loud, the brightness of the room hurting her eyes, the impending doom of her future encasing her in a shaky embrace, a sort of numbness eclipsing her from the sparkle of Ezra. The future she wanted to grab hold of.

Her future was irrevocably tied with him now.

The blurred image of a life she hadn't ever thought she would have with him, one she never planned on, pierced her like a knife. It branded her heart, a burning hot coal settling amidst the flowers that had bloomed and spread their sickly-sweet fragrance, burning to ash. She knew she needed to tell him, she needed to find the fragmented words and string them together, in a way that made sense.

He deserved to know.

She needed to figure out her new plan.

Beside her, Sabrina shifted, hand coming to lightly rest on Sabah's shoulder. A comforting gesture. Sabah inhaled deeply and let the breath out, trying to ease the tension in her body. She repeated it five more times. She tried to focus on all her senses, count everything around her, take control of the warring thoughts in her mind.

She dropped the stick down with a clatter onto the countertop, her fingertips pressing against the ceramic white sink. Her heart was thundering in her chest, slamming against her ribcage with every breath she took.

"What do you want to do?" Sabrina asked, her voice softer than Sabah had ever heard it.

"I don't know." Sabah's voice wavered, unsure even as the thought slithered through her mind, the hazy image flitting by far too quickly. Her whole life was unravelling and tearing at the seams.

Her world was imploding as she closed her eyes, ignoring the burst of laughter that filtered through the closed door.

She had known what the result would be, even before she took the test.

Sabah's mouth was dry as she sat in Ezra's bedroom, comforted by the warmth of his hand curled around hers. The gentle glow of his lamp filtered away the anxiety knotting itself in her chest, skin flaring red and hot. Her breaths were staggered, uneven as she tried to control the roaring in her mind, amidst the swirling thoughts creating a cacophony of feelings warring in the centre of her very soul. She felt unsettled, squeezing Ezra's hand tighter, her knuckles white and her nails leaving behind moon imprints on his life and love lines.

They were bound together, an invisible string turning into something so much more permanent, pulling them against each other as every shattered edge glistened. Her chest ached, hazy pictures of their future bursting through her mind like a cannonball. She could barely breathe, as she repeated the words silently in her head, unable to think of anything else.

It shot an arrow through her, everything building and growing into a tower.

His name was sunshine on her tongue as his arms slipped around her, pulling her onto his lap. Her legs wrapped around his waist, one arm lifting up to curve around his shoulder, the shiny and soft strands of his hair brushing her fingers. They still held hands, a tethering calmness, a welcomed pull away from the thoughts of her carefully planned future falling apart at the seams.

"Ezra," Sabah said again, quietly. Her voice cracked and split. She cleared her throat and looked up at him. The gentleness in his gold and amber flecked hazel eyes brought tears to hers, choking at her throat, stealing the words from her. She took comfort in knowing he would be there. Knowing he would stay.

It made it easier to breathe.

"It's okay," Ezra soothed, rubbing tender circles on her back, his fingers dipping along her spine in a caress she loved. His touch was a salve to the vortex of fear dragging her into its clutches. "I'm here, bella ragazza." His eyes searched her face, concern and worry lacing his expression. "You don't have to tell me anything now if you're not ready."

Sabah swallowed, her lips quivering. She didn't know what she was going to do, but she knew everything would be easier with Ezra. And it wasn't like she was completely alone. Not anymore. But even still, the anxiety of losing him, and a future she had been working towards the last few months rose like a tidal wave, crashing down over her with the heaviness of Thor's hammer. It burned inside her bones and trailed through her veins, a slow crawl of tears coursing down her cheeks.

She breathed in and out, closing her eyes tightly for a few seconds. Ezra continued rubbing soothing circles against her skin, fingertips a soft brush of comfort.

"Ezra," she repeated. "I, uh . . . I'm pregnant."

For a second, his hand stilled on her back. She held her breath, the heaviness weighing her down. But when he resumed stroking her and then lifted his hand to cup her face, his thumb rubbing her cheeks, brushing away the tears glossing her face, the darkness lifted away. Chased away by the sunshine smile and the warmth in his eyes, a glimmer of fear seeping through.

"How far along are you?" he asked, brushing a kiss to her forehead. Sabah closed her eyes. His kiss felt like a balm, calming the torrential anxiety ripping her apart.

"Two months," she replied, smiling nervously. "I haven't thought of what I want to do just yet, but I want to include you in the decision."

"Whatever happens," Ezra said, his voice rippling with a gentle melody that swept through her like wishing stars. "I will be here. I will support you, whatever you choose. Whatever you decide. It's your body and it's your choice, and I'm here."

Tears brimmed her eyes again, spilling over in a waterfall of raw emotion. The muted lighting made them look like sparkling glitter, the war in her mind and the knot in her throat easing into serenity. She tilted her face up, her fingers sweeping into his hair, and lightly kissed him.

His smile curved against her mouth as he kissed her back, warmth flooding her veins. He reminded her of cinnamon hot chocolate topped with whipped cream and chocolate shavings, of the warmth of a thick waffle blanket while watching a film on those rainy evenings. He was the lazy lie-in on Saturday morning, burrowing into soft blankets and pillows. He was pancakes and bacon, scattered with berries and drenched with maple syrup. He was a hot August morning in twisted bed sheets, eating gelato and drinking chilled rosé wine, on a cold February afternoon. He was jumping into the deep end of the pool, taking the leap of faith when everything was terrifying and changing and full of the promises of something new.

He was what chased away the memories that lingered like bad perfume. Every road lead to him, bringing her back to the warmest bed she's ever known, soothed by his gentle soul and incandescent smile.

"I think," Ezra said softly, pressing his forehead against hers. "You're the most wonderful person I've ever met. I'm glad I found you."

"You're such a softie," Sabah said through her dried tears, laughing. "But," she smiled, the light of a million stars shining through, "you've made me fall in love with Christmas."

He grinned and kissed her again. "Is that your way of saying you've fallen in love with me?"

"You wish," she snorted. She knew she loved him then, when he pulled back and looked at her as if she hung the stars and moon, the sun sinking into his wide smile. He was everything that wishes and dreams were made of and she couldn't get enough.

Read Sabrina's story in
The Art of Faking It

The Art of
Faking It

CHAPTER ONE

THE FIRST TIME SABRINA FELL IN LOVE, SHE WAS thirteen.

It was with a boy she was introduced to do by a girl she had once thought to be her best friend, someone who would forever be in her life. She had naïvely thought all friendships could withstand the test of time, amidst all the bitterness, heartbreak and dead-eyed smiles that came with Growing Up. Sabrina was tethered to her best friend by a fraying thread, one that continued to unravel the more she got to know Harris, the more she gushed about him with stars in her gullible thirteen-year-old eyes.

Somehow, everything revolved around him—her entire solar system orbited around him, as if he was the only sun in existence. It was the dreamiest of dreams, a hazy cocoon of pastel pinks and lavenders shading her world kept safe in a glittery snow globe. Until he left. The first time.

This was when she realised her entire self worth, her life, was muted in lightning silvers and blacks, an old Hollywood movie where the starlet was always on the brink of falling apart. She broke inside of herself, reduced to the ashes of a burning forest.

But when he came back, it was like colour flooded her world again. Everything flushed pink and she soared with the birds again, kvelling in his presence. His attention, when he deigned to grace her with it, when he thought she was worth it, was lit with a thousand stars under the pale moonlight. It never did anything to ease the darkness, the knot in her chest, when night fell across the earth in a whisper soft caress.

By the time year eleven came around, Sabrina's friendship with Zoya, the girl that introduced her to Harris had waned, torn open with bloody hands because the betrayal was too strong. Zoya had liked him first. Zoya had fallen for him weeks before, had dated him and lost him in a matter of weeks.

Sabrina let him flirt with her heart, a dangerous dance that told her to accept the way he flitted in and out of her life, a moth always seeking a brighter light. She accepted his sweet, honey-coated words, burying the lies underneath, thinking this was what she deserved.

It took four years before their lives forked onto different paths, years after Zoya had stopped speaking to her.

The second time Sabrina fell in love, she was eighteen. And this was the love that destroyed her. This was the love that tore its way into the dark crevices of her soul, staining it with blackened hands marred by the charcoal of the bleeding earth. It scorched its way inside her, as she thought that this would be forever.

But when he broke up with her over text, like every other guy, she slipped into a comatose state. Watching life slip by until she was forced to snap out of it and poured everything she could into studying.

And when she met Elle at Naveda's birthday dinner, their friendship bloomed into a flower bursting with life—a new kind of love that helped Sabrina breathe a little better, knowing that even with all the hurt, all the heartbreak and all the tears, she could still let people into her life.

At times, she felt like she'd come to a standstill, watching the world go on without her and moving robotically through life. She was stuck in the same place she'd been in, the night they'd ended. Sabrina was sledging through each day, doing everything exactly the way she knew she should, but wishing she could go back to 2017. It was the only time she'd ever been truly happy. And she missed that. She missed him. The small accomplishments she made, being top of her class, shadowing and learning how to be a counsellor that children felt connected to, finishing her dissertation, made her feel relief but wish she could share these things with him.

It was silly, she knew, still holding to someone who had already left. But she was still hoping he would come back. Her attempts at rebounding with a guy she met on Twitter a year ago failed epically, and she had found herself comparing what she had with Soran to

Musa, after that not-really-a-relationship crashed and burned into something platonic. It was wrong. It was an automatic thought process: *it wasn't like this with Musa.* While Soran was devastatingly beautiful and showed her how she deserved to be treated, he wasn't Musa. The sex, though, god, the sex was like every unspoken desire she'd had answered: sex in paradise, brimming with endless orgasms.

Sabrina couldn't bring herself to regret sleeping with him, even though the guilt she felt afterwards burned in her veins, as she sat on the train home, a cup of hot chocolate clasped in her palms. The warmth heated up her hands in the cold January night, liquid sloshing around, as she brought the drink up to her mouth, her lip gloss leaving behind a faint shimmer on the lid. There were two other passengers on the carriage she was in, one of the women had her head tilted back resting against the seat, slouched down with her legs stretched out in front of her. The other was reading *We Need to Talk About Kevin*, a book Sabrina read in year eleven, borrowed from her English teacher, Mr. Haines, a beanie pulled down low over her head. Beneath the empty seat opposite Sabrina, there were a pair of burgundy gloves, and next to them, was an empty, clear *Starbucks* cup.

Her phone dinged with a text, quieting Thank U, Next by Ariana Grande. She glanced down at her phone, resting on her lap.

Soran at 01:23 PM: *Remember to text me when you get home, Sabi gyan*

Sabrina had smiled, but didn't reply.

Soran had been a potential relationship that never happened, ending before it ever truly began and it *sucked* a little bit, a small part of her had wanted it to work out with him. He could have made her happy. He could have erased all the shadowy parts of a past she tried to hide from.

But he wasn't Musa.

They were different in every way, and she appreciated that. In the moments she found herself wishing they were a little more alike, wishing she could see a glimpse of Musa in Soran's eyes, she remembered their differences and felt a quiet relief in the way she no longer had to tiptoe on broken glass to earn a love that was never real. Still—*he wasn't Musa* and they fell apart when he decided that one day, they were better off as friends.

But now that she didn't have the distractions of essays and her dissertation, or Soran, she was thinking about Musa again, too much. And the feeling of loneliness in her chest rose to her throat, making her blink back tears, as she sat in front of her dressing table, staring into her reflection.

Sabrina let out a sigh and put the lid back onto her Luminous Silk foundation, making a mental note to order another from John Lewis. She tilted her head slightly, feeling the strands of her newly dyed golden hair brush against her neck and collarbone. Her phone dinged with a message from Veda, asking if she was ready to go. *No*, Sabrina thought as she quickly applied lipstick. She wasn't sure why it was happening *now*, but there was a sinking feeling in the pit of her stomach. A hollow kind of emptiness that ate away at her. For months now, she'd been doing . . . not good, but ok. And that was enough.

But today, it seemed as if she going to stumble around, trying to find her footing, because it was like something was going to happen, something was going to go wrong—or maybe it was that she was thinking about green eyes flecked with amber around the iris, a voice that was all red wine and dark chocolate, and a devastating smile. That goddamn smile.

Absentmindedly, Sabrina applied her lipstick, trying to shake away the thoughts burning through her mind. She'd plied herself with alcohol for months on end, a futile attempt to numb the pain that had been tearing her apart.

Letting out a sharp exhale, Sabrina stood up, phone in hand. She grabbed her leather jacket from off her bed, and jogged down the stairs.

"Hey," she said, voice soft, to Veda.

"Finally," Veda replied, leaning against the shoe rack. "You take forever."

"Sorry."

"You good?"

"Yeah, man. Just one of those days, you know."

"Mm, I do know," Veda said, sympathetic. Her makeup was flawless, lips shaded a crimson red. It matched the heeled boots she wore.

"Only you can pull off red boots," Sabrina's smile was fleeting.

"You're acting as if you can't pull of kameezes and trainers," Veda teased, her expression changing from concerned to amused.

"Bring up my past crimes again, and I'll kill you."

"I'd like to see you try."

"Say wallah."

Veda's laugh was loud and long. "I will if you tell your parents you're not Muslim."

"I'll do that if you do it too," Sabrina shot back, shoving her boots on. She'd been sad to throw away her other pair. They were her favourite.

"I plan to."

At Sabrina's raised eyebrow, Veda's expression changed into a small smirk. "On my deathbed."

"Well," Sabrina replied. She opened the front door, glancing over her shoulder at Veda. They both had put their hijabs on loosely, waiting 'til they were in the train to take it off. "That *is* what deathbeds are for. To confess to long buried secrets."

☼

The Breakfast Crew was, surprisingly, not too busy when Sabrina and Naveda got there, with Elle already waiting for them. Between the swell of breakfast and lunch time rushes, Sabrina sought the comforting lull the cute little café on Belgrave Avenue provided, when customers were few and the pounding of her heart returned to its normal rate.

An elderly couple sipped on tea, not talking—there was an air of ease surrounding them, the kind of familiarity you get with someone who's your best friend, a bowl of porridge in front of them both, filled to the brim with pecans, berries, pumpkin seeds and edible pink flowers. A little further away sat three young women, laughing, three large glasses of milkshakes and plates of stacked pancakes placed on the table they occupied.

There was a young family of four sitting a few booths away from where Sabrina, Elle and Veda usually sat, on the other side of the café. There were three waitresses on this morning's shift.

The girls' usual booth was by the window, closest to the door, and they always chose to get the same thing at each of their top three hotspots for brunch. Despite already knowing what they wanted, Sabrina and Veda still perused the menu, eyes flicking from each breakfast dish to the next, thinking *oh it sounded nice but—no, I want the full English breakfast with a side of pancakes and fruit.*

Between leaving their house, arriving at *The Breakfast Crew*, and having their food arrive, Sabrina found herself thinking about Musa again. It had been a while since he crossed her mind like this, since before her mind was heavy with the stress of her final year and the upcoming exams she pushed out of her head.

"What the hell are you so deep in thought about?" Elle asked her, scooping up a hash brown with the fork clutched between her fingers and used it to mop up the beans on the plate. Sabrina looked up at her, and paused, mouth on the reusable metal straw *The Breakfast Crew* provided their customers with, sipping on her coffee. Blinking, she took a large sip from the frothy goodness and sighed, shaking her head.

"Uh," tucking a few flyaway strands of hair behind her ear, she forced a smile onto her face, hoping it didn't resemble a grimace. "Nothing."

"Right," Elle nodded. "*Sure*. What the fuck were you thinking about?"

Sabrina rolled her eyes, "seriously, for fuck's sake, nothing. Drop it."

"Jheeze," Veda muttered. "Someone woke up on the wrong side of the bed this morning. What happened? Didn't get enough beauty sleep?"

"As a matter of fact, no. I did not."

"Why's that, sugarplum?"

"I was too busy masturbating," Sabrina said casually, the forced smile on her face widening into a full-blown smirk, as she chewed on the slightly warm but sweet and juicy strawberry, powdered sugar dusted over the red berry. The pair of her companions stared at her, faces blank, but amusement was slowly crossing over Elle's face, an almost deliberate, flirty grin tugging on the corners of her mouth.

"What were you thinking about?" she tilted her head a little and lifted her mug of coffee, taking a slow sip, eyes on Sabrina.

Unable to resist, Sabrina replied, "you."

"I'm sorry," Veda interrupted just as Elle was about to say something. "Do I need to leave you two alone to resolve your sexual frustration?"

"Not at all," Sabrina drawled. "I think we're doing just fine here. If anything, we can fix our sexual tension with a very heated make out session tonight, right?"

"But of course," Elle nodded, winking at her. "Maybe a little heavy petting, too."

"Don't you mean a lot?"

"Please stop," Veda groaned loudly.

"Are we making you uncomfortable?" Sabrina sniggered.

"Yes," she stared at Sabrina. "You *are* fucking making me uncomfortable."

"My apologies, darling."

"Shut the fuck up."

"Eat my—"

"Arse?" Eleanor interjected, laughing.

Sabrina smirked in response, turning her attention from her cousin to her friend. She tilted her head to the side as Elle stared her, face unimpressed. "You know," she said, as she cut up the pancake, glancing at her two friends briefly, before she stabbed a strawberry into the piece of pancake on her fork. "I think I want to volunteer with the Citizens Advice Bureau."

"Wait, what? Since when and why?" Veda demanded, raising her eyebrows.

"Well, to get more experience and it would look good on my resume. Also because I need something else to do with my life after exams are over—it gets quite boring, you see."

"How can masturbating get boring?" Elle stared at Sabrina, clearly fighting back the laughter that made her seem like she was a little bit unhinged.

Sabrina grinned wickedly, "Oh, I'm not talking about touching myself. That's fun. That will *always* be fun. Like, the other day, I wasn't even horny, but I decided to get out my friendly, battery-operated-boyfriend, just in case."

"God," shaking her head, Veda scooped up the scrambled egg with beans dropping from the fork and lifted it to her mouth, slowly chewing. "You're fucking crude."

"Says the girl that slept with two best friends," Sabrina replied sweetly.

"I didn't know they were—" she stopped, sighing. "*Whatever*. Fuck off."

"That's a bit rude," Elle pointed out.

"Go fuck yourself."

"Listen *here*, you lil shit," Elle was saying, pointing her index finger at Veda, before she lifted her rather large mug of hot chocolate with both hands, and began sipping it slowly. The two girls waited for her to finish drinking, amusement plastered on their goddess-like faces. "Don't tell me what to do."

"Unless you're fucking," Sabrina added.

"Okay—we're changing the subject," Veda announced loudly, glaring at both Elle and Sabrina. The ghost of a smile played on the edges of Sabrina's mouth and as the conversation drifted from sex and masturbating to exams and their already handed in dissertations and essays, as well as their upcoming exams, Sabrina was thinking about summer 2017, when she found and lost the love of her life, within a span of three months—the weeks before everything began to fall apart and suddenly, it was like she was hit with a wave of nostalgia. Perhaps it was the South Asian blood in her, the need to watch something ripen with age before it was touched . . . because for *days* now, she hadn't thought of him.

And then she handed in her fucking dissertation and her mind felt a little less heavy without all the clutter of literature reviews, analysis of her research into the stigma and silencing of survivors, and the late night studying.

Everything hit her all at once and it was like she was struggling to differentiate between what really happened and what only happened in her head. There wasn't really much difference between the ending that happened in reality and the ending that took place on her end—they both left her heart bruised, left her alone to a pack of savage wolves, crumbling like an old cathedral, raw and bloody while everything around her was blurring, fragmented, distorted.

So that was why, while she was sitting in *The Breakfast Crew* with Veda and Elle, she was lost in fermented nostalgia, the kind that took away the air needed to breathe and the logic needed to realise that nothing was ever as good as the memories made it seem. Because while everything tasted better with age—wine, sex, music, it somehow seemed like memories were the only thing that ended up tasting bitter in her mouth: sharp and cold and *bitter*.

It kind of sucked, when you thought about it—the way the world screwed you over, because here she was, thinking about a man that left her more than a year ago, maybe even before he finally told her. He had been playing a ruthless game with her heart, never calling it anything more than a summer fling when they were dead and gone and buried.

It had been the greatest three months of her life, until reality poured cold water over the rose-tinged glaze she wore, a fiery burn that felt painful and sweet all at once, the kind of pain that you got used to after a while. And Sabrina thought it was something forgotten, but now she was thinking about it, about the monsters in her closet, stacked up in boxes, with months and months of dust collecting on top of it all.

But she probably shouldn't be thinking about it all—about the love she had and lost, about the man that was her beginning and end, and everything in between. She looked at Elle as she turned her attention to Sabrina, asking why she wanted to volunteer with the Citizens Advice Bureau, the Camden branch in particular, because that was a little far from her, especially when she had several close to home. Swirling her finger in the powdered sugar that had been sprinkled over the pancakes and scattered onto a small part of the plate, Sabrina sighed quietly, fighting back a smile. *It's not because of Musa*, she wanted to say.

"I already told you," she said instead. "I need to get more experience and make my CV look good, and I need something to do."

"Then why don't you volunteer to teach at a summer school or find a mental health related job?" Veda tossed back, arching one perfect eyebrow. There was that hint of a smirk on her crimson lips, the kind of smirk that said: *you're doing it because of Musa—all of this is because of Musa and you can't let go of the man that's already left you behind.*

Sabrina didn't think it was meant to be a cruel smirk, with those words that had gone unsaid ringing in her ears, as if screamed, but it was like being stabbed, all the same.

"Because," Sabrina slurped from the mug that holding her coffee, eyeing Elle over the rim. "Volunteering with CAB is a good idea for me to do and it incorporates both mental health and the legal sector."

"Uh huh," Elle said, exchanging glances with Veda.

"Fuck the both of you," Sabrina snapped, slamming the mug down on the table. She swallowed, taking in deep breaths. Veda frowned, looking at her carefully. *Calm, Sabrina. Calm. Stay calm.* "God, I need to get laid," she mumbled.

"I quite agree," Elle tilted her head a little, watching Sabrina.

Sabrina raised an eyebrow. "Are you offering?"

Elle started laughing, "You're not my type, sweets. If you want though, I could get one of—"

"Fuck no," Sabrina interrupted, shaking her head. "I'm capable of finding someone to get down and dirty with on my own, thank you very much."

She smirked and said, "If you say so."

"Sabah's hooking you up with Daniel though, no?" Veda hummed.

Not bothering with a reply, Sabrina glanced around *The Breakfast Crew*; a young couple with two daughters were sitting near the window that overlooked the street outside, cars blurred, as they cruised speedily down the road. The traffic lights changed from red to amber to green and back again, over and over.

The couple were arguing—he was waving his hands about, gesturing wildly as he spoke, looking angry and furious and like he wanted to hit something, someone, and she looked like she was going to cry, exhausted, *tired* of it all, as if the world was weighing her down. Their daughters were quietly eating, not looking at their parents as they fought, voices slowly rising and the elderly couple and the other three young women were starting to look over at them, frowns etched on their faces, and soon, Sabrina was not the only one watching as they started screaming at each other. One of the girls started crying.

An image burned itself to the front of her mind, coming together like the last piece of a puzzle finally falling into place: her raven-haired mother sitting in the living room, staring blankly at the TV, strands of inky blackness pulled into a bun on the top of her head, silently crying. It was the worst kind of hurt, when all you could do was just sit there, numb, as tears slipped out.

It was the things that danced on the edges of your consciousness that hurt the most, flickering images that should have been forgotten long ago, but weren't. And there were so many things, numerous moments from years ago that were burning behind her eyelids: her father's yells, dark and veiny hands causing so much damage. Adam walking across the stage to get his certificate. Sultana crawling into her bed the night everyone found out. The two of them wearing baby pink grooms-maid lenghas, diamond hairpins glittering in their hair. Going with Adam to Seville for the first time, a few days of bliss away from their parents, the summer after Sabrina had finished her GCSEs, his hair dark and glossy and wild around his face, eyes crinkling as he laughed at Sultana's joke. Flying out to America for the Christmas break with her siblings to escape reality—she fell in love with New York, finding pieces of herself mending as she stared at the glittering Christmas tree in Rockefeller Center, hand in hand with Adam and Sultana.

But of all these things, Adam was always there—because he became more than just an older brother; he acted as a father figure for them, and he was there for her when her parents failed to be. It was him she went to, crying, when Musa left, choosing to stay with him for a few weeks, wallowing in his guest room. He had been her rock through the months that followed, when she was too distraught to leave the house except to go to university, and it was him she was terrified of disappointing. She never wanted to do anything to make him feel let down.

☼

The streets were illuminated by golden streetlamps, reflecting off the glistening cobblestoned pavements, the tops of the cars parked in the driveways shimmering beneath the light that just about did its job to brighten the already darkened evening, the rain slashing down and seeping in through Sabrina's clothes as she ran, feet pounding against the tarmac streets that was not too far from home. Her grey top was soaked, sticking to her skin, prickles of cold rippling through her, rattling in her bones as the wind chilled her even more, numbness eclipsing her, raw and icy. But it did nothing to stop her from glancing up at the glorious blanket of stars that she ran beneath.

Sabrina quickened her pace, and stumbled, the top of her left trainer getting caught in a crack on the pavement. A sound of irritation escaped her, as she shook her foot free, and continued to run, eyeing her house in the distance. Every pathway had a tree lining up, standing tall and proud, its recumbent, bare limbs arching up and bending down, the world fading to a dull, dreary greyness in the spring night, awaiting the summer of 2019, much like Sabrina was. She had a plan for this summer: she'd already booked the flight tickets to go travelling around parts of Asia in August with Elle; they had seven countries down on their list that they wanted to hit up within five weeks.

Though Sabrina hadn't made her parents aware of that particular plan just yet.

It didn't matter though—they couldn't say no. She was graduating.

Sabrina slowed down to a jog, her breaths coming in quick, shallow gasps from having run for more than an hour, with only a few minutes rest in between. She only properly began working out several months after her breakup with Musa, a name that sent a jolt of pain through her system, made her swallow back tears that threatened to spill each time he came up in conversation. It hurt her heart, and she didn't know, even after all this time, how to perfectly block out the memories of the very person who completely destroyed her, ruined her for all other relationships, made the word love mean heartbreak, broke her soul to the point she gave up on the idea of religion altogether, after a year of pleading prayers that went unanswered, a river of salt streaming down her cheeks, flushed with cries that didn't seem to stop.

As she continued to slowly jog towards her house, voices to her left captured her attention. She went still, pushed back her hair, rain seeping through her, making her lashes stick together. There was a girl, tall, angry, motioning with her hands as she talked to the person in the black BMW. The light from the streetlamps cast a gold glow on the girl's dark brown skin, giving her an almost otherworldly look. She swore loudly, piercing through the music pumping in Sabrina's ears, and stepped back just in time, as the car peeled away. Sabrina swallowed and turned her attention back to continuing to jog to the front steps of her house.

She ran a hand through her hair, plastered to her head with the rain, droplets running down her face and sinking into her wet top, a droplet of water cascading down the nape of her neck and beneath the cotton material. She shivered, getting her keys out from the pocket of the running belt around her waist, fingers cold and slightly numb. Clutching onto the keys tightly, she unlocked the front door. Stepping into the warmth was a relief, and she shuddered from the cold and wet, quickly shutting the door behind her. She kicked off her Reebok trainers and peeled off her wet socks, hearing the sounds of the TV.

"Veda?" she called, walking in the general direction of the living room. She spotted her niece and close friend lounging on the sofa, a packet of Sensations crisps on her lap.

"Oh, good, you're back," Veda smiled. "I was thinking, since you start late tomorrow and I have nothing to do, let's do a Harry Potter marathon tonight."

"Sounds good, let me have a quick shower."

"Ok. Hurry up though."

"Don't tell me what to do."

"Bite me."

"Kinky."

"Go have a fucking shower, Sabrina."

"Yes, daddy."

"Save that for your fuck buddy."

"Which one?" Sabrina called, as she was walking upstairs.

"Whoever the next one is," Veda shouted, laughing.

A few hours later, after Sabrina was done with her steaming hot shower and dressed in the Central Perk pyjamas she'd bought from Primark, hair loose and damp around her shoulders, face scrubbed free of makeup and Veda had set up the living room with a blanket and cushions on the floor, one bowl filled with sweet and salty popcorn mixed in with a few M&Ms, one with Sensations and the other with McCoy's crisps, and two Volvic water bottles, they were halfway through *Harry Potter and the Prisoner of Azkaban*.

Sabrina reached her hand in, throwing popcorn and chocolate into her mouth as Sirius lunged for Peter Pettigrew. Honestly, Harry really should've just let Remus and Sirius kill the dickhead.

Nobility and heroic acts of kindness can only get you so far. Like, seriously—Sirius, Remus, Tonks, Fred, Mad-Eye Moody, Dobby and Dumbledore would all still be alive, hadn't it been for fucking Peter. But then again, perhaps Remus and Tonks wouldn't have become a thing, got married and had Teddy. The whole sequence of events would've changed and Peter wouldn't have owed Harry, paying his debt at the Malfoy's. She sighed quietly as she continued watching the movie, trying to take out a popcorn kernel stuck between her teeth.

The whole scene right now, with her long time closest friend beside her, eyes on the large TV screen, watching Harry Potter for the umpteenth time was something that warmed her bitter insides—like butterscotch poured over vanilla ice cream, the kind of thing that stayed with a person, way into later adulthood.

And honestly, there were a lot of things that would stay with her even when she was in her late forties, and away from the life she was living now—because these things made and shaped and defined a person, and half of it had already shaped her into the woman she was now, and she didn't know whether she loved it or hated it. Maybe something in between, or maybe it was something akin to indifference. She breathed out slowly, the moving coming slowly coming to an end, closing her eyes as Sirius flew away on Buckbeak.

As the credits began to roll, Veda moved away, taking out the DVD of the *Prisoner of Azkaban* and switched it for the *Goblet of Fire*. She sat back down beside Sabrina, shivering a little and pulled up the blanket to her chin, grabbing a handful of popcorn and M&M's

with the other hand as the movie started. Sabrina lifted a hand, covering her mouth as she yawned.

"You're tired?" Veda asked, not glancing away from the screen.

"No shit, Sherlock," Sabrina mumbled in response, rubbing her eyes.

"So original," she snorted, laughing. "Your wit never fails to shock me."

"Eat shit."

Veda leaned back a little, stretching a leg out and pulling her hair into a low ponytail. She glanced at Sabrina, eyes bright and brown. "You know," she said. "I think you should try actually dating someone. Getting into a relationship and all that."

Sabrina raised her brows. "Sorry?"

"You're still so fucking hung up on Musa, and it's just so sad and—like I get you love him and he's everything to you. But you need to move on. And the only way you'll be able to do that is if you start dating again. I know things with Soran didn't—"

A smile forced its way onto Sabrina's face and she thought, *girl gets heart broken by boy . . .*

Almost as if that explained everything—because it *should*, it really should, and yet, it was like it didn't explain anything at all. Not the ending, not the beginning, but at the same time, it was enough of an explanation to know that there were some questions that couldn't be answered, some things that were left better not knowing, some things that were better left unsaid, something things that scared you so much, you didn't want to go through it again—and this was one of those things. Because here was the thing: Sabrina didn't want to be with anyone ever again.

She wasn't ashamed to admit that it was him that completely fucking enraptured her, taking her in, reeling her into his world of getting high and drunk and fucking shamelessly all night long, all day when they were supposed to be at work—it went a little like this: she now knows how to properly give the kind of blowjob that drove guys insane. God, she was so bad at that before she met Musa. And now she wasn't.

He turned her into this girl, this soulless, not-believing in god kind of girl, so in love with someone even when he left, that she couldn't see she was *better off* without him. No, she thought, her smile hardening as she looked away from Veda, telling her that *no, I don't want to be with anyone*—she was more like a god fallen from the throne she once sat on because everything else has turned to smoke and ash.

The movie continued playing, and she was no longer paying attention, staring almost unseeingly as Harry's name got called. She was thinking about how she couldn't seem to find anyone to replace Musa, because none of them measured up, and how she was fucking sick of feeling this white-hot anger and hurt rising up inside her, like a wave of nausea, every time she remembered the way things ended, compared it to the final chapter of them in her head. It made everything tainted and grey and foggy, and here she was, one year and six months and twenty two days later, watching *Harry Potter and the Goblet of Fire*, unable to stop thinking about him.

But god, it had been a really long time since she last had sex.

"It kind of sucks that the last movie got ruined," Veda commented after a while. "I mean, what the fuck—Voldemort was supposed to fall to the floor, like his corpse and shit, not turn into fucking butterflies or whatever. And god," she shook her head, letting out a laugh. "Harry was supposed to repair his wand. Why the hell didn't the producers follow that?"

Maybe she could really get over him if she tried to get under someone else again. Shoving every thought of Musa back into that box that is covered in dust and half-ripping in her head, she clenched her fists.

Dumbledore was talking, "Now the pain we all feel at this dreadful loss reminds me, and reminds us, that though we may come from different countries and speak in different tongues, our hearts beat as one."

"In light of the recent events, the bonds of the friendships made this year will be more important than ever. Remember that, and Cedric Diggory will not have died in vain."

Swallowing, she shifted on the blanket, crossing her legs beneath. "The producers are fucking cheap, that's why."

Veda laughed, "Nah, they're good producers—you know that. I just wish the ending was the same as the book." She paused. "But the epilogue sucked."

"You remember that, and we'll celebrate a boy who was kind, and honest, and brave, and true. Right to the very end."

The thing about being honest was that sometimes all it does is tear your world apart; destroying everything that ever meant something—because sometimes lies were better than the truth. *Or maybe that's just me.* Her breath came out in a loud sigh, her shoulders caving in beneath the grey pyjama top she was wearing, and she ran a hand through her hair, thinking, *I don't want to be sad.*

That was the thing about not wanting to feel a certain emotion—the harder you denied it, the harder it ended up hitting you, full force, like a tidal wave, crushing down on your chest and *this* was what she was feeling now, something inside her burning like liquid metal, scorching and painful, hatred mixing in with this aching sadness. She laughed, as the Golden Trio arrived at King's Cross Station. Naveda looked at Sabrina, a question on her face.

"You okay?" she asked.

An almost bitter smile was playing on the edges of Sabrina's lips, and she looked back at Veda, brown eyes on brown eyes—sad on concerned. "I'm fine," she replied, smiling, smiling, smiling. "I'm gonna go up to bed."

"Okay," Veda nodded, still looking at Sabrina. She frowned.

Sabrina laughed, "god, stop looking at me like I'm about to slit my fucking wrists or something."

Veda raised her eyebrows but said nothing as Sabrina pushed the blankets away from her and stood up.

"You okay to clear up down here? I'll do the cleaning later this week."

"Mhm, yeah, of course. We do need to do a massive spring clean," Veda said, briefly glancing back at the TV.

Sabrina wished she could do the same to her own life. She

wanted to press a **RESET** button and start again. She wanted to be someone new.

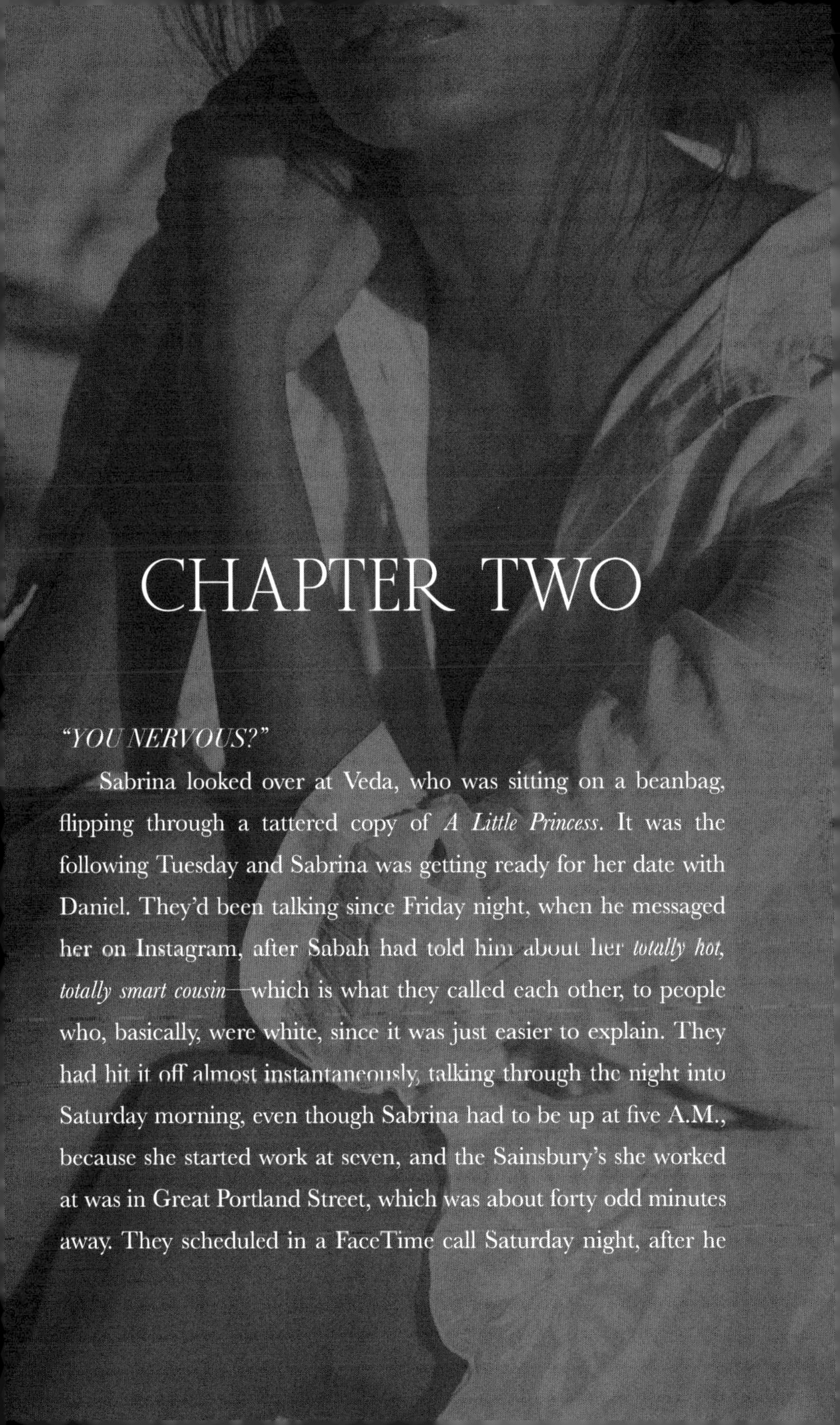

CHAPTER TWO

"YOU NERVOUS?"

Sabrina looked over at Veda, who was sitting on a beanbag, flipping through a tattered copy of *A Little Princess*. It was the following Tuesday and Sabrina was getting ready for her date with Daniel. They'd been talking since Friday night, when he messaged her on Instagram, after Sabah had told him about her *totally hot, totally smart cousin*—which is what they called each other, to people who, basically, were white, since it was just easier to explain. They had hit it off almost instantaneously, talking through the night into Saturday morning, even though Sabrina had to be up at five A.M., because she started work at seven, and the Sainsbury's she worked at was in Great Portland Street, which was about forty odd minutes away. They scheduled in a FaceTime call Saturday night, after he got back from an engagement party and it was, well, nice.

"Not particularly," she responded, turning back to face the mirror, as she swept her brush lightly across her cheeks, dusting blusher on to bring some colour to her face. Other than the fiery red lipstick she planned on wearing. Sleek's All Fired Up liquid lipstick was one of her top three favourite reds. "It's just a date. I've been on plenty of those."

"No, you haven't."

"Shut up."

"You're *so* nervous," Veda laughed.

"I am *so* not!"

"Ok, if you say so."

"I do," Sabrina deadpanned, turning back round to look at Veda. "I'm not nervous. I'm actually kind of excited. It's been a while."

She was also feeling kind of guilty.

It felt like she was cheating on Musa. But she was doing her best to brush those feelings aside. It wouldn't help any, to be thinking of him on this date with an extremely attractive, extremely talented guy who, by the looks of his page, was an artist. She let out a slow, whistling exhale, and put The Body Shop blusher brush down, part of a sixteenth birthday gift from her cousin, Nafisa. Ever since her cousin had gotten married a few years ago, she'd felt a distance in their relationship.

She supposed marriage came with change, but it wasn't like she'd ever been particularly close with Nafisa anyway. Sabrina's relationship with Layla, a friend of five years since they'd been paired together in first year Psychology class in sixth form, had changed somewhat since she'd gotten married a little more than three years ago—they rarely talked, but when they did, everything was fine and it was as if no time had passed at all since they last spoke, often spanning a few months.

Carefully lining her lips with a brown lip liner from Barry M, Sabrina again thought over her choice of outfit. She was wearing the same skirt she'd worn when she met Soran, the first guy she'd slept with after Musa, a black and white dogtooth skirt with a paper bag waist from Primark, paired with a black ribbed V-neck top, showing just a hint of her cleavage. Under her clothes, she wore a new black silk and lace bra and thong, with sheer black stockings, bought from Agent Provocateur last Wednesday. She leaned back, briefly staring at herself, thinking she did a pretty damn good job with her makeup. Sabrina slowly applied the red lipstick, mouth parted. She hadn't really heard of the diner Daniel was taking her to, *The Shack* based in Central London, with a modern American theme.

"Are you taking a jacket?" Veda asked.

"Yeah, my leather one," Sabrina replied, twisting the lid back into the lipstick tube.

"The All Saints one or the Missguided one?"

"Missguided. And I'm thinking of wearing the black Chelsea boots?"

"Sounds good. You're gonna be tiny next to him."

Sabrina grinned, "He's a whole fucking foot and two inches

taller than me."

"You're just a midget."

"Leave me alone, you *rude* ass doo-doo head."

"Remind me again, how old are you?"

"Younger than you."

"Clearly," Veda snorted, dropping Sabrina's book onto the floor.

"Why are you putting my book on the floor? Put it back on the shelf, man."

"You're becoming more and more like your mother every day."

There was a beat of silence.

Sabrina gasped loudly, turning round fully to face Veda, as she slid *A Little Princess* back into one of the shelves Sabrina had, taking up an entire wall, weighed down by various other books.

"*Take that back*," Sabrina hissed.

"No."

"You're a bitch."

"Is it really?"

"I'm telling your mum."

"Go ahead," Veda smirked. "She won't give a shit."

"Bite me."

"Tell Daniel to do that."

"I shall," Sabrina said, after she'd spritzed her face with her nearly finished bottle of the All Nighter setting spray. "How do I look?"

"Like you're going to eat him alive."

"Kita?"

Veda laughed. "You look fucking sexy, man. Fifty quid says he's going to get a boner when he sees you."

"I'm not betting on that," Sabrina rolled her eyes. "I know he will."

"Your humbleness never ceases to amaze me."

"Thank you."

Sabah had texted a little earlier, during her break, wishing good luck for the date and to update her on how it went. Sabrina hadn't bothered with a reply, thinking she would message back after the date had ended—and it was now nearing eight P.M., and Daniel would be waiting to pick her up outside Upton Park station, since she hadn't wanted to give him her address, in approximately twenty minutes. But it was fine, since it only took six minutes to walk there.

After putting on a pair of giant gold hoop earrings, Sabrina tidied the clutter on her dressing table; putting the makeup products back in their rightful places, save for her powder and lipstick. Those, she'd be taking with her. She kept her brushes and beauty blender out, thinking she'd give them a wash the next day.

"When are you meeting your friends?"

"Um," Veda furrowed her eyebrows. "Not sure. Probably half nine. Why?"

"Emne zikayram," Sabrina responded. She took her jacket off the back of her bedroom door. Her phone was in her hand, a small black bag with a gold chain over her shoulder. "Let me know when you're with them."

"Acha."

"Great," she smiled, looking over her shoulder at Veda, as they descended the stairs, leading into the hallway where the other three bedrooms and bathroom were.

Her phone vibrated with a text.

Daniel at 19:37: *I'm about ten minutes away from the station. I'll see you soon. Hope you're dressed nice ;)*

A smirk graced Sabrina's lips. She quickly typed out a response.

Sabrina at 19:39: *are you worth dressing nice for though . . .*

Daniel at 19:43: *Ouch. And here I thought you liked me*

Sabrina at 19:44: *who lied to you? and stop texting. focus on ur driving. thanks x*

Daniel at 19:45: *Aw, are you worried about me? :)*

Sabrina at 19:45: *no. why would i be?*

"Is that Daniel?" Veda asked, as they stood at the bottom of the stairs, Sabrina's gaze locked to her phone.

"Hmm?" she hummed, distracted. "What?"

"*Interesting*," Veda laughed.

"What is?"

"Nothing," Veda said, though the widening smile on her face implied otherwise. "It's just . . ."

"*What*?"

"You're into him."

Sabrina gaped, speechless. "I haven't even *met* the guy."

"You will be, in a few minutes."

"Not the point at all."

"Oh, but it is. You're so into him."

"No, I'm really not."

"Mhm, if you say so," Veda's smile was still intact.

Sabrina rolled her eyes, choosing not to respond, as she slipped her ankle-length boots on. It was no point arguing with Veda when she made her mind up about something. Her teasing was relentless.

"Share your location with me, by the way," Veda was saying, as Sabrina grasped the cool, gold door handle. "So I know where you are at all times. I mean, he's still a stranger. So."

"Sure, yeah, I'll do it now, babe," Sabrina replied, pausing in the doorway. "I'm sharing it on four different apps."

"Good," Veda laughed.

The Shack was lit up with geometric ceiling pendants, making the diner bright in the darkened night outside. Its floors and counter tops were a light brown marble, walls covered in mahogany panelling and lined with black and white pictures of the London skyline, along with New York and Seattle. The seating consisted of light grey booths and tables, and a tall counter with a long row of bar stools, more than half of them occupied, matching the rest of the décor. On the far right were two doors, labelled **STAFF ONLY**, and a little further down from those doors, behind a wall almost shielding it from view and away from all the booths, were another two doors, leading into the bathrooms. There were only two, one for men and one for women, and they were just as pretty as the rest of the diner. Between the two doors was a potted yucca elephantipe. While the décor of *The Shack* was all modern, the food they served and the way the booths were all in the centre and against one wall, with the counter on the opposite wall, kind of reminded Sabrina of *Pop's*, from *Riverdale*.

It was a little after ten P.M., and Sabrina and Daniel each had milkshakes in front of them, having finished their meal about half an hour ago. The reviews she'd read were right, and the pictures she'd seen *definitely* didn't do the place any justice. It was like a little piece of heaven—and the price of the food they'd ordered didn't make Sabrina wince in Broke Student; thankfully it cost much less than what she made in an hour. Their total was less than twenty pounds, to her relief, including the strawberry milkshake she'd ordered, and the chocolate one he was sipping on, eyes locked on her face.

"Can't get enough of my face?" she asked him, red lips tilting up into a small smirk.

He grinned. "Is it that obvious?"

"Little bit," Sabrina raised her eyebrows. "*Some* would say it's a little creepy."

"Do you think so?" He was smirking back at her, and it took all her willpower to not grab his face in her hands right then and kiss the fuck out of him.

"Personally, I'm totally fine with you admiring my beauty."

"Someone's a little vain."

"Just telling it how it is, b."

Daniel laughed, the low sound making Sabrina clench her thighs together. "I like your honesty."

"I think there's a whole lot more that you'll like."

"*Oh?*"

She rested her chin on her hand, meeting his crystalline blue eyes. "Come with me to the bathroom?"

His eyes glinted with a look Sabrina couldn't decipher, tongue darting out to lick his lower lip. She wanted his tongue on other parts of her body.

Sabrina breathed out slowly when he nodded.

They stood up, heading towards the bathroom quickly, hand-in-hand. Sabrina ignored the loud thumping of her heart, the excitement rushing through her veins.

Pushing open the door to the women's bathroom, they slipped inside. Daniel locked the door. Sabrina faced him, eyes trailing over his face, the tanned skin of his neck, the broad shoulders and muscles, accentuated by the pale grey top he wore, paired with black jeans and black Timberlands. He was a male Adonis, looked every inch like a god.

Sabrina inhaled. She took off the bag from her shoulder, dropping it onto the bathroom counter.

Daniel took a slow, measured step towards her, and she tilted her face up, looking into his eyes. He grabbed her face in his hands, gently, and leaned down to kiss her. Her eyes fluttered shut and she lifted her arms, looping them around his neck, kissing him back instantly, with no hesitation. His lips were softer than she could've imagined and he tasted like chocolate. Daniel's hands swept through the golden strands of her hair, down to her back. She moaned quietly.

That was enough for him to lift her up into his arms. Sabrina gasped a little against his mouth, and he took that as an invitation to sweep his tongue into her mouth. Placing her down gently onto the counter, Daniel stood between her legs, holding Sabrina close against his body.

He pulled back slowly, kissing along her jaw line, slowly pressing open mouthed kisses against her neck. "You absolutely sure you want to do this?" His words were murmured against her neck, biting down gently on the skin.

Sabrina ran her fingers through his silky hair, "yes. One hundred per cent."

Daniel kissed her on the mouth again. Paused. Moved back. Gazed at her intensely. "Tell me, at any point, if you want to stop, ok? If you feel uncomfortable or anything at all, tell me." He kissed her again.

"Safe word's *bubblegum*," Sabrina said against his mouth.

He smiled.

☼

A little more than an hour later, Sabrina and Daniel were seated in a little bar in Notting Hill, laughing. The bar had dark wooden flooring, deep brown leather booths and matching bar stools, the wall behind the counter they were sitting on entirely shelved with bottles of alcohol, from wine to rum to vodka to whiskey. Soft music played overheard. They were both tipsy, blackberry juice mixed with rum coursing through Sabrina's bloodstream, while Daniel was drinking whiskey neat. A slow smile graced his face as he looked at her.

"So, tell me," Sabrina was saying, taking a long sip of her drink. "How does a teacher afford a Porsche?" she pointed at him, then her eyes widened. "Wait, oh my god, don't tell me. You're a fucking undercover mafia boss aren't you?"

Daniel laughed, "No. My family is, uh, rich, I guess. And I make a lot of money from selling my paintings. They're actually featured in that new gallery that just opened up four months ago, in Shoreditch."

"Ah," she nodded solemnly. "Your family's part of the bourgeoisie, huh? The elite one percent of the, um, population."

"Basically," He shrugged, embarrassed.

"So why are you a teacher then? Shouldn't you be, like, I don't know, CEO of a major multibillion pound company?"

Daniel laughed again, lifting the glass to his mouth. He took a long sip. "No, my father is still CEO. He will be, for a long time. My older brother, Caleb, is COO of the company, but my sister and I decided to step out of that mould and chase our own dreams. Neither of us were particularly interested in running the company. So my brother took the reigns—he'd been groomed to take control of it, anyway. He wants to. It's his. Completely will be. After my dad decides to hand it over to him." Daniel paused. "Or dies, I guess."

"And how's his health?" Sabrina hid a smirk..

Daniel raised his eyebrows. "It's good, thankfully. He's dedicated to living a healthy lifestyle." There was a hint of laughter in his voice, his eyes glimmering with amusement as he thought about his father. "Dad always participates in marathons and exercises all the time, eats as healthy as possible." He put his hand on her thigh, beneath the skirt revealing an inch of the lace on her stocking clad leg. The warmth of his hand seared through her skin, and she caught her breath, meeting his eyes. "If I could," he continued saying. "Somehow stop my parents dying at any point in their life, I would. My dad is one of my best friends."

"That's nice. That's really nice," Sabrina murmured, then frowned. "*Jesus* . . . you know what I never got about Christianity? Jesus. Like, how can he be the son of god and god in human form? I just don't get it. Because in Islam, Jesus is just a messenger. The second to last one, I mean. After him is Muhammad."

Daniel smiled wryly, "I don't know. Uh, yeah, I was never really one for religion. My family isn't religious at all. The only time we ever go to church is during weddings or funerals."

He runs his finger over the edge of the glass before lifting his eyes back up to her face, his gaze probing. "Are you Muslim?"

She tilted her head as his arm curled around her waist, pulling her in closer with a drag of her stool. Her heart trembled in her chest.

Sabrina laughed a little, "no. I mean, I was. I'm not now."

"What do you mean?"

"I was born into a Muslim family. But I left Islam a while back."

"How come?" Daniel asked. His fingers traced patterns into

her skin, sending a delicious shiver down her spine, goosebumps spreading across her skin.

Sabrina hesitated a little. "Uh well . . ." she bit her lip. "I guess there were just aspects of the religion I didn't really agree with. It just felt like rules and regulations to me, some of it was just so . . . *restricting* and I felt stifled. Don't get me wrong, it is still a beautiful religion, and like if I were to believe in any religion at all, if I didn't disagree with the religious ideologies as a whole, I would choose Islam. But I just don't like religion in and of itself." She paused. She'd offered up too much information. "There were just some minor parts of Islam that I didn't want to adhere to, and I found myself questioning it more and more every day. So I just . . ." she shrugged. "Left it."

Daniel was watching her, a curious look on his face. "You're smart and brave—not because of leaving your religion, but the way you were able to question the things that were bothering you, the ideologies and beliefs you were raised with. It takes a lot of courage to ask questions about something that defines a part of someone's identity."

"I like to think so. I mean, I didn't get Firsts in all my essays for nothing, three years straight. Not that I know what my results are for the last two essays I did. But—"

Daniel cut Sabrina off with a kiss, laughing.

"That's not what I meant. But I'm glad to know you're achieving Firsts," he murmured against her lips. He moved back, smiling at her.

"Mmm, it is pretty amazing." Sabrina smiled tipsily. "Kiss me again."

He complied with her request, laughing as they kissed. She tasted his laugh in her mouth, threading her fingers through his hair.

Her bag vibrated on the bar top, buzzing against the slightly scratched up wood with a few dents scraped in.

"It's pretty late, I should take you home," Daniel said.

"We both drank alcohol. You can't drive and—" Sabrina kissed him. "I *really* want to go down on you right now."

His car was parked in the parking lot of the bar, a sleek black Porsche amidst other fancy, ridiculously expensive cars.

"My place isn't too far from here," he winked, still smiling, and stood up.

Sabrina got to her feet, fingers grasping the bar top for support—the stool she had been sitting on was slightly high, and her feet didn't even touch the ground. She swung her bag over her shoulder, watching as Daniel left a twenty pound note beside their glasses, waving a quick *bye* to the bartender when he bid them adieu.

They stumbled out of the bar, laughing and kissing.

Around them, the usually bustling street was silent, save for a few cars cruising down the road, headlights a bright beam in the black. The streetlamps standing on the pavements did a good job in lighting up the night, as the couple walked towards a line of three black cabs waiting just down the road. A group of four women were laughing, chattering loudly, as they pulled open one of the cab's doors, the fluorescent light shining down on their hair. One of the women had been wearing a sash labelled *BRIDE*, whilst the other four women's sashes read *TEAM BRIDE.*

"We'll get a cab to make it quicker, even though it's just a few minutes' walk," Daniel said quietly, as they paused in the street, his arms encircling her waist. She smiled prettily up at him.

They got into one of the cabs, and Daniel gave his address to the driver, his gaze never once leaving Sabrina's face. Her hand was on his thigh, creeping closer to the bulge in his jeans. His fingers tipped her chin up, as he brushed his lips across hers. Sabrina hadn't planned on going round to his, but she wanted to feel his hands and mouth on her again, and she wanted his dick in her again. It had hurt a little, but not in a painful way—it was more like an uncomfortable stretching as she'd taken in his length, because *fuck*, he was just as big as Soran had been, maybe an inch longer, and thicker. And she really shouldn't be comparing, shit. Not that she *was*. It was just—he was so *big* and she hadn't expected that, at all.

Sabrina hadn't sucked him off when they'd been in the bathroom and it was all she could think about right now, and she really wanted to. She wanted to see the look on his face, make him gasp, and realise that she was the best he'd ever had. Because she sure as fuck *would* be.

It was close to one A.M. when they got to his house, and she didn't even notice Daniel quickly paying the driver, as they tumbled outside. Her legs were wrapped tightly around his waist again, as he walked into the driveway of his home.

He unlocked and opened the front door, the bright light of the foyer making Sabrina blink rapidly. She glanced around a little, noting the grand staircase leading up to the landing. There were two floors from what she could see. Daniel kissed her neck, kicking the door shut, returning her attention back to him instead of the fucking mansion he lived in, with marble floors and a goddamn grand staircase.

Barely noticing him moving, mouth pressing a soft kiss to her forehead, Sabrina gently bit down on his neck, soothing it with a little lick, humming in appreciation.

Doors slid shut in front of her, making her eyes widen in shock. She pulled back, staring at Daniel.

"You have a fucking lift in your house?"

He looked at her, a hint of a smirk glossing his mouth, a twinkle in his eyes. Sabrina's heart fluttered. "I have more than just a lift, babe."

If you have been affected by any of the issues mentioned in *Say Hello to Goodbye*, there are a number of organisations that offer advice and support:

ChildLine is a free, 24-hour confidential helpline for children and young people who need to talk.

Phone: 0800 1111

childline.org.uk

SANEline is a mental health support line available every day from 4:30pm to 10:30pm

0300 304 7000

Email: support@sane.org.uk

Samaritans is available for anyone struggling to cope and provide a safe place to talk 24 hours a day.

Phone: 116 123

nspcc.org.uk/

National Suicide Prevention Helpline UK offers a supportive listening service to anyone with thoughts of suicide 24 hours a day.

Phone: 0800 689 5652

Shout is a confidential texting service offering mental health support.

Text SHOUT to 85258.

Acknowledgements

A massive, massive thank you to Ashley Quick and Murphy Rae for bringing to life the vision I had in my head for this cover. It's everything amazing and wonderful. Thank you a million.

To Sabrina, you're the best writer, graphic designer and friend I could have asked for. Talking about our love for Damon Salvatore and me convincing you to properly watch Friends has been the highlight of this blossoming friendship. I couldn't be more grateful for your support and your kindness. You're an angel.

To Nahima, Shajeda, and Saima, words will never be able to explain how special you ladies are and I am so happy to have found you.

You're the bestest friends anyone could ask for and I can't wait to see you all bloom into the people you're meant to be. I love you.

To John, you're the first person I really saw the best of life with and you push me to become the best version of myself. I can't thank you enough for believing in me in the moments I doubted myself, for supporting my writing and for loving me. You're the best part of my life and I love you, infinitely.

Other Titles by Sumaiya Ahmed

SECOND CHANCE LOVE SERIES

The Art of Faking It

Say Hello to Goodbye

About The Author

Sumaiya Ahmed is a freelance writer, aiming to break down the boundaries of cultural stigma and shame attached to mental health and sexuality within the South Asian culture and bring marginalised topics to light.

She specialises in sex and relationships, mental health, and PCOS, having previously written for Metro, The Sun, Lacuna Voices and Hello Giggles, and more. She has published two poetry collections, Lost and Found, and Reality. The Art of Faking It is her debut novel, the first book in the Second Chance Love Series.

Sumaiya is a born and raised London gal, with a love of chocolate, Modern Family and romance novels.

You can find her on:

www.sumaiyaahmed.com

Twitter: @sumaiyawrites

Instagram: @sumaiyaahmedwrites

Email: sumaiyaahmedwrites@gmail.com

MA VICTOIRE
SUR L'AUTISME

Tamara Morar

MA VICTOIRE SUR L'AUTISME

Odile
Jacob

15, rue Soufflot, 75005 Paris

ISBN : 2-7381-1377-X

www.odilejacob.fr

À Maman
À Alexandra, sa bonne fée
À Barbara qui m'a montré le chemin
À Sœur M. qui l'a pris sous son aile
Et à ceux qui y ont cru.

Chapitre premier

LE BONHEUR

Nous avions accueilli Paul avec l'immense bonheur d'avoir un garçon et de donner un petit frère à notre fille, Laure, alors âgée de deux ans et demi. La grossesse comme l'accouchement s'étaient passés sans difficultés et nous envisagions de déménager pour offrir à chacun sa chambre. N'ayant pas été très satisfaite des moyens de garde trouvés pour Laure lorsque je travaillais, je résolus de me consacrer à eux seuls et de prendre le temps de réorganiser notre nouveau nid avant de reprendre mes activités. Laure était la joie de vivre, enthousiaste, rieuse, robuste, et son frère ne dépareillait pas. D'une beauté aussi saisissante, les mêmes traits fins et d'immenses yeux bleus. Toujours actif et en alerte, l'ingéniosité des moyens déployés pour arriver à ses fins, c'est-à-dire découvrir le monde sous toutes ses formes, témoignait de sa curiosité insatiable et de son intelligence. Une amie, témoin un soir de la facilité avec laquelle je l'avais nourri puis couché, m'avait posé la question : « Il est toujours comme cela ? » Apparemment je ne réalisais pas ma chance. Suivirent quelques mois d'un développement tout à fait normal. Paul babillait, souriait beaucoup, s'installait sans réticence sur les genoux de nos visiteurs ou amis, se laissait cajoler et regardait toujours les nouveaux arrivants avec curiosité. Vers onze mois, il se lança dans la marche où il montra une bonne coordination physique. À un an, ses premiers mots furent « maman », « d'accord », « non », « encore ». Il avait apprécié son premier Noël, vécu l'excitation de la fête et le plaisir de revoir ses nombreux cousins. Nous ne pouvions nous empêcher de contempler nos deux enfants jouer le soir sur notre lit, rire et se tortiller comme des vers, adorablement boudinés dans leurs pyjamas d'éponge pastel. La perfection physique des enfants en bas âge, leurs petites mains si curieuses, leur peau lisse, la naïveté de leur regard, la pureté de leur corps, que les maladies et les accidents n'ont pas encore abîmés étaient pour moi un sujet constant d'admiration et de bonheur. Nous les regardions avec la fierté sans limites des jeunes parents : « Nous ne les avons pas trop mal réussis », nous disions-nous, avec cette idée saugrenue : « Comment avons-nous pu fabriquer de telles merveilles ? »

Nous étions loin de penser que le cerveau de l'un contenait déjà, larvées, les déficiences d'une maladie mentale incurable.

Chapitre II

PRÉMICES

Vers l'âge d'un an, à la suite de ses vaccinations, Paul souffrit d'une période de vomissements isolés, suivie de difficultés pour manger, avec pour résultat une cassure de la courbe de poids. Cela fut accompagné d'un changement assez radical de comportement et de tempérament. En quelques mois, Paul cessa de s'intéresser à son entourage, ne nous regardant plus quand nous lui adressions la parole. Il s'isolait de plus en plus, jouait seul, *se désintéressait de son environnement*. De moins en moins malléable, il opposait des refus systématiques même dans ce qu'il aimait faire auparavant. Il pleurait dès qu'il était contrarié, criait pour exprimer sa colère et ne parlait plus. Le contact devenait de plus en plus difficile et Paul, au lieu de venir à nous, se laissait prendre passivement.

Pouvions-nous soupçonner qu'il s'agissait d'une régression significative ? À l'époque, non. La manière de se développer se transformait mais, mis à part ces troubles de l'alimentation et de l'humeur, Paul ne régressait pas réellement. Souvent plongé dans ses pensées, absorbé par les objets plus que par les individus, Paul s'enfermait sur lui-même sans que nous sachions s'il fallait réagir et de quelle manière.

Dans sa bulle

Les débuts de Paul à la halte-garderie vers quatorze mois furent difficiles. Mais les séparations, pénibles au départ, se firent dans une indifférence étrange par la suite. Paul semblait en « prendre son parti », restait assis toute la durée de la garde dans sa poussette. Confrontées à ses hurlements lorsqu'elles essayaient de l'en sortir, les assistantes maternelles en abandonnèrent l'idée et Paul fut dès lors conduit dans sa poussette au square contigu où les enfants pouvaient jouer dans le sable, à la balançoire et aux différents jeux. Deux heures plus tard, car je n'osais pas le confier plus longtemps, je le retrouvais tel que je l'avais laissé, assis dans sa poussette dont il n'avait pas même voulu détacher la sangle, parfois endormi ou le regard perdu dans le vague. Je m'inquiétais de ce refus de partager les activités des autres enfants et plus encore de cette *capacité à se retrancher sur lui-même* physiquement et mentalement. Je sentais confusément que quelque chose n'allait pas. Que signifiait ce besoin de se couper du monde extérieur ? Avait-il peur des autres, peur du monde qui l'entourait ?

Paul eut dix-huit mois l'été suivant, son comportement alimentaire était devenu aberrant. Il refusait tout ce qu'il prenait habituellement (bouillies, purées, poisson et viande en morceaux) pour n'accepter que des biberons de lait et des biscuits. De plus, il réclamait à manger à des heures inhabituelles et refusait tout à l'heure des repas. Sa maigreur s'accentuait et il s'alimentait de nouveau avec l'irrégularité d'un nourrisson.

Par ailleurs, nous n'étions plus les seuls à remarquer sa volonté de s'isoler. Le contact visuel était de plus en plus difficile à obtenir et son regard paraissait vide, comme tourné à l'intérieur de lui-même. Même son visage n'exprimait plus les émotions courantes et ses crises de pleurs étaient difficiles à contenir et à comprendre. Les jeux de plage – nous passions ces vacances au Pays basque – que sa sœur appréciait le plongeaient parfois dans une *panique incompréhensible.* Paul avait pris l'habitude de partir seul, subitement, se promener sur la plage, sans se préoccuper de savoir si nous pouvions le surveiller et s'il saurait nous retrouver. Notre présence lui était totalement indifférente. D'ailleurs, il ne revenait jamais de lui-même et les angoissantes poursuites à sa recherche commencèrent à ce moment-là. Le réprimander ne servait à rien. Les mots ne paraissaient pas franchir cette barrière d'indifférence. Nous nous efforcions de nous habituer à ce comportement étrange dont nous ne soupçonnions pas l'origine. Nous lui mettions des vêtements reconnaissables de loin et avions toujours sur nous des biscuits pour le calmer ou apaiser sa faim à toute heure. C'était peut-être une erreur que de se plier à cette façon d'être, mais, déjà, il ne nous entendait plus, ne nous comprenait plus. Opposer des refus, le contraindre à une certaine discipline était quasiment impossible.

Nous pensâmes que ce n'était qu'une mauvaise période, que « cela s'arrangerait avec le temps ». Comme ils me manquaient, ses sourires radieux, ses regards malicieux, ses petits bras qui se tendaient vers moi au réveil et son délicieux babillage.

Chapitre III

EMMURÉ VIVANT

À la rentrée suivante, Paul avait presque deux ans. Je l'inscrivis à la halte-garderie de Laure qu'il connaissait bien pour y être souvent allé la chercher avec moi. Il s'y est tout de suite senti plus à l'aise. Mais il ne se remit toujours pas à parler. Pas plus qu'il ne recherchait la présence des autres, ni les contacts, jouant seul, à l'écart, si possible dans une autre pièce. Il paraissait ne pas entendre quand on lui parlait, ne manifestait aucune réaction à notre présence. Je fis un test avec sa peluche hochet et la secouai à l'autre bout de l'appartement : il entendait cette petite bille secouée – alors que ce bruit est à peine perceptible – et venait chercher sa peluche. Il *sélectionnait donc les sons d'une façon anormale*. Progressivement, à la maison comme à l'extérieur, l'évitement de l'autre se faisait systématique : il devenait évident que Paul refusait les contacts visuel et physique.

Devant tous les premiers signes, nous avions tout d'abord pensé que c'était son évolution naturelle, preuves d'une maturation, de l'acquisition d'une certaine indépendance et d'un tempérament autonome. Je me souviens de commentaires de la part de personnes de notre entourage : « Finalement, il n'aura pas si bon caractère », « il a une vie intérieure intense », dit sur le ton de la plaisanterie. Ou encore : « Il est très indépendant. »

L'absence totale de langage commençait à nous apporter les réactions et réflexions d'autrui, qui devinrent vite pénibles. Nous étions persuadés que cela tenait du blocage et non pas d'une incapacité. Paul ne voulait pas parler. Il refusait le langage et ses raisons étaient difficiles à cerner. Comprenait-il que, dès qu'il parlerait, il n'aurait plus d'excuses pour ne pas se plier aux exigences des autres. Était-ce pour ne pas avoir à obéir ? Nous le pensions capable de ce calcul : faire semblant de ne pas comprendre, de ne pas parler pour ne pas rentrer dans notre système. Pourquoi refuser notre système ? Parce qu'il ne le comprenait pas ou parce qu'il lui faisait peur ?

À cette époque, Paul évitait d'avoir à demander quoi que ce soit à autrui. Il préférait construire un échafaudage d'objets pour atteindre ce qu'il désirait plutôt qu'avoir à demander l'aide d'une autre personne, se servant seul dans les placards ou dans le réfrigérateur lorsqu'il avait faim ou soif. Il ne recherchait de contact que lorsqu'il avait besoin de quelque chose, et que cette chose était réellement hors de portée. À ce moment-là, il prenait ma main et la dirigeait vers l'objet désiré sans un mot. Je refusais d'accéder à ses demandes en exigeant qu'il parle :

« Qu'est-ce que tu veux ?... ça ? alors tu me demandes : "Je voudrais cette cassette"... répète : "Donne-moi cette cassette"... » Contrarié, il se mettait à pleurer devant mon insistance. Convaincue qu'il connaissait tous ces mots courants, je finissais par lui donner l'objet, pensant que le braquer ne résoudrait pas ce blocage.

J'espérais qu'il prenne exemple sur Laure qui parlait avec beaucoup de facilité. Mais, dans ce domaine comme dans les autres, je comprendrais peu à peu qu'il n'avait *pas la capacité d'imiter*. Je pouvais déjà constater qu'il n'imitait personne, ni dans la parole, ni dans les gestes. Retranché dans son univers, il n'attachait aucun intérêt aux autres.

Un intérêt exclusif pour les objets

De plus en plus, il s'intéressait aux objets et négligeait, évitait même, les personnes. Était-ce qu'il ne leur faisait pas confiance, qu'il en avait peur ? Il passait des heures à examiner le fonctionnement des portes de placards qu'il ouvrait et fermait indéfiniment, en examinant les gonds. Ou encore à faire fonctionner des appareils sauf ceux qui faisaient du bruit. Sa façon même de jouer était anormale. Il ne faisait pas circuler ses petites voitures pour reproduire une rue, un accident, une course, mais, le nez collé aux roues, il faisait avancer et reculer la voiture des heures durant en examinant la rotation des jantes. Ses petits personnages ne reproduisaient aucune scène vécue ou imaginée, il les rangeait dans un ordre établi et il ne fallait pas les déplacer. Il était habile de ses mains, manipulant les objets avec une grande précision. Je m'efforçais tous les jours de lui montrer comment animer ces jouets en représentant des scènes, en les faisant parler, en inventant une histoire, mais il ne le supportait pas.

Sentant confusément qu'il ne fallait pas qu'il s'enferme dans ces *jeux répétitifs*, j'intervenais pour rompre cet ordonnancement immuable. Il se montrait extrêmement contrarié que je bouscule ses habitudes. Je lui imposais des jeux nouveaux, puzzles, lotos, *memory*, mais ses réactions étaient parfois violentes, il jetait tout à travers la pièce et s'enfermait dans son mutisme habituel. Malgré son opposition, je ne le laissais pas jouer seul longtemps et j'intervenais régulièrement dans le cours de ses jeux obsessionnels. Il m'en voulait et se révoltait. Je le forçais quand même à essayer de jouer d'une autre manière pour tenter d'empêcher ses comportements singuliers.

Son *attachement à certains objets* devenait préoccupant. Pendant plusieurs mois, il n'acceptait pas de lâcher tel objet, le tenait de jour comme de nuit serré dans sa main. Il l'emportait partout avec lui, à table, pendant la toilette, au square, à la garderie, en week-end à la campagne, et le gardait dans son sommeil. Quand il lui arrivait de le perdre dans son lit, il nous réveillait en pleurant et en criant. Il fallait le retrouver sinon il ne se rendormait plus. Le perdre était pour lui catastrophique et le plongeait dans une violente angoisse. Il changeait parfois d'objet, mais l'attachement était tout aussi obsessionnel.

« *Il n'écoute rien* »

Le fait qu'il n'obéisse à aucune consigne nous a alertés. Entendait-il ? Comprenait-il ? Ni l'un ni l'autre en apparence. Il ne retenait rien de ce que je lui expliquais. Au lieu de m'épuiser à chaque instant pour qu'il obéisse, je décidai de me limiter aux situations les plus importantes ou les plus dangereuses. Je me posais la question : est-ce vraiment essentiel de le faire obéir sur ce point précis ? Naturellement, plus le temps passait, moins nous étions exigeants. Nous en arrivions à un laxisme qui pouvait paraître choquant. Mais Paul étant aussi insensible à un discours qu'à une fessée, je dus trouver le moyen d'éviter des accidents graves. Le fait qu'une voiture arrivant à toute allure ne l'empêche pas de traverser montrait qu'il ne traitait pas l'information normalement en se représentant l'idée du danger. Il n'avait pas conscience des risques et j'étais terrorisée à l'idée qu'il pourrait ne jamais l'acquérir. J'avais beau lui représenter, à l'aide de ses voitures et de ses personnages, un accident où le personnage était renversé brutalement, immobilisé, blessé, souffrant, il ne le comprenait pas. Il m'est même venu à l'esprit de me procurer un film de la Sécurité routière qui montrerait un piéton renversé dans un accident.

En attendant, puisqu'il ne voulait pas rester assis dans sa poussette pendant les promenades ou à la sortie de l'école de Laure, je l'attachais avec une laisse pour enfant que j'accrochais à la poussette. Il se débattait et tirait comme un chien qui aurait voulu s'échapper. Dans la rue, les passants me jetaient des regards outrés. Si, au début, j'avais eu honte en public de ses bizarreries, à ce moment-là, le regard des autres m'indifférait déjà. J'avais cessé de m'inquiéter du jugement d'autrui.

Il en était de même au square : je ne pouvais pas quitter Paul des yeux une seconde, il passait la grille et disparaissait en un clin d'œil. Il fallait alors nous lancer à sa poursuite en demandant aux passants s'ils l'avaient vu. Paul ne se rendait pas compte que j'allais le chercher ou m'inquiéter, il n'avait *aucune conscience des sentiments ou des pensées d'autrui*. Quelques secondes suffisaient pour qu'il lâche la poussette, entre dans un magasin ou traverse la rue. Combien de fois Laure et moi avions-nous dû le chercher, tremblantes d'inquiétude, en courant dans tous les sens.

Face à ce comportement risqué, je décidai de le marquer physiquement à chaque désobéissance. Un pas hors du square signifiait une fessée immédiate. Il jouait indéfiniment à ouvrir et refermer la grille sans plus sortir. Il lui arrivait d'avoir ce genre de comportement quand il était bouleversé, il répétait alors indéfiniment les mêmes gestes ou les mêmes sons.

Ces comportements répétitifs ont quelque chose de sinistre, d'effrayant même, qu'on prête aux déments. C'est insupportable à regarder, on a peur de les interrompre. On craint une réaction disproportionnée. J'avoue que j'y allais sur la pointe des pieds, comme on réveille un somnambule. J'avais bien l'intuition qu'il s'agissait d'une régression en réaction à une agression trop forte du monde extérieur, un retranchement si profond qu'il conduisait – qu'il nécessitait ? – à une gestuelle aussi aberrante. Je lui prenais doucement les mains, lui mettais une peluche dans les bras, en essayant d'attirer son attention sur autre chose ou je le prenais dans mes bras. Mais dans mes bras, il fallait un balancement ou marcher sur un rythme lent pour le calmer.

Entre deux et trois ans donc, Paul n'eut *aucune relation* avec les enfants du square ou de la garderie. Ceux qui, même en bas âge, s'approchaient et tentaient d'établir le contact s'apercevaient en quelques minutes de l'anormalité de son comportement. Pas de regard, pas de réponse. Aucun signe qu'il les ait remarqués. En cas d'insistance de l'enfant, un geste de refus ou fuite, parfois même, il les repoussait sans ménagement. Les autres enfants n'insistaient pas et n'y revenaient plus, ce que Paul cherchait très exactement, et il passait quatre heures à la garderie à jouer seul *sans aucune interaction visuelle, physique ou verbale.* Malgré les efforts des responsables de la garderie, il refusait tous les jeux et toutes les activités en commun.

Nelly, je craignais que son comportement parfois difficile ne vous pose des difficultés : vous étiez responsable du bon fonctionnement de la halte-garderie. Des enfants ou des parents auraient pu se plaindre de sa présence. Beaucoup à votre place auraient été tentés de se débarrasser de cet enfant très visiblement anormal et souvent imprévisible. Mais devant ma détresse et ses besoins, vous avez tenu bon. Non seulement vous ne l'avez jamais refusé, mais vous lui avez consacré beaucoup de temps, imposant vos règles avec douceur et souplesse. Ces trois années chez vous ont contribué à sa guérison. Vous avez toute notre reconnaissance.

Toujours actif, très organisé, Paul choisissait ses jeux sans hésitation, jouait avec les dînettes ou les voitures, ne demandant l'aide ou la participation de personne. Il utilisait le matériel approprié, quand il faisait de la peinture, par exemple, mais il refusait de porter le tablier de protection bien que ce fût la règle.

Ce refus des règles était déjà habituel. Il était extrêmement difficile de contraindre Paul à quelqu'usage que ce soit. Il fallut beaucoup de temps, d'explications répétées pour qu'il accepte certaines règles et ce uniquement lorsqu'il en avait compris le bien-fondé ou le bon sens. Mais au début, les explications ne servant à rien, il fallait empêcher physiquement ses comportements aberrants. Par exemple, Paul ne mangeait qu'avec ses doigts alors que son habileté manuelle lui aurait permis d'utiliser des couverts facilement. Il s'essuyait constamment les mains dans les cheveux ou sur tout autre objet proche y compris ses vêtements, ou les nôtres, et les meubles alentour, car il ne supportait pas le contact de la serviette en papier et hurlait quand on lui lavait les mains. Je sévis en lui donnant une légère claque chaque fois qu'il le faisait. Ces tapes données de façon immédiate et systématique, sans violence et sans cris ou discours, finissaient par lui faire perdre ses habitudes.

Que les enfants fassent cela à un certain moment n'est pas inhabituel. C'est la durée du comportement – des mois sans comprendre – et la violence des réactions au lavage des mains et au shampooing qui font la différence.

Nous pensions que ces trois demi-journées par semaine au contact d'autres enfants inciteraient Paul à parler et à solliciter les autres, à découvrir l'intérêt sinon l'utilité du langage, mais en réalité son indépendance et son autonomie ne firent que croître et Paul devint expert dans l'art d'éviter toute interaction avec autrui. Il était sensiblement le même à la maison. Certaines peurs et réticences s'accrurent. Paul devenait de moins en moins « gérable » et ce dans tous les domaines.

Une violence inquiétante

C'est à ce moment que les frustrations conduisirent Paul à des attitudes plus violentes. Lorsqu'on lui opposait un refus, il se mettait à hurler, à se débattre, à donner des coups de poing et des coups de pied. Dans la rue, j'avais du mal à le rasseoir dans sa poussette et à le rattacher pour éviter qu'il ne se roule par terre et ne se blesse. Il devenait insensible à la douleur. Ni les tapes ni les claques, les paroles encore moins, n'avaient d'effet sur lui. Il était muré dans sa colère.

Ces crises de violence, ces hurlements et ces pleurs sans fin le plongeaient dans un abattement alarmant : il n'avait plus la moindre réaction et cette apathie était inquiétante. Il finissait par s'endormir dans sa poussette ou, lorsqu'il était à la maison, allait se coucher dans son lit et dormait une à deux heures comme pour oublier, disparaître. Ces crises nous anéantissaient et choquaient profondément Laure. Nous cédions lorsque la raison ne nous paraissait pas essentielle, en limitant notre opposition lorsqu'il y avait danger pour lui-même ou pour d'autres.

J'avais consulté, à cette période, un cardiologue du quartier qui, comme tous les bons médecins, allait au-delà des courbes et des chiffres que fournissent les appareils sophistiqués. Mes réponses à ses quelques questions lui avaient naturellement suffi pour comprendre l'origine de mes symptômes. Il m'avait alors parlé d'une jeune femme qui avait fait un travail extraordinaire avec son fils autiste. J'ai écouté sans me sentir concernée. Comme si en lui parlant d'un bras dans le plâtre, il me répondait d'un tétraplégique. Je n'y ai plus repensé.

Des terreurs incompréhensibles

L'habiller posait de plus en plus de problèmes. Tout d'abord, il ne supportait pas les chaussures et les vêtements neufs. Était-ce parce qu'ils représentaient un changement et que, *hostile à tout changement*, il ne les acceptait pas ou parce que le contact physique avec des tissus ou cuir neufs lui était insupportable ? Paul portait donc la plupart du temps les vêtements et chaussures usagés de Laure. Par ailleurs, les vêtements serrés (chemises, pantalons à ceinture), les chaussures ou chaussons paraissaient le blesser. Habillé le matin, je le retrouvais systématiquement nu au bout d'à peine une heure. J'avais ainsi à le rhabiller plusieurs fois par jour avec des vêtements amples sans col ni boutons. Il hurlait chaque fois qu'on lui mettait un manteau et des chaussures. À la campagne, comme il pouvait sortir sans mon aide, je le retrouvais pieds nus et sans manteau dans le jardin indifférent au vent ou à la pluie.

Il me parut important dans ces situations de ne pas le braquer puisque, visiblement, notre fonctionnement et nos règles lui échappaient. Je compris qu'il fallait pénétrer son monde avant de l'attirer progressivement dans le nôtre. Je sortais donc sans manteau, l'accompagnant en silence. Puis, lorsqu'il paraissait prêt pour un contact, je lui faisais comprendre qu'il faisait froid, que j'avais froid en accompagnant mes paroles de gestes explicites. « Et puis, tu vois, je mets mon manteau et alors là, je suis bien, je n'ai pas froid, on est bien dans un manteau... » Je lui montrais le sien : « C'est doux, c'est chaud, essaie... » Il n'acceptait pas au premier essai et je recommençais les jours suivants. Lorsqu'il consentit enfin à le mettre, il fit un grand pas vers notre monde. Il avait accepté de quitter son univers et ses règles, insensées pour nous, mais rassurantes pour lui. C'était une victoire. Je recommençais indéfiniment pour ses chaussures... et pour tout le reste.

Il en allait de même pour les bains ou la toilette, qu'il avait aimés auparavant comme tous les bébés. Maintenant, il était terrorisé par le bruit de l'eau dans la baignoire se remplissant. Pour le réhabituer, il fallait que je le garde dans mes bras en rentrant dans la baignoire avec lui. Il hurlait de terreur dès que je relâchais mon étreinte. Les shampoings le plongeaient dans un tel affolement, avec des hurlements quasi insoutenables pour nous, que nous avons renoncé pour plusieurs mois en utilisant des shampoings secs.

Toucher certains objets lui causait un malaise physique et il fallait immédiatement frotter ou enlever l'objet. Il ne supportait pas le contact de l'eau, du savon ou de toute autre substance humide ou collante.

Il ne supportait pas non plus qu'on lui touche la tête. Pour lui couper les cheveux, nous étions contraints de lui donner un somnifère afin qu'il dorme profondément. C'est seulement ainsi que je pouvais lui couper des mèches d'un côté puis de l'autre, en le retournant avec précaution. J'en profitais également pour lui couper les ongles et nous éviter non seulement des hurlements mais aussi le risque de le blesser. Paul n'a pu supporter de bonnet, casquette ou chapeau de déguisement jusqu'à l'âge de 6-7 ans et encore... il les enlève très vite.

Il était clair que la plupart des *contacts sur sa peau* le faisaient souffrir. Pour éviter ces combats permanents et des traumatismes inutiles, il valait mieux trouver des solutions d'attente et rééduquer très progressivement. Au bout de quelques mois, je pus le laisser dans la baignoire, mais il fallut plusieurs mois supplémentaires avant qu'il y reste seul et plus longtemps encore avant qu'on puisse quitter la salle de bains, porte ouverte. Séance après séance, le rassurer, lui montrer des objets, jouer avec des personnages en mousse, attirer son attention sur autre chose quand il panique. Il fallut plusieurs mois également pour qu'il ne hurle plus chez le coiffeur. Dans un premier temps, je l'y emmenai avec sa sœur afin qu'il puisse voir qu'elle n'y souffre pas, puis je le gardais sur mes genoux avec un objet nouveau pour le distraire. Je prévoyais de l'emmener à jeun pour qu'il se calme avec quelques biscuits pendant la coupe : la plus simple et la plus rapide au début. Je prévenais le coiffeur à l'avance, en prenant le rendez-vous, pour ne pas être stressée par sa réaction qui de toute façon s'avérerait sans doute désobligeante.

Les réactions face à des parents d'un enfant difficile sont dans la plupart des cas déplorables. Tant que l'enfant n'est pas dans un fauteuil roulant ou atteint de façon évidente, c'est l'éducation de la mère qui est mise en cause. Si on laisse hurler, on est laxiste, si on punit, on est monstrueux. De toute façon, on nous regarde de travers parce qu'on ne sait visiblement pas s'y prendre et qu'un quelconque handicap ne vient à l'esprit de personne.

J'avais aussi remarqué que Paul pouvait être totalement indifférent à certains bruits même forts, et *réagir anormalement à des bruits de type sifflements aigus ou sirènes*. Il me revient un exemple frappant lorsqu'il avait environ deux ans et demi. Nous nous trouvions à une réception en province, près de l'endroit où les pompiers avaient installé leur sirène. Lorsqu'elle retentit, la centaine de personnes présentes s'immobilisa et se tut en attendant qu'elle s'arrête, toute conversation étant impossible. Cette sirène plongea Paul dans un état de panique tel qu'il se mit à hurler sans discontinuer en courant pour me retrouver, parmi les autres enfants de son âge qui attendaient passivement et sans crainte. Je l'emmenai à l'intérieur où le bruit était moins fort, mais il fallut une demi-heure pour qu'il se calme et retrouve son état normal. Ne pas comprendre ce bruit le terrorisait et cette fréquence devait lui être particulièrement pénible.

J'ai gardé le souvenir de cette scène comme la séquence d'un film où seules deux personnes sont en mouvement au milieu d'une foule figée, statues par dizaines dont les yeux suivent un enfant au regard fou qui court et s'abat sur sa mère qui l'a deviné, et le porte à l'abri.

Étrangement, Paul était capable de reproduire à la perfection des sons ou des notes entendus à la télévision ou ailleurs. Il appréciait certaines musiques, mais était complètement indifférent à d'autres. Il m'arrivait de mettre le même morceau en boucle : il l'écoutait indéfiniment. Mais, si j'en changeais, il partait aussitôt.

Par ailleurs, je compris assez rapidement que Paul ne faisait pas le lien entre un objet et le son qu'il émet, entre un objet et l'odeur qu'il peut avoir. De la même façon, lorsqu'il se blessait ou se cognait, il était incapable de faire le lien entre cet objet et la partie de son corps qui lui faisait mal, et n'arrivait pas davantage à savoir à quel endroit il avait mal. Son ressenti de la douleur me laissait perplexe. Parfois, il paraissait ne rien sentir, à d'autres moments, il hurlait de façon disproportionnée par rapport au coup ou au choc reçu.

Débuts à la maternelle

En septembre, son entrée en maternelle, à un peu moins de trois ans, suscita très rapidement des interrogations. L'institutrice nous demanda de faire vérifier son audition puisqu'il paraissait ne pas entendre et n'obéissait pas aux consignes. Le fait que l'école nous ait convoqués pour nous signaler ces difficultés nous poussa à consulter.

Les résultats de l'audiométrie à l'hôpital Necker apparurent normaux au médecin bien que les réactions de Paul aient été infimes ou inexistantes à mon sens. Nous avions décidé de poursuivre les investigations à l'hôpital Saint-Joseph à Paris où furent pratiqués différents examens. Électroencéphalogramme, chromatographie des acides aminés, analyses d'urine et de sang, recherche de l'X fragile ne révélèrent rien d'anormal et le chef de service de pédiatrie nous laissa partir sans la moindre piste.

Au cours du deuxième trimestre, nous consultâmes le Dr N... qui pensa qu'il ne s'agissait pas d'autisme, mais prononça le mot... et nous recommanda l'intervention d'un spécialiste des psychoses infantiles. Une thérapie fut mise en place à raison de deux séances par semaine. Ce terme était employé pour la seconde fois (la première lors du passage d'une assistante sociale dans sa classe qui avait parlé de comportement autistique à son sujet), je ne voulais toujours pas l'entendre. Je ne ressentis que de la colère : « Ils disent n'importe quoi ! » me disais-je. Pour la plupart des parents qui n'y ont jamais été confrontés, de près ou de loin, l'autisme est une maladie gravissime, impensable dans le cas de son propre enfant. On imagine des êtres possédés, des malheureux attachés sur leur lit ou menottés pour qu'ils ne se blessent pas, même sous camisole chimique. Quel rapport avec un enfant renfermé ou sans langage ? Non, décidément, ils se trompaient.

Nous avions espéré que l'école aiderait Paul à surmonter ses difficultés : cette absence de langage et de communication, de relations avec ses pairs et de curiosité d'autrui. Je n'avais pas besoin des regards lourds de sens et des réflexions on ne peut moins anodines pour comprendre que quelque chose n'allait pas et empirait même. Tout dans son comportement se révélait de plus en plus anormal jusqu'à sa façon de marcher ou de jouer comme un automate. La pédiatre du quartier ne manquait pas de me signaler tout ce qu'il aurait dû faire à son âge, mais ne faisait pas, dès l'examen du vingt-quatrième mois par exemple : « Obéit à un ordre simple, nomme au moins une image, superpose des cubes... » Rien de tout cela. Et le décalage s'accentuait au fil des mois. Hélas, elle, comme tant d'autres, n'était pas formée pour détecter au plus tôt l'autisme infantile. Je sortais des consultations démoralisée, extrêmement inquiète, mais sans aucun recours. Plus le temps passait, plus l'*absence* de Paul et son *aphasie* étaient évidentes aux yeux de tous.

Je luttais quotidiennement, plus ou moins consciemment, contre son enfermement progressif. Bien que je n'aie eu aucune réponse de sa part pendant des mois, je continuais à parler à Paul comme s'il entendait et comprenait. Face à un sourd-muet, je poursuivais des monologues, posais des questions et donnais les réponses. M'entendait-il ? Je n'en avais aucun signe mais je ne lâchai jamais prise. Toutes nos activités servaient de prétexte à cette rééducation que je menais sans même le savoir. Rentrer de la garderie ou de l'école permettait tous les jours de lui faire remarquer, en accompagnant mes mots de gestes explicites, une voiture, le bruit d'un camion, un objet dans une vitrine, un arbre, de lui cueillir une fleur, de la lui mettre dans la main, la lui faire sentir. Je répétais inlassablement les mêmes mots, les mêmes phrases.

Mon existence finissait par tourner autour de ce que me disait l'institutrice à la sortie de 11 h 30. Tantôt encourageante, tantôt désespérante, malgré les efforts qu'elle faisait pour l'aider. Les progrès étaient lents, peu convaincants. Je vivais avec cette angoisse : qu'y aura-t-il de catastrophique aujourd'hui ? Va-t-on encore me rapporter qu'il a bu l'eau des flaques de la cour et que tous se sont moqués de lui ? Qu'il s'est échappé à nouveau dans les escaliers et qu'on l'a retrouvé à errer dans les couloirs des étages supérieurs interdits aux enfants ? Que son petit voisin l'a poussé contre un mur : « Mais on n'a pas vu... je n'étais pas dans la cour... », me répondait-on. Qu'il a saigné du nez... « – Mais est-il tombé ?... – Non, mais untel est un enfant violent et il s'en prend toujours à Paul... » La directrice de l'école avait fini par le prendre en grippe et je vis plus tard, trop tard, les traitements injustifiables qu'elle faisait subir aux enfants qui lui déplaisaient ou qui lui causaient des problèmes, pas lui plus qu'un autre d'ailleurs, mais de toute sa mauvaise volonté elle chercherait à l'exclure de son école. De son côté, Paul, s'il ne pouvait raconter ses journées, ne semblait pas mécontent d'aller à l'école. Il en sortait souvent amoché et, le connaissant, ce n'était pas lui qui avait cherché la bagarre. Il ne se pliait que difficilement aux consignes et ne s'intégrait toujours pas, bien que l'institutrice m'ait signalé des progrès en ce sens vers la fin de l'année. En réalité, cette année-là a certainement aggravé sa défiance à l'égard des autres enfants, son manque de confiance dans l'entourage, sa peur du bruit et sa tendance à se replier sur lui-même dans un milieu agité. Mais nous pensions qu'il devait faire cet apprentissage-là, nous ne voulions pas le couver. C'était une erreur et nous aurions dû opter dès le début pour un environnement un peu plus sécurisant, plus protégé, des effectifs réduits et une directrice compréhensive.

Au troisième trimestre, la directrice me proposa un « marché » que je vécus comme un chantage : « Faites-le suivre dans le centre dont je vais vous donner l'adresse et je le prendrai à la rentrée en moyenne section. » Je l'emmenai donc consulter un psychiatre dans ce centre.

Celui-ci, me voyant probablement dangereusement fragilisée par deux ans de difficultés croissantes avec mon fils, rongée d'une inquiétude rarement formulée et obsédée par les progrès ou les régressions de chaque jour, de chaque instant, ne voulut pas me dire la vérité qu'il connaissait sûrement. J'avais droit à des discours lénifiants et à un leitmotiv « Posez vos valises. » Tout cela commençait à être trop lourd à porter et je frisais certainement la dépression nerveuse sans le savoir. Il me faisait comprendre que j'avais frappé ici à la bonne porte et que je pouvais me décharger de ce fardeau, et les laisser faire. Également que, ici, on m'aiderait moi, personnellement. Je n'ai pas pu me laisser endormir. Le discours était trop inconsistant : que proposait-on concrètement ? Pas de réponse claire. Je n'avais pas l'intention de poser mes valises, parce que justement c'étaient les miennes. D'autre part, ce n'était pas moi qui avais besoin d'aide mais mon fils. Il nous a sans doute trouvés trop peu malléables, mon mari et moi-même, et n'a pas insisté pour nous voir souvent. Il nous a recommandé une séance hebdomadaire de psychomotricité avec une jeune femme douce, attentive et compatissante qui est vite devenue indispensable à Paul, bien qu'aucune parole ne soit sortie de lui avant longtemps.

Forcer les contacts

Pendant l'été de ses trois ans, comme pour toutes les vacances scolaires, j'essayais d'entourer Paul d'enfants. Neveux, voisins, quel que fût leur âge, il me paraissait important qu'il soit en présence de jeux, d'activités diverses, de rires ou de disputes, même s'il les ignorait. Jour après jour, je le forçais à suivre la troupe où que l'on aille : promenades, plage, visites, courses au supermarché, tout était bon pour lui faire suivre le mouvement et le rythme des autres enfants. Il était naturellement récalcitrant au départ et il était rare qu'il ne hurle pas la première demi-heure. Petit à petit, il opposait moins de résistance, mais cela lui demandait de gros efforts. Renoncer à son silence, à sa solitude était certainement une souffrance pour lui.

À la fin des vacances, il nous apparut un peu moins en retrait, plus ouvert au monde extérieur, regardant plus souvent les autres. Cela suffisait à nous rendre optimistes pour la rentrée scolaire. Nous misions énormément sur cette deuxième année qui, pensions-nous, encouragerait cette évolution favorable.

En réalité, certains comportements déviants s'étaient cristallisés, solidifiés. Dans de nombreux domaines, Paul était encore moins malléable, muré dans cette rigidité, cette *immuabilité* qui le sécurisait. Il vivait mal les changements de son existence. Quant à le confier à une autre personne, c'était totalement impensable. Il était devenu à ce point ingérable qu'il n'était pas question pour moi de reprendre mon travail. Cependant, il avait évolué et nous avions retrouvé un peu d'optimisme... pas pour longtemps.

Chapitre IV

DESCENTE AUX ENFERS

En me présentant à l'école avec lui à la rentrée de septembre de l'année suivante, la directrice nous refusa l'entrée en prétextant que les premiers jours étaient une période trop mouvementée pour lui et qu'il valait mieux revenir la semaine suivante, quand « les choses se seraient calmées ». La semaine suivante, nouveau refus avec pour prétexte que c'était à la précommission de la CCPE (Commission de circonscription de l'enseignement préélémentaire et élémentaire) de décider des modalités de son admission en petite section (à nouveau). Stupéfaite, je demandais des explications, ne sachant pas même ce qu'était la CCPE et encore moins une précommission. C'était le début d'un combat inutile contre l'administration, sa toute-puissance, son inertie.

L'école, un combat perdu d'avance

Je suis alors devenue le témoin de l'application arbitraire des lois de l'Éducation nationale sans que ni les parents ni les médecins ne soient entendus, bien que convoqués à des simulacres de réunions qui ne servent qu'à entériner des décisions déjà prises en leur absence. Témoin jugé de plus, les parents étant non seulement incapables mais coupables. Ne voulant pas passer pour une mère hystérique à leurs yeux, en plus de tout le reste, je retenais ma colère pendant ces réunions cauchemardesques. Ils m'avaient recommandé de prendre rendez-vous avec des psychologues scolaires, ce que j'avais fait, en espérant qu'ils puissent influencer les décisions prises, mais c'était peine perdue. Ils déguisaient à peine leur certitude que tous les problèmes venaient des parents et surtout de la mère : mon fils avait des difficultés parce que j'étais angoissée. C'était donc de ma faute et il conviendrait que je me soigne. Il ne leur venait pas à l'esprit que je pouvais être angoissée parce que j'étais quotidiennement confrontée aux problèmes que me posait mon fils. Quelle que soit l'origine des troubles du comportement d'un enfant, les parents sont suspectés. En ce qui concerne les troubles autistiques, cette idée de responsabilité et de culpabilité de la mère a été abandonnée aux États-Unis depuis au moins vingt ans. En France, et pas seulement dans le cadre de l'école, puisque j'en ai fait l'expérience ailleurs, nous en sommes toujours là : les mères sont d'emblée soupçonnées d'être hystériques ou dépressives, et d'ailleurs on recommande que l'enfant aille en hôpital de jour – il y sera mieux qu'avec sa mère –, l'école ne pouvant se charger de cas particuliers.

Je sortais de ces réunions blessée au plus profond de moi-même, anéantie par l'injustice et le sentiment d'impuissance de tous les parents dont on exclut les enfants du système pour des raisons inconcevables. L'école maternelle, dont le but officiel (et suffisamment déclaré) est la sociabilisation et l'apprentissage du langage : pour qui ? Pour ceux qui n'en ont pas besoin ? Ceux qui en ont vraiment besoin, allez voir ailleurs. On n'est pas là pour aider ceux qui ont des difficultés. On n'a pas le temps. On n'a pas le personnel pour ceux-là. Il faut rentrer dans le moule dès deux ans et demi. À trois ans et dix mois, c'est trop tard, alors dehors, et débrouillez-vous.

Le « contrat d'intégration » mis en place devait permettre une intégration progressive de Paul dans son école à raison de trois quarts d'heure par semaine. Nous réagîmes immédiatement devant cette décision aberrante. Mis au courant, il apparut évident à tous les thérapeutes qui suivaient Paul que cette durée n'était pas faite pour l'intégrer mais pour l'exclure. Suivit une contre-offensive de notre part, acharnée mais parfaitement inutile ; envoi de courriers et rendez-vous avec la commission d'appel, la CDES (Commission départementale d'éducation spécialisée), qui n'a jamais daigné répondre, lettres et interventions des médecins qui trouvaient la décision dangereuse pour l'avenir de Paul, mais qui n'ont pas été écoutés non plus. Suppliques et menaces, aucun résultat. Notre demande d'accès au dossier n'a jamais abouti.

Or Paul vivait mal l'issue de ces quarante-cinq minutes de classe. La directrice nous faisait quitter l'école avant la récréation et il ne comprenait pas pourquoi il était le seul à s'en aller à cette heure-là. C'était un crève-cœur que de le voir pleurer et supplier de rester.

Sa nouvelle classe lui plaisait et il paraissait s'adapter à ses rythmes et à ses activités. Il ne s'échappait plus pour aller se promener dans les couloirs. Je l'épiais avant de partir ou en venant le chercher, comme toujours pour analyser son comportement, comprendre ses lacunes, chercher des idées pour y remédier. Je le trouvais souvent en train de regarder les autres et leurs activités du moment. Il était curieux de voir ce que ses camarades faisaient mais n'osait pas le faire. Il écoutait sans en avoir l'air mais se gardait bien de le montrer de peur qu'on s'adresse à lui. Cette attitude distante le protégeait. On aurait dit qu'il faisait tout pour ne pas se faire remarquer. Si on lui demandait de se joindre au groupe ou de faire comme les autres, il se repliait aussitôt dans sa coquille, refusant par son attitude toute autre proposition. Lorsque les autres avaient quitté la table, il se faufilait prudemment pour aller voir ce qu'ils avaient peint, dessiné ou fabriqué. Cette curiosité discrète me paraissait bon signe. Il n'était plus indifférent à ce qui se passait autour de lui. Il s'intéressait mais ne voulait pas qu'on le sache : il écoutait les chants et les comptines mais n'acceptait pas de s'asseoir parmi les autres. Le contact physique et verbal lui déplaisait toujours. Le fait de lui adresser la parole le mettait parfois en colère, comme s'il vivait les mots ou les regards comme une agression physique. Cela me sembla encourageant dans la mesure où c'était une réaction, là où auparavant il n'y en avait aucune.

En si peu de temps, et pour une durée si courte chaque fois, il s'était bien adapté et l'institutrice était optimiste. Elle était d'accord pour l'accueillir davantage. Mais la « commission » ne l'écouta pas non plus et ne voulut jamais augmenter son temps de classe. En juin, nous en étions toujours à quarante-cinq minutes par semaine.

Je reste convaincue que, s'il avait pu venir tous les matins, il se serait progressivement ouvert à cette classe restreinte, calme, contrairement à la première année où deux petites sections étaient souvent réunies dans un brouhaha et une agitation difficilement supportables, qui ne pouvaient que renforcer son repli sur lui-même. Il se plaisait visiblement dans cette petite classe, et l'en sortir de force parce que les quarante-cinq minutes étaient écoulées me paraissait cruel et dangereux pour son équilibre mental.

Après les crises de la sortie de l'école, Paul, à la maison, allait se coucher sans un mot, sans un regard, comme un zombie. Sa détresse était si poignante que, bientôt, je prétextais des rhumes, des rendez-vous, des empêchements quelconques pour lui éviter ces moments traumatisants. Je tenais à ce qu'il garde un pied dans l'école plus que tout, mais pas à ce prix. Mieux valait pas d'école du tout que cette souffrance absurde. Quelle explication lui donner ? Moi qui mettais un point d'honneur à expliquer, démontrer, justifier nos règles et notre fonctionnement, que pouvais-je lui dire ? Qu'on ne voulait pas de lui à l'école ? Bien qu'il n'ait jamais montré la moindre violence ou agressivité, bien qu'il ne soit plus un danger ni pour lui-même, ni pour les autres, bien qu'il ne fasse aucun bruit, qu'il ne soit mêlé à aucune bagarre, qu'il n'ait fait aucune bêtise qui aurait justifié une remarque... ou alors, c'est qu'on ne me l'a pas rapporté, ce qui m'étonnerait fort, vu qu'on montait en épingle ses gestes les plus anodins.

À l'époque, nous étions accablés plus encore par ce combat contre l'Éducation nationale que par les déficiences de notre fils, croyant en lui malgré tout et convaincus que le temps arrangerait les choses, si seulement, en plus des thérapies, de notre attention constante, des demi-journées à la halte-garderie, il y avait un peu plus de temps en classe...

Du diagnostic à la compréhension

Bien que nous n'ayons pas obtenu d'aide efficace de la part des nombreux médecins consultés, nous nous sommes laissé convaincre par un ami neurologue à San Francisco de prendre de nouveau un rendez-vous à l'hôpital Robert-Debré, cette fois, avec un confrère parisien. Nous venions de fêter les 4 ans de Paul et j'avais le sentiment que nous ne pouvions pas connaître pire situation que celle que nous vivions. Je me trompais.

Les mois qui ont suivi cette consultation m'apparaissent confus aujourd'hui, comme si ma mémoire avait voilé cette période la plus désastreuse de mon existence. Nous sortîmes de cette consultation sans avoir réellement compris de quelle maladie il s'agissait. Le neurologue était probablement resté dans le flou pour éviter tout acte de désespoir, nous laissant ainsi du temps pour découvrir petit à petit l'étendue et les conséquences de cette calamité. Nous avions conscience qu'il s'agissait de quelque chose d'épouvantable dont le pronostic n'était pas rassurant. Il avait préféré nous parler de *Pervasive Developmental Disorder*, pensant peut-être que ce terme valait mieux que d'autres plus connus, qui auraient induit un caractère irréversible à la maladie, ce qu'il ne voulait pas. J'avais retenu que ce « désordre » rendait impossible une scolarité normale et que le médecin recommandait une méthode d'apprentissage américaine qu'il connaissait peu, mais dont il avait entendu parler. Je retenais de la conversation que 20 % des cas s'en sortaient et réussissaient à vivre sans aide, les autres conservaient des séquelles plus ou moins importantes et, parmi eux, 30 % régressaient dramatiquement.

À partir de ce jour et pendant les deux ans qui suivirent, j'avais, au moment du réveil, lorsque le rêve s'effiloche et qu'il nous échappe, quand la conscience affleure, une conviction insidieuse, funeste que quelque chose d'imminent et de terrifiant allait fondre sur moi. Ah !... oui... le désastre... la chape de plomb... à porter jusqu'au soir, jusqu'à l'oubli d'un sommeil artificiel... jusqu'au prochain réveil... à tous les réveils... jusqu'à la fin ?

À la sortie du rendez-vous, je me sentais vidée de toute émotion, de toute conscience des choses extérieures, accomplissant comme un automate les mouvements nécessaires : retraverser les couloirs de l'hôpital, remonter en voiture, rentrer à la maison et préparer le dîner. Une angoisse sourde, lente et lourde remplissait peu à peu ce vide. Je ne me sentais pas la force de parler et mon mari, anéanti lui aussi, gardait le silence. Je ne me rappelle pas des jours qui ont suivi. Peu à peu, cette ignorance est devenue insupportable. J'en voulais au médecin de ne pas nous avoir expliqué plus précisément de quoi il s'agissait, et je m'en voulais de n'avoir pas su lui poser les bonnes questions. Il fallait que je sache, à n'importe quel prix.

Je me suis donc rendue avec cette redoutable abréviation de PDD, d'autant plus terrifiante qu'elle ne signifiait rien de précis, à la librairie Joseph-Gibert, sachant que j'y trouverais de nombreux dictionnaires bilingues et des ouvrages de médecine. Au bout d'une demi-heure de recherches vaines, abandonnant les ouvrages de médecine générale, je finis par tomber sur un dictionnaire de psychiatrie anglais-français. Il n'en donnait pas la signification, mais situait ce *Pervasive Developmental Disease* dans une classification des maladies liées à l'autisme. À la lecture de ce mot que je n'avais voulu entendre, je fus prise de sueurs froides et, la tête bourdonnante, je dus m'asseoir par terre, craignant de tomber et d'attirer l'attention des rares personnes qui se trouvaient là. Le dictionnaire s'était refermé et semblait peser une tonne sur mes jambes. Ma vision était devenue floue et il me fallut quelques instants avant de pouvoir la focaliser à nouveau... sur le mot *psychiatric* de la couverture. Je respirai mal, il fallait que je sorte. Mais, cherchant de nouveau, je recopiais d'une main moite et tremblante les quelques mots attachés à PDD, sans vouloir aller plus loin que ce terme d'autisme qui était déjà insoutenable. Je rentrai comme un zombie. Pas le moindre souvenir de ce trajet de retour et de ce qui s'est produit par la suite.

Le choc ressenti prouvait-il que j'avais accepté le diagnostic ? Le processus d'acceptation allait être long. Pendant plusieurs semaines, je cherchai tous les moyens de récuser le diagnostic : toutes les bonnes raisons, « rien de ce genre dans nos familles respectives », tous les signes prouvant l'erreur, « il était parfaitement normal à la naissance et jusqu'à 14 mois... On me l'aurait dit bien avant... Ce n'est pas ça, l'autisme... », etc. Je devais aller vérifier que c'était une erreur... ou peut-être savoir de quoi il s'agissait... besoin de savoir... même le pire ? La curiosité revenait, les questions : d'où cela vient-il ? Pourquoi lui ? Que s'est-il passé à partir d'un an ? Est-ce cela qu'on appelle autisme ?

Je résolus de m'inscrire à la bibliothèque de la faculté de médecine. Et là, dans le silence des étudiants plongés dans leur étude, je parcourais les rayons, piochais au hasard des ouvrages en anglais, en français qui me paraissait correspondre. « L'autisme est le plus connu des troubles envahissants du développement, lisais-je, ces troubles peuvent apparaître dans les premiers mois de la vie ou se déclarer au cours de la deuxième année... Leur taux d'incidence est de 22 personnes pour 10 000... cela fait 1 pour 500 environ... Quatre fois plus fréquents chez les garçons... en augmentation marquée selon les chercheurs. » Emportant la pile sur une table, je les parcourais, l'un après l'autre, m'emplissant des définitions, descriptions, analyses. « Les TED sont fréquemment caractérisés par un changement soudain et notable du comportement jusqu'alors normal (arrêt du langage, repli sur soi-même, absence de contact visuel, intérêt exclusif pour les objets, refus de communiquer avec autrui, anorexie) »... Ingurgitant les récits d'expériences, les bilans de chercheurs, les synthèses d'études de cas, les comptes rendus cliniques, je cherchais à me persuader que le neurologue s'était trompé, mais en réalité, l'idée faisait son chemin.

Je commençais à cette époque à me réveiller vers trois heures du matin. Une phrase lue à de nombreuses reprises, comme un verdict sans appel, qui ne m'avait pas arrêtée de jour, s'était gravée dans mon esprit, pour resurgir la nuit, comme en lettres de feu : « L'autisme est une maladie incurable... autisme... maladie... incurable... *Autism is a lifetime disease... lifetime disease.* » Mon cerveau paraissait ressasser de son propre chef cette effroyable litanie.

Un jour, assise à la bibliothèque et consciente que je cherchais à nier ce diagnostic, malgré l'évidence accumulée au fil des lectures, je pris la résolution de regarder la vérité en face. Je résolus de prendre note, dans tous ces ouvrages, de ce qui était vrai dans le cas de Paul, de ce que j'avais constaté à la maison et à l'extérieur... et de remplir ce questionnaire. Il s'agissait d'une liste de critères permettant d'établir un diagnostic de façon certaine. Je le remplirai honnêtement, le mieux possible... non, pas le mieux possible, c'est déjà un mensonge. Je devrais dire la vérité, rien que la vérité... « Levez la main droite et dites : je le jure. » Je faillis éclater de rire à cette repartie et levai les yeux pour voir si quelqu'un avait deviné ce fou rire que je contenais difficilement. Il fallait que je réponde à ce questionnaire, aller au bout de la torture en quelque sorte. Je me contraignis à ne pas lire les indications pour l'interprétation qui m'auraient peut-être permis de tricher.

J'étais donc devant les définitions du DSM IV [1] (*Diagnostic and Statistical Manual of Mental Disorders*) regroupant les 5 catégories de troubles envahissants du développement (TED), traduction française de *Pervasive Developmental Disease* (PDD). Passant outre la terreur qui s'insinuait en moi à la lecture de ces mots qui sonnaient comme le glas de mes espoirs, je cherchais la bonne catégorie. 1. Trouble autistique, 2. Syndrome de Rett, 3. Syndrome désintégratif de l'enfant, 4. Syndrome d'Asperger, 4. Troubles envahissants du développement non spécifiés (PDD-Nos.)

Je commençais par les critères diagnostiques du trouble autistique.

1. *DSM IV, Manuel diagnostique et statistique des troubles mentaux*, traduction coordonnée par J.D. Guelfi, Paris, Masson, 2003.

A – *Un total de 6 (ou plus) parmi les éléments décrits en 1., 2. et 3. dont au moins 2 de 1., 1 de 2. et 1 de 3. :*

1. *Altération qualitative des interactions sociales, comme en témoignent au moins 2 des éléments suivants :*

a) Altération marquée dans l'utilisation, pour réguler les interactions sociales, de comportements non verbaux multiples, tels que le contact oculaire, la mimique faciale, les postures corporelles, les gestes.
(Oui, hélas, impossible de ne pas cocher.)

b) Incapacité à établir des relations avec les pairs correspondant au niveau de développement.
(Oui, pas de doute.)

c) Le sujet ne cherche pas spontanément à partager ses plaisirs, ses intérêts ou ses réussites avec d'autres personnes.
(Oui, puisque nous n'existons pas.)

d) Manque de réciprocité sociale ou émotionnelle.
(Pour ce que j'en comprends, oui.)

2. *Altération qualitative de la communication, comme en témoigne au moins un des éléments suivants :*

a) Retard ou absence totale de développement du langage parlé (sans tentative de compensation par d'autres modes de communication, comme le geste ou la mimique).
(Oui, absence totale sans compensation.)

b) Chez les sujets maîtrisant suffisamment le langage, incapacité marquée à engager ou à soutenir une conversation avec autrui.

(Pas de langage.)

c) Usage stéréotypé et répétitif du langage, ou langage idiosyncrasique.

(Idem.)

d) Absence d'un jeu de faire-semblant varié et spontané, ou d'un jeu d'imitation sociale correspondant au niveau de développement.

(Oui, incapable de faire semblant et aucun jeu d'imagination.)

3. *Caractère restreint, répétitif et stéréotypé des comportements, des intérêts et des activités, comme en témoigne au moins un des éléments suivants :*

a) Préoccupation circonscrite à un ou plusieurs centres d'intérêt stéréotypés et restreints, anormale soit dans son intensité, soit dans son orientation.

(Oui, c'est une bonne définition.)

b) Adhésion apparemment inflexible à des habitudes ou à des rituels spécifiques et non fonctionnels.

(Oui, également résistance aux changements.)

c) Maniérismes moteurs stéréotypés et répétitifs (par exemple, battements ou torsions des mains ou des doigts, mouvements complexes de tout le corps).

(Non, enfin une caractéristique absente !)

d) Préoccupations persistantes pour certaines parties des objets.

(Oui, souvent.)

B – ***Retard ou caractère anormal du fonctionnement, débutant avant l'âge de 3 ans, dans au moins un des domaines suivants :***

1. *Interactions sociales.*
(Oui, après 14 mois.)

2. *Langage nécessaire à la communication sociale.*
(Aucun après 13 mois.)

3. *Jeu symbolique ou d'imagination.*
(Aucun.)

Le compte était vite fait : en **A**, nous avions 9 réponses sur 12, 6 étant suffisantes. En **B**, au moins 1 réponse et nous avions les 3.

Les critères diagnostiques concernant les autres maladies soit ne correspondaient pas à notre cas, soit comptaient des critères communs au trouble autistique. Il fallait bien se rendre à l'évidence, mes lectures m'y avaient préparée, mais cocher des définitions et faire le compte ne laissaient pas de doute. Cette classification correspondait aussi à la CIM-10[2], c'est-à-dire la classification internationale des maladies. Des médecins l'avaient conçue et s'y référaient pour établir les diagnostics. « On est en plein dedans », me répétai-je indéfiniment. « Pas de doute, on est en plein dedans. » Je repensais à toutes ces bonnes âmes qui depuis plus de deux ans cherchaient à me rassurer, à me convaincre que cela allait s'arranger, que tous les enfants « faisaient ça » à un moment ou à un autre. Elles me revenaient en écho, nous nous étions tous trompés... ou plutôt

2. CIM-10, 10e révision, OMS, 1992.

personne ne pouvait savoir que tout cela était défini précisément comme une maladie mentale… « maladie mentale »… Mon petit bonhomme atteint d'une maladie mentale ? Ce visage adorable, ce corps sans défaut et, à l'intérieur, comme une bête monstrueuse tapie dans les circonvolutions de son petit cerveau qui en grossissant allait éteindre, étouffer, détruire, dévorer ce petit être et en faire quoi ? Un être hébété au regard vide qui n'aura plus rien d'humain, un demi-sauvage fixant méchamment les visiteurs croisés dans les couloirs de l'hôpital psychiatrique, un monstre dans une camisole. Comment est-ce possible ? Que s'est-il passé ? Qu'est-ce qu'on lui a fait ? Qu'est-ce qu'on nous a fait ? À qui la faute ?

Encore des questions… à n'en plus finir. Qu'ai-je fait pour mériter cela ? De quoi me punit-on ? N'est-il pas innocent ? L'empreinte de culture judéo-chrétienne… on est coupable… on naît coupable… mais de quoi ? Un châtiment ? Je ne suis coupable de rien. Moi, entre toutes, qu'on disait, lorsque j'étais petite, bonne, aimante, généreuse, dévouée aux miens, serviable envers tous, incapable de garder rancune. Moi qui observais les préceptes chrétiens, sans même avoir conscience d'une morale à respecter, mais parce que j'étais née comme cela. Quel mal avais-je fait ? Que de monologues dans les églises que je trouvais sur mon chemin, pour tenter de comprendre la raison de cette épreuve et espérant trouver un secours et le courage d'accepter. En ressortir avec l'envie rageuse de lever le poing au ciel, profondément convaincue : « Il n'y a personne là-haut, il n'y a jamais eu personne. »

« Aide-toi, le ciel t'aidera », tu parles, qui peut m'aider ? Alors, arrête de gémir et remue-toi. Je n'ai pleuré à aucun moment, je n'avais pas de larmes, pleurer sur mon sort ne me venait pas. Il fallait que je passe à l'action. Quelque chose de constructif. Il doit bien y avoir une solution, des remèdes. Ne rêve pas... Si on guérissait de l'autisme, cela se saurait. En prendre son parti ? Impossible. Comment accepter une telle monstruosité ? Non, jamais... pas lui, pas moi. Ce n'est pas envisageable, je ne peux pas vivre avec ça.

Me faire à l'idée d'avoir un enfant en hôpital psychiatrique, en institut spécialisé pour le restant de mes jours... de ses jours. Je ne pourrais jamais me faire à cette idée. Cela revient à dire que je n'aurai plus le droit d'être heureuse, de profiter de moments de bonheur sans me sentir coupable et, d'ailleurs, il n'y aura plus de moments heureux. Rire, être joyeuse, plaisanter ? À rayer du vocabulaire et des possibilités. Prendre plaisir à des voyages, des rencontres, des réunions entre amis ? Inimaginable. Jouir d'un repos mérité avec la satisfaction d'un travail bien fait, des enfants épanouis dans leur vie d'adulte ? Impensable. Toute source de bonheur tarie, tout sentiment de bonheur disparu, sachant que j'ai mis au monde un être qui souffre et ne vit qu'à moitié.

Un autre monde

J'ai basculé dans un autre monde. Rien ne sera plus comme avant. Il y aura maintenant un avant : insouciant, léger, libre, et un après : lourd de peine, de chagrin, de souffrance, de culpabilité. Tous ces mots seront valables à un instant ou à un autre, mais leur contraire n'existera plus. Voilà, je n'accepte pas cette situation, je ne pourrai pas vivre avec, je ne pourrai pas la vivre. Cela ne sera pas une vie, mais on n'a rien trouvé entre la vie et la mort. Je me suis inventé cet état : je marche, je respire, je pense, mais je ne vis pas. Mon cœur ne s'est pas arrêté de battre, ma vie s'est arrêtée de battre. Aujourd'hui, j'ai enterré ma vie. Un bon titre de roman, mais ce n'est pas un roman, c'est une réalité des plus cruelles.

À la sortie de la bibliothèque, des étudiants discutant avec entrain, des touristes le nez au vent. Dans le métro, des hommes et des femmes qui vaquent, plongés dans leurs pensées. Je les examine comme des cas, si différents de moi maintenant. Vivent-ils des drames aussi ? Certainement, mais cela ne se voit pas.

Commence alors cette sensation de décalage qui ne me quittera plus. Je les regarde : rentrent-ils de leur travail ? Vont-ils faire des achats ? Choisir leurs vêtements avec soin, hésiter devant les rayons d'alimentation, aller au cinéma, se disputer avec un collègue de travail ou avec leur femme, harceler leur mari, tout paraît futile et sans importance. Comment peut-on prêter une quelconque attention à de tels détails ? Comment ai-je pu faire tourner, moi aussi, mon existence autour de ces bricoles ? Plus rien n'avait d'importance. J'étais aliénée, j'avais mis le pied sur une autre planète encore inconnue qui n'avait plus rien à voir avec celle-ci. C'était le début d'une transformation qui recentrerait tous mes intérêts vers un but unique, qui lui-même tournerait à l'obsession.

Je continuais mes lectures, mais l'angle de vue différait. Je m'imprégnais de la maladie et de ses conséquences concrètes, toujours plus terrifiantes cas après cas, analysées, objets de statistiques précises qui paraissaient inéluctables. Qu'aucun cas ne paraisse en réchapper anéantissait l'espoir auquel je cherchais à me raccrocher dans cette chute vertigineuse. Un précipice sans fond : saura-t-il un jour comprendre et répondre à une seule question ? Pourra-t-il un jour se situer dans une ville, traverser seul, observer les feux (ne pas attendre le rouge toute la matinée parce que le feu est en panne), retrouver son appartement ou son lieu de travail ? Faire ses courses et se nourrir seul ? Apprendre un métier, mener à bien une tâche, avoir un travail rémunéré, conserver son emploi ? Résister à des gens malveillants, se défendre ? Sera-t-il capable d'aimer quelqu'un qui pourra prendre soin de lui, l'écouter, lui obéir ? Sa sœur portera-t-elle ce fardeau ? Et lui confiera-t-on ? Échappera-t-il aux crises d'épilepsie de l'adolescence ? Quelle sera l'influence de la puberté sur son comportement, maîtrisera-t-il ses pulsions ? Deviendra-t-il agressif, violent et devrons-nous lui faire quitter l'appartement familial pour ces raisons ? Serai-je obligée de suivre une psychothérapie dans le but de me détacher de lui pour être capable de l'abandonner dans un hôpital psychiatrique où l'on me déconseillera d'aller le voir ?

Les parents devaient s'attendre à toutes ces questions qui me tenaient éveillée nuit après nuit. Fallait-il que j'en passe par là ? Au pied de mon lit, ces piles de livres achetés, empruntés, ces photocopies de rapports et de documents trouvés sur Internet, que je lisais jusqu'à l'écœurement. Quand s'arrêterait cette descente aux enfers ?

Chapitre V

PASSER À L'ACTION

Un jour, une nuit peut-être, mon intérêt s'est déplacé. Jusqu'à présent je m'étais efforcée de comprendre la maladie pour accepter ce diagnostic. J'avais bien saisi l'ampleur de la catastrophe ; je me tournais alors, peu à peu, vers les moyens d'en sortir. Internet me fournissait toutes les méthodes, traitements et thérapies existantes, notamment aux États-Unis et au Canada, qui me paraissaient très en avance sur nous. Les piles continuèrent de grimper, mais cette fois j'étudiais ces méthodes d'apprentissage et de rééducation et je gardais les adresses des centres et écoles spécialisés. Certains parents avaient sorti leur enfant de cette « forteresse » et écrit leur expérience. Je me procurais leurs livres. Ayant compris les mécanismes de cette maladie, je commençais à entrevoir les moyens de remédier aux anomalies qu'elle provoquait. La compréhension de ces troubles, d'un point de vue scientifique avec l'analyse des dysfonctionnements du cerveau et leurs répercussions, fut le déclencheur.

À mieux connaître et mieux comprendre, la peur avait reflué. Comme un noyé qui touche le fond, donne un grand coup de pied pour remonter, cette curiosité a été mon élan. Avec la compréhension est venu le besoin d'agir. J'allais mettre en place quelque chose, tâtonnant au début, j'allais gagner en assurance et en confiance. Il fallait agir vite, le temps jouait contre nous. Je suivais donc toutes les pistes, triant au fur et à mesure, élaguant dans le tas, retenant celles qui me seraient utiles. Je renonçais pour l'instant à aller suivre une formation parentale dans un centre spécialisé aux États-Unis, craignant de perdre un temps précieux.

Je me préparais à la bataille. Dans ma vie aussi, je fis le tri. Se débarrasser des boulets et du superflu pour être plus libre. Des freins de tous genres : ceux qui ne croyaient toujours pas au diagnostic malgré l'évidence, ceux qui me tiraient vers l'inertie, « ne t'inquiète pas, cela va s'arranger ». Des belles-sœurs intransigeantes qui, dans leur ignorance, me soupçonnaient de manquer d'autorité ou qui éloignaient leurs enfants par crainte de contagion. Ceux qui pensaient que les parents sont responsables car mauvais éducateurs... Et tous les indifférents.

Sabrant dans les relations qui ne me seraient d'aucune aide à ce moment-là je refusais les invitations et les sorties pour me concentrer sur cette tâche de tous les instants. Excusant mon comportement auprès de ceux, bien peu nombreux au fond, qui même au courant s'en formalisaient, par un « tu sais, j'ai la tête dans le guidon » et un vague « on a un petit problème à la maison » aux autres. Je fis disparaître l'accessoire pour consacrer tout mon temps, toute mon énergie et toutes mes ressources mentales et physiques à l'essentiel : tirer

Paul de son enfermement avant qu'il ne sombre irrémédiablement et préserver Laure du mieux possible.

Très vite, j'avais eu besoin de comprendre l'origine de ces troubles. Ce développement anormal d'une petite partie du cerveau et les différentes anomalies que les chercheurs avaient observées : comportementales, psychologiques, neurocomportementales, neurologiques, neurochimiques, neuroanatomiques et génétiques. Je me passionnai pour leurs causes éventuelles à la lumière des récentes découvertes dans les domaines de la biologie et de la biochimie et des progrès de l'imagerie médicale (IRM et TEP). Tous ces ouvrages et articles scientifiques m'aidèrent à comprendre la maladie de mon fils. Cette compréhension me fut très utile d'abord pour accepter un diagnostic si difficile à entendre, puis pour surmonter ce sentiment de culpabilité inévitable ; qu'ai-je fait de mal pendant ma grossesse, pendant les premiers mois, de quelles erreurs sommes-nous responsables ? Rien et aucune. Il fallait s'en persuader. La lecture de ces articles médicaux si peu accessibles servait à m'en convaincre. Nous n'étions ni coupables ni responsables de ces troubles. Je me forçais à penser que la génétique est une grande loterie : on tire parfois le mauvais numéro. Il fallait l'accepter, mais réagir. La lecture des ouvrages (voir la bibliographie non exhaustive à la fin de cet ouvrage) m'avait aussi permis de changer d'état d'esprit. C'était une condition essentielle du succès : arrêter de se lamenter et se mettre au travail. Comme un savant analyse, déduit, théorise, applique, échoue et recommence, sans jamais se décourager, je devais tenter l'expérience. Sans passer la blouse blanche, je devais être le thérapeute de mon enfant. Observer, comprendre, déduire, formuler des hypothèses, trouver des remèdes, les essayer, analyser le succès ou l'échec des tentatives, en tirer des conclusions qui permettront de nouveaux essais. Enfin, j'étais passée des rapports purement médicaux à des descriptions de cas cliniques qui me permettaient de comprendre les mécanismes et d'analyser les grands principes d'un mode de fonctionnement si différent du nôtre. C'était indispensable pour dégager des moyens de traitement concrets. Un modèle de thérapie se dessinait peu à peu, des principes essentiels émergeaient.

Un des principes qu'il me paraît important de garder à l'esprit en toute occasion est que les enfants atteints de ces troubles n'apprennent pas par osmose, ce qui est la règle dans l'évolution du petit enfant. Attentif dès les premiers jours aux comportements et aux réactions de son environnement social, l'enfant n'apprend pas sciemment, ce n'est pas un processus conscient et volontaire. Il enregistre et reproduit parce qu'il est imprégné de ce qu'il voit et entend, d'où son aptitude aux jeux d'imitation.

Chez Paul, tout apprentissage par osmose était impossible, il fallait donc le faire par un processus intellectuel basé sur une réflexion, un raisonnement, des mots. Mais cet apprentissage par processus conscient, raisonné se heurtait à l'absence de langage. Comment franchir cette barrière, qui le coupait de nous, comment instaurer un mode de communication ?

J'avais lu et constaté d'une part que, chez l'enfant autiste, les perceptions sensorielles (goût, vision, odorat, audition, sensibilité à la douleur, etc.) sont déformées, désorganisées par rapport aux nôtres. D'autre part, que le cerveau n'a pas la capacité de traiter l'information globalement en la reliant aux autres perceptions et en l'« expliquant » afin que cette perception ne soit pas perçue comme un danger. Ce traitement parcellaire de l'information explique que toutes les perceptions constituent un *bombardement de stimuli* inexplicables, incompréhensibles donc terrorisants. Cela provoque un retranchement dans le monde sécurisant car prévisible des objets. Par ailleurs, non analysée, l'information ne peut entrer dans le registre des choses connues donc s'ajouter à une somme d'expériences.

Je compris qu'il fallait non seulement essayer de rééduquer les anomalies de la perception mais également rétablir les connexions qui ne se font pas entre ces différentes perceptions. Comprendre les processus cognitifs pour rétablir les associations ou connexions qui permettent d'appréhender le monde environnant pour ne plus le craindre.

D'autres principes de fonctionnement, schématisés et simplifiés ici, découlaient de ces constatations, d'où l'importance d'une observation objective et continue. Avec l'habitude d'analyser les moindres faits et gestes d'une façon claire venaient les automatismes : trouver un remède, une solution, le biais, les moyens de corriger la déficience, l'anomalie, le comportement déviant.

Rééduquer les perceptions

Les trois quarts d'heure d'école par semaine nous laissaient beaucoup de temps. Je le conduisais trois demi-journées par semaine à la halte-garderie pour qu'il y soit en présence de personnes étrangères et surtout d'enfants. Paul avait aussi, tous les mercredis, une séance de psychomotricité dont je ne voyais pas bien, au début, l'utilité puisqu'il n'avait pas de problème moteur. En réalité, la psychomotricité avait un grand rôle à jouer.

Je consacrais donc tout le reste du temps à la rééducation de Paul. J'apparentais cette tâche à un travail de réparation, mais je repris l'ensemble au début, comme avec un bébé. Chaque acte était morcelé, expliqué, répété et, bien sûr, verbalisé clairement.

Pour l'habiller le matin, par exemple, je lui expliquais tout point par point. « On enlève le pyjama (lui mettre le pyjama sous les yeux et que le mot coïncide avec son regard) et on le met sous l'oreiller pour ce soir. On met le T-shirt, en haut (détailler les épaules, le cou), il est blanc, répéter blanc lorsque son regard est dessus. Les chaussettes sont pour les pieds (prendre un pied, lui montrer, le masser pour qu'il sente qu'il est à lui), un pied, deux pieds, une main, deux mains. Il n'avait pas vraiment conscience que tout cela lui appartenait, pas plus qu'il n'appréhendait son corps comme un tout distinct de son environnement. Je pense que sa terreur des aspirateurs lui venait de sa peur de disparaître à l'intérieur comme s'il était volatil. Il fallut du temps et de nombreux exercices quotidiens devant un miroir pour qu'il se sente comme un tout, solide, entier. Au début, il n'osait pas se regarder dans la glace. Il fallait le forcer ou il se détournait aussitôt. Répéter son nom des dizaines de fois. Détailler son corps, en touchant chaque partie pour qu'il fasse bien le lien entre ce qu'il voyait et ce qu'il sentait. Plus tard, lorsqu'il se prêterait au jeu, lui demander de faire pareil : je lève le bras, la jambe, etc. Les massages aussi l'aidaient à prendre conscience des sensations sur sa peau et à distinguer les différentes parties de son corps en fermant les yeux.

Même chose dans la salle de bains. Se laver les mains était une torture. Trouver là encore le moyen de le détourner de ces angoisses. Faire flotter des jouets de bain dans le lavabo pour qu'il ait envie de les faire bouger. Et relier toujours les perceptions, deux par deux, pas plus, afin d'éviter une stimulation excessive qui générerait de l'anxiété. L'eau est froide, chaude. C'est mouillé, sec. Le savon sent bon : faire sentir des odeurs légères d'abord, anticiper la panique qui submerge tout à coup, on ne sait pas pourquoi. Réconcilier avec la brosse à cheveux, puisqu'il ne supportait pas les contacts sur sa tête. Et décrire toujours avec les mêmes mots, cela pique dans la paume. La mousse à raser, c'est doux, ça fond, c'est blanc. Attendre que la concentration revienne s'il est « parti ailleurs ». Retourner le chercher dans son monde avec un objet attirant ou un bruit amusant. Cacher les appareils qui font du bruit (sèche-cheveux, rasoir...) pour ne pas rompre la concentration.

Dans la cuisine, profiter des odeurs et des bruits de cuisson. Montrer le gaz qui brûle, c'est chaud, c'est bleu : faire mine de se brûler. Montrer le plaisir que l'on a à manger, faire goûter quand c'est possible. Paul refusait la plupart du temps, bien sûr, puisqu'il ne s'alimentait pas normalement. Il faudrait aussi trouver les moyens de réduire cette *hypersensibilité aux odeurs, aux goûts* ou *à la consistance des aliments*, mais pas tout à la fois. Jouer avec les couverts. La fourchette, ça pique. Le couteau, ça coupe : faire mine de se couper et d'avoir mal. Se pencher au-dessus du vide-ordures : pas bon ! ça sent mauvais ! À exagérer tous les mots et gestes, j'obtins les premiers sourires et, à ma grande surprise, un certain humour. Plus tard, il mettrait dans nos assiettes des escargots trouvés dans le jardin et, dans un fou rire, nous dirait : « Mange ! » (Il ne pouvait pas imaginer qu'il y avait effectivement des amateurs...)

L'extérieur fournissait naturellement de nombreux sujets d'expériences. Tout était prétexte à une explication. C'était décourageant de n'avoir aucune réponse, surtout s'il y avait des personnes autour de nous, surprises de le voir muet, indifférent. Les arbres, les fleurs : lui mettre dans la main pour qu'il en sente le contact et répéter indéfiniment : c'est rose, ça sent bon, mmh, exagérer les mimiques, jouer la comédie, s'extasier sur les couleurs, la taille des arbres, le toucher rugueux d'un mur, le froid des grilles métalliques...

Le bac à sable nous servait aussi beaucoup. Si, au début, il fallait retirer le moindre grain de sable de sa chaussure pour éviter une crise de panique, il finit par accepter de toucher le sable, bien avant d'autres substances (colle, peinture, qui demandèrent un an encore).

Je remarquais aussi que, lorsque je cachais un objet, ne le voyant plus, il s'en désintéressait. J'allais découvrir le travail sur ce processus de mentalisation plus tard avec mon amie Barbara qui me fournirait bien d'autres pistes encore.

La foule le mettait dans un état proche de la panique. Renonçant à mon envie de le maintenir éloigné de toutes ses sources d'angoisse, je lui faisais subir celles-ci à doses homéopathiques. Si le bus commençait à trop se remplir à son goût, Paul éclatait littéralement en sueur et je sentais une chaleur moite et intense à travers ses vêtements. Je n'avais que quelques minutes avant la crise pour lui parler, le rassurer, avant qu'il ne puisse plus m'entendre. Nous descendions à l'arrêt suivant. Au fil des mois, il réussit à tenir jusqu'à notre arrêt. Faire la queue à la caisse d'un magasin me demandait des trésors de patience. Même dans sa poussette, la présence toute proche des gens autour de lui l'affolait. Quand son énervement devenait visible, les gens nous regardaient, jugeaient cette mère incapable et cet enfant intraitable, détournaient leurs regards méprisants ou dégoûtés, se faisaient entre eux des remarques malveillantes ou même lançaient à la cantonade des commentaires blessants. À moins de les gifler, je ne pouvais rien faire et surtout pas donner d'explications, parce que, en étant un peu attentif, on pouvait deviner que ce n'était pas un simple caprice d'enfant gâté. Voir ses yeux révulsés de terreur pouvait suffire. Mais qui voit vraiment ? En tout cas, je me blindais, sans pouvoir m'empêcher parfois de lancer des remarques acerbes à qui nous provoquait. Paul acceptait difficilement de lâcher un objet que je lui achetais au supermarché pour le mettre sur le tapis de la caissière ; le lui faire poser et attendre pour le reprendre qu'il fût encaissé tenait déjà du miracle. Quand, en plus, j'avais affaire à une caissière qui se mêlait d'inculquer la politesse aux enfants : « Je te le donne que si tu me dis merci » et lui promenait sous le nez, elle avait droit à un magnifique scandale. Même chose, à la bibliothèque, où les jeunes femmes, sympathiques du reste, exigeaient de lui des discours de remerciements ou d'excuses. Nous y allons toujours. S'en souviennent-elles, des crises d'hystérie qu'elles provoquaient ? Et cette vendeuse, assise tranquillement derrière sa caisse, qui papotait longuement au téléphone, pendant que j'essayais de contrôler la crise de Paul hurlant, gesticulant, en sueur dans mes bras. À bout de nerfs, je lançai : « Cela ne vous ennuierait pas d'encaisser mes articles ?... » Et elle de s'exécuter en soupirant : « Ce que les gens peuvent être pressés. » Pour moi, tout cela est indélébile.

À longueur de journée, je poursuivais cette rééducation des sens, dans un travail d'imagination permanent pour attirer son attention, l'apprivoiser, lui faire comprendre notre monde.

À l'affût du moindre signe de panique également. Je le devinais si bien que j'anticipais sur ses craintes, le prenant dans mes bras pour le rassurer pendant qu'un camion de pompiers passait toutes sirènes hurlantes ; me précipitant vers lui lorsque quelqu'un s'apprêtait à mettre en route une machine bruyante, faisant un détour pour éviter le marteau piqueur, pestant contre ces abrutis de motards, qui démarrent brusquement leurs engins trafiqués à côté de Paul tétanisé. Dès que je sentais monter l'angoisse, je venais le prendre, le balançais sur mes genoux en répétant : « Maman est là, maman est toujours là, tu n'as pas peur quand maman est là. Maman revient toujours, maman est toujours là », comme une berceuse pour endormir sa peur.

Je mis du temps à trouver le moyen de rétablir ce *contact visuel* dont on parlait beaucoup. Son absence ne m'avait pas réellement frappée puisqu'il n'y avait pas d'autre contact : pas de gestes d'affection, pas de paroles non plus. Si je voulais qu'il m'écoute, je devais m'agenouiller face à lui, parler lentement et distinctement, avec des phrases courtes et en utilisant toujours les mêmes mots. Je prenais son menton entre mon pouce et mon index pour maintenir son visage face au mien et chercher son regard. « Paul, écoute-moi... Paul, tu m'entends ?... Paul, tu me regardes... » chaque fois que je m'adressais à lui. J'attirais son attention en permanence sur ce que nous faisions. Par la suite, il nous fit la même chose, il prenait mon menton pour que je lui prête l'attention qu'il réclamait. Je le revois tenir le visage de Catherine, sa première maîtresse dans la nouvelle école, de ses mains d'une propreté douteuse. Elle ne s'en formalisait pas, au contraire, et écoutait patiemment les balbutiements qui en auraient découragé plus d'un, sachant que c'était là un gros effort pour lui et un résultat miraculeux pour nous.

Catherine, vous êtes partie enseigner dans une classe d'adaptation l'année suivante parce que vous aviez une passion pour ces enfants-là, puisse votre amour en sauver d'autres.

Ses premiers contacts visuels étaient très brefs, comme pénibles pour lui. Il y a lu tant d'amour et d'attention que, par la suite, il cherchait mon regard pour se rassurer dans les moments inquiétants. Il fallait toujours être à l'écoute, à l'affût, conserver en mémoire les « trucs » qui avaient marché, en rechercher d'autres, déployer des trésors d'ingéniosité, d'imagination et de patience, chaque jour, jour après jour. Cette façon de réfléchir, d'analyser, d'imaginer des solutions devint obsessionnelle. Ces réflexions me tenaient éveillée la nuit, et toutes ces insomnies m'ont fourni de nombreuses solutions que j'appliquais dès le lendemain. J'arrêtais la rééducation avec l'arrivée à la maison de Laure après l'école et jusqu'au coucher. Je m'efforçais de transférer mon attention sur elle tout le temps de sa présence à la maison. Mais j'avais tellement donné à Paul que je n'avais plus guère d'énergie à lui consacrer. Elle en a souffert malgré nos conversations à deux où elle me demandait ce que nous avions fait, et si Paul avait fait des progrès. Je lui demandais son avis, toujours précieux, pour ne pas la laisser à l'écart. Je lui disais toujours, bien qu'elle ne se plaigne pas : « Si ça avait été toi, j'aurais fait exactement pareil. »

Un espoir : le principe de l'intervention précoce

À notre seconde visite, le neurologue avait formellement déconseillé l'hôpital de jour dans le cas de Paul et préconisé une petite école privée. D'ailleurs, nous étions convaincus que la fréquentation d'enfants comme lui ou plus atteints encouragerait ses comportements déviants et ne lui ferait faire aucun progrès. En l'absence d'aide concrète et de structure plus adaptée à son cas (école spécialisée ou classe d'adaptation), il fallait que j'arrive à mettre en place une thérapie. J'avais compris dans mes lectures la nécessité d'appliquer un programme, comme le faisaient ces centres éducatifs et autres structures spécialisées nombreuses aux États-Unis. Dans ces méthodes, les parents avaient un rôle déterminant à jouer dans la thérapie de leur enfant. Ils étaient partie prenante dans ces programmes personnels, adaptés au cas de leur enfant. Des résultats spectaculaires avaient été obtenus par l'approche comportementale d'Ivar Lovaas décrite dans *The Me Book* (1981). Parmi de nombreuses études, j'en retenais une. Les 19 enfants d'un groupe expérimental avaient reçu 40 heures de stimulation précoce par semaine pendant 2-3 ans ; 9 enfants avaient réussi à être intégrés dans une classe normale dès la première année où ils avaient progressé normalement ; 8 autres s'étaient retrouvés dans des classes pour enfants aphasiques ou ayant des troubles de la communication ; 2 seulement dans des classes pour autistes. Le suivi indiquait qu'à l'adolescence les acquis avaient été maintenus. Chez les 19 enfants du groupe témoin, aucun enfant n'avait pu être intégré dans les classes régulières ; 8 étaient suivis dans des classes pour personnes aphasiques et 10 dans des classes pour autistes.

D'autres ouvrages décrivaient les cas de récupération d'enfants ayant suivi des programmes de stimulation précoce intensive. Parmi eux, *Let Me Hear Your Voice* de Catherine Maurice. Des cliniques utilisaient cette méthode d'analyse du comportement appliquée (ABA) et affirmaient récupérer 40 à 50 % des enfants autistes qui entrent dans leurs centres. Mais à quel âge y entrent-ils ? Et à quel degré sont-ils atteints ? Certains centres de rééducation préconisaient 40 heures d'intervention hebdomadaires grâce à la présence d'un personnel hautement qualifié (orthophonistes, psychomotriciens, ergothérapeutes...)

Parmi les chercheurs et cliniciens reconnus mondialement, je lisais toutes les études menées par le Dr Bernard Rimland, directeur de l'*Autism Research Institute* (ARI) de San Diego en Californie. Il assurait que ces méthodes n'étaient plus expérimentales et étaient également efficaces pour les enfants de plus de 5 ans, même si, pris plus tard, une récupération totale s'avérait très rare.

L'éducation structurée du programme TEACCH, qui utilise en partie l'approche comportementale, permettait à 95 % des personnes autistes de rester dans la communauté en comparaison des 50 % de ceux n'ayant pas bénéficié du programme. Cette méthode prône le développement de l'autonomie de l'enfant dans les trois sphères importantes de sa vie : son milieu familial, le milieu scolaire et la communauté, grâce à un enseignement structuré. Le programme d'intervention d'Ivar Lovaas reprenait des principes semblables. Quels étaient-ils [1] ?

1. Lovaas O.I., Ackerman A.B., Alexander D., Firestone P., Perkins J., Young D., *Teaching Developmentally Disabled Children : The Me Book*, Austin, Pro-Ed, 1981.

1. Un lieu d'apprentissage dépourvu de distractions.

2. Un moment de la journée qui ne varie pas et une durée de travail adaptée au niveau de l'enfant.

3. La concentration et la capacité d'obéir de l'enfant s'accroissent lorsqu'on lui demande de faire un effort et de terminer sa tâche : il est important de ne pas céder au refus de l'enfant (pas de tâche supérieure à ses capacités naturellement) pour qu'il ne déduise pas qu'une attitude désobéissante ou opposante est un moyen efficace de mettre fin au travail.

4. Le contenu du programme est basé sur un plan d'intervention personnalisé mis au point par le médecin, l'équipe soignante et les parents. Il est important que les deux parents se partagent les séances d'apprentissage bien que les mères soient souvent plus disponibles.

5. Les troubles du comportement pouvant interférer avec l'apprentissage de l'enfant doivent être éliminés ou remplacés par des comportements moins nuisibles.

6. Les techniques basées sur le conditionnement opérant, renforcement, punition, sont utilisées : récompenses immédiates et concrètes pour les plus jeunes (alimentaires ou matérielles), approbation sociale et récompenses différées pour les autres (félicitations, etc.). Les punitions peuvent aller des réprimandes, des « non » fermes à la suppression du jouet avec lequel l'enfant s'autostimule – ou de la récompense attendue, à la réprimande physique.

Tout cela était bien théorique, et je n'imaginais pas un instant Paul se soumettre à cet apprentissage structuré puisqu'il n'écoutait rien et n'obéissait en rien. Ce programme était-il conçu pour des enfants beaucoup plus passifs, malléables ou obéissants ? « Éliminer ou remplacer les troubles du comportement », facile à dire. Je m'imprégnais des exigences de ces différents programmes que j'avais analysés : l'importance d'établir une routine, les heures fixes, le même déroulement des activités, les rituels d'ouverture et de fin sécurisants pour l'enfant donc favorables aux acquisitions. Là encore, je retrouvais le même leitmotiv : morceler chaque acquisition, découper chaque activité, faire acquérir ces petites portions l'une après l'autre en respectant une certaine logique, diviser chaque apprentissage en étapes, vérifier que l'une soit bien acquise avant de passer à la suivante et les reprendre régulièrement pour conforter les acquisitions et donner un sentiment d'assurance et même de fierté à l'enfant.

Chaque activité devait développer les capacités dans des domaines précis et aboutir aux objectifs suivants (entre autres) :

1. Développer le langage.
2. Développer la conscience de son corps souvent floue, stimuler par des massages et des mouvements de gymnastique, des exercices de motricité globale et de motricité fine.
3. Développer l'interaction avec les autres.
4. Rester dans le concret avant de développer l'étape suivante qui sera un travail sur l'imagination car les représentations mentales nécessitent une appréhension de la réalité déjà bien établie.
5. Lecture et mime de contes et d'histoires pour apprendre les comportements sociaux. Par la suite, ils permettent d'enseigner les émotions et leur langage, de décoder ses sentiments propres et ceux des autres afin de parvenir à les exprimer.

Je concevais très bien les principes et les objectifs de ces thérapies. Il me restait à construire ce programme point par point, en respectant une certaine logique dans les apprentissages, établir des degrés de difficulté pour chaque tâche, ne pas faire d'erreur qui le bloquerait, ne pas aller trop vite, ne pas ajouter aux dégâts... Comment m'y prendre concrètement ? Par quelle activité commencer ? Quel matériel utiliser ? Une amie américaine habitant San Diego avait eu la gentillesse de se déplacer pour aller se renseigner dans ces centres. Elle s'était fait conseiller de nombreux ouvrages qu'elle m'avait envoyés ainsi que toute la documentation et les livres que je lui avais demandés. Je commençais à les traduire en fiches pour pouvoir m'en servir avec Paul, mais elles me paraissaient d'un niveau bien supérieur à ce qu'il était capable de faire ou de comprendre. De plus, la vision d'ensemble et les imbrications des différentes activités qui permettraient les progrès manquaient de cohérence et de netteté. Je craignais de jouer les apprentis sorciers dans la mise en place de ce programme qui pouvait se révéler au mieux inutile, au pire néfaste. Il me fallait des exemples concrets. Ces programmes devaient avoir leur équivalent en France : y avait-il des spécialistes dans des centres de rééducation ? Où les trouver ? Des parents parisiens avaient peut-être suivi ces stages de formation, monté des programmes semblables. Les quelques contacts pris ne conduisirent nulle part. Je commençais à céder au découragement avant même d'avoir commencé.

Des soutiens décisifs

Il me revint alors que quelqu'un, quelque part, m'avait parlé d'une mère qui avait accompli un travail extraordinaire avec son fils autiste. J'avais entendu cela deux ou trois ans plus tôt. Il fallait à tout prix que je retrouve cette piste. Je me remémorais alors cette visite chez le cardiologue à qui j'avais fait part en quelques mots de mes difficultés et de mon désarroi. C'était bien chez lui. Dans la minute, je composai son numéro et obtins un rendez-vous en espérant qu'il ait gardé le contact avec cette patiente et qu'il accepte de me donner ses coordonnées. Je fus soulagée d'apprendre qu'elle habitait le quartier, qu'elle serait peut-être disponible. Je pressentis que c'était une chance extraordinaire pour nous, notre salut peut-être. Il ne fallait pas la laisser passer. Je pris contact immédiatement. Si je n'en garde aucun souvenir, Barbara se souvient de ce premier contact. Elle sentit l'urgence de ma demande et mon obsession de mettre en place rapidement un programme comme celui qu'elle avait conçu pour son fils. Nos premiers rendez-vous m'apportèrent un immense espoir. C'était une chose de savoir que des améliorations étaient possibles, de lire que certains enfants avaient pu être « récupérés » outre-Atlantique, mais d'en avoir une preuve vivante en la personne de son fils, écouter le récit de cette expérience vécue aussi récemment et aussi près de moi fut un formidable catalyseur. Barbara expliquait sa méthode avec la clarté d'un sujet parfaitement maîtrisé et l'assurance que donne le succès. L'espoir d'une guérison totale pour Paul allégea le poids de cette chape de plomb qui ne m'avait pas quittée, même si dans l'action de cette rééducation constante, j'avais déjà trouvé un soulagement. J'avais le sentiment que, grâce à elle, nous allions pouvoir passer aux choses « sérieuses ».

Nos deux cas différaient. Barbara avait compris plus tôt, malgré l'incapacité de son pédiatre à lui avouer dès le début l'autisme de son fils, dont les symptômes, contrairement à Paul, avaient été présents dès la naissance. Leur comportement et leurs aptitudes différaient, mais là n'était pas la question. L'autisme se présente sous forme d'un continuum regroupant des troubles, sans limites clairement définies, des atteintes plus ou moins profondes et des handicaps variables. Cette notion de continuum autistique considère le handicap social comme le symptôme central de ces troubles, c'est-à-dire un triple déficit dans les rapports à autrui ; acceptation, communication et compréhension reconnus dans un large spectre de gravité. Des handicaps dans d'autres domaines ont tendance à s'ajouter, dont l'ampleur varie également. On parle ainsi de degré dans l'autisme au sujet d'enfants qui n'en présentent pas le syndrome complet. La dysphasie du développement dont le diagnostic est généralement porté par exclusion comporte des troubles spécifiques du langage auxquels peuvent être associés des traits autistiques. Finalement, peu importe la dénomination de ces troubles, sujette à de nombreuses controverses. Le danger est de cataloguer l'enfant pour en attendre des résultats stéréotypés. Ou de prendre la dénomination pour une explication : « Paul ne peut avoir de relations avec autrui puisqu'il est autiste. » Le résultat est que nous ne croyons plus qu'une évolution soit possible. L'état d'esprit qui en découle est évidemment catastrophique.

Il me fallut un certain temps pour intégrer cette idée et je dois en remercier le Dr N... qui m'a mise sur la piste de ce nouvel état d'esprit à acquérir. Je lui avais téléphoné pour lui raconter notre rendez-vous. Je l'accusai avec violence d'oser nier un diagnostic médical établi par un neurologue de renom. Il le récusait d'une façon incompréhensible pour moi : « Tout est ouvert, tout est possible. » Ses propos ont fait leur chemin et je compris par la suite que sa colère venait du fait qu'un médecin avait, ce jour-là, condamné un enfant dans la mesure où il lui avait collé une étiquette indélébile sur le dos, qu'il ne s'était pas étendu sur les solutions possibles puisqu'il n'y croyait pas lui-même, et que tout le monde prendrait le parti d'enfermer Paul dans un tiroir et ne l'en sortirait un jour que pour l'enfermer de nouveau dans des études de statistiques. Vous aviez raison, docteur N... : « Tout était ouvert, tout était possible », du moins pour lui, pour nous et à ce moment-là.

L'essentiel était maintenant de concevoir un programme adapté, construit avec logique et précision. Barbara avait l'expérience et le recul nécessaire, je pataugeais dans trop d'informations, la logique globale d'un programme, le matériel nécessaire et son utilisation me manquaient, même si j'en avais compris le principe.

Depuis la guérison de son fils à la suite de trois ans de rééducation structurée intensive et un suivi sans faille pendant quelques années encore, Barbara avait été contactée par de nombreux parents qui avaient entendu parler de ce « miracle. » Elle avait adapté pour d'autres cas sa méthode et son travail, et acquis la capacité de concevoir et rédiger des programmes qu'elle expliquait aux parents et suivait avec leur enfant le cas échéant.

Les résultats étaient toujours positifs et la progression plus ou moins rapide, en fonction des capacités de l'enfant et du degré d'implication des parents dans le programme de leur enfant.

Après une analyse du cas de Paul, Barbara mit donc au point un programme qu'elle m'expliqua dans le détail. J'étais admirative de la façon dont elle faisait le lien entre la déficience et l'exercice à faire pour la corriger. Je ne voyais pas le lien entre les deux mais elle connaissait si bien les processus d'acquisition mentale que, effectivement, je ne pouvais que constater qu'elle avait frappé juste. Mener à bien les activités de chaque atelier mis en place apportait la solution à l'incapacité à laquelle elle s'était précisément attaquée. Elle accepta de prendre Paul pour deux séances par semaine en ma présence, où elle détaillait précisément la manière de s'y prendre et le résultat qu'elle escomptait, afin de faciliter la mise en route du programme.

À bras-le-corps

Les débuts à la maison furent très difficiles et très pénibles. Nous nous enfermions dans une chambre réservée à cet usage avec le matériel nécessaire que j'avais acheté sur les recommandations de Barbara. La leçon commençait par les crises de rage de Paul qui ne supportait pas d'être enfermé dans cette pièce et cherchait à ouvrir la porte en hurlant. J'attendais qu'il se calme, en réfrénant mon envie d'ouvrir et de partir avant même d'avoir commencé. La première activité consistait à faire rouler une balle de l'un à l'autre en essayant de capter son regard le plus souvent possible et en répétant : « À toi... à moi... » Lorsqu'enfin il accepta ce jeu, il se montra habile et visa avec justesse. Nous passions alors à un jeu de formes à encastrer dans un plateau. Refus à nouveau, hurlements. Couché par terre, Paul refusait de regarder le jeu que je lui proposais. À ces moments-là, je le prenais dans mes bras, de force, l'asseyant sur mes genoux et le maintenant serré pour qu'il ne s'échappe pas. J'essayais de rester calme malgré ses hurlements perçants. Je lui prenais la main, lui faisais saisir une forme pour la déposer dans le trou correspondant. Il résistait, lâchait l'objet, se débattait, pleurait.

Combien de séances a-t-il fallu avant qu'il accepte ce contact forcé de ma main, et combien d'autres avant qu'il saisisse l'objet de lui-même. Je m'interrogeais sur cette violence, sachant que Barbara n'y avait jamais recours, mais Paul, pensait-elle, se mettrait à coopérer avec de moins en moins de difficultés par la suite. Il avait parfaitement vu la forme de ces pièces et compris l'exercice (et je répétais chaque fois : « Je prends le carré... le rond... le triangle... le losange... et je le mets dans le trou carré... », etc.), mais il résistait par principe.

L'étape suivante était un jeu de topologie développant les facultés de repérage spatial. Une cinquantaine de photos représentaient des scènes à reproduire à l'identique avec les mêmes objets fournis dans la boîte. Prenant la scène la plus simple, je lui détaillais ce qu'il fallait faire, toujours à voix haute et distincte. « Sur l'image, en haut, il y a un cube jaune avec un toit rouge dessus, comme une maison, un arbre à droite, une vache à gauche. On va faire la même chose sur notre planche vide, la maison en haut, l'arbre à droite, la vache à gauche. » Je prenais les objets dans la boîte pour les disposer de la même façon que sur l'exemple. Il fallut plusieurs semaines avant que Paul accepte de tenir les objets pour les poser au bon endroit. Il ne formulait toujours pas, je le faisais à sa place. Une fois acquise la configuration du premier carton, nous passâmes avec grande difficulté au suivant. Paul ne voulait pas en changer. Il refaisait donc le premier et je le forçais à faire le suivant en verbalisant à sa place : « Je mets la barrière au fond, le cheval à droite, l'arbre à gauche, la poule devant. » Il finit par y prendre goût et se trompait rarement dans la disposition. Parfois je commençais seule un nouveau carton, en me trompant volontairement. Je voyais son regard aller du carton à ma disposition, et il corrigeait mes erreurs, jusque dans le moindre détail : ce n'était pas l'arbuste mais le sapin, ma barrière était posée à l'envers... J'étais obligée de cacher les cartons qu'il connaissait par cœur pour le forcer à changer. Il les cherchait avec anxiété dans la pile et je lui promettais en récompense, après un nouveau carton, de lui donner son préféré. Il ne voulait rien entendre. Le « si tu fais ça, je te donne ça » n'était pas encore acquis. Lorsqu'il ne s'opposait pas, ses gestes étaient précis, ses mains adroites. C'était déjà cela.

Puis je lui faisais la lecture de livres simples, lui décrivais la scène d'une image. Il se lassait vite, mais j'évitais de céder au premier signe, pour gagner à chaque séance une minute de plus d'attention. Il ne montrait jamais du doigt la moindre image, ne répétait pas les cris d'animaux, ne montrait aucun signe qu'il écoutait. Après la crise d'opposition qui nous laissait épuisés l'un et l'autre, il restait passif jusqu'à un certain point. Les premiers jours, j'avais donc quelques minutes d'attention entre deux crises où il se débattait et voulait partir. Nous nous arrêtions à la deuxième si les quelques activités, d'une ou deux minutes chacune, étaient terminées.

Si la durée de chaque activité s'allongea progressivement, l'ordre en était immuable, ce qui le rassurait. Il savait à quoi s'attendre, donc il restait calme. Je constatais que son temps de concentration et d'acceptation s'allongeait. Hélas, il y avait aussi des moments de régression. Pendant deux ou trois jours, il me semblait que tous les acquis étaient perdus, Paul se roulait à terre et hurlait si j'insistais. Nous étions revenus à zéro. J'en sortais au comble du découragement, avec l'envie d'abandonner.

J'appelais Barbara : « Je n'y arriverai jamais, je vais y laisser ma peau... – C'est si tu t'arrêtes que tu vas y laisser ta peau, continue, ne t'interromps surtout pas. C'est normal, ces enfants fonctionnent en dents de scie, tu auras des régressions, mais de moins en moins profondes et de moins en moins fréquentes, alors, pour aujourd'hui, ça suffit, et, demain matin, tu reprends exactement où tu t'es arrêtée comme si de rien n'était. »

Elle avait raison, mais il me fallut des mois avant que ces régressions ne m'atteignent plus. Je me revois un an plus tard, « consoler » l'orthophoniste, désespérée par deux ou trois séances pénibles de régression où Paul avait refusé toutes les activités habituelles : « Ne vous inquiétez pas, ça va revenir, avec moi non plus, ça ne marche pas ces jours-ci. » La semaine suivante, il était effectivement « reparti ». Je remarquais aussi que lorsqu'il était grippé ou avait attrapé une de ces « gastro-entérites » si fréquentes dans les haltes-garderies ou à l'école, il régressait très nettement, et ce dans tous les domaines : comportements anormaux, manque de contrôle de soi, crises d'angoisse. Je savais que c'était temporaire, mais serait-ce ainsi toute sa vie ?

Si au début, puisqu'il ne supportait pas la contrainte, je le laissais choisir ses activités préférées, il était important d'imposer un ordre précis dans leur déroulement et leur durée. Ce n'était pas à lui de choisir – on ne choisit pas à l'école –, il devait au contraire accepter la contrainte et obéir aux consignes. Nous en étions bien loin, mais, lorsqu'il est devenu un peu plus malléable, j'eus la possibilité de construire des séances dans l'ordre prescrit par Barbara.

« *Regarde-moi* »

Je débutais chaque séance en essayant d'établir le contact visuel par différents moyens. Le jeu de « je te tiens, tu me tiens par la barbichette... » permettait, grâce à son aspect ludique, de prolonger ce contact, si difficile à obtenir au départ de façon naturelle. Les jeux de balle, l'un en face de l'autre, nécessitaient également ce contact parce que me regarder permettait d'anticiper la façon dont je lui enverrai la balle : va-t-elle la faire rouler par terre ? la lancer vers le haut, en direction de sa gauche ou de sa droite ? le tromper : faire semblant de partir à gauche et lancer à droite pour le faire rire ? Cela lui demandait une certaine concentration : je gagnais ainsi, séance après séance, quelques minutes d'attention de plus. Cela signifiait également, pour lui, se concentrer sur une action extérieure à lui-même, dépendante de la volonté d'une autre personne. Le troisième aspect important de l'activité était de décrypter mes attitudes et d'anticiper un mouvement. Si tout cela lui demandait un effort au début, je comptais qu'il le ferait de plus en plus naturellement, par réflexe, dans sa vie quotidienne.

Ce contact établi, je devais garder son attention qui divaguait facilement, je sortais alors la boîte de cubes, confectionnés par mon père, chaque face peinte d'une couleur différente avec les lettres de l'alphabet en capitales, en cursives... les chiffres arabes, romains, la ponctuation sur une autre face... Je pensais que nous étions bien loin encore de cet apprentissage des lettres, s'il en était capable un jour. Pour le moment, j'empilais les cubes, un à un, lentement, toujours en verbalisant. Il fallut de nombreuses séances avant que nous mettions chacun à notre tour notre cube : longtemps il garda le cube dans sa main avant d'oser le mettre sur la pile, mais l'important était qu'il accepte et obéisse. Là encore, trouver une conclusion plaisante : d'une pichenette, voir s'effondrer la tour de douze cubes dans un grand fracas ; il était pressé de la reconstruire pour avoir le plaisir de la démolir.

L'étape suivante nécessitait l'imitation : chacun son tas de cubes et « tu fais comme moi : j'en pose un, tu en poses un, un deuxième à côté, tu poses l'autre à côté aussi... » Tout verbaliser clairement et lentement, bien qu'il ne répète rien encore, il enregistrait certainement tous ces mots : dessus, dessous, à gauche, à droite, à côté, etc. Les changements le contrariaient toujours. L'habitude d'un jeu, le même pendant des jours, était difficile à modifier. Faire deux colonnes au lieu d'une, puis faire un mur, le même que le mien, toujours en maintenant le contact visuel le plus souvent possible. Des semaines plus tard, nous nous servîmes des couleurs : la face rouge dessus, la face jaune du côté gauche. Lorsque c'était trop difficile, je le savais tout de suite : Paul lançait les cubes dans tous les coins de la pièce, énervé, puis se couchait par terre et reprenait ce regard tourné vers lui-même, oubliant ma présence.

C'était déjà plus supportable que ses hurlements, sa rage de ne pouvoir sortir quand il frappait la porte de toutes ses forces. Nous changions alors d'activité, mais il fallait qu'il m'aide à ranger les cubes dans la boîte. Pendant longtemps, il les jetait pêle-mêle... mais ils ne rentraient pas tous dans la boîte de cette façon, il fallait qu'il les aligne et les empile couche après couche pour enfin reposer le couvercle : revenir donc à des gestes précis et ordonnés, maîtriser sa frustration.

Ces petites tâches imposées durant les leçons étaient reflétées dans la rééducation quotidienne : jeter son manteau sur le portemanteau avec impatience, pour aller jouer plus vite dans sa chambre n'était pas l'accrocher ; je le rattrapais au vol pour lui faire ranger manteau et chaussures avec précision. Leçons et rééducation se réfléchissaient comme dans un miroir pour conserver un parallèle logique entre toutes ces activités, la même manière de faire quelle que soit cette activité. Je gardais toujours à l'esprit que mon travail était un travail de reconstruction cérébrale et de réorganisation des sens. Tout était utile à cette reconstruction de sa personnalité.

Dans l'activité suivante, il fallait aussi reconstituer le lien entre les choses. En effet, dans le Loto des objets usuels, Paul devait remettre l'un à côté de l'autre les petits cartons représentant des objets connus : retrouver le marteau pour le mettre à côté du clou. La pièce de monnaie devait retrouver son porte-monnaie, le pinceau sa boîte de couleurs, etc. Il connaissait la plupart des objets, mais si certains lui étaient inconnus, je retenais qu'il faudrait les lui montrer et les lui expliquer : dans l'après-midi, je sortirais la boîte à outils, lui ferais visser et dévisser une quelconque charnière, lui ouvrirais une boîte de conserve et lui laisserais l'ouvre-boîtes à examiner longuement pour imaginer son fonctionnement.

Je décrivais à sa place les objets et leur usage. Le travail était équivalent avec le jeu des animaux. Lorsqu'il se lassait, je mettais exprès le bocal à poisson à côté du lapin ou le poisson à côté du nid d'oiseau pour le faire sourire ou réagir.

« *Écoute-moi* »

Je constatais que, si son acuité visuelle était bonne, ses capacités auditives étaient un réel problème. Il ne semblait pas interpréter les sons ou les mots. Il n'établissait pas de lien s'il n'avait pas de support visuel. Les *Comptines et jeux de doigts* en cassette le laissaient indifférent et il restait passif sans reproduire les gestes ou le mime qu'exigeait la comptine. Il ne décodait pas. Il fallait donc rétablir un lien entre ce qu'il entendait et la gestuelle correspondante, et surtout qu'il comprenne ce qu'il entendait. Tous ces sons lui parvenaient sans doute brouillés et incompréhensibles ; les phrases : des amalgames confus, indéchiffrables. Nous utilisâmes donc pendant longtemps un support visuel. Des images pour chaque son et chaque parole en les découpant dans leur expression la plus simple. C'était décourageant de constater cette incapacité, à quatre ans et demi, de comprendre des cassettes éditées pour les enfants de deux ans à peine. Lorsque je lui présentais le livre d'images correspondant à l'histoire lue en même temps, il ne regardait que les images, tournant les pages trop vite sans faire le moindre lien avec ce qu'il entendait, sans chercher à comprendre l'histoire. Cela correspondait bien à son incapacité à suivre et à comprendre l'histoire d'une cassette vidéo comme les histoires du Père Castor. Tout enfant de son âge décodait les signes, les gestes puis les mots de chaque personnage, en déduisait la logique des actions puis des paroles. Lui en était incapable. Notre logique lui échappait totalement.

Pour remédier à cette défaillance de sa concentration auditive, nettement moins bonne que sa concentration visuelle, le Loto des sons nous a beaucoup aidés. De grandes planches représentaient des scènes quotidiennes : une cuisine, la campagne, la ville, un jardin... de façon très détaillée. Sur une cassette étaient enregistrés les différents sons correspondant aux scènes. Dès que j'entendais un son, je montrais du doigt l'objet sur la planche correspondante : le robinet qui coule dans l'évier, le mixeur dans le bol, la moto qui démarre, le chien qui aboie, le tracteur qui passe au loin, la tondeuse à gazon... Paul résistait toujours lorsque je lui prenais la main pour lui faire désigner l'objet. J'ai insisté pendant des semaines, mais quelle victoire lorsqu'il a montré de lui-même le bonhomme jouant du violon à sa fenêtre, l'abeille bourdonnant dans le jardin. Je l'applaudissais et le félicitais. Il ne nommait toujours pas les objets, mais chacune de ces avancées était pour moi un miracle, il faisait enfin le lien entre les objets et leur bruit, cette connexion-là était rétablie.

Parallèlement à ce travail sur les sons, il fallait une étude des comportements des personnages pour l'aider à comprendre les actes de chacun, et leurs conséquences, ce qui lui permettrait de décrypter les codes sociaux. Je trouvais une collection d'histoires très simples et j'en découpais chaque scène avec toujours ces mots importants ; d'abord, ensuite, après, enfin... « Winnie est un ourson, un bébé ours. Winnie a faim, il cherche du miel. Winnie mange du miel, les ours aiment le miel. Winnie est gourmand, il mange trop de miel. Winnie a mis trop de miel dans son ventre, il a un gros ventre. Il a grossi. Il est trop gros. La fenêtre est petite. Winnie veut sortir. Mais Winnie est trop gros pour passer par la fenêtre. Il est coincé. Il ne peut plus bouger. » Pour chaque phrase, je montrais l'image et mimais la scène, exagérais les gestes, posais des questions : où est Winnie ? Ici ! Où est le miel ? Dans le pot ! Que fait Winnie ? Il mange, mange, mange, je répétais et mimais pour faire rire Paul. Je m'efforçais de bien en montrer la logique : il ne peut pas sortir parce qu'il est trop gros... La même histoire tous les jours, guettant une réaction après des heures de passivité indifférente, essayant de ne pas penser aux réponses vives et enthousiastes de Laure devant la même histoire non pas à quatre ans mais à deux ans.

Pour conforter les acquis, pour donner confiance à Paul aussi dans ses capacités, je revenais régulièrement sur des activités qu'il maîtrisait bien en le félicitant chaque fois. Nous reprenions le Loto des voitures où il avait simplement à poser sur sa planche le carton qu'il piochait ou à me la donner s'il ne l'avait pas. Cela servait différents objectifs : lui donner confiance en constatant qu'il maîtrisait bien une activité, donc pourquoi pas les autres aussi ? Mais c'était également le prétexte à « blablater », comme je pensais en mon for intérieur : « Tiens, c'est moi qui ai le camion de pompier, c'est beau un camion rouge, et puis on le voit de loin dans la rue. Tu te souviens du bruit qu'il fait le camion de pompier ? Pin-pon, pin-pon... Et puis il va vite... » Je mimais le chauffeur au volant qui prend des tournants serrés dans un crissement de pneus. « J'ai pioché la voiture de course, tu sais la bleue, comme celle que tu as ? On l'avait achetée où celle-là ? Ah oui ! dans le magasin de jouets à côté de l'école... »

C'était lassant de parler toute seule, de faire indéfiniment les questions et les réponses, mais je savais qu'il écoutait de plus en plus souvent, et de plus en plus longtemps, mes monologues interminables.

Puisqu'il ne comprenait pas instinctivement les attitudes et les réactions des autres, nous avons pensé au mime. Le jeu de Séquences photo comprenait une douzaine d'histoires, chacune photographiée en quatre ou six scènes distinctes. Il s'agissait de remettre l'histoire dans l'ordre logique, de commenter chaque photo et de les mimer. Il fallut plusieurs semaines avant que Paul se prête de bonne grâce à des reproductions de scènes. Je décrivais les quatre photos posées au sol dans le désordre et posais des questions. Que fait la petite fille ? Pourquoi est-elle par terre ? Pourquoi tombe-t-elle ? Je répondais et il remettait dans l'ordre les photos et je répétais à sa place : d'abord... ensuite... et puis... enfin... et mimais la scène : « La petite fille monte sur son vélo, elle roule, (je pédalais), tout à coup elle tombe « aïe ! mon genou », elle remonte sur son vélo et s'en va. » Paul devait mimer en même temps que moi. Je faisais semblant parfois de ne pas savoir le nom d'un objet, mais les questions directes le mettaient en colère. Peu à peu, je réussis à introduire le « donnant-donnant » : si tu fais ça, je te donne ça. Nous allions alors régulièrement au magasin de jouets où il apprit à attendre. Au début, il lui fallait tout immédiatement et il hurlait si nous sortions du magasin sans ce qu'il désirait. Je devais tenir bon, le temps qu'il comprenne qu'il aurait son jouet s'il obéissait. Pendant les leçons, mais aussi pour les choses de la vie courante, j'instaurais le « si tu fais ces deux planches, je t'achète la figurine que tu veux : tu voudrais la Belle au bois dormant ou la sorcière ? Tu sais à La Grande Récré ? » Ce sésame nous ouvrait bien des portes. J'achetais les jouets à l'avance pour pouvoir lui donner dès que l'effort serait accompli. La récompense était donc immédiate et le poussait à toujours plus d'efforts.

Chapitre VI

Y CROIRE

Le Magné-B6

Parallèlement, j'avais poursuivi mes recherches sur Internet et lu de nombreux articles sur les différents traitements possibles. Des traitements à base de vitamines étaient préconisés. À part les traitements lourds, dont le neurologue ne m'avait pas parlé et que je voulais éviter le plus longtemps possible, je me laissais convaincre par les nombreuses études sur les résultats très positifs d'un traitement au magnésium associé à la vitamine B6. Celui-ci fait l'objet d'études depuis les années soixante et les résultats positifs de ce traitement semblent aujourd'hui indiscutables. Un complément alimentaire, la Diméthylglycine (DMG), était recommandé pour les TED sur certains sites d'Internet, mais les médecins que j'avais interrogés ne connaissaient pas ce produit. Je le commandais aux États-Unis. Paul prenait tous les jours deux ampoules de Magné-B6, une gélule de DMG et de l'Alvityl. Son alimentation était si déséquilibrée que je craignais des carences. De plus, j'avais lu que les troubles intestinaux sont fréquents chez les autistes et provoquent une mauvaise assimilation des vitamines, des oligo-éléments et sels minéraux. Je constatais des améliorations très rapides des troubles du sommeil : des nuits complètes, un sommeil moins agité (coups de pied, sursauts, réveils...). Dans l'ensemble, un comportement beaucoup plus calme, des crises moins fréquentes, une diminution des angoisses de Paul (bruits, foule, environnement inconnu), une amélioration dans la « gestion » de ses frustrations. Les crises de colère suivies d'un retrait total disparurent. Sa concentration et sa patience lors des séances augmentèrent au fil des semaines. Je constatais aussi que ses difficultés revenaient quand j'arrêtais le Magné-B6. Barbara l'avait utilisé plus ou moins à longueur d'année pour son fils et je n'hésitais pas non plus, m'étant assurée qu'il n'y avait pas d'effet secondaire gênant ou nocif à ce traitement au long cours.

L'utilisation de la sécrétine faisait également l'objet de nombreuses études où l'on remarquait une amélioration des problèmes intestinaux chroniques, des nuits complètes, l'établissement du contact visuel et la verbalisation. Aucun médecin ne m'ayant répondu au sujet de ce type de traitement, j'imagine qu'il n'est pas utilisé en France ou trop peu connu. Je consultais régulièrement les *Newsletters* du DAN (*Defeat Autism Now*). Le DAN dépend de l'ARI (*Autism Research Institute* à San Diego). Cette association américaine de chercheurs et de médecins travaille depuis trente ans sur l'identification et les traitements des causes de l'autisme et des troubles apparentés. Elle a la possibilité de rassembler des milliers d'informations envoyées par des parents et des médecins sur les traitements essayés comme sur les programmes suivis. Les comptes rendus des conférences sont disponibles sur Internet, le plus difficile étant de trouver l'aide appropriée en France (un médecin connaissant ces traitements ou prenant la peine de répondre à leur sujet, par exemple...). À la lecture de ces études, on en arrive à se demander si les causes de cette maladie ne sont pas justement ce que l'on pense être des conséquences : et si ces troubles du développement dont les chiffres sont en augmentation provenaient de ces anomalies biochimiques ? Et si ces études sont connues en France, pourquoi les enfants atteints de TED ne sont-ils pas systématiquement dépistés et soignés, ne serait-ce que pour rétablir l'équilibre, prévenir les dysfonctionnements et diminuer les handicaps dont ils sont l'objet ? Les résultats de ces recherches ne sont-ils pas connus en France ? Le retard pris dans le traitement de ces maladies et leur prise en charge est manifeste et l'ignorance ou la réticence de nombreux médecins français face aux innovations américaines témoignent du peu d'intérêt porté à l'autisme par les autorités de tous bords. À mes yeux, l'information, le débat et les connaissances sur les troubles envahissants du développement manquent grandement.

L'orthophonie

Dans les récits d'expériences de thérapies parentales que j'avais lus, l'orthophonie me paraissait jouer un grand rôle. J'avais demandé une ordonnance pour mettre en place des séances pour Paul, mais ni le neurologue ni la psychologue clinicienne vers laquelle il m'avait orienté pour les « détails » ne m'avait fourni cette ordonnance. Cela me donnait l'impression qu'ils ne pensaient pas Paul capable de parler un jour. J'avais donc pris rendez-vous pour un bilan. La psychologue clinicienne tenta ce jour-là de faire une évaluation, pour mesurer ses aptitudes et ses compétences. À mon grand désespoir, Paul refusa absolument tout. Il passa toute la consultation à examiner les jouets à l'autre bout de la pièce. J'enrageais. Nous avions trois mois de « programme » derrière nous et il avait accepté à la maison de faire les activités qu'elle proposait et qu'il pouvait reconnaître. Mais, obstiné, il y avait à peine jeté un regard, pas même curieux de voir ce qu'elle avait dans sa mallette... et résisté à mes suppliques. L'attitude de Paul la confortait dans son appréciation de la gravité de ses troubles. Je cherchais à lui démontrer – me démontrer ? – que des progrès étaient possibles. En sortant, je bouillais de colère contre lui. Je sortis de l'hôpital en marchant si vite que Paul avait peine à me suivre. Je l'aurais giflé. Je décidais de m'asseoir sur un banc et d'avoir une « explication » avec lui. Je lui demandais pourquoi il n'avait rien voulu faire, pourquoi il n'obéissait pas, pourquoi il n'écoutait pas. Mon attitude et le ton de ma voix l'inquiétèrent. Il était comme tétanisé par cette agressivité qu'il sentait à son encontre. J'ai dû le terrifier. Sur le chemin du retour, il vomit. Je me revois dans la rue, l'essuyant, le consolant, le prenant dans mes bras et m'excusant. Me sentant affreusement coupable, je m'arrêtais dans un magasin de jouets et lui offris tout ce qu'il désirait et, dans sa joie, il oublia aussitôt son chagrin. Chargée comme un baudet d'énormes sacs dans chaque main, je me répétais : « Que cela te serve de leçon, tu n'as rien à prouver à personne, tu te fiches pas mal de ce que pense cette psychologue, l'essentiel c'est lui, et le reste n'a aucune importance. Les bilans, terminé ! Je trouverais bien quelqu'un pour me faire cette fichue ordonnance, même si personne n'y croit, l'orthophonie on la fera. » En tout cas, plus jamais ça. Lui en vouloir de ne pas être à la hauteur, de ne pas être comme les autres, était inévitable à certains moments, mais le lui dire était inadmissible. Plus jamais ça, me disais-je. Garder mon calme, être patiente. Rien dans mes attitudes ne devait refléter cette souffrance.

Quelques jours plus tard, je pris rendez-vous chez notre pédiatre du quartier pour la convaincre de m'accorder de l'orthophonie à raison de deux séances par semaine. Elle le fit sans me demander pourquoi le neurologue n'avait pas lui-même fait cette ordonnance et me conseilla une orthophoniste qu'elle connaissait : elle était tout près, c'était important. J'avais décidé d'arrêter de promener Paul dans tout Paris inutilement. Je n'ai jamais eu à regretter mon choix. Il me sembla même plus tard que nous avions trouvé l'idéal. Paul commença aussitôt et bien que les débuts, sans aucun langage, n'aient pas été simples pour l'orthophoniste, Paul accepta au bout d'un mois de rester avec elle pendant que j'attendais dans la salle d'attente. Malheureusement, il avait tendance à s'échapper pour venir me rejoindre ou vérifier ma présence. Je lui expliquais à plusieurs reprises que j'allais le laisser seul le temps de la séance, parce que « j'avais des courses à faire » et que je reviendrais le chercher à la fin. Il accepta cet arrangement au bout de quelques jours, et aussitôt l'orthophoniste constata qu'il était plus attentif et se prêtait de meilleure grâce aux activités. Elle me félicita d'avoir eu cette initiative, de m'y être tenue malgré la difficulté. Tout compliment était bon à prendre dans cette période d'expériences et de tâtonnements aux résultats plus qu'incertains. Un travail important, qui allait durer presque trois ans, avait commencé. Obtenir l'aide et le soutien d'un professionnel était important pour moi, bien que je fusse résolue à ne pas trop attendre des autres, surtout des professionnels...

Laure à la rescousse

Malgré ses progrès, l'absence de langage était lancinante. Ce blocage était inexplicable. Paul entendait et comprenait visiblement. Cinq mois de séances quotidiennes et de rééducation constante commençaient à porter leurs fruits. Laure lui parlait constamment et l'empêchait, comme moi, de s'enfermer dans son monde. Sa présence était infiniment précieuse. J'avais sous-estimé sa compréhension en cherchant à la protéger de ce cauchemar pour éviter qu'elle ne le vive aussi dramatiquement que nous. Cependant, peu après le diagnostic et au début de mes recherches, lorsque je sus que ce ne serait jamais un petit problème passager, je résolus de lui en parler. Ma connaissance était encore succincte et mes mots inadéquats.

« Je voudrais t'expliquer quelque chose au sujet de Paul. Tu sais que depuis des mois nous allons voir des médecins pour comprendre pourquoi il ne grandit pas comme tous les enfants, pourquoi il ne parle pas. À l'hôpital, on nous a expliqué qu'il n'était pas comme les autres...

– Ça, je le sais bien, il n'a jamais été comme les autres...

– Euh... si peut-être au début, mais tu étais trop petite pour te souvenir... enfin voilà, tu sais, on a tous un cerveau dans la tête, c'est comme un ordinateur qui voit tout et qui enregistre, il nous permet de penser, de réfléchir, de parler...

– Eh bien, son ordinateur à Paul, il ne marche pas bien.

– Euh... oui c'est un peu ça, il ne marche pas comme le nôtre... imagine que les circuits... enfin les chemins ne soient pas bien dessinés, alors quand il voit ou qu'il entend des choses, elles ne prennent pas le bon chemin, alors il ne sait pas ce qu'elles veulent dire... il ne les comprend pas bien.

– Il comprend rien.

– Si, mais pas comme nous, alors toutes ces choses, elles lui font peur...

– Oui, c'est vrai, il a peur de tout...

– Donc il faut l'aider à comprendre...

– Moi j'essaie, mais il écoute jamais.

– Parce que, d'abord, il faudrait qu'on refasse ces chemins, qu'on répare ce qui ne marche pas bien...

– Mais comment cela se répare ?

– Je ne sais pas bien encore, mais je lis beaucoup de choses pour comprendre ce qui ne marche pas et comment je peux réparer.

– Et moi, je peux t'aider à réparer ?

– Oh ! oui, mon joujou, tu peux m'aider, on s'y mettra tous. Et, ensemble, on va y arriver.

– C'est quand qu'on commence ?

– Dès que j'aurais construit un programme, on fera tous les jours des leçons.

– Moi aussi, je vais lui faire des leçons. »

Je pensais que j'aurais du mal à lui expliquer, qu'elle aurait du mal à comprendre, qu'elle serait peinée. J'étais bien loin de me douter qu'elle avait déjà tout compris, qu'elle avait souffert, qu'elle avait déjà essayé... et qu'elle en avait pris son parti. Mais, à six ans, l'espoir renaît vite. Elle est devenue une aide précieuse grâce à sa patience, à son intelligence et à son bon sens. Paul l'admirait, à juste titre.

À partir de ce moment-là, je la mettais au courant de tout ce que nous pouvions faire pour aider son frère. Je lui expliquais comment lui apprendre les choses, comment lui parler pour qu'il écoute, comment morceler les apprentissages pour qu'il suive. Elle avait une connaissance innée des problèmes de Paul, en les vivant sans s'interroger, elle apportait des solutions qui n'étaient pas le fruit de réflexions longtemps mûries mais des réactions de bon sens qui m'étaient très utiles. Ne sachant pas qu'il s'agissait d'autisme et encore moins d'une maladie incurable, elle s'attaquait à toutes les difficultés sans le moindre doute de réussir un jour. Même si son « ordinateur » ne marchait pas bien, on pouvait toujours le réparer. Je la voyais tenter de lui faire comprendre des jeux qui me semblaient trop difficiles, en réalité du niveau de son âge, mais je résolus de ne pas lui dire qu'elle plaçait la barre trop haut. Elle exigeait, sans s'en rendre compte, énormément de lui : forçant son attention, le faisant obéir, imposant le langage, détruisant ses défenses, le tirant de son univers solitaire de toute la force de ses certitudes. J'en tirais des leçons. Par amour pour sa sœur, pour sa mère aussi, il faisait des efforts incommensurables.

Le regard des autres

J'avais depuis longtemps constaté que Paul parvenait à décoder certains comportements chez sa sœur parce qu'il la connaissait bien, mais il n'en était pas de même avec des inconnus. *Il ne transposait pas* ses émotions ou ses expériences aux autres. Il ne décryptait pas les attitudes ou les visages. J'avais lu que certains de ces enfants ne lisaient pas les visages comme un tout mais observaient séparément les yeux, la bouche, le front, etc., comme des parties distinctes. Paul ne rassemblait pas le puzzle et ne saisissait pas non plus le langage des gestes comme nous le faisons de manière innée. Je m'aperçus qu'il ne comprenait pas nos réactions mais les apprenait « par cœur » et les reproduisait lorsqu'il reconnaissait une situation. Il grondait notre chatte, qui mettait le nez dans nos assiettes, parce qu'il nous avait vus le faire, mais le soir même, il lui en facilitait l'accès sans comprendre que le refus que nous exprimions était valable dans toutes les situations. Il regonflerait le pneu d'un vélo qui n'en avait nul besoin rien qu'en voyant la pompe. Ses réactions tenaient donc du « copier-coller ». Elles étaient stéréotypées puisque le fruit d'un processus tel que : « Cette situation me rappelle un dessin animé où..., le moment où Laure a dit que..., donc je fais pareil » ; mot pour mot, geste pour geste, il reproduisait une réponse apprise et non vécue, ni ressentie par lui-même mais copiée sur les autres. Rien n'était instinctif, tout était raisonné, stocké dans sa mémoire et reproduit d'une façon figée, anormale qui surprenait les autres, comme une leçon apprise mais mal adaptée à la situation.

Il ne se rendait pas compte non plus de l'effet produit par ses gestes (ou ses paroles par la suite), *n'ayant pas la faculté de lire sur le visage des autres, ni de décrypter leurs réactions*. Il ne voyait pas l'étonnement ou la réprobation qu'il provoquait car il n'avait pas encore l'habitude d'étudier les autres ou d'analyser leur réaction qu'il n'aurait d'ailleurs pas comprise à ce moment-là. Il n'avait donc aucune retenue ou aucune gêne, ne sachant pas bien ce qui se fait ou non. Il était immédiatement catalogué comme bizarre. Je souffrais pour lui, moi qui déchiffrais sans peine les expressions des visages qui l'entouraient. Au moins ne voyait-il pas qu'il n'était pas sur la même longueur d'onde, si ce n'est complètement à côté de la plaque. Les enfants sentent tout cela immédiatement et je souffrais du regard des autres. Les plus jeunes l'oubliaient aussitôt, les autres le regardaient comme une bête curieuse. Dès qu'il était en présence d'autres enfants, la bizarrerie de son comportement ressortait. J'étudiais ces différences pour trouver des remèdes et rendre ce comportement moins étrange. Lorsque nous attendions Laure à la sortie de l'école, il ne se passait pas cinq minutes avant que les autres mères ou les enfants le remarquent. Seul à ne pas comprendre les remontrances de la directrice de l'école qui ne tolérait pas que les petits frères ou petites sœurs jouent sur les marches d'entrée... Les autres s'enfuyaient comme une volée de moineaux à son approche, il fallait que j'aille le chercher sous le regard désapprobateur et la critique acerbe, essayant de modérer la colère disproportionnée de Paul qui s'obstinait à vouloir sauter les marches, malgré l'interdiction qu'il n'avait bien sûr pas comprise, et subir les regards interloqués des parents devant cette crise incompréhensible d'un enfant trop âgé pour jouer de cette façon-là. Son mutisme était devenu évident lorsqu'on lui adressait la parole. Il était trop grand pour détourner le regard sans répondre, ne pas dire son prénom lorsqu'on le lui demandait ou répondre à des questions évidentes. Que leur dire ? Il a quatre ans et demi mais ne sait dire ni son prénom ni son âge ? Je ne répondais pas, mais cela n'empêchait pas ces regards appuyés. Comme je les enviais, ces petits garçons vifs, bavards, agités mais prévisibles, qui devaient jouer, parler, manger et dormir normalement. J'enviais la normalité des autres enfants, des autres familles, des autres vies. Pouvaient-ils imaginer un instant ce que nous vivions ?

Un quotidien inimaginable

Un enfant sans langage, au comportement incompréhensible qu'il fallait endormir au moyen d'un somnifère le soir sinon il ne se coucherait pas. Qui refusait de dormir seul dans sa chambre, hurlait des heures durant et vomissait derrière sa porte si nous avions le malheur d'« essayer quelque chose ». Qui se levait toutes les nuits pour jouer bizarrement pendant deux heures, tout seul, puis se recouchait sans un mot entre nous deux. Qui ne se nourrissait que d'un seul type de pâtes que nous emportions en stock partout où nous allions. Qui hurlait à s'étouffer, vomissait de rage si on tentait de lui faire goûter une bouchée d'autre chose ou de lui donner un quelconque médicament. Qui luttait avec acharnement contre qui voulait l'habiller, le laver. Qui posait un problème insoluble à chaque instant de la journée. Qui ne donnait aucun signe de tendresse, n'appelait jamais personne et repoussait tous et toutes avec indifférence ou colère. Non, c'était inimaginable. Il me paraissait tout aussi inimaginable que tout cela puisse rentrer dans l'ordre un jour. Il fallait continuer à y croire. Tout subir, tout accepter en attendant.

Au moins étaient-elles révolues ces séances houleuses du début, où je sortais de la pièce de travail les jambes flageolantes, vidée de toute énergie, atteinte profondément par cette violence, la sauvagerie de ses réponses qui ne pouvaient qu'être physiques. Le forcer était un viol, pour lui, pour moi. Mais, malgré les doutes qui m'assaillaient, j'avais cette conviction qu'il fallait briser ce mur qui montait autour de lui, chaque jour un peu plus. Défaire une à une ces pierres, au prix de cette violence quotidienne, pour le libérer de cette prison où il se laissait enfermer.

Chapitre VII

MÉTAMORPHOSE

Le fait que Paul surmonte avec beaucoup moins de difficulté ses frustrations pendant les leçons s'observait aussi dans les actes de la vie courante. Ses crises violentes se raréfiaient et leur intensité s'amenuisait. La réflexion et l'acceptation prenaient le pas sur la colère ou l'anxiété. Les changements dans la routine étaient mieux acceptés, parce que compris petit à petit dans le cadre très régulier, répétitif et organisé des leçons. Si aujourd'hui nous allions introduire une activité nouvelle, les autres activités resteraient semblables. Il fallait casser très doucement ce désir d'immuabilité qui le caractérisait.

Les leçons obligeaient Paul à réfléchir pour comprendre ce qui lui était demandé, exigeaient de lui un effort d'analyse pour appréhender des situations données. Cette habitude prise, il l'appliquait de la même façon aux événements extérieurs auxquels il était confronté. Si ses premiers réflexes devant une situation inconnue avaient été dominés par la peur ou le refus brutal, ils avaient été suivis par un repli indifférent et silencieux : je ne comprends pas, je rentre dans ma coquille. Enfin, la curiosité venait, la peur était refoulée et le regard attiré. À ce moment-là était venue la réflexion : « Qu'est-ce que c'est ? Que fait-elle ? » Et enfin : « Que veut-elle que je fasse ? » Je montrais et remontrais indéfiniment ce que j'attendais de lui, jusqu'à ce qu'il accepte. J'avais remarqué au cours des séances cette particularité de ne pas refaire ou imiter comme un perroquet sans comprendre. Dans ce domaine, il lui fallait comprendre pour accepter de reproduire et il le faisait de plus en plus souvent, preuve qu'il acceptait et assimilait de nouvelles règles plus facilement.

Le jeu de repérage logique nécessitait un travail de raisonnement et de logique assez élaboré. Les nombreuses planches de difficulté croissante nous servirent pendant des mois. Elles se présentaient sous forme de tableaux à double entrée. Nous avions en haut, horizontalement quatre couleurs : rouge, bleu, jaune, vert ; verticalement, à gauche : une voiture, un ballon, une fleur, un crayon. Seize petits cartons représentaient tous ces objets dans les quatre couleurs. Je prenais un carton et je disais : je mets la voiture bleue dans la ligne voiture (je montrais la ligne) et dans la colonne bleue (je la suivais du doigt également). Je remplissais ainsi tous les espaces avec les cartons en verbalisant clairement et lentement. Il fallut du temps pour qu'il les y place lui-même, mais assez rapidement il me montrait du doigt l'espace. Au début, il changeait de planche avec difficulté, la nouveauté l'effrayant toujours.

Cette résistance aux changements diminuait cependant lorsqu'il reconnaissait le type de travail déjà effectué. Je le voyais observer avec attention les éléments proposés par une nouvelle planche. L'exercice était le même sous différentes formes mais je regardais ma montre : nous allongions de jour en jour sa capacité à se concentrer sur une tâche. Sa concentration qui ne dépassait pas deux ou trois minutes au début, se maintenait, après cinq à six mois de leçons, jusqu'à dix minutes si l'activité lui plaisait. Lorsqu'il commençait de nouveau à s'agiter ou à refuser, nous revenions à une activité physique qui le détendait. J'allais régulièrement me fournir chez *Nathan Petite Enfance* où je pouvais trouver de nouvelles activités ou de nouveaux jeux parfaitement adaptés à son niveau du moment et qui permettaient de rompre un peu la monotonie, parfois décourageante, des séances, ou d'aborder des expériences nouvelles dans les moments de loisirs.

À la halte-garderie où il passait deux à trois demi-journées par semaine, les animatrices percevaient aussi des améliorations. Elles le trouvaient beaucoup plus à l'écoute, rendant parfois service à un plus petit que lui qui n'arrivait pas à attraper l'objet désiré. Il n'en était pas encore à venir s'asseoir à la table commune lorsque c'était l'heure de l'atelier de collage ou de pâte à modeler mais il s'y intéressait de loin. Il ne paraissait pas aussi coupé des autres qu'auparavant. Il observait et imitait parfois. Je ne le retrouvais plus systématiquement dans la pièce laissée vide par les autres enfants, mais dans le groupe. Il côtoyait les autres sans gêne et prenait conscience de leurs gestes. Qu'ils le touchent pendant les jeux ne le dérangeait plus. Bousculé, il ne s'en allait plus à l'autre bout du jardin mais suivait des yeux les mouvements de chacun. Il tenait compte des réflexions qu'on lui faisait et commençait à obéir. Le trouver au milieu des autres pendant les activités de chant ou de lecture était plus fréquent. Il se laissait apprivoiser.

Grâce à la rééducation du toucher que nous faisions à la maison, il avait enfin accepté de prendre un pinceau. Ce blocage qui existait chez lui depuis deux ans face aux feutres et aux crayons, qu'il refusait, en hurlant, de prendre dans ses mains, commençait à céder. J'avais pour cela « dédramatisé » l'usage du crayon. Puisque son véritable usage – dessiner donc laisser des traces – l'affolait, je résolus de l'utiliser de bien d'autres façons. Le faire rouler, le planter dans de la pâte à modeler, le mordiller, en faire deux personnages qui se battent ou plus prosaïquement lui gratter le dos avec. Je l'amenais à accepter de le garder en main sans que cela le gêne. Lui donner une feuille blanche et lui montrer comment dessiner le plongeaient dans une inquiétude qui le faisait frénétiquement tenter d'effacer les traces laissées. Frottant avec ses mains sans y parvenir, essayant maladroitement avec une gomme, il a même tenté un jour d'effacer ces traces avec un gant de toilette mouillé qu'il avait couru prendre dans la salle de bains. Non, la page devait rester blanche, peut-être à cause de ce besoin de netteté, de propreté.

Il voulait que les choses restent propres, rangées, en ordre. Le fouillis le mettait mal à l'aise. Un livre abîmé aussi, un jouet cassé l'a longtemps bouleversé. Pour le dessin, il fallait trouver un autre biais. Ce fut la peinture, avec Laure. Tous deux à la même table, avec de nombreuses feuilles de toutes sortes, Laure barbouillait sans réticence, il regardait puis essayait timidement. Les feuilles souillées le dérangeaient encore. Il se lança finalement sur le grand panneau de la halte-garderie qui ne pouvait s'effacer. Les enfants y peignaient les uns sur le travail les autres, son propre travail s'y mélangeait. Ensuite, voyant que l'on pouvait y accrocher des feuilles blanches que l'on rangeait, une fois peintes, dans un dossier au nom de chacun, et les renouveler aussi souvent que l'on voulait, ses réticences ont finalement cédé. Rater son dessin n'était pas grave, on pouvait recommencer aussitôt, le stock de feuilles était suffisant. Cependant, il refusa longtemps de mettre le tablier protecteur, ou de se laver les mains comme les autres.

Le lavage des mains était un travail quotidien qui l'angoissait de moins en moins à la maison. Mais, là encore, l'exemple des autres enfants qui pouvaient « jouer à l'eau » dans le long lavabo de la garderie facilita les choses. Il commençait à apprivoiser ce monde étrange en observant les autres. Banal, bien sûr, pour tous les enfants dans la norme, mais exceptionnel pour nous.

Contrairement à Barbara, qui avait longuement approfondi ces relations de cause à effet, je ne concevais pas clairement pourquoi et comment ce que nous faisions pendant les leçons se répercutait dans ces acquisitions du comportement quotidien. Mais il n'y avait aucun doute, cela marchait. Paul changeait, c'était indubitable. Ces changements étaient encore plus perceptibles pour notre entourage, amis ou membres de la famille, qui d'un mois sur l'autre pouvait constater les différences. Paul paraissait beaucoup moins attiré par les objets, sa présence autour de nous n'était plus celle d'un petit fantôme, silencieux, absorbé dans ses activités solitaires. Nous nous étions efforcés d'être réceptifs à toutes les indications qu'il nous donnait, il avait peu à peu pris conscience qu'il pouvait avoir de l'impact sur les personnes présentes, susciter des réactions, obtenir ce qu'il désirait. Il était maintenant présent à chaque réunion de parents ou d'amis et tenait à ce que tous soient conscients de sa présence. *Il émettait de drôles de bruits*, qui ressemblaient à une conversation : « Il parle en clics comme les Bushmen », disait mon père. Il circulait dans nos jambes, cherchant à attirer l'attention par différents moyens. Il insistait pour que je le prenne dans mes bras lorsque je conversais avec les personnes présentes, cherchait à avoir le visage à la même hauteur que nous. Tournant de force mon visage vers lui comme pour dire : « Arrête ton blabla et occupe-toi de moi. » Il était très attentif aux expressions des visages qui allaient lui fournir des indications sur la conversation. Il observait, écoutait, mettait son grain de sel, nous interrompait, mais en utilisant son sabir comme pour se moquer de nous.

Il découvrait aussi la valeur du contact humain. Il réclamait que nos amis le prennent au sérieux, l'écoutent « parler », jouent avec lui ou fassent semblant de le lancer en l'air ou de le faire tomber lorsqu'il était dans leurs bras. J'étais émue aux larmes de l'entendre hurler de joie, de surprise, de peur et de rire ensuite aux éclats. Il commençait à apprécier les contacts physiques, même avec les inconnus – qui savaient s'y prendre – et réclamait leur attention. Il avait une mémoire phénoménale de ce qu'il avait fait avec chacun. Notre invité à peine arrivé, il pouvait réclamer ce petit jeu de doigt qu'il lui avait appris six mois auparavant. Se précipiter sur un autre pour détacher cette montre qui lui avait tant plu quatre mois plus tôt.

Cette mémoire était frappante lors de nos déplacements. Il reprenait ses marques aussitôt dans une maison quittée huit mois auparavant. Il y retrouvait ses objets, sans la moindre hésitation sur l'endroit où il les avait laissés. Il remarquait des changements infimes et je le voyais réfléchir à ce qui s'était passé, chercher dans les tiroirs des objets manquants. Même dévoré de curiosité, il évitait de demander. Il préférait se donner le mal de chercher plutôt que d'essayer de poser la question qui lui aurait permis de retrouver immédiatement l'objet qu'il cherchait.

Premiers mots

Très ingénieux, lorsque je lui posais des questions, il trouvait un moyen de me répondre autre que la parole, mais je lui prenais la tête entre les mains en disant oui-oui-oui, en lui faisant hocher sur chaque oui, il riait et réclamait que je lui fasse : non-non-non de la même façon. Parfois quand je disais non à ce qu'il réclamait, il prenait mon visage et me forçait à hocher pour dire oui. Je disais non-non-non en hochant la tête ; dérouté, il riait de ce piège. Pendant les leçons aussi, je cherchais à le piéger. Je faisais semblant de ne pas comprendre, de ne plus savoir, il me relayait, pas dupe probablement, mais toujours sans parler. Nous savions qu'il comprenait beaucoup de choses et nous nous demandions s'il ne faisait pas exprès de ne pas parler. Accepter de parler, c'était aussi accepter les contraintes du langage : être obligé de répondre, d'obéir, c'était beaucoup plus ennuyeux que de faire semblant de ne pas entendre ou de ne pas comprendre, et ainsi conserver une totale liberté. Il aurait fallu entrer de plain-pied dans cette communication permanente qui avait de nombreux inconvénients. Nous le soupçonnions d'être largement assez malin pour ce calcul. Mais cela avait un inconvénient de taille, comment se faire obéir ? Et cela, c'était important pour quelqu'un d'aussi déterminé et résolu, « qui avait des jugements tranchés », comme avait dit son psychiatre qui le trouvait très déterminé dans sa façon d'être et d'agir.

Je ne pouvais m'empêcher de tester sa compréhension en lui donnant des ordres simples ou en l'attirant avec un cadeau, mot magique auquel il ne résistait pas, mais si j'exigeais qu'il me dise : « Donne » ou : « Qu'est-ce que c'est », il se renfrognait et se braquait. Je cessais de lui imposer cette pression, attendant qu'il se décide. Tous ces changements dans son comportement me rendaient impatiente.

Il progressait également dans les leçons qui se déroulaient d'autant plus paisiblement que ses progrès me donnaient bon espoir et qu'il me sentait moins inquiète. L'humour et le rire que je pouvais maintenant y introduire allégeaient l'atmosphère. En gardant une certaine rigueur, j'étais plus souple quant à la façon de parvenir au résultat. Si nous avions fait un exercice difficile, je le félicitais et lui permettais de choisir l'activité suivante.

Il choisissait soit des livres, que je lui racontais en mimant, soit le jeu de topologie. Il était sur son terrain lorsqu'il fallait reproduire un des cartons qu'il avait sous les yeux. Il avait plaisir à le faire même quand il s'agissait d'une nouvelle scène. Je n'avais pas besoin de le guider mais je verbalisais ce qu'il faisait, à sa place. Un jour, cherchant à le piéger, je dis : « À côté de la barrière, il faut mettre la vache… – Non cheval… »

J'en restais abasourdie, muette, il avait voulu corriger mon erreur mais, au lieu de le faire silencieusement comme d'habitude, il avait rectifié avec des mots. J'en aurais sauté de joie ou pleuré peut-être, mais je contrôlais mon émotion, sentant que des débordements ne lui auraient pas plu. « Ah ! oui, tu as raison c'est le cheval qu'il faut mettre… » balbutiai-je, les larmes aux yeux. Le miracle était arrivé, son premier mot enfin. Allait-il continuer ?

Pas si facilement. Il nous fallut attendre plusieurs jours avant qu'il ose reparler à nouveau. Il s'était risqué une fois mais ne paraissait pas vouloir recommencer. Je n'avais pas rêvé pourtant, il l'avait bien prononcé ce mot. D'une voix neutre, très doucement, presque un ronronnement. Les jours suivants, je multipliais les questions. Tu as faim ? Tu veux des frites ? Mais malin, il me prenait la main et la tirait vers le panier de pommes de terre. Tant pis, il fallait sans doute lui laisser le temps. Peut-être fallait-il qu'il le décide : je veux parler ou je ne veux pas ? En tout cas, il en était capable. Je maîtrisais mal mon impatience d'entendre d'autres mots et je le plongeais malgré moi dans un tourbillon de paroles et de questions. « Non » fut l'acquisition suivante. Cela ne m'étonnait pas de lui. Entêté, toujours à vouloir décider de tout, cédant difficilement. Pas de doute, ce non correspondait bien à son caractère volontaire. Le « oui » est venu beaucoup plus tard. Je continuais à lui poser des questions : c'est ça que tu veux ? Pendant longtemps, il se cantonna à l'essentiel et répondait « ça » ou « veux » tout court.

Le plus difficile pour moi fut de m'empêcher d'anticiper ses besoins, ses désirs, comme je le faisais depuis si longtemps, pour lui imposer la nécessité de parler : faire semblant d'être distraite, de n'avoir pas vu, de ne pas comprendre vers quel objet il tendait ma main. Il parlait lorsqu'il était pris au piège en quelque sorte : contre sa volonté. Surpris par une question ou une affirmation fausse, la réponse venait malgré lui. Il se reprenait aussitôt comme s'il se disait : « Zut ! J'ai parlé ! » On sentait qu'il avait envie de ravaler sa réponse. Comme s'il y avait un danger à parler. Je n'insistais pas, soulagée de voir qu'il en était capable et qu'il saisissait bien le sens de ce qui se disait autour de lui.

Je réalisais que nous avions jusqu'à présent parlé assez librement, pensant qu'il n'écoutait pas vraiment. Qu'avait-il entendu et depuis combien de temps ? Il fallait revoir nos comportements et surveiller nos paroles. Nous avions là un petit espion qui paraissait encore souvent plongé dans une méditation profonde, aveugle à ce que nous faisions, sourd à nos conversations. Qu'en était-il vraiment ? Sa grand-mère paternelle nous disait : « Il entend tout, il comprend tout cet enfant-là, il vous surprendra... » C'était bien difficile à croire à une certaine époque. Sa conscience s'ouvrait au monde extérieur très certainement, ses sens s'aiguisaient, l'amélioration de ses perceptions lui permettait de « capter » mieux et davantage.

Appréhender l'environnement

Les séances avec moi ont peu à peu aidé à développer sa conscience du monde extérieur. Paul semblait mieux se rappeler les choses apprises ou vécues et se servir davantage et à bon escient de ce qu'il savait. Son regard n'était plus vide, comme tourné vers l'intérieur, mais traduisait peu à peu ses émotions, sa curiosité, son étonnement. Son visage était plus expressif. Il y avait comme un questionnement, absent auparavant. Il réagissait aux événements extérieurs et tentait de les comprendre, surmontant sa peur, il raisonnait sur ses perceptions du monde environnant. Son esprit commençait à analyser, à faire des déductions, à stocker des informations, à les trier d'une façon qui se rapprochait de la nôtre. Il apprenait à se servir de sa mémoire pour enregistrer des images durables qui, par conséquent, lui resservaient plus tard. Avec cette compréhension plus globale, ses peurs l'abandonnaient. Avec les mots, il apprivoisait les phénomènes. Ceux-ci n'étaient plus aussi surprenants si on pouvait les expliquer et les nommer. Et si tous les gens donnaient le même nom à ces choses et à ces phénomènes, c'était quelque chose d'immuable, donc de rassurant. Je lui montrais que la fonction et le nom des objets ne variaient pas. C'étaient des codes communs à tous et à lui aussi maintenant. Il en tirait une grande fierté. Il observait et commençait à comprendre quand et comment les autres s'en servaient. Faire comme les autres était sa motivation. Comprendre et imiter. Un pas immense.

Laure le mit aux jeux d'ordinateur, qu'il accepta facilement puisqu'il était fasciné par les images. Pendant longtemps, il ne fit pas le lien entre la souris et le curseur sur l'écran. Nous faisions donc toutes les manipulations à sa place. Je désespérais : quand fera-t-il cette connexion entre le mouvement de sa main sur la souris et sa représentation à l'écran ? J'entends encore défiler les 500 images et les mots correspondants de l'*Imagier* du Père Castor, qu'il fallait lui mettre en boucle pendant des heures. Il ne parlait qu'à peine et mon cœur se serrait de chagrin et de jalousie d'entendre ces voix d'enfants si jeunes, répéter ces mots et rire pendant la ritournelle du générique. L'émotion me submerge encore aujourd'hui lorsque Paul met ce CD-Rom pour sa petite cousine.

« *Rain Man* »

Un jour, pendant que les images défilaient accompagnées des mots et que Paul « bricolait » dans sa chambre, je l'entendis répéter les mots à voix basse... un chuchotement presque inaudible, machinal. Tendant l'oreille sans me déplacer, je fus stupéfaite d'entendre qu'il ne répétait pas les mots, mais les anticipait : il prononçait le mot de l'image qui n'était pas encore à l'écran, il connaissait les 500 images par cœur et dans l'ordre, et les récitait de la pièce d'à-côté avec une intonation strictement identique à celle de l'enregistrement. J'avais bien lu quelque part que les enfants autistes ont des capacités de mémorisation un peu particulières, mais cette façon robotique de mémoriser me fit froid dans le dos. Je courus lui trouver en librairie un autre CD-Rom qui donnait la définition des objets en phrases complètes et cherchais le moyen d'assouplir son mode de pensée et de mémorisation. Allait-il devenir un dictionnaire ambulant, récitant des définitions apprises par cœur sans en comprendre le premier mot ? Un *Rain Man* récitant l'annuaire par cœur ? L'écholalie allait-elle devenir son moyen d'expression ? Les quelques mots qui lui échappaient ne permettaient pas de le savoir. Beaucoup en passaient par là, selon Barbara.

Il fallait trouver le moyen d'éviter ce stade ou de le raccourcir. J'introduisis au cours des séances, un atelier basé sur le dialogue. Laure avait des marionnettes et j'inventais des petits dialogues entre elles. Elles devinrent le mime préféré de Paul et j'obtins des éclats de rire, un peu bizarres, comme un son de poupée cassée. Minnie et Babar se rencontraient donc au début de chaque séance :

« – Bonjour madame, comment allez-vous ?

– Oh ! Très bien monsieur, et vous-même ?

– Avec ce beau temps, c'est bien agréable d'aller se promener. Regardez ces belles fleurs, des rouges, des jaunes, des bleues et ces papillons comme c'est joli !

– Et ces oiseaux qui chantent, vous les entendez ?

(Il suivait avec attention mais les éclats de rire, c'était quand il y avait bagarre.)

– Quels oiseaux ? Ce sont des canards !

– Mais non, ce sont des oiseaux : ils font cui-cui...

– Pas du tout, ce sont des canards : ils font coin-coin !

– Mais si !

– Mais non ! !

– Je vous dis que SI !

– Je vous dis que NON !

(Les marionnettes se battent.)

– Paf !

– Boum !

– Aïe ! »

Il riait et réclamait « encore, encore ». Il fallait recommencer encore et encore. Je changeais d'histoire pour varier les mots et les réactions mais il fallait que la chute soit la même. Pendant longtemps, il refusa d'enfiler une marionnette pour me répondre : l'échange ne lui venait pas, les mots sortaient difficilement. Je n'insistais pas, le découragement venait vite quand il constatait ses incapacités et il se repliait dans sa coquille aussitôt.

Son langage se développait de façon étrange. Sa voix tout d'abord était inhabituelle. Plutôt haut perchée, mais sans la moindre intonation, plate. Lorsqu'il commença à répondre à nos questions, il reprenait la fin de la phrase : « Tu veux un cookie ou un BN ? » « Ou un BN ? » était répété avec strictement la même intonation que la mienne. Il ne reposait pas la question bien sûr, il y répondait à sa façon. C'était à chaque fois surprenant.

« Paul, tu ne veux pas mettre tes bottes ? » « Mettre tes bottes ? » signifiait qu'il était d'accord. C'était difficile à corriger. Lui dire : « Tu dois répondre : *je* veux mettre *mes* bottes » était compliqué pour lui. Maman me fait un reproche ? Pourtant j'ai dit oui ! Alors pourquoi me reprend-elle ? D'autre part, le *je* n'était pas acquis. Pour cela, il fallait encore travailler sur l'image qu'il avait de lui et de son corps, encore très floue. Pendant longtemps il nous dirait en pleurant : « J'ai mal à l'horloge » ou « J'ai mal au mur ». Il faudrait du temps avant qu'il puisse exprimer une douleur en précisant qu'il avait mal *au* genou parce qu'il s'était cogné *sur* l'horloge.

Il était encore à un niveau bien inférieur à un enfant de son âge sur le plan du langage et de la socialisation, mais sur celui de la motricité fine et de la motricité globale, ses capacités correspondaient à son âge. Malgré tout, nous étions encore loin d'un comportement normal. Sa frustration, lorsqu'il ne pouvait exprimer ses émotions, le poussait toujours à se frapper des poings sur la tête. C'était le signe que nous étions allés un peu trop loin pendant la séance, qu'il s'était senti débordé probablement. Je lui écartais les poignets aussitôt, pour le prendre dans mes bras et le balancer doucement, le consoler d'une litanie qui le calmait toujours : Paul est formidable, Paul est intelligent, Paul comprend tout, Maman est fière de Paul, fière de toi. Maman t'aime beaucoup, beaucoup, beaucoup.

« *La* » *bonne école*

Nous avions eu le diagnostic du neurologue en novembre, les leçons avaient commencé en décembre. Rudimentaires au départ, elles s'étaient peu à peu étoffées. Nous avions réadapté chaque semaine le programme de Paul en complétant ou en modifiant constamment les ateliers en fonction de ses refus, de ses insuffisances ou de ses progrès. En cinq mois, ces leçons de plus en plus élaborées et diversifiées avaient permis des progrès certains dans de nombreux domaines. Cependant, sans école nous étions toujours dans une impasse. Je consacrais les demi-journées de halte-garderie à poursuivre mes recherches pour trouver une petite école, à effectifs réduits, sécurisante pour lui et adaptée à ses besoins.

Les contacts avec les directeurs d'établissement étaient tout d'abord chaleureux et positifs, j'essayais d'expliquer au mieux la situation, sans dissimuler l'absence de langage de Paul et ses difficultés de communication. Observant Paul qui visitait couloirs et salles de classe, on m'assurait qu'« il y en avait d'autres dans ce cas » et qu'on le prendrait en charge volontiers. Je sortais des rendez-vous pleine d'optimisme et d'espoir. Or, étant dans l'obligation de se faire communiquer le dossier scolaire de Paul, puisque je m'adressais à des écoles privées sous contrat, ces mêmes directeurs m'envoyaient quelques jours plus tard des refus catégoriques sans même prendre la peine de les motiver. La CCPE avait dû, à notre insu, mentionner dans son dossier une psychose infantile qui, contrairement aux troubles envahissants du développement, l'excluait d'une prise en charge scolaire.

L'Éducation nationale se défausse ainsi des éléments embarrassants. Faute d'école, les parents sont contraints de placer leur enfant en hôpital de jour, en attendant que de rares places se libèrent dans des écoles ou des classes spécialisées.

Chaque refus était une offense dégradante et nous plongeait dans la consternation. J'étais anéantie par cette injustice que je n'avais pas même les moyens de combattre. Notre recours en annulation auprès de l'instance supérieure, la CDES, de la décision de la CCPE de n'accorder qu'une heure et demie par semaine était restée sans réponse. Cette absence de réponse nous démontrait que la CDES était complice des décisions de la CCPE et que nous n'avions aucune chance de sortir Paul de ce piège. Je tentai alors ma dernière adresse.

J'avais à nouveau emmené Paul avec moi par souci de franchise en espérant qu'il ne montre pas trop de comportements bizarres. Je n'avais aucune intention de cacher ou de minimiser les difficultés. La directrice lui dit bonjour, et, bien que je meure d'envie d'attraper mon fils pour le forcer à la regarder et à lui répondre, je m'en abstins. Il murmura quelque chose en lui jetant un coup d'œil et se précipita pour examiner les nombreuses cassettes vidéo et les jeux qu'elle avait dans son bureau. Elle l'observait avec attention pendant que j'expliquais pour la énième fois le parcours de Paul, son suivi médical et psychologique, l'orthophonie, la psychomotricité. Je lui parlai aussi de mon travail avec lui et des résultats obtenus. Elle m'écouta patiemment jusqu'au moment où j'expliquais nos démêlés avec l'Éducation nationale, et je sentis à sa réaction qu'elle désapprouvait la situation. Je reprenais espoir, enfin, quelqu'un paraissait être « de notre côté ». À la fin de l'entretien, se levant, elle me dit : « Revenez avec votre mari, parce qu'on va lui donner sa chance... à Paul. » Et haussant la voix, elle dit : « Tu es d'accord Paul pour venir dans notre école ? » Le cœur battant, les yeux embués, je lui serrais la main, au bord de la syncope. J'avais livré une bataille importante, ce n'était pas la dernière mais elle était décisive. Sœur M. m'avait donné de nouvelles forces. Nous avions encore cinq mois devant nous avant la rentrée pour qu'il soit capable de saisir cette chance. Il fallait réussir à tout prix.

J'appelais Barbara aussitôt pour partager cette nouvelle. Enchantée elle aussi, mais toujours pragmatique, elle dressa immédiatement le plan de bataille : « Apporte-moi les notes que tu as prises sur les dernières leçons pour que je sache exactement où il en est, je les veux demain ! » Pour elle, il n'y avait jamais un instant à perdre, elle allait me concocter un programme toujours plus adapté, toujours plus approfondi. Nous fêtâmes quand même cette victoire au restaurant, où Barbara me remonta comme un ressort pour mobiliser toute mon énergie et ma volonté – comme si j'en avais besoin à ce moment-là ! – pour lever les nombreux obstacles restants avant la scolarisation en septembre.

Un psychiatre stupéfait

J'avais une conscience globale des progrès que Paul faisait mais c'est avec des personnes extérieures que je voyais réellement le chemin parcouru. Lorsque je revenais dans des lieux que j'avais quittés quelques mois auparavant, par exemple. Les rendez-vous très espacés chez le psychiatre ou le pédiatre me fournissaient aussi l'occasion de mesurer les progrès, puisqu'en y arrivant je me revoyais avec Paul et son comportement d'alors, dans tous ses détails. Je pouvais comparer et, grâce aux réactions de cette autre personne, vérifier l'exactitude de mes souvenirs. Parmi ces visites, je fis un retour chez le psychiatre recommandé par l'école, qui n'avait pas revu Paul depuis le début de notre programme.

Ce jour-là, Paul entra dans la pièce d'une démarche assurée, retira son manteau d'un geste délibéré, son regard résolu a fait le tour de la pièce, se remémorant probablement ses rares visites. Il ne répondit pas au « Bonjour, Paul » mais regarda posément le psychiatre d'un air de dire : « Ça va, je t'ai vu, je t'ai reconnu mais ce n'est pas toi qui m'intéresses ici. » Aussitôt, il alla ouvrir l'armoire pour en sortir la caisse de jouets contenant des animaux en plastique dont il se souvenait parfaitement. Le médecin l'observait médusé et il pouvait constater, à ma grande fierté, que Paul « savait véritablement jouer ». Il faisait lui aussi la différence entre ces manipulations bizarres, dénuées de sens, des séances antérieures et le fait que là le dinosaure s'attaque au lion, que le lion contre-attaque mais que le dinosaure et ses grandes mâchoires finissent par égorger le lion qui s'affale immobile. Normal, logique... Paul les replaça dans leur boîte, se releva pour chercher la maison Fisher-Price. Plus rapide que le médecin qui se penchait pour l'aider, il tira la petite chaise, s'installa en face de la table et, de ses gestes précis et mesurés, ouvrit et ferma les portes de la maison, cherchant quelque chose à y introduire. Interdit, immobile, le médecin l'observait toujours. Paul continuait, non sans lui jeter régulièrement des regards ni curieux, ni craintifs qui semblaient signifier : je t'ai à l'œil mais tu peux parler avec Maman, j'attendrai.

Finalement, le psychiatre dit en s'éclaircissant la voix : « Paul a beaucoup changé. » Je souris à l'euphémisme. Il se reprit un peu vexé pour me demander de façon alambiquée ce que j'avais fait pour obtenir ces résultats. Je lui racontai succinctement mes recherches, mes lectures et lui demandai s'il connaissait ces méthodes d'apprentissages américaines. Il prit un air dubitatif :

« J'en ai entendu parler.

– Vous en êtes-vous déjà inspiré dans le travail que vous faites avec les enfants que l'on vous confie à l'hôpital de jour ? Pourriez-vous me détailler leur emploi du temps hebdomadaire individuel ? »

Il ne voulait pas répondre, j'aurais trouvé cela insuffisant quoiqu'il dise.

« Et vous, qu'est-ce que vous avez fait ? »

Je le sentais sincèrement curieux.

« Euh... Six heures de rééducation permanente et une heure trente d'enseignement structuré, quotidiennement.

– Étonnant... »

Je commençais à détailler le principe d'intervention précoce, la rééducation continue, les leçons et leurs ateliers.

« Étonnant... »

Je parlais de Barbara, de son aide, de ses programmes, des enfants qu'elle faisait travailler et de ses résultats, des parents qui s'étaient mis, eux aussi, au travail grâce à ses programmes. Le voyant passionné, je lui proposais une rencontre qui lui aurait permis de mieux connaître ces méthodes :

« Mmm... et vous comment vous sentez-vous ?

– Je n'ai vraiment pas le temps de me pencher sur la question ! Paul reprend l'école en septembre, il y a encore du travail...

– Une école... euh...

– Une école *normale* oui, dans une classe *normale* ! »

J'insistais sur le normal sachant qu'il évitait toujours ce mot.

« Étonnant... »

Un peu lassée, même si sa stupéfaction me flattait, je me levais.

« Hum ! Paul, tu reviendras me voir ? »

Je savais qu'il pouvait répondre, et le médecin devait aussi le pressentir, mais Paul était encore très avare de ses mots. Il se leva, rangea sa chaise, me regarda, un demi-sourire de connivence aux lèvres, hocha la tête comme pour dire : « Si ça peut vous faire plaisir... » Il remit son manteau, ouvrit la porte et se retourna d'un air de dire : « Moi j'y vais, pas de discussions interminables, s'il vous plaît. »

Des discussions, il y en avait eu, pas très nombreuses mais plutôt houleuses. Au premier rendez-vous, je n'avais pas voulu « poser mes valises », mais j'avais en revanche posé trop de questions. J'avais cependant accepté l'heure hebdomadaire de psychomotricité.

Au second, sachant qu'il aurait son mot à dire à la prochaine réunion de la commission, j'avais quémandé quelques heures d'école supplémentaires pour Paul. J'avais essayé de le convaincre que Paul ne ferait aucun progrès au rythme de trois quarts d'heure par semaine. Ce qui naturellement donnerait raison aux membres de la commission : « On vous l'avait bien dit. Vous voyez bien qu'il n'est pas scolarisable ! »

« C'est ce que vous voulez, *vous*, me dit le psychiatre, mais est-ce bien ce dont votre fils a besoin ?

– Je ne sais pas exactement ce que l'hôpital de jour lui apporterait, mais c'est non, pour l'instant. Aujourd'hui, je suis convaincue qu'il a surtout besoin d'école. Alors, je vous demande de faire votre possible pour influer sur cette décision de la commission. » J'étais de plus en plus convaincue, en voyant le résultat des leçons et de cette rééducation constante, d'une part que les parents obtenaient certainement plus de résultats que des étrangers, même spécialistes, et d'autre part qu'il régresserait à l'hôpital avec des enfants comme lui ou plus profondément atteints, dont on ne corrigeait pas forcément efficacement les comportements déviants. À ce sujet, j'avais d'ailleurs cessé de parler à la psychomotricienne de ma rééducation avec Paul, car elle avait d'évidence trouvé mes méthodes beaucoup trop énergiques, mes exigences sans doute traumatisantes pour l'enfant (puisque l'on sait qu'il n'en est pas capable, pourquoi insister ? Pourquoi espérer le rendre normal ?) et elle désapprouvait le fait que je ne m'en sois pas totalement remise à des services spécialisés.

Au deuxième trimestre, la commission avait encore refusé d'augmenter son temps d'école, il était clair que ce psychiatre n'avait pas voulu – pas pu ? – nous soutenir. Mon mari se chargea alors seul du règlement de compte au troisième rendez-vous. Le psychiatre l'accueillit en s'excusant de son retard, le fit entrer dans son bureau et attendit que mon mari engage la conversation. À son retour, mon mari m'en fit le récit :

« Que pensez-vous de la situation ? commença mon mari.

– Elle me paraît satisfaisante.

– Ah bon ! Eh bien vous êtes le seul à trouver cela satisfaisant. Et que préconisez-vous pour l'avenir ?

– La poursuite de la fréquentation de l'école à raison d'une demi-journée par semaine et plus de mobilisation vers l'hôpital de jour. Faites-nous confiance, il faut poser vos valises !

– Il ne s'agit pas d'une question de confiance mais de pertinence d'un diagnostic. Devant un cas aussi sérieux et face aux conséquences de vos préconisations du mois d'octobre dernier, nous sommes allés consulter le Pr X au mois de novembre.

– Je le connais, c'est un neurologue de réputation internationale.

– Il a eu un diagnostic et des recommandations résolument opposées aux vôtres et nous a incités à placer Paul dans une petite structure scolaire à temps plein car il craint que le peu de fréquentation scolaire ne le fasse régresser. Par ailleurs, il présente l'avantage de l'avoir vu récemment contrairement à vous, qui préconisez des mesures lourdes de conséquences pour l'avenir de l'enfant... mais quand l'avez-vous vu la dernière fois ?

– Je trouve vos questions pressantes.

– Non, elles sont précises. Ne cherchez pas, c'était il y a six mois. »

Ce troisième rendez-vous nous avait donné le sentiment d'une collusion totale entre deux administrations qui se soutiennent au mépris de leur mission fondamentale. L'une se débarrassant d'éléments ne rentrant pas dans la norme tandis que l'autre les accepte en remplissant ses hôpitaux de jour dans une mixité thérapeutique qui broie ceux qui sont à la marge. Ce sentiment étant confirmé par le fait que ce psychiatre n'avait jamais posé le moindre diagnostic, mais s'était attaché uniquement à l'avis de quasi-exclusion de l'école en faveur de l'accueil dans son service. Dès que nous souhaitions en savoir un peu plus, nous avions droit à la formule incantatoire plus digne du gourou ou de la secte que de la faculté de médecine, « posez vos valises ».

Nous sommes tombés d'accord sur le fait que revoir ce psychiatre n'était d'aucun intérêt pour Paul. Je tenais cependant à ce qu'il reconduise l'année suivante l'heure hebdomadaire de psychomotricité où Paul allait avec grand plaisir. Il me fallait donc retourner le voir et j'étais curieuse de voir sa réaction à la transformation de Paul.

Je ressortais donc de ce dernier rendez-vous avec des sentiments mêlés. Le psychiatre avait reconnu le succès de la méthode mais n'avait pas un instant remis *ses* méthodes en question. Je pensais à tous ces enfants broyés dans ce système, à qui on n'avait pas laissé la moindre chance, à ces parents accablés qui finissent en désespoir de cause par condamner leur enfant à des voies de garage avec l'approbation de tous les médecins et psychologues qui n'ont pas d'autre solution à proposer. J'enrageais de constater que ces méthodes d'intervention précoces étaient sûrement connues en France, mais que les médecins n'en parlaient pas aux parents qui venaient les consulter. Pourquoi ? N'y croyaient-ils pas ou se sentaient-ils menacés par ce moyen qui aurait permis aux parents d'avoir de meilleurs résultats qu'eux ? Se seraient-ils sentis dépossédés de leur pouvoir de guérir au profit de parents prêts à d'immenses sacrifices pour leur enfant ? Je commençais à cette époque à me dire : « Il faut faire quelque chose. »

J'avais toujours cette impression qu'école et médecins se soutenaient pour éloigner les enfants du système scolaire, puis les soustraire à l'influence des parents en les mettant en hôpital de jour : « Ils y font des progrès remarquables... », mais alors pourquoi ne les reprend-on pas à l'école après ces semaines, ces mois passés dans ces services ?

On fait miroiter aux parents que l'enfant pourra retourner un jour à l'école parce que c'est ce qu'ils veulent entendre par-dessus tout : seul gage évident de normalité, rester dans le système ou y revenir par la suite. On leur ment. Le pire étant que, par-là, on cherche à les décharger de leur responsabilité et de leur rôle de parents en leur disant qu'ils ne peuvent rien faire. « Faites confiance aux médecins et à l'équipe soignante… » Non pas qu'ils ne soient pas en mesure de faire un excellent travail, mais exclure les parents de leur rôle d'éducateurs est inadmissible, exclure un enfant de l'école avant quatre ans, empêcher sa réinscription dans une autre école malgré l'accord des personnes concernées et le condamner par là à l'hôpital et aux instituts spécialisés sachant qu'il n'aura guère de chance d'en sortir, est criminel.

J'appelai Barbara pour lui raconter cette entrevue, déçue par le peu d'intérêt qu'avait montré le médecin pour les thérapies parentales. Elle n'en était pas du tout étonnée, elle avait déjà rencontré cette réaction. Elle ne s'attarda pas sur le sujet et me dit : « Il fait partie de ceux qui, même avec des preuves évidentes sous les yeux, ne veulent pas admettre la réussite si elle ne vient pas d'eux, alors laisse tomber. »

Branle-bas de combat

Il nous restait trois mois avant la rentrée de septembre et Paul était loin d'être prêt à tout ce qu'une scolarisation supposait. Barbara m'expliqua la nécessité d'un programme beaucoup plus structuré que celui que j'avais suivi jusqu'à présent. Il lui paraissait indispensable de diviser les leçons en ateliers qui permettraient des apprentissages plus spécifiques. Nous avions dépassé le stade où il fallait lui donner envie d'apprendre et de participer puisqu'il me tirait de lui-même vers notre espace de travail, même s'il rechignait à de nombreuses activités. Ce programme plus diversifié reprenait les axes importants : le développement de la logique et du raisonnement, l'appréhension du temps, de l'espace et son intégration dans cet espace grâce à la motricité.

En premier lieu, *l'atelier de motricité,* qui reposait sur des exercices de gymnastique, de yoga, de jeux favorisant la communication à l'aide de ballon, de quilles, de cerceaux et divers instruments de musique. Les exercices devaient aussi favoriser la perception des objets et leur trajectoire dans l'espace et par rapport à lui ; anticipation de ces trajectoires et adaptation de ses gestes à ces trajectoires très diverses et plus ou moins rapides. Enfin, ajuster ses mouvements, proportionner ses réactions pour maîtriser son corps. Dans ces activités, Paul s'appliquait un moment, puis se mettait à faire n'importe quoi. Je changeais alors d'activité un moment puis reprenais la précédente pour qu'il surmonte sa difficulté. Obtenir un petit progrès tous les jours lui faisait prendre conscience de ses capacités et l'encourageait.

L'atelier d'écoute comprenait l'identification des sons et leur comparaison grâce à divers objets et instruments de musique. Le plus difficile étant d'amener Paul à « se poser » : faire doucement les bruits demandés, se concentrer, s'appliquer à suivre l'ordre. Également, l'appréhension du silence par rapport au bruit, la capacité à se déplacer silencieusement, le jeu avec sa voix, la reconnaissance d'une comptine dont on n'entend que la mélodie. Enfin, un travail sur le rythme et la compréhension avec des cassettes de comptines et de chansons : *Enfance et Musique*, *Jeux chantés-Jeux dansés*, *À l'écoute du monde sonore*, *Vivre le son*... Dans ce domaine aussi, nous utiliserions les CD-Roms (*Père Castor*, *À la découverte des mots*, *Petit Ours Brun*, *Winnie l'Ourson*, *Atout-Clic*, *Éveil-lecture*, *Oui-Oui*, etc.) et puis, bien sûr, le Loto des sons dont j'ai parlé précédemment.

Les cassettes et les CD-Roms servaient aussi pour *l'expression corporelle* à mi-chemin entre la motricité et l'écoute. Enchaîner des mouvements, reproduire les situations suggérées par les images et les sons, se voir dans un miroir et se reconnaître en train de faire des mouvements. Accepter sa maladresse et surmonter ses réticences ou sa gaucherie, oser le mouvement et vaincre sa timidité. Très peu conscient de son corps, ces exercices étaient difficiles pour lui. Il lui faudrait deux à trois ans encore pour surmonter son manque de confiance et réaliser l'étendue de ses capacités physiques.

L'atelier langage était basé principalement, dans ce premier temps, sur le commentaire d'images de toutes sortes. Paul aimait particulièrement regarder et m'entendre commenter les photos des albums. Elles servaient à repérer des lieux, des personnes, des situations, des époques : dans l'ancienne maison... cousine Élisabeth petite... cousine Élisabeth plus grande... à la plage, l'été... à la plage, l'hiver... quand Laure était bébé, quand Paul est né, etc. Au début, je les commentais toujours de la même façon en utilisant les mêmes mots pour les situations similaires, cela afin de lui donner des repères fixes : questions formulées de la même manière, phrases courtes, vocabulaire précis. J'avais aussi de nombreux livres d'histoires simples qui permettaient d'enrichir et de préciser son vocabulaire. J'essayais au fur et à mesure d'approfondir une idée, un thème par jour en regroupant des livres et des images, des photos ou des publicités, des jeux parfois. Par exemple, je prenais pour thème le visage et le corps ; il fallait détailler toutes les parties, les décrire et commenter leur usage : la bouche sert à manger, à rire, à parler, à sourire, à se taire, à respirer, à souffler. Elle peut-être de forme fine, grande, ronde, étirée... Quand je ne trouvais pas d'images, je lui dessinais des bonshommes, des gros, des maigres, des bossus, des laids et je lui disais : « Il est beau ? – Bah ! Pas beau, faisait-il. – Si, il est très beau ! – non, beurk ! » Cela permettait de petits dialogues chaque jour plus élaborés. Puis, je prenais le thème de la ferme : les animaux et leurs bruits, qu'il devait imiter par la voix et par le corps ; les thèmes de la ville, de l'habitat, des métiers, des sports, des saisons, etc. Les nombreux puzzles que j'avais achetés lui permettaient également de construire des petites phrases. « Je mets le soleil en haut à gauche », de même que commenter la disposition des objets avec le Jeu de topologie ou de Repérage logique.

L'atelier tactile et olfactif reprenait de façon plus structurée la rééducation des sens que je faisais pendant la journée avec des objets à toucher et à sentir, grâce à différents jeux comme le Loto tactile ou le Loto des odeurs. Je m'efforçais de faire utiliser à Paul un vocabulaire de plus en plus précis, de lui faire deviner, en regardant simplement l'objet, sa consistance, son poids, son goût. Ensuite, je mettais des objets dans un sac de tissu : en plongeant sa main dedans et en touchant l'objet, Paul devait deviner ce que c'était. Plus tard pour exercer sa mémoire, je cachai l'un des quatre ou cinq objets, et il devait me dire duquel il s'agissait, une fois tous les objets sortis du sac : j'étais un voleur qui lui avait pris son sac, il me poursuivait pour me le reprendre et je lui demandais : « Qu'est-ce qu'il a pris le voleur dans ton sac ? » Paul montrait encore beaucoup de réticences à toucher de nombreux objets, en particulier ce qui lui paraissait humide, collant ou gluant et, bien sûr, tout ce qui « laissait des traces ».

L'atelier graphisme servait d'abord à le réconcilier avec les feutres, les pastels, la craie et la peinture. J'avais rassemblé toutes sortes de coloriages, de dessins à compléter et de cahiers d'apprentissage de l'écriture. Paul refusait de repasser sur des courbes ou des boucles, des traits verticaux et horizontaux, comme s'il avait peur de laisser quelque chose de lui sur ces pages. Je luttai longtemps pour qu'il fasse une page par jour, en m'ingéniant à lui faire oublier cette peur d'écrire. Il passa le cap avec le jeu Crayon vole : il devait repasser sur des figures géométriques ou sur des lettres au feutre sur un plastique transparent, effaçable à volonté. Il effaçait donc immédiatement la boucle ou le trait qu'il venait de faire. À force de s'entraîner et d'être félicité, Paul finit par ne plus avoir peur de laisser cette trace de lui : quelque chose lui appartenant et qui pourrait lui échapper. Il avait le contrôle du support : il pouvait effacer cette trace ou déchirer ce support, donc le faire disparaître. Et tout cela n'avait pas de conséquences sur lui, sur son intégrité physique. Peu à peu, il accepta plus facilement de dessiner, de laisser tel quel son dessin sans le détruire. Nous pûmes commencer les cahiers de graphisme, mais il se lassait vite si ce n'était pas un jeu. Lorsqu'il fallait repasser sur des traits ou rester entre deux lignes, je lui disais que c'était une voiture sur la route, qu'il ne fallait pas aller dans le fossé et je faisais le bruit de la voiture, des accélérations ou d'un accident. Le poussin rejoignait sa maman en pointillé sur le chemin, le lapin courait vers sa carotte, l'avion faisait des loopings, etc. Il fallait toujours imaginer un contexte pour qu'il oublie qu'il était en train d'écrire. Je trouvais chez Nathan suffisamment de matériel ludique, crayons, feutres, craies, papier, cahiers de dessins et d'écriture qui lui donnait davantage envie de collaborer que le matériel d'écriture classique.

Pas de répit pour les braves

Lorsque Paul s'était remis à parler, j'avais eu un sentiment de délivrance tel qu'il me semblait que, pour la première fois depuis deux ans, je pouvais à nouveau respirer. J'avais retenu mon souffle si longtemps que j'avais l'impression de redécouvrir le monde. Je m'ouvrais à des pensées et à des activités que je m'étais interdites tout ce temps. Prendre une demi-journée pour déambuler dans Paris, entrer dans des boutiques ou des librairies au hasard me semblait d'une futilité délicieuse. J'avais naturellement des scrupules à ne pas être à la maison en train de préparer la séance du soir, mais je les étouffais en me disant qu'« il était finalement reparti », que si une école l'avait accepté, c'st qu'il serait capable de suivre et qu'il ferait certainement d'énormes progrès l'année suivante. La réaction du psychiatre aussi m'avait confortée dans la confiance que je pouvais faire à Paul à présent. Je savourais la sensation de renouveau du printemps et vivais la saison comme si c'était la première. Relâchant mes efforts et la pression sur Paul, je sautais des séances pendant le week-end, le faisais travailler dans sa chambre plutôt que dans notre pièce réservée et dans une atmosphère moins contraignante.

« Où en es-tu ? me demanda un jour Barbara au téléphone.

– Euh, je n'avance pas tellement, avec tous ces week-ends et ces ponts à la campagne, j'ai modifié un peu les activités...

– Tu n'avances pas dans le programme ?

– Si, si mais j'ai relâché un peu la pression... »

Elle se mit dans une rage folle.

« Et tu t'imagines que tu vas y arriver ! Alors, pour toi, ça y est, c'est fini, il a dit trois mots et tu considères qu'il est sorti d'affaire ! À quatre ans et demi, il fonctionne comme un enfant d'un an et demi et tu t'arrêtes...

– Tu exagères, il a fait d'énormes progrès...

– Mais ça ne suffit pas ! Est-ce que tu te rends compte que même si tu suivais ce programme d'arrache-pied pendant trois ans, on ne serait même pas sûres encore de l'en sortir ? Rien n'est joué, alors tu vas te remettre au boulot, encore plus qu'avant, pour avoir une toute petite chance d'y arriver. »

Elle avait raison, bien sûr. Je regardais avec consternation les valises que je préparais l'instant d'avant avec tant de joie à l'idée de ce mois entier dans la maison que nous louaient des amis sardes. Un mois de plage, d'enfants bronzés courant se jeter dans cette eau turquoise, si limpide et si chaude qu'on ne pouvait envier la Polynésie. Un mois de soirées sur la terrasse, d'amis italiens venant dîner, de conversations et de rires. Un mois de journées décontractées, libérées des soucis, légères enfin. Je repoussai, écœurée, ces valises remplies de maillots de bain, de tenues d'été que j'avais choisies avec plaisir pour la première fois depuis longtemps. Il me faudrait un sac de voyage entier pour emporter tout le matériel nécessaire à ces leçons qui nous gâcheraient nos journées comme d'inévitables corvées. Il le faudrait pourtant... à l'heure de la sieste peut-être, quand il fait trop chaud pour sortir. Ce ne serait pas pire que l'année précédente : Paul et ses scandales en public, Paul et ses disparitions qui nous rendaient fous. Je me souvenais trop bien du soir de notre arrivée...

Disparition

Nous avions débarqué du bateau dans la matinée et j'avais eu le temps de montrer aux enfants la plage toute proche avant le soir. Pendant le dîner, nous avions laissé Paul jouer dans la voiture garée en contrebas de la terrasse où nous étions attablés. Appelant les enfants pour les coucher, je vis que la voiture, allumée, toutes portes ouvertes était vide. Je cherchai Paul dans le jardin, tout autour de la maison, et l'appelai. Je n'attendais pas vraiment de réponse, mais au moins qu'il se montre. Personne. Mon mari l'avait cherché dans la maison. Il n'y était pas non plus. Depuis combien de temps était-il parti ? Sentant l'angoisse monter comme on remplit une bouteille et s'arrêter dans ma gorge pour l'étreindre, je dis à mon mari, statufié sur la terrasse : « Toi, sonne chez les voisins, prenez des torches, faites des groupes et remontez vers le haut du lotissement et vers la route. Je fais le bas, il a sans doute voulu retourner à la plage. Vite ! », lui criai-je, le voyant pétrifié, probablement avec la même idée que moi – y a-t-il encore des rapts d'enfants en Italie ?... en Sardaigne... on ne doit pas en retrouver des masses... « Et appelez les *carabinieri* si on n'a rien dans une heure. » Je descendis en courant le sentier menant à la plage, arrivai à la porte du lotissement restée ouverte sur la route, dégringolai les marches et sautai sur le rivage. J'appelai... scrutai la plage dans l'obscurité... remontai vers le parking en appelant toujours. Je déboulai dans le restaurant ouvert le soir et demandai, essoufflée, baragouinant un mélange d'italien et de français : « Vous avez vu un enfant, *bambino, solo, tre anni, francese*, tee-shirt blanc ? » Ils me regardaient éberlués : « *No, no, non lo visto.* » Je repris ma course vers les maisons et leurs jardins, perçant l'obscurité à la recherche d'une petite forme blanche, m'arrêtant et essayant d'entendre un appel, un cri, des pleurs par-dessus les battements désordonnés de mon cœur et repartant sur le sentier. Mon Dieu... pas lui... même si des gens le trouvent... il ne saura pas dire son nom... encore moins décrire la maison... Je finis par rencontrer un groupe de voisins qui le cherchaient toujours, ma fille avec eux. Je vis ses pieds nus, elle n'avait sans doute pas voulu rester seule à la maison.

« Où est Papa ?

– Je sais pas, il est parti avec des gens vers le haut.

– Rentrons à la maison, il faut que quelqu'un y soit. »

Je remerciai le groupe de voisins que je connaissais à peine, quelle gentillesse, quel dévouement ces Italiens, quand il y a des *bambini* en jeu, ils sont prêts à tout, pensai-je indûment. Revenant vers la maison, je vis mon mari, au milieu d'un autre groupe, qui nous expliqua qu'en sonnant aux portes quelqu'un leur avait dit que la baby-sitter d'une famille allemande avait elle aussi sonné, un enfant endormi dans les bras. Elle avait expliqué qu'elle avait trouvé cet enfant qui pleurait, qu'il n'avait pas répondu à ses questions et qu'elle cherchait ses parents... Aurait-elle l'idée de descendre jusqu'en bas du lotissement ? Je décidai de la retrouver avant qu'elle n'abandonne et rentre chez elle avec Paul ou qu'elle le dépose au commissariat. Je repartis sans courir cette fois, j'en aurais été incapable, je me sentais au bord de la syncope de soulagement, il était retrouvé : c'était forcément lui. Je parcourais à nouveau les allées sombres, les grands eucalyptus cachaient la lune et les buissons de lauriers étaient trop denses pour discerner une silhouette lointaine.

Quand je rentrai, vers minuit, mon mari me dit que la baby-sitter avait retrouvé notre maison grâce aux indications d'un groupe croisé sur son chemin. Il avait couché Paul qui ne s'était même pas réveillé. J'allais le voir. Il avait dû beaucoup pleurer pour que la sueur lui ait collé les cheveux au front de cette façon. Pas terrible, ce premier jour de vacances... « Même si on ferme le portail, les petits murets de pierre qui entourent le jardin ne sont pas assez hauts, il pourra s'échapper comme ça tous les jours... », dis-je à mon mari. « On avisera demain, répondit-il, assez pour aujourd'hui. » Exténués par ces deux jours de voyage et cette soirée éprouvante, nous allâmes enfin nous coucher.

Les jours suivants, je prenais Paul en filature, discrètement, dès qu'il sortait dans le jardin. Il parcourait les allées, examinait avec précaution les cactus et, lorsqu'il arrivait à la petite barrière du fond, il hésitait, attiré par le sentier inconnu. Je ne savais pas si les remontrances et les explications avaient traversé ce voile d'incompréhension, mais, dès qu'il mettait le pied dehors, j'arrivais en hurlant. Il sursautait et retournait aussitôt vers la maison. Il arriva, quand même, qu'une amie nous le ramène de la plage, alors que nous étions à la maison. Il lui fallait si peu de temps pour disparaître que nous étions sans cesse sur nos gardes, demandant à Laure de nous prévenir dès qu'il n'était plus avec elle. Nous le vîmes même une fois revenir seul, alors que nous n'avions pas eu le temps de nous apercevoir de son absence.

Civiliser le « sauvage »

J'avais bon espoir pour ces vacances-ci. Paul ne s'échappait plus des squares, ne rentrait plus seul dans les boutiques. Sans réellement prévenir, il s'assurait que nous l'avions vu ou que nous le suivions. Il nous gardait au coin de l'œil, sans pour autant s'inquiéter quand nous disparaissions de sa vue. Je l'avais tellement « briefé » à ce sujet-là, qu'il lui en restait quand même quelque chose. Viendrait plus tard la période où il ne supporterait pas que je ne sois plus dans son angle de vision, me suivrait partout comme un petit chien, collé à la porte de la salle de bains si j'y étais, appelant vingt-cinq fois par jour : « Maman ! – Oui, oui, je suis là… » Et si je ne répondais pas assez vite, il hurlerait des « Maman ! » angoissés et furieux qui me feraient sursauter à longueur de journée.

Pour le moment, les vacances s'annonçaient plus calmes que les précédentes, mais aussi très studieuses. Notre matériel encombra le séjour pendant tout le mois et les premiers jours furent désespérants. Paul refusait tout et se traînait par terre. La matinée de plage le fatiguait, mais il n'était pas question pour autant de dormir… Les 40 degrés qu'il faisait dehors à l'heure du déjeuner ne lui donnaient pas non plus envie de sortir. Finalement, le plus dur étant de réinstaller les habitudes dans un autre environnement et à d'autres heures, il s'y mit de nouveau, bien que cette façon moins ludique et plus structurée lui ait déplu. Je le forçai cependant, pensant que, si l'on attendait l'école pour le contraindre, il y aurait un gros risque d'échec.

Qu'il prenne l'habitude d'obéir aux consignes était indispensable. J'avais tout l'été pour augmenter son temps de concentration sur les exercices, imposer une certaine rigueur et le rendre plus malléable pendant les leçons, mais pour tout le reste aussi. L'enjeu était trop important. J'annotais les pages de son programme de remarques sur son travail et de réflexions sur ses difficultés, de même sur les comportements déviants qui subsistaient, car Barbara en aurait besoin pour établir un nouveau programme à la rentrée.

Ces notes m'étaient également utiles pour mieux me rendre compte de ce qu'il y avait à corriger au jour le jour et le garder à l'esprit. Il fallait que je sois plus exigeante dans la lutte contre ce comportement de petit sauvage : dire bonjour, merci, écouter ce qu'on me dit en m'arrêtant et en regardant la personne qui me parle et prendre le temps de lui répondre ; cesser de me promener tout nu parce que je pense les vêtements inutiles en cette chaleur ; accepter la douche sans crier ; ne pas manger debout ou dans le jardin, ni grimper sur les tables ; ou visiter les maisons des amis de fond en comble en réclamant l'aspirateur, leur demander de l'eau poliment au lieu d'aller me servir seul dans leur réfrigérateur... Il y avait du boulot pour le rendre présentable mais au moins maintenant il écoutait... un peu mieux et obéissait... un peu plus.

Si les gens auparavant le percevaient immédiatement comme anormal, aujourd'hui ils le jugeaient plutôt comme un enfant difficilement contrôlable et surtout très mal élevé. Je préférais passer pour une mère laxiste que pour la mère d'un enfant anormal. Et comme il était drôle, attirant et très attachant je voyais que nous passions pour ces parents complètement sous le charme de leur infernal rejeton, qui lui passent tout parce qu'il est « tellement mignon », sans se rendre compte que les autres rêvent de lui mettre une bonne toise. Ces parents qui craignent de gronder leur enfant parce qu'ils ont peur de se le mettre à dos, et qu'ils veulent par-dessus tout rester dans les bonnes grâces du petit tyran. Ce n'était pas vraiment notre cas. Nous revenions de si loin que tout ce qu'il faisait nous paraissait miraculeux.

Je pensais parfois que c'était si injuste par rapport à Laure, qui avait fait tout cela sans que nous nous soyons extasiés sur ses moindres faits et gestes. Nous étions très fiers d'elle, si vive, si intelligente, si précoce... Son frère, qui faisait la même chose aujourd'hui, avec au moins deux ans de retard par rapport à elle, lui, on l'admirait... J'étais consciente qu'il ne fallait pas tomber dans ce travers et je corrigeais ces réflexes dès que je m'en rendais compte pour la mettre en valeur aussi souvent que possible. Mais quand même, elle devait en souffrir. Elle a si bon cœur, elle était si contente pour lui et pour nous tous que je ne lui ai jamais vu de signes de jalousie. Elle aurait pu devenir mesquine et en vouloir à Paul. Elle s'est parfois plainte : « Tu ne t'occupes que de lui. » Je veillais alors à lui consacrer du temps pour elle seule et à rester à son écoute. Nous ne lui refusions rien qui puisse lui faire plaisir. Elle est aujourd'hui encore très gâtée, mais tout cela ne l'a pas « abîmée », pour moi, elle reste quasiment parfaite. Je lui serai à jamais reconnaissante pour tout ce qu'elle a donné, tout ce qu'elle a toléré et j'espère que Paul aussi, un jour, se rendra compte quelle part immense elle a eue dans le « sauvetage » de son petit frère.

Chapitre VIII

NOUVEAU DÉPART : LE RETOUR À L'ÉCOLE

Nous étions convenus que Paul referait une moyenne section, puisqu'on ne pouvait considérer les trois quarts d'heure par semaine comme une année normale. Les avantages d'une classe enfantine où les trois sections étaient réunies lui permettaient de passer d'un groupe à l'autre en fonction de ses capacités. Son langage encore très restreint et ses capacités de communication inégales le rapprochaient des enfants de la petite section ; il s'y sentirait à l'aise pour progresser. Ses acquis dans les autres domaines lui permettraient de s'intégrer avec les moyens. Il pourrait prendre exemple sur les enfants de grande section, qui étaient de son âge. Nous avons eu aussi beaucoup de chance avec l'institutrice, particulièrement patiente et compétente avec les enfants en difficulté.

J'allais le chercher à 11 h 30, essayant de croiser le regard de l'institutrice, que je me refusais à harceler tous les jours, pour savoir comment s'était passée la matinée. Elle me faisait de loin un signe d'approbation rassurant, mais je questionnais son auxiliaire dès que je le pouvais. Celle-ci me disait qu'il ne se pliait que rarement aux consignes, avait beaucoup de mal à s'intégrer, ses rares paroles allant plutôt dans le sens du refus. Cependant, il était toujours actif, paraissait content d'être là et s'intéressait aux activités tout en refusant de les partager. Elles restaient toutes deux optimistes disant qu'il lui faudrait du temps. Elles ne le forçaient jamais, mais lui proposaient les activités qui lui plaisaient. Dans cet environnement attentif et souple, il prit confiance et vint bientôt de lui-même se joindre au groupe pour les activités de chants et de comptines, puis pour les ateliers de jeux. Sa maîtresse était ravie qu'enfin il la prenne par la main pour lui demander quelque chose. Elle le poussait naturellement à verbaliser, mais sans insister. Peu à peu, dans ce climat de confiance, il se lança. Les mots devinrent plus fréquents, des phrases s'ébauchèrent. Cinq ans, il était temps !

À la fin du premier trimestre, Paul se pliait aux consignes la plupart du temps, suivait l'activité de son groupe sans rester à l'écart, s'exprimait pour demander des objets. J'avais si peur que l'on me dise que ce n'était pas suffisant que je mettais les bouchées doubles à la maison. Je craignais les régressions si fréquentes encore qui décourageraient l'institutrice et lui feraient signaler des handicaps insurmontables. Allait-on le laisser dans le groupe de moyenne section ? Passerait-il dans la classe supérieure ? Que d'inquiétudes encore. Et pourtant, il fallait lui faire confiance. Lui seul pouvait décider.

Tout au long de l'année, l'obligation dans laquelle je le mettais de faire un travail précis et de le finir selon des consignes bien établies le conduisit à une attitude d'acceptation, d'analyse des différents paramètres, puis d'action réfléchie adaptée aux circonstances, et ce également en dehors des leçons. L'obéissance à des ordres simples avait suivi dans la vie courante. Son acuité auditive s'était améliorée, mais il était loin de réagir correctement à tous les signaux. Il ne faisait plus le sourd lorsqu'il avait correctement entendu l'ordre, qu'il l'avait compris et que cet ordre rentrait dans le registre de ses acquisitions. Cependant, s'il n'en comprenait pas le bien-fondé, il n'obéissait pas. Il fallait donc lui en expliquer les raisons. Pouvaient-elles lui consacrer tout ce temps à l'école ? Quarante enfants, les trois sections réunies, était-ce possible pour lui ? Elles étaient si bien organisées que cela ne semblait pas poser problème.

Une entrave sérieuse, sa peur de l'échec

Au deuxième trimestre, l'institutrice et l'auxiliaire remarquèrent qu'il y avait un autre blocage : la peur le retenait dans de nombreux domaines. Il arrivait encore souvent que Paul refuse d'obéir à certaines consignes que donnait l'institutrice parce qu'il craignait de ne pas savoir faire. Parfois, il commençait le travail et l'abandonnait ou s'interrompait et le reprenait d'une autre façon. Il refusait de le finir comme elle l'exigeait car il avait peur de ne pas savoir et de se tromper. Il craignait l'erreur ou l'échec au point de refuser tout en bloc, sans même essayer l'activité proposée. Il fallut une grande patience à l'institutrice, par ailleurs suffisamment intuitive pour percer son comportement à jour. Dans ces cas-là, son mutisme et son indifférence apparente n'étaient qu'une protection, et non le signe d'une incapacité. En dépit des apparences, l'institutrice voyait qu'il comprenait ce qui lui était demandé mais elle savait qu'il fallait attendre que son blocage disparaisse. Cela devait poser des difficultés par rapport au groupe. Pourquoi Paul, et lui seul, n'était-il pas contraint de faire les activités imposées à tous, même aux plus jeunes ? C'est l'immense chance que nous avons eue. L'institutrice toléra cette distance le temps nécessaire. Savait-elle qu'il finirait par s'y mettre ? Comment lui fit-elle surmonter ses réticences et ses peurs ? Elle commença un travail qui dura longtemps. Lui donner confiance en ses capacités et lui faire accepter l'erreur, l'échec en les dédramatisant. Prendre le risque d'essayer, même sans être sûr de réussir. Ne pas calculer ses chances, mais se lancer spontanément sans cette peur paralysante de l'échec. Rater quelque chose mit longtemps Paul dans un état proche de la panique. Lorsqu'il put formuler son refus, il disait : « Non, je sais pas, je vais me tromper. » C'était très clair dans son esprit, mais trop souvent insurmontable.

Pendant un an et demi encore, c'était la réponse qu'il allait me faire pendant les leçons et probablement à l'école aussi. Alors, dans la vie courante, je ne manquais pas une occasion de dire : « Zut ! Je me suis trompée », en prenant un air très dégagé pour bien lui montrer que cela n'avait aucune importance. J'enrôlais Laure dans ce petit jeu d'« échecs » pour qu'il voie bien que tous pouvaient se tromper et ne s'en formalisaient pas. Par la suite, la colère a remplacé la peur. Il chiffonnait rageusement le dessin qu'il venait de faire parce que ce n'était pas ce qu'il voulait. Entre-temps, il exigeait que nous fassions pour lui tout ce qu'il avait envie de construire mais n'osait pas faire de lui-même. Et ce n'était pas un petit travail...

Des obsessions encombrantes

Cette manie commença vers la fin de l'année scolaire, se prolongea tout l'été et l'année suivante encore jusqu'à ce que, lassée, je commence à refuser toutes ces constructions pour l'inciter à les faire seul, lui montrant qu'il en était aussi capable que moi. Mais, en attendant, j'allais chercher deux à trois fois par semaine des cartons vides au supermarché. Il fallait reproduire à la perfection tout un ensemble électroménager, qui devait rester dans chaque maison de vacances jusqu'au prochain séjour. Je découpais et collais à l'aide d'un gros rouleau de Scotch un lave-vaisselle : il me montrait où dessiner les boutons qui devaient avoir la forme et la couleur exactes de celui de la cuisine. Je faisais semblant de ne pas savoir : il est rond, carré ? Je le mets ici, là ? Je colorie ou pas ? Ah ! d'accord, je dois mettre *on-off*... Tout y passait : le lave-linge, la cuisinière et le four, l'appareil photo, la tondeuse, le magnétoscope et ses cassettes qu'il acceptait de colorier quand même. En vacances, nous avions sur la terrasse de la maison, une enfilade d'appareils de toute sorte. Les visiteurs s'extasiaient, le voyant enfourner des plats dans son petit four minutieusement dessiné. Il mettait son maillot de bain dans le tambour de son lave-linge en rentrant de la plage. Il servait le café à nos amis en ayant préalablement moulu le vrai café en grains acheté à cet effet dans un moulin à main, jouet d'autrefois, mais qui fonctionnait réellement.

À Paris, l'appartement était encombré de ces appareils. Le couloir était bouché par une voiture à sa taille, faite de cartons peints à la gouache, de roues empruntées à un autre jouet, d'un rétroviseur de vélo, d'un klaxon, de la pédale de ma machine à coudre... Tout était imité dans le moindre détail, l'à-peu-près ne lui suffisait pas. La camionnette rouge de Postman Pat resta garée six mois dans l'entrée. Un ascenseur à sa taille bloqua l'entrée de sa chambre quelques mois également. Lorsque nous ne pouvions plus faire un pas dans sa chambre, je jetais discrètement une des plus vieilles constructions, abîmée par un usage immodéré et qu'il ne regretterait pas, vu le nombre de constructions plus récentes. Il pouvait passer des heures entières à fignoler ses appareils, ajouter des détails, exiger que je répare ce qui avait été déchiré. J'observais les réactions des témoins de cette période de folie constructrice : l'ahurissement total – ils sont timbrés ! – ou l'enthousiasme admiratif – mais c'est génial ! – selon le degré de fantaisie de chacun. Les plus sérieux arguant qu'il existait des jouets semblables, que c'était plus simple d'acheter le mixer, le grille-pain ou la dînette dans le magasin du coin. Pour l'instant, Paul n'en voulait pas. Façonner le carton selon ses désirs, très précis, lui convenait. Plus tard, effectivement, nous dévaliserions La Grande Récré de ses fours avec lumière et tournebroche, son lave-linge se remplissant d'eau et imitant si bien le bruit de l'essorage, sa tronçonneuse, ses quatre aspirateurs différents que Paul interdirait à sa sœur de mettre en route pendant longtemps. Je pus d'ailleurs constater qu'il se lassait beaucoup plus vite de ces jouets si perfectionnés, sans doute parce qu'il ne pouvait pas les modifier à sa guise.

Attention : terrain miné

Cependant, ces jouets ont servi à le réconcilier avec le bruit. Si, au début, il hurlait de peur lorsque quelqu'un mettait en marche un appareil bruyant, il s'y accoutuma peu à peu. Ainsi, à la campagne, il ne courait plus s'enfermer en hurlant au fond de la maison, quand mon mari sortait la tondeuse à gazon ou la tronçonneuse pour couper quelques bûches. L'aspirateur le terrorisa longtemps. J'avais attendu pendant des mois que Paul soit à la halte-garderie pour le passer dans la maison. Si j'ouvrais le placard de l'aspirateur pour en sortir un quelconque objet, il s'enfuyait en hurlant. Je tentais un jour l'expérience de faire passer l'aspirateur par la femme de ménage en notre présence. Il courut s'enfermer dans les toilettes où je pus le rejoindre et essayer de le rassurer. Peine perdue, il hurlait comme un possédé dans mes bras, couvert de sueur, et ne se calma que quand tout fut fini et l'aspirateur bien enfermé dans son placard. J'en sortis en nage, tremblante, aussi traumatisée que lui. Bon, il fallait trouver autre chose.

D'abord, lire une bonne cinquantaine de fois *Léo et Popi et l'aspirateur*, puis utiliser ses aspirateurs jouets sans les mettre en route, enfin sortir le vrai sans toucher au fil de branchement et l'examiner de très loin. Encore un temps avant qu'il se décide à le toucher, à s'asseoir à califourchon dessus, à prendre le tuyau pour la trompe de l'éléphant, sans toucher au bouton surtout. Quelques semaines plus tard, Paul finit par accepter que je le passe – il fallait le prévenir avant – à toute petite puissance pour ne pas faire trop de bruit, et il répétait : « Fini ?... Fini ?... Fini ? » toutes les cinq minutes, passant avec précaution la tête au coin des couloirs ou restant à l'affût derrière les portes. L'aspirateur rangé, il allait vérifier ensuite que les portes étaient bien fermées et interdisait à quiconque, d'une façon générale, de toucher à ce placard.

Au cours de cette première vraie année d'école, l'orthophoniste le fit énormément progresser. Si, les premiers mois, son travail avait consisté à lui donner envie de parler, en lui soutirant quelques mots par séance, il surmontait avec elle sa crainte de communiquer. Elle me faisait part de l'amélioration de la compréhension et de l'attention. Elle utilisait, elle aussi, des CD-Roms, beaucoup de jeux d'images pour le faire commenter avec elle et lui laissait le choix des activités pour gagner sa confiance et sa bonne volonté. Elle le trouvait logique, précis, mais très peu malléable. Elle avait beaucoup de mal à le faire obéir, puisqu'elle ne voulait pas le contraindre et prendre le risque de le bloquer. Dans ces conditions, naturellement, il allait aux séances avec plaisir, sachant qu'il y ferait ses activités préférées sans qu'elle ne s'y oppose. C'était le but pour l'instant, favoriser le développement du langage en le félicitant à chaque pas, allonger sa capacité de concentration, aller au bout de l'activité sans renoncer à la première difficulté, accepter de changer de jeu, ne pas se braquer devant la nouveauté.

Toute l'année, cependant, elle se heurta au même obstacle que l'institutrice et moi-même : cette résistance, variable selon les jours, qui devenait parfois une opposition ouverte à certaines contraintes individuelles ou imposées par la vie en communauté, à ce refus plus ou moins net des règles applicables à tous. Le groupe respectait ces règles mais lui refusait encore souvent d'appartenir à ce groupe. Restant à l'écart, il ne se sentait pas obligé d'obéir. Il était clair que son intégration posait parfois problème, mais le langage qui démarrait véritablement semblait résoudre les obstacles peu à peu. S'il pouvait expliquer pourquoi il refusait telle consigne, on pouvait alors lui répondre en lui en expliquant la raison. Et, s'il comprenait cette réponse, il lui était plus difficile de n'être pas d'accord, plus encore de dire pourquoi il refusait. Comme si ces explications données pour le convaincre d'obéir, que je m'efforçais de garder courtes et claires pour qu'il ne décroche pas, aplanissaient le terrain.

J'avais cette image d'un champ d'obstacles et de bosses, de mines parfois, qu'il fallait, à chaque arrêt brutal, désamorcer, contourner, niveler devant lui pour qu'il accepte de surmonter l'écueil, la contrariété qui entravaient ses progrès. Nous avions ainsi toutes trois, chacune à notre manière, persévéré pour lui faire acquérir cette capacité d'acceptation, une plus grande malléabilité, pour qu'il puisse enfin se soumettre à une certaine discipline commune ou individuelle.

L'ennemi veille

Les réunions de la commission pendaient au-dessus de nos têtes comme une épée de Damoclès. L'ambiance avait néanmoins changé du tout au tout. La directrice, qui l'avait accepté contrairement aux autres écoles, avait bien l'intention de mener les choses à sa manière. La commission avait suggéré quelques matinées par semaine, la directrice avait très rapidement imposé tous les matins. À peine un mois plus tard, elle m'avait enjoint de le ramener l'après-midi. Réunie au deuxième trimestre, la commission ne pouvait faire marche arrière devant le fait accompli. Les assurances de l'institutrice avaient stoppé net leurs velléités de réduire les heures de Paul au profit d'autres thérapies. J'avais le sentiment qu'enfin le destin de Paul commençait à échapper à ses ennemis. L'école le soutenait courageusement et la commission se plia, dubitative, à la décision de la directrice. Elle me reprocha naturellement l'absence de suivi psychologique et je me défendis en disant qu'il avait eu cette année un emploi du temps bien chargé : des journées complètes à l'école, deux séances d'orthophonie et une de psychomotricité par semaine. Elle m'imposa donc de le faire suivre chez un psychologue ou un psychiatre, mais je refusai de retourner dans le centre qui nous avait été « recommandé » l'année passée, avec ce psychiatre qui, pour nous, faisait partie de cette mafia contre Paul. Contrainte, je fis des recherches pour trouver un psychiatre dans le secteur privé.

Du baume au cœur

J'allais donc consulter le Dr N... qui m'avait toujours apporté de précieux conseils. À plusieurs reprises, j'étais venue vider mon sac de toutes mes interrogations et incertitudes. Son expérience et son habileté lui permettaient d'éclaircir les données confuses que je lui soumettais. J'arrivais toujours déboussolée avec le sentiment d'être dans une impasse totale. Avec talent et perspicacité, il démêlait l'écheveau et me fournissait des solutions. Je n'étais pas forcément capable à ce moment-là de résoudre mes difficultés ou n'avais pas la clarté d'esprit nécessaire, mais ses indications, pas toujours bien saisies sur le moment, me fournissaient des pistes, et il me fallait parfois plusieurs semaines ou plusieurs mois, pour que ces idées mûrissent en moi et fassent leur chemin. Je réalisais alors qu'il avait tout compris bien avant moi, à qui il avait fallu tant de temps pour réaliser la portée de ses conseils et les mettre en œuvre, plus ou moins consciemment d'ailleurs. J'admirais alors le talent d'un homme qui avait, à mes yeux, atteint l'excellence dans son domaine.

Arrivant à la porte de son cabinet et trouvant que la porte était trop longue à s'ouvrir, Paul frappa des poings cette porte qui s'ouvrit tout à coup devant le Dr N... étonné. Me serrant la main, il nous fit entrer dans son bureau. Surprise par son silence, je le vis examiner Paul et n'osais parler. « C'est absolument miraculeux... Tout à fait incroyable », dit-il enfin.

J'étais interloquée, il ne l'avait pas vu depuis si longtemps, comment pouvait-il se souvenir si bien de ce qu'il était et voir à ce point les changements. Je lui exprimai mon doute.

« Comment ! Je ne me rappelle pas ? ! » Il se mit à me donner une multitude de détails sur Paul, ce qu'il avait constaté, ce que les médecins m'avaient dit, les conversations que nous avions eues, comme si c'était hier. Je vis qu'il n'y avait pas de dossier ouvert sur son bureau et je savais qu'il prenait fort peu de notes. Cet homme-là a une mémoire phénoménale... ou le cas de Paul l'avait particulièrement marqué. Je relatai mon expérience dans les détails. Suivit une heure d'explications interrompues sans cesse d'interjections de surprise et d'enthousiasme et d'éloges dithyrambiques de sa part. Enfin, je lui demandai :

« Mais pourquoi, vous, médecins, ne dites pas aux parents à qui vous annoncez de tels diagnostics qu'il y a des choses à faire, que les parents peuvent dans une certaine mesure remédier à certains handicaps. Ce que j'ai fait, d'autres parents peuvent le faire, s'ils savaient, ils se lanceraient certainement, comme je l'ai fait.

– Ne croyez pas cela. Vous ne vous rendez pas compte que de nombreux parents ne peuvent accepter le diagnostic et la maladie de leur enfant. C'est une blessure d'orgueil qu'ils ne surmontent pas. Ils se disent : "Comment ai-je pu mettre au monde un enfant pareil ? Ce n'est pas possible !" Et le résultat, c'est qu'ils préfèrent le confier à un centre spécialisé ou à un hôpital, parce qu'ils l'aiment sur un mode tel qu'ils ne supportent pas de le voir ainsi. »

J'avais du mal à le croire. Cependant, je me souvenais de cette cruelle période pendant laquelle j'avais eu une sorte de haine pour Paul, me disant que s'il lui arrivait « quelque chose », ce serait épouvantable, mais peut-être en fin de compte plus supportable pour nous tous que ce fardeau jusqu'à la fin de nos jours. Je savais que de nombreux couples se brisaient, des familles éclataient, usées par des situations insoutenables. Oui, je me l'avouais, je l'avais pensé... et j'avais cherché à me détacher de lui. Je n'avais pas été loin de renoncer, moi aussi, pendant ces semaines de terreur abjecte. Moi aussi, j'avais pensé : Comment ai-je pu enfanter un monstre ? Je n'étais plus dans cet état d'esprit, puisque j'avais foi en lui, mais cela ne me donnait pas le droit d'oublier. Cela n'avait aucun sens de blâmer ces parents. L'idée de trouver le moyen de les aider se fit jour à ce moment-là. Non pas par le biais de médecins incrédules mais directement : de parents à parents.

Lui faisant part des nombreux soucis que j'avais encore concernant, entre autres, les nuits difficiles et l'alimentation toujours aussi restreinte de Paul, il me recommanda de retourner voir un spécialiste des psychoses infantiles. Ce psychanalyste avait suivi Paul quelques mois pendant sa première année d'école. J'avais beaucoup de mal à savoir ce qui se passait lors des séances qui ne duraient pas plus de cinq minutes. Paul ne parlait pas du tout à cette époque et j'avais décidé d'attendre le début du langage avant d'y retourner. L'année suivante, le programme, la halte-garderie, la psychomotricité et mes recherches pour trouver une école nous prenaient tout notre temps. Enfin, l'année du retour à l'école se trouva si chargée que j'hésitai à lui imposer cette heure et demie de métro deux fois par semaine. Je promis au Dr N… d'y réfléchir. En réalité, à la rentrée, j'optai pour un psychiatre du quartier pour nous éviter les transports, mais je l'ai regretté. Non seulement Paul était réticent, refusait de rester seul pendant les séances, mais l'atmosphère devint si tendue et si pénible au bout de quelques mois que je décidai d'arrêter. La CCPE me le reprocherait naturellement et nous serions à nouveau obligés de reprendre une thérapie l'année suivante avec un autre médecin, qui lui, soupçonnerait des difficultés de couple d'être à l'origine des difficultés de Paul !… (Notre couple va bien, merci !) Les séances n'avaient eu aucun résultat visible – je conçois bien que les résultats ne soient pas quantifiables –, ce qui me confortait dans l'idée, que j'avais lue dans différents rapports médicaux, que les psychothérapies pour ce genre de troubles s'avéraient au mieux inutiles, au pire néfastes.

Conforter les acquis

Grâce au bilan qu'avait dressé l'institutrice à la fin de cette première année et aux remarques de l'orthophoniste sur le travail de Paul, nous avions à présent des indications précieuses. Pendant l'été, j'avais pris de nombreuses notes sur son comportement global et au cours de nos leçons. À l'aide de toutes ces données, Barbara analysa ses difficultés et ses handicaps pour mettre au point un nouveau programme centré sur ses défaillances auditives et sur le travail d'imagination nécessaire à la représentation mentale de concepts concrets, l'abstraction venant plus tardivement. Je vous livre ici, à titre d'exemple, le programme que nous devions suivre pendant deux ou trois semaines avant une réadaptation qui serait faite une fois ces acquisitions en bonne voie.

MENTALISATION ET ANTICIPATION PAR LE RYTHME

Exercice quotidien

Inventer tous les jours une histoire différente et le faire raisonner sur ce que croit chacun des personnages dans l'histoire. Pour une meilleure cohésion, écrire le texte de façon à pouvoir le lui redire plusieurs fois de la même façon.

Lundi et jeudi

Rythme : s'asseoir face à lui et taper dans ses mains cinq fois. Reproduire le même exercice avec un tambourin et des maracas. Il doit taper dans ses mains au même rythme. Accompagner de la voix si nécessaire.

Psychomotricité : se mettre tous les deux debout face à face. Travailler le rythme du corps en alternant un membre droit et un membre gauche simultanément. Par exemple, tendre le bras droit devant, tout en tendant la jambe gauche vers l'arrière.

Avec une chanson : montrer comment trouver le rythme de la chanson avec la voix d'abord, en faisant pom... pom... Lorsqu'il est à l'aise avec sa voix, le faire frapper dans ses mains au rythme de la chanson.

À l'aide de la cassette *Vivre le son*, travailler le rythme jusqu'à ce que les frappers de mains passent à quatre mains simultanément. Pour ne pas créer de blocage devant la difficulté, lui prendre les mains pour l'aider au début et accompagner de la voix.

Anticiper en s'exprimant oralement : inventer chaque semaine une histoire nouvelle rédigée au préalable. Elle doit se présenter sous forme de dialogue tantôt avec les questions seules, tantôt avec les réponses seules. Il devra deviner le contexte général (un anniversaire par exemple) puis retrouver les questions ou les réponses logiques qui manquent.

Anticiper sur une trajectoire :

– placer une corde au bout de la pièce et lui demander de lancer des balles de façon à s'approcher le plus près possible de la corde ;

– même exercice en plaçant une quille au milieu et

en lui demandant de lancer la balle soit à droite, soit à gauche de la quille et ce avant d'atteindre la corde ;

– lui demander de s'exprimer en même temps sur ce qu'il est en train de faire.

Anticiper visuellement : découper incomplètement une image dans un magazine de façon à ce qu'il reste des bribes qui le mettront sur la voie. Il devra dire ce que cela représente et éventuellement son usage ou sa fonction s'il s'agit d'un objet.

La mentalisation par l'écoute et par l'image : lui lire tous les jours une histoire différente et le faire raisonner sur ce que croient les personnages de l'histoire afin de vérifier qu'il a bien saisi les opinions de chacun et la raison des divergences de ces opinions. Dans le cas contraire, reprendre la même histoire car ce n'est qu'en terrain connu qu'il pourra comprendre. Ne pas le bousculer avec trop d'histoires qui pourraient le submerger.

Les images séquentielles : utiliser chaque jour une série de photos, par exemple le jeu de cache-cache entre plusieurs enfants. Travailler l'aspect chronologique en remettant les photos dans l'ordre de l'histoire et en le commentant. Travailler également l'exercice de projection dans l'esprit de l'autre, en posant des questions sur ce que chaque enfant voit, croit, et par conséquent ce qu'il fait.

Mardi et vendredi

Le rythme et le corps : exercice de sauts et reproduction de gestes suivant des rythmes variés, selon l'exemple montré auparavant.

Le parcours : à l'aide de dalles de motricité, de quilles et de coussins, inventer un parcours avec des gestes variés : saut en avant, en arrière, tourner autour de... le lui montrer au préalable et lui faire suivre la consigne, verbaliser en même temps.

Avec la cassette Avec ton corps : commencer avec la chanson *Ton corps est tout à toi*, écouter les paroles, en parler et danser sur la musique. Lorsqu'il danse aussi, lui rappeler ce qu'il a dit qu'il pouvait faire avec son corps.

Comptines et frappers : « Un, deux, trois, je vais dans les bois... » Frapper dans les mains ou sauter au rythme de la comptine en chantant.

Adaptation au tempo : au son d'un tambourin, il doit prendre un crayon à gauche, le reposer à droite en respectant le rythme imposé. Dire en même temps : « Je prends, je pose. »

Apprendre à structurer le temps : prendre trois objets pour commencer et donner trois consignes de spatialisation différentes à la fois, avant qu'il commence l'exercice. « Tu mettras le foulard sur la télévision, puis la balle sur le fauteuil, enfin le livre sur le canapé. » Dans la mesure du possible, ne pas répéter les consignes. Lui demander de s'évaluer : qu'il dise s'il pense s'être trompé ou non. Puis, à son tour, exécuter les consignes qu'il donne. Se tromper volontairement de temps à autre pour voir s'il a bien retenu ses propres consignes et s'il est capable de corriger l'erreur.

Utiliser des inducteurs de langage oraux : écrire chaque semaine un petit texte différent où manqueront les inducteurs de langage suivants : avant que, après que, puisque, parce que, il faut que, afin que, à condition que... et lui demander de retrouver les notions dont on a besoin pour comprendre la logique de l'histoire et les mots qui manquent en posant la question : de quelle précision avons-nous besoin pour comprendre l'histoire ?

Anticiper sur la suite d'un récit :

– par l'écoute : raconter une petite histoire et lui demander de la terminer. Plus tard, à lui de commencer l'histoire, de s'interrompre pour que l'on invente la suite. Dernière étape, chacun donne une phrase ou deux à son tour.

– par l'image : en se servant des images séquentielles, inventer une suite qui soit logique.

Mercredi et samedi

Rythme : le faire frapper dans ses mains cinq fois avec des rythmes et des instruments variés. Même exercice avec l'instrument de son choix en accompagnant également de la voix.

Rythme et motricité : lui préparer un parcours avec des dalles de couleurs et de formes différentes en lui donnant des consignes : tu sautes une fois sur le triangle bleu, deux fois sur le carré vert... Puis refaire l'exercice une seconde fois en disant ce qu'il est en train de faire. Même exercice en y ajoutant des frappers de mains.

Avec la cassette Vivre le son : ne travailler que le début de la cassette jusqu'à quatre frappers ; faire à la fois les mains et la voix.

Anticiper en dessinant : sur une feuille, préparer un début de dessin ; lui demander à quoi cela lui fait penser, puis lui demander de le compléter.

Coopérer pour atteindre un objectif commun : ici encore, il s'agit de s'ajuster à une situation, de deviner l'attitude de l'autre, afin de coopérer avec lui ; tenir un long bâton à la main et lui demander d'enfiler sur le bâton six petits anneaux. Modifier son attitude pendant l'exercice afin qu'il soit toujours en situation de réajustement.

Parcours : placer des quilles sur le sol et lui demander de les contourner avec une petite balle qu'il fera rouler dans l'ordre prescrit (à gauche de la rouge, à droite de la bleue). Il devra respecter parfaitement les consignes données au préalable et on augmentera petit à petit le nombre de consignes à retenir.

Réagir à un stimulus sonore : jouer au jeu de la statue en y ajoutant des cerceaux dans lesquels il devra se trouver quand la musique s'arrêtera ; lui préciser dans quel cerceau il devra se trouver à l'arrêt de la musique. En changer chaque fois.

Travaux manuels : lui découper de nombreux morceaux de papier dans un magazine et lui demander de les coller pour que cela représente un bonhomme, une maison...

Mime : lui demander de mimer un oiseau, un soleil, une maison, une chaise, une table. Il s'agit d'un exercice de transposition pure : savoir s'adapter à une forme, comme on s'adapte à la « forme » d'une situation, essentiel pour entrer dans celle-ci et en imaginer tous les aspects.

Dimanche

Rythme et expression corporelle : mettre de la musique et lui donner diverses consignes de sauts, de voix, de frappers de mains à exécuter dans l'instant pour s'adapter à l'imprévu et au changement permanent.

Réagir à un stimulus sonore : élaborer au préalable des consignes ; quand je frappe une fois dans mes mains, tu lèves une fois les bras ; quand je frappe deux fois, tu avances de deux pas ; quand je frappe trois fois, tu tournes trois fois sur toi-même. Plus tard, aller jusqu'à cinq.

Exercice de formulation d'hypothèses : trouver une image d'enfant qui pleure, par exemple, ou dans une situation qui lui est familière. Lui demander de déduire ce qui s'est passé avant ; puis ce qui pourra logiquement se passer après.

Anticiper sur la nature d'un objet : choisir la partie détachable d'un objet inconnu, la sortir de son contexte habituel, lui demander ce que cela peut être et à quoi cela pourrait servir.

Photos séquentielles : choisir deux séries de photos : l'une qui nécessite de se mettre à la place d'une autre personne afin d'en deviner les motivations et l'autre non, afin de lui faire percevoir la différence.

À l'écoute du monde sonore : sélectionner dix bruits différents et lui faire reconnaître, en parler pour les remettre dans leur contexte général, s'exprimer sur leur qualité, leur utilité, leur nuisance.

Ce mode d'apprentissage m'apparaissait au début très mécanique, presque robotique. En réalité, tous ces exercices favorisaient la « reconstruction mentale », le rétablissement des mécanismes mentaux qui ne s'activaient pas tous seuls. Contre toute attente, ce travail aide aussi à rétablir les émotions, à apprendre leur langage et leur expression, à développer la conscience de ses propres sentiments, etc. En réalité, tout est inextricablement lié.

Inutile de dire que réussir ce programme a nécessité non pas quelques semaines mais plusieurs mois. Je rencontrais une telle résistance qu'il a fallu le réduire et le découper en petites portions, tout en le « mélangeant » à d'autres activités et en l'adaptant à son niveau de langage, qui était insuffisant pour certaines activités. C'était pourtant exactement ce dont Paul avait besoin.

Et cela correspondait si bien à ses handicaps qu'il refusait pratiquement tout au départ. Se sentant encore mal à l'aise dans son corps, puisqu'il en avait une conscience déformée et incomplète, il se fermait comme une huître dès que j'arrivais avec mon matériel. Si la connexion entre les sons et l'objet correspondant avait été rétablie, faire correspondre des gestes à un son était très difficile pour lui. Il commençait par se buter, se détournant complètement des objets que je voulais lui faire prendre ou lançait les crayons à travers la pièce au premier essai, au premier échec. Je sautais sur les dalles de sol en nommant leur couleur et lui demandais de me suivre, il faisait n'importe quoi, exprès, pour me faire comprendre qu'il ne le ferait pas suivant les consignes mais à sa manière. Je le laissais faire puis, quand il se lassait, je lui demandais : saute sur la bleue, sur la rouge. À ma voix et sur une consigne à la fois, il acceptait de le faire voyant que j'attendrais, que je ne changerais pas d'activité tant qu'il ne ferait pas un effort. D'autres exercices le perturbaient au point qu'il se repliait sur lui-même, triturant l'objet qu'il avait dans la main, et n'écoutait plus. Les changements de rythme dans les exercices, par exemple, lui faisaient perdre toute son assurance, au point de le déséquilibrer physiquement. Il n'arrivait pas davantage à anticiper ou à modifier le cours d'une histoire. En revanche lorsqu'il s'agissait de lancer un objet en visant, il se montrait habile. Lorsqu'un seul sens était sollicité, l'exercice lui convenait. Lorsqu'il fallait enregistrer une consigne, puis une seconde, les visualiser dans son esprit, afin de les reproduire même peu de temps après, c'était déjà trop difficile.

Frapper dans ses mains le dérangeait, sauter le mettait mal à l'aise. Il faisait d'ailleurs rarement des mouvements amples ou souples avec son corps. Malgré nos exercices de l'été, ses gestes étaient réduits à l'essentiel, par une conscience encore floue de son propre corps. Sa latéralité était mal définie. Lever la jambe gauche, le bras droit sur un son défini, était difficile. Tout ceci est venu bien plus tard, avec le jeu Twister composé d'un tapis de plastique blanc sur lequel étaient peints des cercles de couleur alignés. Une aiguille tournant sur un cadran indiquait qu'un joueur devait mettre la main gauche sur le rouge, le suivant le pied droit sur le bleu, le troisième la main droite sur le vert, et ainsi de suite, sans que les joueurs tombent. Ce qui se produisait inévitablement, quand bras et jambes imbriqués, Laure, Paul et leurs cousins s'écroulaient, les uns déséquilibrés par les autres, dans de grands éclats de rire.

Mais, en attendant, cette période fut décourageante. Barbara avait si bien trouvé ses lacunes ou défaillances que je me heurtais à un rejet constant de Paul. Petit à petit, en modulant, en inventant d'autres moyens de parvenir au même but, il avançait. Plutôt que de lui imposer ces activités au cours de leçons formelles qui ne lui laissaient aucune échappatoire et nous crispaient tous les deux, j'introduisais ces exercices comme des jeux au cours de la journée et particulièrement lors de nos week-ends ou vacances scolaires à la campagne ou dans le Midi.

Jouer pour réussir

Contrairement à ce qui se passait dans le cadre assez strict des leçons où il se braquait facilement, j'arrivais à des acquisitions semblables en me basant sur le principe de l'exercice donné par Barbara, mais dans un esprit plus décontracté et ludique. Par exemple, dès que nous avions un petit moment, je le faisais jouer à la brouette, je lui attrapais une jambe pour qu'il saute à cloche-pied, puis l'autre en essayant toujours de le faire rire pour que, dans son esprit, ce ne soit pas du travail mais un jeu. Nous imitions ensuite le flamant rose, debout immobile sur une patte, les ailes repliées, puis nous faisions le chat qui s'étire, ou sautions comme des grenouilles.

Tout était prétexte à quelque exercice : lancer les cailloux du jardin dans un seau métallique faisait du bruit donc l'amusait. On changeait de main en disant la gauche, la droite. Puis le jeu de « Jacques a dit » qu'il acceptait si je prenais soin de donner régulièrement des consignes qui l'amusaient. Jacques a dit : « Va faire pipi sous le pommier. » Suivre les consignes d'un parcours donné passait beaucoup mieux s'il avait un œuf dans une cuillère serrée entre ses dents, encore mieux si l'œuf tombait. Il ne faisait le parcours que pour voir l'œuf exploser sur le carrelage... mais il le faisait. Marcher à reculons au signal était beaucoup mieux accepté si le signal était un véritable coup de gong sur une grande marmite... tant pis pour les voisins.

La campagne était riche de possibilités : « chercher des pièces d'or » avec Laure au bord des rivières, sauter dans les flaques et patauger dans la boue le réconciliait beaucoup plus naturellement avec l'eau dont le contact était impossible à éviter, à l'automne du moins. Les jours de mauvais temps, je rassemblais toutes sortes d'objets pour le « bricolage », mot magique. Je déplumais le plumeau de ma grand-mère pour les leur faire coller sur des feuilles de papier Canson. Nous obtenions des poules et des canards, que nous faisions converser après les avoir découpés. Ma grand-mère avait également une boîte à couture impressionnante qui contenait un stock de boutons proprement hallucinant : de toutes tailles, de toutes couleurs, Paul les jetait en l'air et disait : « Il pleut des boutons. » Il les secouait dans la boîte de métal et nous comparions les bruits différents selon le remplissage de la boîte. Le but étant de lui faire trier par grosseur, couleur, nombre de trous, etc., car, malgré une bonne acuité visuelle, le tri était un exercice difficile pour lui. Il lui a fallu beaucoup de temps avant d'être capable d'aligner horizontalement un grand, un moyen, un petit marron, un grand, un moyen, un petit noir... dans le tas d'une douzaine seulement que je lui donnais à trier selon des consignes variées.

Grâce à une liste d'activité que j'emportais avec moi dans nos déplacements, j'avais ainsi à tout moment de la journée des idées de choses à faire avec lui, quel que soit le temps. Pour mesurer ses progrès d'un week-end à l'autre ou d'un séjour au suivant, j'écrivais en face de chaque exercice le signe – lorsque ce n'était pas acquis, = lorsqu'il faudrait le refaire et + quand il l'avait fait de façon satisfaisante. Dans ce cas, je compliquais un peu la consigne ou lui faisais faire deux exercices simultanément. Voici la liste que j'utilisais à ce moment-là.

Motricité globale :

– Marcher à quatre pattes comme un chien, un éléphant, une souris, un canard, en levant la tête très haut comme une girafe, sauter comme une grenouille.

– Marcher sur les genoux, bras tendus devant, sur les côtés.

– Fermer les yeux et se diriger comme un somnambule.

– Suivre les consignes et dire ce que l'on rencontre sur son chemin.

– Passer sous une table, sous une chaise en rampant.

– Se cacher sous une couverture et sortir au signal.

– Se tenir sur un pied le plus longtemps possible, puis sur l'autre.

– Se tourner bras tendus à gauche, à droite sans bouger les pieds.

– Courir à quatre pattes, comme Mowgli et les éléphants, en avant puis en arrière, sans mettre les genoux au sol.

– Marcher droit, un livre sur la tête sans le faire tomber.

– Frapper dans ses mains en sautant.

– Marcher autour de la table sur la pointe des pieds, puis sur les talons.

– Donner des coups de pied en l'air avec la jambe gauche, puis la droite.

– Ramasser des objets au sol le plus vite possible.

– Marcher en rythme lorsqu'on frappe des mains.

– Faire le robot : avancer tout droit, demi-tour à droite, toucher ses pieds, se relever, trois pas à gauche...

– Tracer des lignes et des cercles au sol : les suivre sans déborder, puis à reculons.

– Marcher en glissant les pieds sur le sol, puis en levant les genoux très haut.

– Couché sur le dos, faire de la bicyclette lentement, rapidement.

– Marcher sur trois pattes, en tenant un objet dans la main gauche puis la main droite.

– Placer un sac de riz sur le pied et marcher sans le faire tomber.

– Marcher avec une cuillère sur le dos de la main sans la faire tomber.

– Marcher entre deux lignes tracées au sol, espacées de 15 centimètres sans les toucher, puis à reculons.

– Sauter à pieds joint dans un cercle en disant : dedans, dehors, dedans, dehors.

– Courir sans toucher les obstacles dans la pièce ou dans le jardin.

– Monter sur une chaise et sauter dans le cercle tracé au sol.

– Sauter par-dessus une corde tendue, de plus en plus haut.

– Organiser des parcours d'obstacles, de relais, de sauts.

Motricité fine :

– Lancer des balles dans un seau de plus en plus éloigné.

– Empiler des cubes, les aligner, reproduire à côté ou en dessous symétriquement.

– Assembler des vis et des écrous. Enfoncer des chevilles dans une planche trouée.

– Visser, dévisser les couvercles de pots de différentes tailles.

– Enfiler des macaronis, des boutons sur une ficelle.

– Modeler des boules de différentes tailles avec de la pâte à modeler, les classer par ordre, par couleur.

– Transvaser de l'eau dans divers récipients, d'un petit verre dans un grand, d'un plus grand verre dans un plus petit, sans renverser.

– Mettre des pinces à linge autour d'une boîte à chaussures.

– Empiler des pièces de monnaie le plus haut possible.

– Plier des feuilles en ajustant les coins.

– Ouvrir les lettres, coller des timbres.
– Faire des nœuds sur une corde, les défaire.
– Boutonner et reboutonner sa veste.
– Perforer des feuilles de papier.
– Tracer des lignes avec une règle.
– Suivre les tracés sur une feuille avec un feutre.
– Relier les points dessinés sur une feuille.
– Tracer des carrés, des ronds autour de ceux déjà tracés, puis à l'intérieur.
– Découpage de journaux et collages.
– Coloriages avec des crayons, des feutres, des pastels, de la peinture.

Pour favoriser son aptitude à jouer avec les autres enfants, je demandais à Laure de jouer avec nous. Nous faisions des parties de cache-cache, seules au début, car il refusait de se cacher : si on ne pouvait plus le voir, on l'oublierait. Peut-être qu'en disparaissant à la vue des autres on cessait d'exister ? Pour surmonter cette peur, nous commençâmes par le jeu de cache-tampon. Nous cachions l'objet en exagérant nos gestes et nos recherches et nous lui disions : « Tu chauffes... tu brûles ! Ah ! non, là c'est froid de nouveau... », lorsqu'il s'éloignait de l'objet dissimulé. Il constatait donc que l'objet était caché mais ne disparaissait pas pour autant. On le retrouvait toujours. D'autre part, il commençait à comprendre aussi que l'autre ne pouvait pas savoir où était caché l'objet s'il n'avait pas vu la personne le cacher. Cela nous paraît évident, mais cela ne l'était pas pour Paul.

Dans la peau de l'autre

Ce processus de projection dans l'esprit de l'autre vient tout naturellement aux enfants. Si, pendant les premiers mois, l'objet qu'on dissimule à leurs yeux cesse d'exister, ils en viennent à se le représenter mentalement de façon instinctive. Très vite, si on leur montre un biscuit, qu'on le cache l'instant d'après dans notre dos, ils vont nous contourner pour le retrouver de l'autre côté. Ils savent qu'il est là, derrière. Pendant longtemps, pour Paul, *l'objet que l'on dissimulait n'existait plus*, il s'en désintéressait. De même, à ce moment-là de son évolution, il était difficile pour Paul de concevoir que les autres pensaient différemment dans un contexte lui paraissant similaire. Il s'attendait donc à ce que les réactions des autres soient les mêmes que les siennes et ne comprenait pas pourquoi elles différaient. Je lui expliquais que c'est parce que les autres n'avaient pas vu la même chose que lui. Comment Laure pouvait-elle deviner où j'avais caché un objet si elle s'était retournée quand je le cachais ? Lui m'avait vue, il pensait donc que Laure l'avait vu aussi. Il lui était si difficile de faire cet exercice, de projection dans l'esprit de l'autre, que nous y passâmes de longues semaines.

L'exemple de l'histoire de Poule Rousse était frappant. Poule Rousse invite son amie la tourterelle chez elle. Le renard les guette et, dès que la tourterelle repart, il attrape Poule Rousse dans son sac. La tourterelle, appelée au secours, détourne l'attention du renard qui essaie de la capturer elle aussi. Pendant cette diversion, Poule Rousse coupe le sac avec ses ciseaux, met de grosses pierres à l'intérieur, le recoud et s'enfuit chez elle. Voyant Poule Rousse libérée, la tourterelle s'envole. Le renard, déçu, repart avec son sac.

Lorsque je demandais à Paul : que crois-*tu* qu'il y a dans le sac ? Il me répondait : des pierres. Mais lorsque je lui demandais : Qu'est-ce que *renard* croit qu'il y a dans le sac ? Il me répondait : des pierres. Il était très difficile pour lui de concevoir que le renard, lui, pensait que la poule était toujours dans le sac. « Toi, Paul, tu as vu Poule Rousse s'enfuir, mais le renard n'a *pas vu cela*, puisqu'il courait après la tourterelle. Pour le renard, Poule Rousse est toujours dans le sac. »

Nous dûmes prendre beaucoup d'exemples, dans des livres et dans le quotidien pour qu'il analyse les situations sous des angles de vue différents, afin de concevoir que chacun pouvait avoir des perceptions variées d'une même réalité, donc des opinions différentes.

Cette difficulté allait de pair avec celle de *se mettre à la place de l'autre pour deviner ses émotions ou ses pensées*. Sans cet instinct d'empathie avec l'autre, il ne pouvait prévoir ou comprendre ses réactions, ni les anticiper par des gestes ou des attitudes appropriées, celles que les autres attendaient de lui. Il fallait travailler sur ses perceptions d'autrui pour qu'il surmonte ses difficultés de contact et de communication.

Lorsque, grâce à de nombreux jeux et aux exercices prescrits par Barbara dans les programmes, il fit cette acquisition importante, je constatais effectivement qu'il acceptait, sollicitait même parfois le contact avec les enfants du square. Il commençait à comprendre les autres d'instinct, à accepter leurs demandes plus facilement plutôt que d'imposer ses jeux répétitifs qui les déroutaient et finalement les éloignaient. Une véritable communication commençait à s'établir. J'en profitais pour inviter le plus souvent possible ses cousins à la maison. À la campagne, je conviais tous les jours nos trois petits voisins à venir jouer dans notre jardin. Ayant ainsi été en contact permanent avec des enfants et des adultes, pendant de nombreux week-ends et pendant les vacances scolaires, son comportement s'était beaucoup modifié. Il avait de moins en moins souvent besoin de s'isoler. Il était rare maintenant de le trouver seul dans une pièce, à « bricoler » dans son coin. Il lui arrivait souvent encore de jouer seul, mais il avait besoin d'une présence près de lui. Il lui arrivait de déplacer ses constructions ou ses objets dans la pièce voisine pour être en présence de quelqu'un d'autre, même sans lui parler. Il était ainsi en position d'écouter ce qui se passait autour de lui et de participer dès que cela l'intéressait. Je voyais bien qu'il tendait l'oreille car il se levait comme un ressort dès qu'il entendait quelqu'un proposer une activité qu'il aimait faire ou la voix d'un nouvel arrivant avec qui il voulait jouer.

Paul s'apprivoise

Fait nouveau également, Paul se mit à prendre parfois *l'initiative du contact*, des jeux, des activités. Pendant des mois, il n'avait pas voulu prendre ses repas à la table commune, la présence des autres le dérangeait. Il emportait donc son assiette dans sa chambre ou dans le jardin. Nous avions cédé pour ne pas batailler du matin au soir, nous préserver des moments de calme, au moins pour le repas. Maintenant, la présence des autres enfants l'attirait et il prenait volontiers ses repas avec ses cousins ou les enfants de nos voisins, invités également. Il participait à la conversation, très succinctement au début, mais l'attitude des enfants l'aidait dans ses efforts. Ils semblaient ne pas remarquer les comportements étranges, ne posaient pas de questions insistantes comme le font les adultes, n'insistaient pas lorsqu'il refusait quelque chose, cette attitude d'acceptation lui permettait d'oser être lui-même.

D'autres comportements aberrants disparaissaient aussi. Les autres ne criaient pas pendant les shampoings, acceptaient qu'on leur coupe les ongles, enlevaient ou remettaient leurs vêtements sans réticence. Il observait tout cela. Enfin terminées, ses lubies avec certains vêtements ou chaussures. Pendant plusieurs mois, nous avions eu des hurlements pour qu'il accepte de mettre des chaussures pour sortir. Ensuite était venue une période où il n'acceptait pas qu'on les lui retire. Je me souviendrai toute ma vie de ces petites bottines fourrées qu'il ne tolérait pas qu'on lui enlève. Il dormait donc avec toutes les nuits, entre mon mari et moi, puisqu'il n'y avait pas moyen de le faire dormir dans son lit à cette époque. Le ridicule de la situation ne nous faisait plus tellement rire... Nous attendions qu'il dorme pour les lui retirer, non sans d'immenses précautions pour ne pas le réveiller, lui laver les pieds avec un gant de toilette à la température idéale pour qu'il ne sente rien. Souvent, il se réveillait et nous nous précipitions pour lui remettre des chaussettes propres et ses chaussures. Nous aurions pu refuser sans doute, et attendre qu'il s'écroule d'épuisement après avoir hurlé comme un possédé pendant une heure ou deux, parce qu'il avait d'étonnantes ressources malgré son petit gabarit... Mais nous pensions qu'il valait mieux attendre pour certaines choses, de toute façon, nous ne pouvions pas lutter sur tous les fronts. Il fallait s'économiser et faire le tri, cerner les priorités. Faire porter tous nos efforts sur une ou deux choses à la fois, pour avoir plus de chance de succès et ne pas devenir fous.

En acquérant des connaissances sur le monde extérieur et sur les autres, il commençait à percevoir les dangers. Que je l'empêche de courir à sa guise dans la rue ne lui paraissait plus aussi aberrant. Il répondait quand je l'appelais ou du moins s'arrêtait. Je profitais aussitôt de ses bonnes dispositions pour lui imposer de s'arrêter sur le bord des trottoirs et de m'attendre avant de traverser. Nous conduisions donc une voiture virtuelle, avec force bruitage, qui s'arrêtait pile au « stop » retentissant que j'émettais. Ce fut la première indication d'un travail d'imagination totalement absent auparavant.

Faire semblant commençait à signifier quelque chose pour lui. Cependant, cette activité a été pendant longtemps mêlée au réel, sans signe qu'il fasse la différence. C'était un peu inquiétant. Il passait d'un monde de silence qui l'absorbait entièrement à un monde imaginaire qu'il pensait être réel et l'absorbait tout autant. Il ne disait pas : « On dit que... On dirait que toi tu serais la maîtresse... On dirait que toi tu serais malade et que je serais le docteur... », ainsi que le faisait toujours Laure comme pour bien faire comprendre qu'à partir de maintenant « c'est pour de faux ». La limite était nette et formulée. Pour Paul, c'était impossible de savoir. Il « partait » dans des histoires, mimées, commentées comme dans le réel, mais faisait-il vraiment semblant ? J'avais le sentiment qu'il s'y croyait vraiment quand il hurlait : « Attention ! Tu marches sur Zulli ! » en désignant une place vide à mes pieds ! « Oh, pardon ! Je ne l'avais pas vu... » et je « le » contournais, perplexe. J'eus pendant longtemps cette interrogation : le croit-il vraiment ? Fait-il vraiment la distinction entre le réel et l'imaginaire ? Pas du tout, je le comprendrais plus tard, lorsqu'il parlerait beaucoup plus. Mais c'était un grand progrès.

L'absence de tout jeu d'imagination chez un enfant est très inquiétante. Ne pas reproduire ou inventer, donc s'inspirer d'une réalité observée puis déformée ou transformée, est anormal. Je déduisais des quelques bribes que j'avais observées que, si Paul s'était mis à imaginer, c'était le signe qu'il commençait à s'approprier le réel pour le modifier selon son désir. C'était une étape importante à encourager.

Chapitre IX

SUR LES RAILS

À la rentrée en grande section, Paul retrouva sa grande classe mais une nouvelle institutrice. Dans l'école, il y avait aussi une intervenante spécifique qui prenait en charge de petits groupes de quatre à cinq enfants une ou deux fois par semaine. Paul fit régulièrement partie de ces groupes et cette « maîtresse sans classe », comme on l'appelle à l'école, me dit que Paul avait encore des difficultés à suivre les consignes pour mener à bien un travail déterminé. Il se montrait bavard et elle était obligée de lui dire souvent : « D'accord, tu me raconteras cette histoire plus tard, pour le moment on travaille. » Bavard, il devenait bavard ! Un comble... alors que son mutisme nous avait hantés si longtemps.

À la maison aussi, il se lançait dans de grandes explications, lentes, laborieuses, il avait tant de mal à choisir ses mots et à construire ses phrases que beaucoup n'avaient pas la patience d'attendre. Moi bien sûr, j'attendais, sans le brusquer ou le corriger sans arrêt pour ne pas le décourager. Je le reprenais avec délicatesse de peur de le vexer. Je réorganisais ses phrases dans la conversation, sans exiger qu'il les répète. De lui-même, il se reprenait, attentif et exigeant quant au vocabulaire employé. Chez l'orthophoniste aussi, ses progrès de langage étaient extrêmement rapides. Elle notait que le vocabulaire était employé à bon escient avec une volonté de précision étonnante.

Tout cela bien sûr ralentissait son débit, ses efforts d'élocution étaient visibles physiquement sur son visage crispé et sa langue qui lui obéissait difficilement. J'avais parfois l'impression de voir, dans son petit cerveau, sa pensée prendre ces chemins détournés, allongés pour remplacer ceux qui avaient fait défaut. J'entendais presque ces rouages compliqués se mettre en branle dans un effort fastidieux, soutenus par cette volonté tenace d'arriver au bout de son discours. J'avais envie de l'aider mais je me retenais, cessant mes activités pour le regarder, l'écouter de toute mon attention, l'encourageant mentalement dans cet effort démesuré que je percevais si bien... bravo... bravo... continue... c'est bien... je comprends... Lisait-il ces encouragements dans mon regard ? Ses yeux ne quittaient pas les miens et je partageais ce travail, épuisée moi aussi par ces efforts incommensurables que j'admirais. D'où lui venait cette volonté de parler ? J'espérais que tous ceux qui l'entouraient montreraient la même patience, la même indulgence pour qu'il ne renonce pas. Il exigeait des explications précises aux questions qu'il posait. L'à-peu-près ne lui suffisait pas et je cherchais le mot exact, même très technique, qu'il répétait alors à voix basse après moi, à plusieurs reprises.

Il avait une excellente mémoire des mots, des faits, des détails qui nous échappaient à tous. Il se souvenait des cadeaux reçus pour tel ou tel événement ou de l'endroit précis où nous les avions achetés. Il me faisait douter de ma propre mémoire, dans son exigence de précision. Parfois même, il venait à mon aide lorsque je cherchais mes mots ou il me corrigeait lorsque j'avais employé un mot équivalent, mais qui ne lui convenait pas. Les histoires devaient être racontées avec les mêmes mots ou il me reprenait :

« Non, ce n'est pas ce que tu as dit hier... le petit garçon...

– Euh ! Qu'est-ce que j'ai dit : il n'était pas content... en colère ?

– Non ! Pas ce mot-là ! »

Mon imprécision l'irritait.

« Ah ! Je sais : le petit garçon est contrarié, c'est ça ?

– Oui, contrarié... contrarié... » répétait-il à voix basse, comme pour sentir le mot dans sa bouche.

À d'autres moments, il me réclamait des mots plus savants :

« Comment on dit déjà quand on ne peut pas lire ?

– Quand on ne sait pas lire, on dit illettré.

– Non pas ça, quand on n'arrive pas à lire parce que c'est mal écrit !

– Ah oui ! On dit que c'est illisible !

– Illisible... illisible. »

Que je ne connaisse pas le nom des moissonneuses-batteuses, lieuses et autres grosses machines agricoles qu'il voyait à la campagne l'agaçait. Je cherchais donc pour lui à la bibliothèque les livres qui détaillaient les différentes parties des engins avec leurs noms techniques.

À d'autres moments, cette mémoire étonnante lui faisait défaut. Lorsque nous passions devant sa première école et que je le questionnais sur les souvenirs qu'il en avait, c'était le trou noir. Comme s'il n'y avait jamais mis les pieds. Sa mémoire avait dû oblitérer les moments pénibles et je me gardais bien de les lui rappeler. Il ne gardait aucun souvenir des périodes précédentes non plus et les photos de bébé ne lui disaient rien ou l'inquiétaient. D'une certaine façon, il était né à nouveau à l'âge de quatre ans, et ses souvenirs ne remontaient jamais plus tôt, contrairement à Laure qui avait des impressions familières en revoyant ces photos ou des jouets qu'elle avait eus bébé.

Par ailleurs, je m'inquiétais d'un développement qui n'était pas très homogène. Il commençait à avoir un vocabulaire très étendu, il dépassait dans certains domaines les capacités de sa moyenne d'âge et, en même temps, il n'avait pas acquis cette espèce de culture générale, superficielle mais étendue, que tous les enfants de 6 ou 7 ans se sont construite au fil des années. Pas un savoir encyclopédique certes, mais des idées générales sur le monde, les pays étrangers, les différentes langues parlées, la science et les découvertes, l'évolution des civilisations. Je me rendais compte que nous marchions souvent sur des nénuphars lorsqu'il était avec d'autres enfants de son âge, qui eux avaient cette espèce de « science infuse », et il les surprenait par son ignorance de choses évidentes pour eux (par exemple que, dans d'autres pays, il fait plus froid, que l'on y parle une autre langue, que les hommes des cavernes ont bien existé, etc.). Il fallait combler ces trous, ces lacunes pour le rendre plus homogène.

Grosses lacunes et savoir encyclopédique

Paul avait beaucoup de mal à se repérer dans le temps. Dans ce domaine, il était très en retard. Il aimait utiliser des mots tels que l'année dernière, la semaine prochaine, mais je voyais bien qu'il n'en saisissait pas bien le sens.

Je trouvais donc des calendriers où il devait cocher les jours qui passaient et, surtout, je coloriais nos différentes vacances, d'été ou d'hiver, les week-ends prolongés et je lui faisais compter les jours avant tel ou tel événement : Noël bien sûr mais aussi les anniversaires ou l'arrivée du printemps. Pour les jours de la semaine, j'avais affiché sur le réfrigérateur un carton représentant les jours sous forme de crayon de couleur (*Je découvre l'heure et le temps*, Nathan). Paul devait chaque matin décaler par rapport aux autres le crayon correspondant au jour. J'ajoutais d'autres repères lorsqu'il déplaçait les crayons : hier, dimanche, nous avons vu tes cousins ; avant-hier, samedi, nous avons déjeuné chez Mimi. Mercredi prochain, nous irons à l'Aquaboulevard...

Tout le travail que nous avions fait au départ, basé sur l'acquisition des sens, vue, ouïe, toucher, odorat, puis la reconnexion entre ces sens avaient porté ses fruits. Il agissait maintenant tout à fait normalement dans ces domaines. Par la suite, les exercices de topologie, de repérage logique, de motricité fine et globale et de prise de conscience de son corps avaient permis de combattre ses anomalies de comportement. Ce que les psychiatres appelaient des « particularités » et que j'appelais sans illusion des comportements déviants ou des anomalies avaient presque disparu.

Loin d'être renfermé ou silencieux, il parlait sans arrêt jusqu'à en être saoulant. Un jour, alors que Laure essayait de me parler et que Paul dans son blabla interminable, m'empêchait de l'entendre, je lâchais : « Paul, tais-toi un peu !... »

Qu'est-ce que j'ai dit là ? Qui aurait crû qu'un jour je lui demanderais de se taire ? ! Il devenait très bavard pendant les réunions de famille et en cela faisait une concurrence ardue à mon père qui ne pouvait en placer une... « On le préférait quand il ne parlait pas ! » fit mon mari, avec un clin d'œil à mon père, interrompu pour la énième fois, qui approuva, souriant à l'énormité de la réflexion. J'étais parfois un peu gênée par l'exubérance de Paul à laquelle nous n'étions guère habitués. Il abordait dans la rue des gens de tout âge : « Qu'est-ce qu'il y a dans ton caddie, madame ? » « Hé ! le garçon ! comment il s'appelle ton chien ? » Il n'hésitait pas non plus dans l'ascenseur, surprenant nos voisins habitués à un silence indifférent de sa part, à leur demander leur prénom, leur âge ou la marque de leur voiture. Surpris, ils répondaient, mais je les sentais un peu dérangés par son sans-gêne. Il n'avait aucune conscience de lui-même, de la distance que l'on met généralement quand on s'adresse à des inconnus ou du respect envers des personnes plus âgées. Cette familiarité m'inquiétait un peu. N'aurait-il pas suivi, dans cette confiance immédiate qu'il accordait aux inconnus, n'importe qui dans la rue ? Je tentais de lui faire comprendre tout cela, mais il était comme les enfants de 3-4 ans qui, dans leur innocence et leur naïveté, n'ont pas encore cette timidité par rapport à l'autre... ou cette méfiance. À 7 ans, il paraissait trop âgé pour agir de cette façon, et son langage bizarre attirait l'attention. Haché, lent, maladroit, il paraissait artificiel comme des mots collés les uns à la suite des autres sans vue d'ensemble. Il employait souvent le nous et s'obstinait à mettre les négations. Ni Laure ni moi-même n'insistions sur le « je *ne* sais pas » ou « ce *n*'est pas possible » mais lui, le faisait toujours, ajoutant à cela des mots peu courants qui donnait à son langage un air précieux surprenant dans la bouche d'un enfant. Le « nous sommes égarés » faisait un effet bœuf sur la passante qui nous renseignait dans la rue. Nos efforts devaient porter maintenant sur l'expression orale, la construction des phrases pour faciliter son élocution, la rendre plus souple et plus fluide. Pour cela, la lecture me paraissait importante.

Cette année-là, nous commençâmes à fréquenter assidûment la bibliothèque, qu'il connaissait déjà, mais qu'il découvrait de façon beaucoup plus consciente. Nous étions si chargés en sortant que je pris l'habitude de prendre la roulante du marché, que Laure rebaptisa la « croulante » pour l'occasion. Nous rapportions ainsi la vingtaine de livres, magazines, cassettes et disques pour la semaine.

Apprendre plus tardivement les choses avait un avantage. Paul approfondissait le sujet comme il ne l'aurait pas fait à 2 ou 3 ans. Il passait donc de passion en passion à chaque nouveau sujet qu'il abordait pour la première fois, contrairement aux autres pour qui c'était déjà familier et moins digne d'intérêt. Il se lançait à corps perdu dans chaque découverte, il fallait trouver les livres et les objets correspondants et cela tournait à la *manie*. Il lassait tout le monde avec de longues explications sur le sujet qu'il venait d'approfondir. Puis il abordait un autre sujet et s'y plongeait avec la même passion.

Je cédais à son obsession du moment tout en essayant de l'intéresser à autre chose, quand je ne trouvais pas ce qu'il cherchait, par exemple. Dans sa période *Oui-Oui*, j'allais acheter les livres, les CD-Roms ou les cassettes. Nous avons même acheté la frise à coller sur les murs et à la parure de lit. Vint ensuite Woody de *Toy Story* qu'il ne lâchait pas, de jour comme de nuit, connaissant par cœur la moindre réplique du film. Puis les voitures et camions de toute sorte, les *monster trucks* américains qu'il apprenait par cœur dans ses livres. Je tentais régulièrement de varier nos nombreuses lectures, pour lui donner des repères sur l'histoire et la géographie, les différentes civilisations. Je cherchais aussi des activités qui lui donneraient le sens de la logique du temps et de l'espace, qui lui manquait. Mais, comme pour le reste, il fallait que cela vienne de lui. Dans sa période animaux, il récitait les commentaires d'un CD-Rom qu'il mettait sans arrêt et je l'entendais marmonner des choses sur les reptiles, batraciens et autres amphibiens...

Dans le domaine des apprentissages fondamentaux, des blocages ralentissaient ses progrès en écriture et en lecture. Chez l'orthophoniste aussi, Paul se « braquait » dès qu'elle lui présentait un travail plus scolaire. Elle devait toujours passer par une forme ludique pour lui faire accepter les exercices. Je m'inquiétais : on ne joue plus en CP, je commençais à oser l'imaginer en CP. Impensable, il y a si peu de temps encore... cela entrait maintenant dans le domaine du possible. Quel chemin parcouru ! De son éviction fatale de l'école à 3 ans et demi, il entrerait peut-être en CP à un peu moins de 7 ans... un vrai miracle. Je craignais donc ces blocages qui pouvaient à tout moment entraîner ces régressions décourageantes.

Le quotidien amélioré

En m'adressant à un « spécialiste », un psychiatre du quartier, j'avais l'espoir que tous les problèmes restants seraient résolus. J'expliquais sa crainte de l'échec, ses réticences à essayer tout ce qui lui était inconnu, cette peur de la nouveauté et du changement, en espérant qu'il parvienne à débloquer ce qui l'empêchait souvent de progresser. J'en demandais trop. De même que pour le sommeil et l'alimentation rien ne se réglerait si facilement.

Grâce aux différents apports en vitamines et en magnésium qui semblaient lui réussir, nous avions des nuits un peu plus calmes selon nos critères. Il ne se couchait plus à minuit. Il ne venait plus jouer sur notre lit à 2 heures du matin en déplaçant bruyamment son garage et ses voitures sur le parquet. Il avait le sommeil un peu moins agité, ne sursautait plus aussi souvent. Cependant, il n'était toujours pas question de dormir dans son lit. Nos essais se soldaient par des hurlements et des pleurs sans fin qui nous mettaient les nerfs à vif et perturbaient Laure. Nous hésitions à employer le sirop calmant tous les soirs et nous l'utilisions pour avoir une nuit complète de temps en temps. Nous avions essayé de l'endormir dans son lit en lui lisant des histoires, chacun à notre tour, mais soit il se réveillait en sentant notre mouvement pour partir, soit nous nous endormions avec lui, pour nous réveiller perclus de crampes en pleine nuit. Le soir, épuisés l'un et l'autre nous cédions : il s'endormait plus vite entre nous. Et encore, il ne dormait pas tant que la télévision marchait ou que nous lisions. La feinte consistait à éteindre le temps qu'il s'endorme pour rallumer ensuite nos lampes de chevet recouvertes d'un tissu pour éviter qu'une lumière vive ne le réveille. Inutile de dire que la feinte était un piège pour nous aussi. De plus, il fallait qu'il soit en contact avec nous deux, nous touchant de son dos ou de ses mains. Sa présence avait chassé notre chatte de sa place favorite, couchée de tout son long entre nous, sa tête reposant sur l'oreiller, et le drap sous le menton. Incroyable mimétisme qui nous faisait sourire. Nous trouvions beaucoup moins drôle son remplaçant, aussi chaud mais beaucoup plus encombrant. Nous essayions souvent de l'emporter endormi dans son lit. Malgré d'immenses précautions, il se réveillait et protestait ou revenait au bout d'une demi-heure, marchant comme un somnambule dans le couloir qui séparait nos chambres, et se couchait sans un mot, pas même réveillé. En plus des grincements de dents, crissements bruyants comme deux pierres que l'on frotte l'une contre l'autre, et des coups de pied, il lui arrivait souvent de ronfler. Cet hôte si charmant nous chassait, nous aussi, de notre lit. Je partais dormir dans celui de Paul laissant mon mari à son triste sort. Lorsque nous eûmes installé un lit à deux places dans la chambre de Laure, espérant que Paul irait y dormir, je la rejoignais parfois en pleine nuit, laissant ainsi la possibilité à mon mari de déserter, lui aussi, le lit conjugal que Paul toujours de travers occupait tout entier. Réveillé brutalement par un coup de tête, des genoux pointus dans le dos ou des pieds repoussant sa nuque, mon mari s'avouait vaincu et essayait de gagner encore quelques minutes de sommeil avant la sonnerie du réveil, en migrant dans le lit de Paul ou dans le canapé. La chatte, désorientée, essaya un moment de me suivre dans mes pérégrinations et, de guerre lasse, abandonna l'idée de nuits paisibles, comme nous tous. Souvent, le matin, je ne savais plus où je me réveillais. Avais-je fini dans le lit de Paul, dans celui de Laure ? Ou étais-je restée dans le nôtre, grâce à un somnifère qui me rendrait insensible à ce va-et-vient ? Au réveil, nous mettions un certain temps à reprendre nos marques. Je trouvais parfois notre lit vide. Le contact d'un corps chaud et rassurant avait dû manquer à Paul au cours de la nuit et il était par conséquent venu se coller à son père dans le lit d'enfant de sa chambre.

Il était des questions qu'on ne posait plus à la maison. Le « as-tu bien dormi ? » matinal en faisait partie. Nous scrutions plutôt les cernes de l'autre au-dessus de la première tasse de café qui serait suivie de bien d'autres pour tenir le coup. J'essayais de retrouver le moral en pensant à cette expression qui me fait toujours rire « on a la gueule en vrac »... et imaginer un visage à la Picasso : la ligne des cheveux en zigzag, un œil deux centimètres au-dessus de l'autre, le nez partant de biais, la bouche à la verticale et le menton sous l'oreille. Je ne m'arrêtais plus au spectacle désolant qu'offrait mon miroir au-dessus du lavabo le matin. Je n'en étais plus à me préoccuper de mes apparences. On verra plus tard, quand ou si le cauchemar est derrière nous. J'avais le sentiment que l'on se rapprochait du « quand » et tout le reste n'avait pas d'importance.

Ces migrations nocturnes se prolongèrent jusqu'à ce que, récemment, Paul accepte de dormir avec sa sœur. Nous pensions que ce ne serait qu'une solution passagère car nous ne voulions pas que le sommeil de Laure s'en ressente, mais il y a du transitoire qui dure. Apparemment, les cauchemars sont toujours installés sous son lit la nuit et les fantômes se cachent toujours derrière les rideaux à l'heure du coucher... mais, au moins, ils ne nous empêchent plus de dormir.

Les psychiatres qui suivirent Paul cette année-là puis la suivante ne nous ont pas aidés à trouver la solution. Rien n'en est sorti, pas plus pour les blocages alimentaires qui rendaient la cantine impossible.

Depuis son retour au biberon et aux biscuits à quatorze mois, j'avais tenté à maintes reprises de réintroduire d'autres aliments. Au début, anxieuse de cette alimentation si restreinte et déséquilibrée, j'en arrivais à lui faire plusieurs plats au même repas : je commençais par une bouillie de flocons d'avoine qu'il avait aimée petit. Il en prenait deux bouchées et s'en allait. Je tentais alors quelques coquillettes, la viande ou le poisson étant exclus : il en était dégoûté au point de vomir si on le forçait à en prendre une bouchée. Pas plus d'une cuillerée de coquillettes. De guerre lasse, je finissais par lui faire les habituelles pommes de terre sautées. Heureusement, les petits-suisses passaient toujours. Il n'était pas question de pain, il n'en a jamais mangé depuis l'âge d'un an où il suçotait des croûtons, ni de fromage. Ne parlons pas de la purée, des légumes, des fruits ou des jus de fruits. Lui faire avaler un demi-petit pot de compote était un exploit.

Au bout de quelques mois, lassée de ces repas à plats multiples qui me contrariaient et ne donnaient aucun résultat, je résolus de lui donner uniquement ce qu'il mangeait avec plaisir, les frites bien sûr, les pâtes italiennes que je stockais et qu'il appelait « des gros ressorts », et, enfin, plus ou moins à volonté dans la journée, des céréales et des petits-suisses. Il refusait systématiquement de goûter ce que je donnais à sa sœur, « je ne sais pas si c'est bon », « j'aime pas, ça sent mauvais ». L'odeur du fromage fondu ou des viandes en sauce le faisait fuir, les yeux pleins de larmes, et, avec des haut-le-cœur, il se précipitait dans les toilettes. Véritable dégoût, caprice puis comédie... comment savoir ? Je voulais qu'il garde par-dessus tout le plaisir de manger, sans les disputes et les pleurs, même si c'était la même chose tous les jours. Le grand progrès a été le steak haché, le retour du poisson pané, d'autres pâtes, mais toujours pas de purée, de jambon, de fruits ou de légumes.

À la cantine, Paul ne mangeait rien, pas même du pain ou un fruit. Je ne voulais pas attirer l'attention des responsables sur un comportement alimentaire aussi anormal. C'était encore du détail par rapport au reste. Contrainte d'aller le chercher tous les midis en plus de la sortie de 16 h 30, j'avais pris l'habitude de prendre mon vélo qui me faisait gagner beaucoup de temps par rapport à la voiture, les places près de l'école étant rares et les rues souvent bouchées. La contractuelle du quartier semblant prendre un malin plaisir à passer entre 11 h 26 et 11 h 32 pour verbaliser les mères mal garées qui couraient chercher leurs enfants. Maudissant ancienne directrice et CCPE réunies qui nous avaient contraints à cette école éloignée, je supportais la corvée en me disant que cette heure et quart de vélo par jour me servait de sport quotidien et ne pouvait pas me faire de mal… sauf accident, bien sûr, ce qui n'a pas manqué d'arriver. Les probabilités de rouler à vélo à Paris pendant trois ans sans avoir d'accident étaient minces. Paul n'avait rien eu malgré sa chute et je fus emmenée à l'hôpital par les pompiers pour une simple radio de mon bras droit que la portière d'un camion avait violemment heurté. Ce n'était pas trop grave heureusement. Je faillis renoncer, en cédant à la pression de mon mari, décidé à emmener mon vélo à la campagne depuis le début. J'avais cependant gagné tant de temps à ne pas tourner indéfiniment autour de l'école – d'argent à éviter les contraventions – et puis, à l'hôpital, on m'avait trouvé cent pour cent d'oxygène dans le sang, un taux de grand sportif, me dit l'infirmier, restait à savoir la quantité d'oxyde de carbone ingurgitée… En tout cas, messieurs les camionneurs garés en double file, ayez l'obligeance de regarder dans votre rétroviseur lorsque vous ouvrez votre portière à la volée.

Apprendre à lire

Je tenais également à ramener Paul à midi, car ces deux heures, seuls à la maison, nous permettaient de continuer le programme que nous avions du mal à suivre le soir, après les devoirs de Laure et la fatigue de la journée.

J'utilisais de nombreux jeux pour que les lettres et les mots lui deviennent familiers. Il refusait trop souvent d'apprendre de façon scolaire dans des livres de lecture ou des cahiers d'écriture. Je me fournissais toujours chez Nathan Petite Enfance où je trouvais les jeux nécessaires à ses leçons mais aussi du matériel qui me donnait des idées pour diversifier ses savoirs. *Crayon vole* et l'ardoise *Megasketcher* le réconciliaient avec l'écriture puisqu'il pouvait effacer aussitôt. Les jeux de loto qui comportaient le mot sous l'image à poser sur chaque planche étaient utiles. Même si dans un premier temps, il ne regardait que l'image, sa mémoire enregistrait les lettres. Dans l'étape suivante, le carton ne comportait que le mot, qu'il devait poser également sur la planche, dans l'espace correspondant. Cet exercice s'apparentait plus à cette méthode globale tant décriée, mais Paul était fier d'avoir reconnu un mot même sans l'avoir lu.

J'avais aussi trouvé très précieux le catalogue *Playjeux* des collectivités. Outre les nombreux supports pour le bricolage ou la construction, il y avait du matériel très bien conçu pour faciliter l'apprentissage des lettres, des chiffres, poids et mesures, réglette à calcul, bouliers, etc., notamment des pochettes contenant 16 fiches chacune pour s'exercer à reconnaître les lettres et les mots. Nous en faisions 2 à 3 par jour bien que Paul se montre assez réticent, ne voyant pas bien l'intérêt de ces exercices qui lui facilitèrent pourtant grandement la lecture par la suite (Janine Cougnenc : *La Discrimination visuelle : nouveaux prérequis ; Le Mot-tilt 1-2, Entoure, Tableaux* [dans le catalogue Playjeux], etc.).

L'*Ordi-baby*, chez Nathan également, servait de nombreux objectifs grâce à la trentaine de planches qu'il contenait. Nous avions par exemple l'action et l'objet : deux images à relier entre elles : Paul appuyait sur l'épuisette et devait retrouver l'enfant à la plage pêchant des poissons. L'ordinateur lui indiquait son erreur ou lui disait bravo. « Qui vend quoi ? » exigeait qu'il sélectionne les objets vendus par le boucher, le quincaillier, le pharmacien... Dans « Dangereux ou pas ? », il devait choisir une image, un enfant jouant avec des allumettes, par exemple, et appuyer ensuite sur la touche « dangereux » c'est-à-dire un petit bonhomme rouge à l'arrêt. Lorsque l'image montrait des médicaments ou des produits ménagers hors de portée, il devait choisir la touche « sans danger », qui était représentée par un petit bonhomme vert qui court. « L'écriture au quotidien » était très utile pour lui donner envie de lire dans la vie courante : la planche représentait des produits de consommation courante dans sa première ligne : chocolat, œufs, pâtes, beurre, etc. La deuxième ligne représentait les mêmes produits empaquetés avec le mot écrit sur l'emballage. La troisième ligne ne comportait plus que leur étiquette aisément reconnaissable grâce au dessin. La quatrième ligne représentait seulement le contenu avec le mot, enfin la cinquième le mot seul, écrit toujours de la même façon, les mêmes lettres de la même couleur. Paul était très fier lorsqu'il avait réussi à sélectionner le produit choisi dans les quatre lignes et je lui disais : ça y est ! Tu sais lire, formidable !... Nous en étions encore loin, mais cela l'avait convaincu que c'était dans ses possibilités, c'était l'essentiel. C'est un des meilleurs jeux d'apprentissage, ludique autant qu'éducatif, que je connaisse.

Avec chaque jeu, je comblais ses lacunes ou ses difficultés : *Découvrir l'heure et le temps, Découvrir les saisons, Découvrir la lecture, La Maison des mots, Apprendre à lire*, toujours chez Nathan, *J'écris sans faute* et bien d'autres faisaient partie de nos leçons. Un autre jeu, le *Structuro*, lui faisait découvrir la construction dans l'espace : une première approche de la géométrie. C'était beaucoup plus ardu : il devait reproduire un mur, un bloc, une pyramide dessinés sur des cartons quadrillés qui lui permettaient de compter le nombre de cubes à juxtaposer et à superposer. Je l'aidais beaucoup car il avait du mal à visualiser l'ensemble de la construction puisqu'il ne voyait pas la partie cachée sur le dessin. Il devait imaginer la construction dans son ensemble et reconstituer les parties invisibles : deviner le nombre de cubes empilés derrière la façade visible. Nous l'utilisons encore aujourd'hui pour les figures géométriques les plus complexes.

Les Incollables sous forme de petits carnets étaient souvent trop difficiles pour lui bien qu'ils correspondent à son niveau (petite section, moyenne section puis grande section de maternelle). Je mesurais là l'étendue de ses lacunes. En revanche, le grand jeu des *Incollables* qui permettait à Laure de jouer avec nous lui plaisait. Elle me lisait les questions pour adultes, et je lisais avec Paul les questions CP, CE1 ou CE2 pour elle, je lisais les questions de Paul très lentement, plusieurs fois de suite, et en les reformulant si nécessaire pour qu'il les comprenne. C'était très difficile au début pour lui, car il avait besoin d'un support visuel concret, qui lui fournissait des pistes ; sa compréhension des questions s'améliora lentement, mais il se décourageait vite.

Je ne savais pas si la méthode de lecture utilisée pour Laure marcherait avec lui mais j'essayais tout de même. J'avais glané à l'époque quelques idées du livre *La Méthode Arthur*[1] pour Laure. Cette méthode me paraissait intéressante dans la mesure où père et mère avaient environ 14 heures non-stop sur 24 à consacrer à l'éducation d'un enfant, ce qui n'était pas mon cas, même si je m'en étais approchée. J'avais donc fabriqué pour Laure de grands cartons, 35 cm sur 10 cm, et écrit les mots correspondants et scotchés sur le mur, l'armoire, la télévision, etc. L'appartement en était couvert et nos amis se moquaient de nous : « Vous êtes tous amnésiques, ici ou quoi ? » Je les avais donc tous ressortis, sans le forcer à les lire. Laure avait enregistré tout cela machinalement et j'espérais qu'il ferait de même.

Très tôt, Laure avait réclamé qu'on lui fasse la lecture. En plus des commentaires sur les images, je lisais en passant mon doigt sous les mots et les phrases. Je n'exigeais pas qu'elle lise, bien sûr, mais elle pouvait toujours voir le mot au moment où elle l'entendait. Par la suite, j'attirais son attention sur un mot ou une syllabe : tu as vu, il y a écrit PA PA, sans insister, puis POT, il y a un O, avec la bouche on fait un rond, un O ; et là, à ton avis, c'est quoi ? etc. Ces mois de lecture « active » lui avaient permis de déchiffrer sans effort, presque intuitivement les syllabes en grande section et de lire parfaitement, sans difficulté et sans hésitation, dès les premières semaines de son entrée en CP. Je n'avais jamais forcé ou imposé un travail de déchiffrage précoce comme certains parents le font dans l'espoir de faire « sauter des classes »

1. Jaona Ramiandrisoa, *La Méthode Arthur*, Éditions Fixot, 1992.

à leur enfant ou d'en faire des surdoués : je me méfiais des singes savants. Elle avait pris tant de plaisir à dessiner, peindre, fabriquer maintes galettes des rois, arbres et boules de Noël, immenses peintures sur papier Canson, que j'affichais, admirative, dans toute la maison, que la priver d'une année de maternelle pour la jeter dans les « apprentissages fondamentaux », si rébarbatifs à son âge me paraissait absurde. Elle était très demandeuse de cahiers de vacances et de jeux, de lectures et d'activités éducatives et je lui avais consacré beaucoup de temps. Elle avait en conséquence des « facilités » et travaillait très bien. Les difficultés de Paul faisaient naturellement un contraste saisissant et je m'efforçais d'accepter cette différence sans lui en vouloir.

Je suivis donc le même chemin avec Paul, sans savoir s'il enregistrait ces mots et ces phrases que mon doigt soulignait. Certainement pas avec la même facilité, mais sa mémoire visuelle était si bonne qu'il stockait, lui aussi, mais de façon plus consciente. Dans son esprit, la lecture devenait un véritable travail, associant mémoire et reconnaissance non pas instinctive, comme chez Laure mais raisonnée. Le découragement venait vite devant les mots trop longs. Au début, je lui demandais de lire en même temps que moi *Petit Ours Brun, Oui-Oui* ou *Bob le bricoleur* : « Une journée char... (mon doigt sous la syllabe)

– ... mante.
– chargée s'annonçait pour...
– Bob.
– Il lui fallait pré...
– ... venir
– ... parer ! Préparer le champ.
– Bob et Zo...
– ... é

– rassemblèrent les ma...
– ... rteaux
– machines !... »

Il inventait souvent au début la fin du mot ou de la phrase, en s'aidant du contexte. Il finissait par tomber juste, puis par reconnaître des mots et je l'encourageais : « Tu vois, tu sais presque lire. Tu vois que c'est facile... tu y arrives très bien. »

Ensuite, nous lisions chacun une phrase, ce qui l'obligeait à suivre le texte et ma phrase. Souvent, il disait : « Non, pas moi, ça, c'est trop long. » Ce qui avait l'air d'un gros paragraphe lui faisait peur. Je le remplaçais et il prenait les petites phrases. J'avais obtenu avec peine qu'il participe, mais c'était indispensable. Si je lisais seule, il décrochait, son esprit se mettait en roue libre et quand je lui posais une question sur ce que je venais de lire, il n'en avait aucune idée. Pour qu'il accepte ce système, il fallait que la lecture aille assez vite, il était pressé de savoir la suite et tournait les pages avant la fin de ma lecture.

Tout cela prit naturellement des mois, mais à son entrée en grande section-CP, Paul avait les bases nécessaires pour suivre les premiers apprentissages de la lecture en classe. À la fin de sa grande section, la directrice ayant la possibilité de rassembler un petit groupe de CP qui ferait son programme propre à l'intérieur d'une classe de grande section choisit cette solution idéale pour Paul, que nous imaginions avec crainte dans une vraie classe de CP, nombreuse et plus agitée, avec des enfants beaucoup plus grands que lui par la taille et beaucoup plus mûrs. Il s'y sentirait tout à fait à l'aise et le changement se ferait doucement entre la maternelle et la « grande école ».

La fin de la dictature

La CCPE (Commission de circonscription pour l'enseignement pré-élémentaire et élémentaire) avait entériné la décision prise lors de la dernière réunion, à laquelle je m'étais rendue moins angoissée depuis que la directrice de l'école de Paul avait fermement pris en main les rênes de son avenir. Les représentantes me paraissaient toujours aussi soupçonneuses et j'avais bien du mal à me retenir de leur crier : « Reconnaissez que vous vous êtes trompées ! Le voilà admis en CP alors que vous l'aviez cru incapable ! Osez reconnaître votre erreur ! Et maintenant laissez-nous tranquilles. » L'évolution me mettait aujourd'hui en position de force, mais je ne l'avais pas toujours été. J'avais toujours en tête une citation trouvée par hasard et qui avait soutenu ma détermination :

« *Les parents, parce qu'ils ont donné la vie à leurs enfants, ont la très grave obligation de les élever et, à ce titre, doivent être reconnus comme leurs premiers et principaux éducateurs*[2]. »

Je ne pourrais jamais oublier, lors d'une de ces réunions, que lorsque l'inspectrice m'avait enjoint de chercher et d'inscrire au plus vite mon fils dans une CLIS[3] je m'étais rebellée. Il avait à peine quatre ans, mais sans lui donner la moindre chance pour les deux années suivantes, elle supposait qu'il serait incapable d'intégrer un CP normal. En lui obéissant, j'aurais exclu mon fils du système, puisqu'elle préconisait l'hôpital de jour et des classes d'adaptation. Je m'étais levée, furieuse, pour lui dire : « Si vous permettez, on verra à ce moment-là ! »

2. Concile Vatican II, *Gravissimum educationis*, 3 11.
3. Classe d'intégration scolaire.

Vexée, elle m'avait rétorqué : « Je pourrais vous assigner devant les tribunaux pour enfants pour "défaut de soins". » Je faillis m'étrangler. Risible... si ce n'avait pas été aussi grave : moi qui courais les hôpitaux et les psychiatres depuis plus de deux ans, qui n'avais pas repris mon travail pour m'occuper de mon fils à temps plein... Défaut de soin, un comble !

Combien de fois ai-je dû leur dire au cours des réunions suivantes : c'est *mon* problème. C'est *ma* responsabilité. Laissez-moi libre de faire ce que *je* pense être le mieux pour lui. J'avais foi en lui malgré tout ce qu'ils disaient et montraient. Je ne supportais plus leurs airs de commisération, faussement compatissants et leurs hochements de tête complices : « La pauvre, elle n'a toujours pas compris... elle devra bien s'y résoudre... comprendre qu'il n'y a rien d'autre à faire que de le laisser au soin des professionnels. » Eh bien non, je ne le leur avais pas laissé. J'en étais responsable. J'avais « la très grave obligation de l'élever ». « L'élever » dans tous les sens du terme. Je n'avais pas « posé mes valises » à l'hôpital de jour. Je ne voulais pas le confier à des étrangers, si professionnels et compétents qu'ils soient. Nous étions ses « premiers et principaux éducateurs » et nous ne voulions pas nous en remettre à eux si tôt et en tout cas pas sur l'injonction de la CCPE. Nous allions d'abord mettre en œuvre, par nous-mêmes, tous les moyens possibles pour le sauver. Cela a été possible pour Paul. Je n'affirmerai jamais que c'est possible dans *tous* les cas. Loin de là. Mais il faut y croire.

Une fin d'année glorieuse

À la fin de l'année, je suivais avec anxiété les préparatifs de la fête de l'école. Sa classe préparait des danses et des saynètes et ils seraient déguisés.

Il acceptait de mieux en mieux les vêtements, mais pas n'importe lesquels : tous les bonnets, cagoules, chapeaux étaient proscrits sous peine de crise. Il s'était accoutumé aux vêtements neufs, allant de lui-même chercher ce qu'il lui fallait dans les magasins, puisque je l'avais habitué à faire les courses. Il choisissait ainsi ce qu'il mettrait, la couleur, la forme et la matière ne lui étaient pas indifférentes, et dans mon obsession de *normalité,* je pensais que les petits garçons de son âge se fichaient pas mal de leurs vêtements, mais, après tout, s'intéresser, prendre le temps de regarder et de choisir n'était pas mauvais bien qu'inhabituel. (J'accepterais même, deux ans plus tard, parce que c'était pour les vacances, une atroce chemise de nylon avec de grands dragons bleus, puisque c'était sa passion du moment...) Il avait surmonté cette réticence physique, conscient que cela n'était plus douloureux, mais seulement gênant parfois. Mais de là à se déguiser ! Se transformer à la vue des autres... à la sienne. Craignait-il de devenir un autre ? de ne plus se reconnaître ? Bref, sujet sensible encore. Et puis s'intégrer à un groupe, qui aurait besoin de sa présence. Comprendre et accepter ce qu'on exigeait de lui, le faire devant des spectateurs. Suivre le mouvement, donner la main aux autres.

Je prévoyais des drames, et les reproches d'une institutrice beaucoup moins tolérante que la précédente. De celles qui empiètent sur le domaine des parents. Elles devraient rester en marge dans des cas aussi délicats. Elle me disait régulièrement : « Il a besoin d'être cadré votre fils, et il ne faut pas hésiter. » Certes ! J'étais bien consciente que, après lui avoir laissé une si grande liberté (tout valait mieux que de le voir comme un zombie), il était indispensable de resserrer les boulons. J'eus peur toute l'année, je me méfiais de la rigidité de l'institutrice. Ça passe ou ça casse, me disais-je, et je craignais que si ça casse, on en revienne au point de départ. Il tint bon, il se plia petit à petit aux contraintes qu'elle imposait. Je n'avais pas voulu en faire un cas à part, notre but était de le faire rentrer dans le moule, de le normaliser à tout prix. Le risque était important mais je le soutenais sans relâche à la maison, vigilante, guettant les signes de « casse » éventuels, et l'encourageant pour lui faire accepter la difficulté de l'école.

Le jour de la fête, j'attendais dans la cour avec appréhension. Allait-il accepter le déguisement, se mêler au groupe pour le spectacle ou tout refuser d'un bloc ? Je mourais d'envie d'aller dans la classe où les préparatifs avaient lieu, l'aider à enfiler son déguisement et le rassurer. La veille, je l'avais « briefé » en lui disant que j'attendais avec impatience le spectacle, que je prendrais des photos, que je serais très fière de lui. Je guettais leur arrivée dans la cour : mais que se passe-t-il là-dedans ? Est-ce qu'il est en pleurs en train de faire un scandale, sous les yeux ronds de ses camarades, avec l'institutrice en train de lui faire honte. Les instituteurs devraient davantage prendre conscience de l'importance de l'exemple qu'ils donnent face à un enfant en difficulté. En effet, les enfants de la classe se comporteront avec cruauté ou gentillesse selon l'exemple qui leur est donné. Enfin, ils arrivèrent en file indienne. Je vis Paul, déguisé, apparemment à l'aise, se mettre en ligne avec les autres donner la main à ses voisins, avancer au son de la musique, reculer avec la ligne, tourner sur lui-même en suivant le rythme... je crois que mon cœur ne battait plus. À la fin de la ronde, il reculait à nouveau et, trébuchant, il entraîna dans sa chute ses voisines qui lui donnaient la main, et les autres qui s'écroulèrent à la suite. La foule des parents éclata de rire, les enfants aussi, je jetais un coup d'œil à la directrice et aux maîtresses qui s'esclaffaient... la mêlée se redressait dans des rires, échevelée, costumes de travers, et Paul émergea souriant, pas gêné pour un sou. Je cachais mes yeux embués derrière mon appareil photo. Un miracle ! Qui l'eût cru il y a seulement un an ? Cette victoire couronnait une année d'efforts pour se plier aux exigences d'un groupe et de ses activités. Le bout du tunnel était en vue, même s'il restait du chemin à faire.

À la découverte du monde

Pour l'été, sur les conseils de Barbara, je mis au point un programme de « connaissance du monde ». J'approfondissais en quelque sorte ses connaissances sur le terrain et de façon plus concrète. Dans son programme habituel, Paul se prêtait de meilleure grâce aux devoirs écrits et aux nouveaux jeux avec une préférence, toute récente, pour l'écoute de chansons enfantines. Laure et les autres enfants montaient des sketches qu'ils appelaient pompeusement pièces de théâtre ou chorégraphies. Paul était réticent à se donner en spectacle mais acceptait de chanter avec les autres, et j'entends encore sa petite voix juste et pure s'accrocher à celles des autres à la deuxième syllabe de chaque vers de *Manteau de pluie, manteau de neige*...

Les nouveautés du programme étaient basées sur les activités extérieures, la découverte et la compréhension de la nature, par exemple, avec analyse du paysage, des sons, des couleurs, des odeurs, du relief. Lors des promenades avec Paul, nous nous attachions à observer tout avec précision : les bateaux du port, leur nom, leur taille, leurs différences, le bateau à voile, le nombre de mâts. S'imaginer vivre en mer. Le temps, les orages, le vent, la météo à la télévision. Où sommes-nous ? Quelle région connais-tu ? C'est près de l'Espagne, de l'Italie ? Quelle langue y parle-t-on ? Nous nous efforcions de décrire les choses avec précision, cherchant le mot juste, la couleur exacte, précisant nos impressions sur tous les sujets possibles. C'était une habitude à prendre. Pas si facile de s'interroger sur toutes ces choses, si évidentes, qui font partie d'un quotidien sur lequel on ne s'interroge jamais. S'efforcer de formuler ces pensées, ces impressions fugitives, qui nous traversent sans qu'on y prête attention. Encourager sa curiosité et prendre le temps de répondre à ses questions. Faire l'effort de trouver des explications simples mais complètes à ses nombreuses questions, y compris les farfelues ou les trop compliquées : pourquoi la mer est bleue ? Et pourquoi voit-on un objet rouge ? Se lancer dans des explications sans dire : « C'est trop compliqué pour toi. » Essayer quand même.

« La lumière est pleine de couleurs, toutes les couleurs de l'arc-en-ciel, tu te souviens de l'arc-en-ciel ?

– C'est quand il y a de la pluie d'un côté et du soleil de l'autre.

– Eh bien toutes ces couleurs de l'arc-en-ciel vont aussi dans les objets quand ils sont à la lumière, les objets qu'on voit absorbent les couleurs.

– C'est quoi "absorbent" ?

– Les captent, euh, les attirent, mais il y en a une qu'ils rejettent, qu'ils n'absorbent pas, c'est celle qu'on voit.

– Mon pull est rouge parce qu'il rejette le rouge ?

– Euh, oui, c'est un peu cela... » (Vivement la physique à l'école, je ne suis pas à la hauteur...)

Il était naturellement curieux des choses et de leur fonctionnement et cet intérêt facilitait l'acquisition des connaissances. L'étendue et la précision de son langage étaient suffisantes dans ce domaine mais paraissaient bien moindres dans celui de la communication. Si Paul réussissait à instaurer des relations avec autrui, c'était pour lui un domaine difficile à appréhender, semé d'embûches ; écouter, comprendre, répondre représentait un effort, et ses aptitudes à la conversation et à la communication devaient être améliorées.

Chapitre X

LES PIÈGES DE LA VIE SOCIALE

Si, pendant longtemps, Paul avait ignoré les personnes pour ne s'intéresser qu'aux choses, il les avait prises en compte par la suite dans la mesure où elles pouvaient l'aider ou remplir ses besoins du moment. Peu à peu, il s'aperçut que l'interaction avec les autres n'avait pas qu'une dimension fonctionnelle – demander quelque chose et l'obtenir – mais également une dimension affective ou ludique. Être à l'initiative d'un échange pouvait être amusant (provoquer son père au jeu du lancer de bouteilles d'eau minérale vides à la figure, par exemple) ou gratifiant : réclamer qu'on le console après un échec ou une blessure comblait un besoin d'être rassuré mais était aussi prétexte à expérimenter les relations sociales. Pendant longtemps, Paul avait rejeté son père dans la catégorie des étrangers dont on se méfie. Cette attitude avait dérouté son père qui hésitait à forcer le contact que Paul refusait parfois brutalement. À la méfiance avaient succédé l'indifférence, puis une curiosité distraite. Il ne nous paraissait pas idéal que son père fasse lui aussi des leçons car il ne le voyait que très peu le soir et profitait du week-end pour l'habituer à sa présence. Si je pouvais me permettre d'être exigeante, parfois sévère dans la rééducation, c'est parce que je lui consacrais mes journées entières et Paul pouvait y trouver de nombreuses preuves de mon affection. Mon mari préféra rester en retrait, renoncer aux démonstrations d'autorité en attendant que Paul fasse le premier pas. Sa patience fut finalement récompensée quand Paul s'aperçut que son père acceptait les jeux agités, sinon brutaux, que sa mère et sa sœur refusaient. De combat de boxe en prise de judo, une connivence finit par s'établir. Des accords se firent sur la conduite de la voiture sur les genoux de son père dans les chemins de campagne en échange d'une page de cahier ou d'un demi-steak haché. Paul apprenait aussi à surmonter sa frustration de voir que l'autre n'est pas toujours à sa disposition, qu'on ne peut dominer l'échange chaque fois ou avoir gain de cause et qu'il faut faire des concessions pour vivre en harmonie. Il posait aussi des questions assez déroutantes dans ce besoin de comprendre ces relations dont le fonctionnement lui échappait : Pourquoi tu me consoles ? Et pourquoi tu as mal quand j'ai mal ? Et pourquoi tu m'aimes ? Parce que je suis ton petit garçon ? Par ailleurs, il ne comprenait pas tous ces codes sociaux, souvent implicites. Il lui fallait, là aussi, raisonner pour comprendre ce que d'autres apprenaient d'instinct. Toutes ces règles lui paraissaient peu logiques et sans raison d'être :

« Il ne faut pas poser des questions comme ça aux gens que tu ne connais pas.

– Pourquoi ? Ils ne veulent pas le dire ?

– Si, ils peuvent le dire mais pas à tout le monde ; aux gens qu'on ne connaît pas, on ne dit pas son âge, son prénom ou l'endroit où on va. Et c'est indiscret de demander.

– C'est quoi indiscret, c'est secret ?

– Non, ce n'est pas secret mais c'est personnel, il y a des choses qu'on garde pour soi. On ne dit pas tout à tout le monde, cela ne les regarde pas. Il y a la famille, les parents à qui on peut tout dire ou demander et puis il y a les amis ou tes copains de l'école avec qui tu parles mais à qui tu ne vas pas tout raconter.

– Tout quoi par exemple ?

– Tu ne vas pas leur dire tout ce qui se passe chez toi, tout ce qu'on dit et tout ce qu'on fait, cela ne les intéresse pas et cela ne les regarde pas. »

Ce genre de restriction le dérangeait. Ces codes sociaux lui compliquaient la vie et le contrariaient. De plus, Paul était très sensible aux critiques sur son comportement et avait tendance à en voir partout. Je prenais donc des précautions pour lui dire ce qu'il fallait faire ou ne pas faire. La notion de « convenable » ou de « convenu » ne lui paraissait pas utile. Les différents niveaux de langage à employer en fonction des personnes aussi lui paraissaient compliqués et hypocrites bien qu'il n'ait pas acquis la notion véritable de l'hypocrisie. Il avait encore une naïveté d'enfant très jeune par rapport à son âge. Il avait donc du mal à saisir qu'on ne s'adressait pas à sa directrice ou à son psychiatre comme à son copain de classe. Il expérimentait avec délices les premiers gros mots et le langage on ne peut plus direct des petits qui jouent aux grands.

Mes cheveux se sont dressés sur ma tête le jour où je l'entendis dire à son psychiatre alors que j'entrais dans la pièce en fin de séance : « Ta gueule, Comoret, je te l'ai déjà dit ! » d'un ton sans réplique. Horriblement gênée, je ne pouvais pas faire semblant de ne pas avoir entendu, je dis à Paul : « Je ne crois pas que ce soit poli de parler comme cela, tu devrais t'excuser, Paul... » Je vis dans son regard amusé qu'il était conscient que cela ne se disait pas, mais qu'il devait être en train d'expérimenter les limites de la tolérance du psychiatre, qui me fit comprendre que la situation ne lui échappait pas et que tout cela était très bon signe.

Je lui fis quand même la leçon en sortant dans la rue. Je répugnais toujours à le gronder ou à le punir sur le moment, c'est-à-dire en présence d'étrangers. Je passais, là encore, pour laxiste mais les mères qui font des démonstrations d'autorité en public, fessées à l'appui, pour bien montrer « moi, je ne me laisse pas faire » me paraissent manquer d'un sens du respect élémentaire. Elles n'aiment pas qu'on les vexe en public, pourquoi le font-elles à leurs enfants ? Je tenais aussi pour ma part essentiel de ne pas se donner en spectacle en public, et je crois à la force de l'exemple chez les parents.

Une voix nouvelle

J'avais remarqué le changement qui s'était opéré chez Paul dans sa voix et ses intonations. Il passait d'un discours plat, monocorde et plutôt vide d'émotions (il racontait un « drame » à l'école comme il aurait dit « passe-moi le zappeur ») à des intonations pleines de sens même dans une phrase extrêmement courte. Son « Ta gueule, Comoret, je te l'ai déjà dit ! » signifiait à la fois « tu me barbes avec tes questions, c'est toujours les mêmes ; ne crois pas que je ne comprends pas ton manège ; t'as vu un peu comment je te parle et voyons voir ce que tu vas répondre à ça ! » Sa voix était pleine de significations, défi compris.

Ses petites phrases pleines de sous-entendus me rassuraient sur sa compréhension du langage si limitée à une époque. L'humour lui échappait totalement et sa sœur, tout en le taquinant, lui apprenait tous ces sens cachés :

« Oh, la, la ! Tu as perdu ton sens de l'humour ! disait-elle à la fin d'une dispute.

– Eh ben oui ! je l'ai laissé à Paris, dans mes peluches ! » répondait-il dans le feu de l'échange.

Terrassées par le rire, Laure et moi tentions d'expliquer à un Paul furieux et vexé ce qu'était le sens de l'humour. Il prenait souvent les expressions au pied de la lettre. Mais il acquérait lui aussi le sens de l'humour quand il me disait d'un air effaré :

« Regarde, Maman ! en me montrant ses talons.

– Quoi, qu'est-ce que tu as ? Je me précipitais, inquiète...

– J'ai l'estomac dans les talons !

– Oh ! Andouille ! tu m'as fait peur... »

Et il riait aux éclats.

Je lui avais appris toutes ces expressions qui le déconcertaient. Lorsqu'il essayait de « prendre ses jambes à son cou » cela lui faisait faire une bonne gymnastique. « Mais c'est débile ! on ne peut pas courir », concluait-il. Quand pressé de manger, je lui disais : « Je ne peux pas aller plus vite que la musique ! », il me répondait, toujours logique : « Quelle musique ? il n'y a pas de musique ! » sur le ton « encore une de tes expressions farfelues mais bon, ça va, je comprends ».

Ces intonations me montraient également la maîtrise qu'il avait sur son entourage et sur le monde qui l'environnait. Moins trouillard que sa sœur, qui sursautait à une porte qui claque : « Aah ! des fantômes, j'ai peur ! » (elle en rajoutait naturellement).

Le « mais t'as peur de quoi, idiote ? ! » qu'il répliqua un jour était si plein de sens que je ris toute seule dans ma chambre en l'entendant. Il signifiait : « Arrête de brailler comme ça, tu me fais peur », mais aussi : « Ma pauvre, une malheureuse porte qui claque... quelle trouillasse ! » et, en plus, un peu de suffisance protectrice « T'inquiète pas, c'est rien, je suis là, je te protège », comme il l'aurait dit à une petite sœur effrayée par une bricole. Cette richesse m'étonnait et me rassurait quant à son incapacité première à décoder les sens cachés ou implicites de tout ce langage non verbal qui découlait de son manque d'empathie.

Apprendre à communiquer

Il fallait pourtant améliorer son interaction sociale, encore maladroite et sa capacité à déchiffrer le langage du corps ; la signification des gestes et des attitudes d'autrui, auxquels il ne prêtait pas attention. Au début, dans ce peu d'intérêt qu'il portait à l'autre en tant que personne, il y avait probablement de l'incompréhension. Dans le dialogue, il était encore souvent à côté de la plaque, sans s'en rendre compte. Il ne comprenait pas que les autres puissent s'attendre à des réactions précises dans un contexte précis. Ses propres réponses ou réactions n'étaient pas toujours adaptées aux circonstances. Il aurait abordé une personne qu'il n'avait pas revue depuis un certain temps comme si l'échange ne s'était pas interrompu. Il reprendrait, au moment où il s'était arrêté : « Alors, tu l'as vue, la pieuvre de *Vingt mille lieues sous les mers* ? » sans comprendre pourquoi son interlocuteur était déconcerté par la question. Les codes sociaux qui exigeaient qu'il dise d'abord : « Bonjour, comment ça va ? » avant d'introduire une question qui guidera son interlocuteur : « Est-ce que tu as pu voir la cassette dont je t'ai parlé la dernière fois ? », lui paraissaient superflus.

S'il arrivait, dans des jeux, à mimer un personnage, il lui était difficile de se mettre dans la peau de l'autre, au quotidien, lors de chaque rencontre, pour comprendre ses pensées ou ses réactions. Ce réflexe naturel, presque inconscient chez nous, ne l'était pas chez lui. Je devais trouver les moyens d'aiguiser son observation de l'autre afin qu'il capte les signaux émis qui lui fourniraient des pistes. Mais était-il assez curieux de l'autre pour vouloir faire cette démarche ?

Dans ses cassettes vidéo, je cherchais des situations permettant de poser les questions qui lui ouvriraient cette perspective. Pourquoi fait-il ce geste ? Qu'est-ce qu'il veut faire croire à l'autre ? Est-ce qu'il ment ? À quoi le voit-on ? Est-ce qu'il fait semblant ? J'essayais dans ses livres aussi de lui faire décrypter les attitudes des personnages, pour qu'il en déduise les pensées. Ses intuitions, car il en avait, étaient exactes, mais il n'allait pas au bout de ce processus de décodage. Processus pourtant nécessaire à la compréhension des pensées d'autrui, donc de leurs actes.

Il faudrait plus tard lui expliquer aussi que l'on ne pense pas toujours ce que l'on dit et que l'on ne fait pas toujours ce que l'on pense. Je ne ratais pas une occasion de lui montrer aussi les divergences d'opinions ou de sentiments :

« Toi, tu n'aimes pas faire ce travail à l'école, mais la maîtresse pense que tu dois le faire, je pense aussi que c'est important pour toi d'apprendre cela. Et si toi, tu n'aimes pas, les autres peuvent aimer, et si tu les empêches d'écouter, ils n'apprendront pas non plus. Ils t'en voudront peut-être de les empêcher d'apprendre, et la maîtresse aussi sera mécontente que tu la gênes. Si tu la regardes bien, tu verras cela sur son visage. Elle va s'interrompre, te regarder d'une façon qui va te mettre mal à l'aise. Même si elle ne t'a rien dit, elle pense que tu es gênant. Il faut obéir à ces signes même s'il n'y a pas de mots. Cela signifie : « Tais-toi, respecte le travail des autres. » C'est le respect de l'autre, pense toujours quand tu fais quelque chose : est-ce que ce n'est pas gênant, vexant ou méchant pour l'autre ?

De même, il devait apprendre à adapter ses réactions aux gestes des autres. « Si quelqu'un te fait tomber à l'école, il ne l'a peut-être pas fait exprès. Il ne faut pas le bousculer ou te mettre en colère, il ne t'a peut-être pas vu. » Lui apprendre à s'excuser pour désamorcer les situations de crise. Je lui « mettais les mots dans la bouche » pour qu'il les ait à sa disposition plus facilement. « Pardon, je ne t'ai pas vu. » « Excuse-moi, je n'ai pas fait exprès. » Je graissais les rouages de sa communication car tout cela ne lui venait pas automatiquement. Pas plus qu'utiliser le langage plutôt que les cris (ou des coups, car bien qu'il ne soit pas violent, il était vif). « Quand tu veux regarder un dessin animé et que quelqu'un te gêne ou fait du bruit autour de toi, il faut lui dire : "Je voudrais regarder ce film, s'il te plaît, recule ou ne fais pas de bruit." Ce sera plus efficace que de bousculer ou de crier. »

Observer les autres l'ouvrait à d'autres intérêts. Ses passions avaient diminué d'intensité et elles n'étaient plus aussi personnelles. Non seulement, il cherchait à faire partager sa passion du moment, mais il se tournait vers celles des autres. Je ne peux pas dire que j'aie tellement approuvé qu'il se plonge, lui aussi, dans les *Pokémons* que sa sœur affectionnait, mais le voir enfin chercher à comprendre l'intérêt des jeux sur la *PlayStation* montrait qu'il était curieux de savoir ce que ses camarades d'école faisaient chez eux. Sans céder frénétiquement aux modes, il cherchait à savoir, à se mettre au courant. C'était là encore un grand pas vers les autres qu'il n'avait jusque-là pas eu envie de faire. Cet intérêt partagé lui fournissait des sujets de conversation et lui permettait de s'inclure dans un groupe.

J'avais conclu, d'après ses dires, qu'il avait du mal à se faire des amis, qu'il jouait souvent seul dans la cour et que les récréations devenaient parfois des moments pénibles. J'aurais moins souffert de savoir qu'il recherchait la solitude ou que les contacts ne lui manquaient pas. Mais ce n'était pas le cas. Il les recherchait maintenant et je me doutais bien que ce n'était pas le fort des petits garçons de son âge de lui passer ses bizarreries éventuelles. Je le faisais parler pour savoir s'il avait conscience de ses difficultés relationnelles et s'il en souffrait. J'espérais ne jamais avoir à lui dire qu'il aurait à acquérir ces aptitudes à la communication au prix d'un travail plus ou moins long alors qu'elles étaient innées chez les autres. S'il était conscient de ses difficultés, il semblait en prendre son parti courageusement et apprendre sur le tas au prix d'efforts incessants. J'espérais ne jamais entendre : « Maman, pourquoi je ne suis pas comme les autres ? » La peur d'avoir à répondre à cette question un jour me faisait redoubler d'effort, moi aussi.

Pendant les grandes vacances, en plus de notre travail de « découverte du monde », je cherchais toujours à le mettre en contact le plus souvent possible avec d'autres enfants. Ma présence me permettait d'observer les lacunes de son comportement social. Je cherchais à résoudre le problème à l'origine des différents « couacs » dont j'étais le témoin pendant ses échanges. Et, lorsque je n'étais pas à côté, les hurlements des disputes, fréquentes et harassantes, avec les garçons de son âge m'obligeaient à intervenir. Paul s'entendait très bien avec les plus jeunes – il s'entend toujours à merveille avec les petites filles, qui s'attachent beaucoup à lui – ou les plus grands, mais les enfants de son âge lui posaient un réel problème. Il arrivait donc en hurlant et pleurant à la fois, suivi de sa sœur qui voulait fournir ses explications, se méfiant de ma propension à le protéger des plus grands. Ce qui était un tort d'ailleurs car je m'efforçais toujours, malgré mon énervement pour être si fréquemment interrompue dans mon travail, d'écouter les parties en conflit et je n'hésitais à reprocher ses torts à Paul si nécessaire. Il arrivait souvent que Paul exige que le jeu se déroule à sa façon et les autres qui acceptaient tout d'abord finissaient par donner au jeu une autre tournure dont Paul ne voulait pas. J'avais donc souvent à lutter contre ses penchants tyranniques, pour lui faire accepter le principe que les autres avaient leur mot à dire, ou de bonnes idées à soumettre et qu'il fallait parfois se plier aux exigences des autres, ne serait-ce que pour leur faire plaisir.

Distinguer le vrai du faux

Il arrivait aussi, et le problème était plus épineux, que Paul confonde la réalité avec la fiction. Ses jeux d'imagination que j'avais vus se développer avec satisfaction l'emportaient parfois au point de se persuader que son monde imaginaire était réel. Dans sa période mythologique, je voyais bien qu'il s'attendait à croiser des licornes, des chimères et autres griffons à tous les coins de rues. Il reproduisait avec application des visages de méduses avec leurs longs cheveux et me demandait si l'on avait déjà vu le dragon qu'il venait de dessiner, magnifiquement d'ailleurs. Les histoires qu'il se racontait ou les explications qu'il me donnait sur ses lectures, car nous avions dévalisé la bibliothèque de tous les livres sur la mythologie, me confondaient. Il était évident que toutes ces bestioles étaient réelles à ses yeux et que j'allais lui en montrer à notre prochaine visite au zoo.

Dans ces jeux avec les autres aussi, je voyais bien que les dangers imaginés prenaient tout à coup une dimension réelle. Un jour qu'il arrivait en pleurant, je finis par démêler, grâce à Laure stupéfaite, qu'il avait eu peur du pistolet braqué sur lui par le cambrioleur de l'histoire – un de nos petits voisins de 6 ans –, qu'il avait couru se cacher, terrorisé, en hurlant : « Ne me tue pas ! », s'étant persuadé que le pistolet était réel et qu'il allait mourir d'une seconde à l'autre. Je ne grondai pas les petits voisins, atterrés par la réaction de Paul et les proportions que prenait une histoire bien banale à leurs yeux. J'expliquai à Laure l'aspect traumatisant d'un geste comme celui-là pour quelqu'un qui confondait le jeu avec la vie réelle et lui demandai de me prévenir si leurs jeux prenaient une allure un peu scabreuse.

Par la suite, elle m'imita dans mes réflexions : « Mais ça, ça n'existe pas en vrai », « C'est pour de faux », « Là on fait semblant », etc. Encore aujourd'hui, Paul me prévient lorsque nous jouons au restaurant dans la cuisine et qu'il demande à la patronne (moi !)

« un steak-frites, avec une bière, s'il vous plaît, Madame ! *mais ça, c'est du faire-semblant, hein* ? », ajoute-t-il un peu inquiet, comme si j'allais lui servir une bière, à 8 ans !... Je me dis parfois qu'il vit dans un monde bien inquiétant pour avoir à se rassurer ainsi aussi souvent.

Je constatais que son attachement à des *routines rassurantes* disparaissait aussi. Sans que cette caractéristique de l'autisme n'ait jamais pris des proportions inquiétantes chez lui, les changements soudains dans son environnement ou dans son emploi du temps le perturbaient. Je le prévenais toujours à l'avance d'un changement dans nos prévisions, car il aimait savoir ce que nous avions décidé pour occuper le week-end ou les vacances. Savoir comment se déroulerait un voyage était important. Détailler l'emploi du temps des journées le rassurait aussi. Je lui disais donc toujours à l'avance : « On part bientôt, on va profiter des deux derniers jours pour cueillir les dernières oranges, rassembler un peu nos affaires, ranger tes constructions qui sont dans le jardin, parce que sinon elles prendront la pluie. Demain, on rangera la maison, on fera un peu de ménage... » Visualiser ces activités lui permettait de ne pas être pris de court devant l'imminence des départs qui le déstabilisaient toujours un peu. (Comme notre chatte qui se couche dans nos valises de peur d'être oubliée ?) Se projeter dans l'avenir le rassure toujours : « À quel moment on est adolescent ? Quand on est adolescent on peut conduire une voiture ? Le grand A rouge, on le met devant ou derrière la voiture ? » Hélas, à voir sa chambre – aujourd'hui un véritable capharnaüm si je n'y mets pas de l'ordre –, son côté maniaque et son besoin d'ordonnancement précis ont bien disparu pour certaines choses.

Son année dans une classe réduite, divisée en deux groupes (grande section-CP), a conforté ses acquis et lui a donné confiance en lui. Il participait au cours en petits groupes dans lesquels l'intervenante spécifique consolidait les apprentissages en lecture et en calcul. L'institutrice le guidait encore beaucoup dans les activités communes et dans son programme personnalisé. Il était épanoui et heureux d'aller à l'école, nous pressentions la fin de nos ennuis, soulagés de le voir si bien intégré et osant espérer qu'il était définitivement « reparti ».

L'immersion dans d'autres milieux

Ces deux années d'école lui avaient permis d'apprendre à faire partie d'un groupe. Mais serait-il capable de s'intégrer dans un environnement totalement nouveau ? Pendant les vacances de février, nous avons fait le pari de l'inscrire à l'école de ski avec sa sœur. Se plierait-il à la contrainte de porter de lourdes chaussures, mettre des skis, suivre avec peine son groupe, faire la queue dans le froid et apprendre à utiliser le « tire-fesses » ? Devant lui, nous adoptions une façade : « Tout le monde le fait, pourquoi pas toi ? », et une assurance feinte : « Bien sûr que tu vas y arriver. » Je n'étais évidemment pas rassurée quand nous partions de notre côté, le laissant se débrouiller seul avec un groupe d'étrangers dans un environnement totalement nouveau pour lui. Je tâchais de ne pas lui communiquer mon inquiétude, mais je revenais avant la fin des deux heures de cours pour voir comment il se débrouillait. Il est rare de trouver du plaisir au ski lorsqu'on est débutant ; je voyais des petits empotés tomber sans arrêt et la monitrice les remettre debout à longueur de temps, rajuster des skis, ramasser lunettes et bonnets semés dans la neige. Finalement, il ne se débrouillait pas si mal, agile et léger, ses petites jambes comme des ressorts. Dès qu'il me voyait, il se mettait à se plaindre en disant qu'il ne reviendrait pas le lendemain. Nous tînmes bon et, à la fin de la semaine, Paul était fier d'avoir obtenu son flocon alors que d'autres ne l'avaient pas eu. Il venait de franchir une nouvelle étape : se plier à des exigences nouvelles dans un groupe inconnu.

Le spectacle de la fin de l'année, où il était déguisé en rocker, jean, baskets et lunettes noires, et se trémoussait en jouant d'une grosse guitare électrique rouge, entouré d'un groupe de « danseuses » nous a émus de nouveau. En regardant les photos, nous nous disions : « Il n'y a pas si longtemps, ça, c'était de la fiction. »

Pour le mois de juillet, nous avions choisi, à nouveau, le Pays basque. Exactement six ans plus tard, les souvenirs de nos vacances passées au même endroit lorsqu'il avait dix-huit mois affluaient. Je me remémorais notre sentiment d'impuissance face à ces petits riens quotidiens, inexplicables, mais qui l'enfonçaient chaque jour un peu plus dans un détachement de tout. Plus aucune interaction à cette époque, un enfermement qui se consolidait sans que nous sachions comment lutter contre.

Mais, ce jour-là, nous allions l'inscrire au club Mickey. Laure était enthousiaste à l'idée de passer ses journées à la plage, de partager avec des amis les jeux et les activités prévues sur le grand tableau. Elle, elle irait tout le mois, matin et après-midi avec la même hâte, nous pressant à la maison pour arriver plus vite, se faisant des copines que nous inviterions au restaurant, les quittant avec tristesse à la fin du mois et réclamant qu'on revienne l'année suivante. Ce ne serait pas aussi simple pour Paul, rien ne sera jamais simple avec lui. Je m'informai auprès de la directrice pendant qu'il prenait possession des lieux : l'immense portique, repéré la veille, avec ses agrès, ses balançoires, son toboggan. Le coin des plus jeunes séparé par une barrière et les caisses remplies de jeux de plage, la cabine où ils se réfugieraient en cas de pluie. Par bravade, je ne signalai rien de particulier à la directrice qui les inscrivit l'un et l'autre pour la journée entière et pour tout le mois. Voilà, c'était définitif et il faudrait que cela marche. Essayer de ne pas transmettre mes incertitudes à cette petite éponge à côté de moi, qui va en profiter aussitôt pour se défiler et moi avec. C'est ainsi que le lendemain, très décontractée, forçant mon enthousiasme, je le présentai aux animateurs, attentionnés, souriants, qui l'entraînèrent aussitôt pour lui montrer tout ce qu'il pourrait faire. Impatient d'essayer les jeux, il se retourna à peine à mon « à tout à l'heure », avisa la présence sécurisante de Laure, déjà en train de faire connaissance avec les filles de son âge. Sa sœur, appui, soutien, exemple, rivale, objet d'amour et d'agacement, souffre-douleur et tortionnaire tout à la fois. Elle est là, ça va.

Une tentative décourageante

En revenant les chercher à midi, je me penchai audessus du mur de soutènement pour les observer à la dérobée. Paul jouait seul avec une énorme balle sur laquelle il roulait, le corps écartelé. Je descendis aux nouvelles : il n'avait pas voulu partager les activités de groupe, trop occupé à découvrir les jeux. Je ne décelai pas le regard interrogateur, vaguement suspicieux habituel. Bon, il n'y avait pas eu de comportement bizarre trop frappant. Paul se plaignit des jeux qu'on avait voulu lui imposer : « Ils sont idiots, ce sont des crétins, je ne veux plus y aller. » J'en conclus que les animateurs ne laissaient pas les enfants s'isoler et insistaient pour que tous partagent l'ensemble des activités. Excellent pour lui mais, naturellement, il ne le supportait pas. Les dires de Laure confirmèrent sa difficulté, non pas à prendre possession physique d'un nouveau lieu, chose qu'il surmontait bien maintenant, mais à tolérer la présence de têtes inconnues, envahissantes, exigeantes et difficilement compréhensibles. Sur le chemin du retour, j'essayai de dédramatiser.

Le lendemain midi, la directrice me fit un signe discret et prit ce ton plus bas, intime, discret, que je connaissais trop bien et qui déclenchait aussitôt cette angoisse viscérale familière : « On n'en finira jamais... » Elle voulait me signaler des difficultés. Son refus de certains jeux qui, je m'en doutais un peu, reposait sur un lien entre les enfants. Voilà la vraie difficulté : faire partie d'une équipe, gagner face à une autre équipe. Et tous les éléments délicats étaient réunis : l'obligation de s'intégrer pour ne faire qu'un avec les autres, comprendre les règles du jeu, les respecter. L'idée de rivaliser avec d'autres le dérangeait. L'émulation, la compétition, lui étaient étrangères. Faire mieux que l'autre, pourquoi ? Juger la performance de son équipe, sa performance personnelle, dérangeant. Être jugé, critiqué par les autres, inacceptable. Se sentir en position d'infériorité, perdre sa confiance en soi, insupportable. Toujours la peur de perdre, d'être dévasté par l'échec, d'avoir à se reconstruire. Une véritable souffrance. J'expliquai donc à la jeune femme qu'il fallait toujours à Paul un certain temps pour s'adapter à de nouvelles situations et qu'il évitait souvent les activités de groupe par manque de confiance en lui. Elle s'étonnait de sa véhémence et de ses colères, je lui demandai de ne pas le forcer à participer mais de lui en donner envie, en lui laissant le choix du moment.

Je rentrai assez désespérée. L'année scolaire s'était si bien passée, il s'était intégré facilement et on ne m'avait plus signalé ce genre de crise. Je pensais qu'il était capable maintenant de surmonter ses craintes même dans des circonstances différentes. S'agissait-il d'une régression ? Cet épanouissement n'était-il valable qu'à l'école où il connaissait tout le monde ? Tout serait à recommencer à chaque nouvel endroit ? On ne s'en sortira jamais. Le moral au plus bas, j'appelai Barbara à l'aide. Fallait-il renoncer à le conduire au club pour qu'il s'occupe, solitaire, à la maison ou à la plage ? Elle se montra comme toujours prudente, circonspecte et je suivis ses conseils avisés : alléger ses heures de présence au club, ne pas l'y emmener s'il est fatigué ou « dans un creux », organiser avec Laure des situations d'échec progressives, pour qu'il se fasse à l'idée que perdre à un jeu n'est pas grave. Dédramatiser les revers au détour des conversations ou des jeux, valoriser opportunément ses capacités et ses compétences. Avec Laure, nous avions l'habitude de lui instiller nos petites doses d'antidotes contre la peur, l'insécurité, la contrariété, la mauvaise humeur, nous allions y ajouter la confiance en lui, le recul par rapport aux choses qu'il prenait trop à cœur et qui le bouleversaient. La carotte aussi fonctionnait toujours bien : « Si tu y vas cet après-midi et que tu participes au concours, on t'achètera la marmotte toute douce que tu as vue au magasin de la plage. » Quand, furieux d'avoir perdu avec son équipe et que, par conséquent, il ne recevait que des lots de consolation et non pas les vrais jouets que les moniteurs distribuaient à l'équipe gagnante, Laure lui échangeait le sien contre le *Journal de Mickey*, insuffisant à ses yeux par rapport à l'effort que tout cela lui demandait. Elle lui évitait ainsi une trop grosse déception et des larmes qui la désolaient. Il était donc assuré d'avoir l'objet qu'il désirait et ne se formalisait pas s'il perdait.

Perdre, c'est gagner

L'effort que lui demandait cette confrontation à des enfants inconnus pendant ces six à sept heures quotidiennes était visible dans sa nervosité : il se montrait susceptible et s'emportait pour un rien. J'hésitais à l'emmener tous les jours : fallait-il continuer ce travail de sociabilisation à ce prix ? Cet aspect-là était important pour ses relations sociales futures. Mais n'était-ce pas trop d'un coup ? Je ne pouvais pas rester assise sur le muret à l'observer pendant trois heures pour aller le chercher si cela tournait mal. Il fallait, là encore, lui faire confiance et assurer ses arrières. Pas très reposant pour des vacances. Je lui redonnai donc du magnésium qui rétablissait son égalité d'humeur, le rendait plus calme, plus patient, moins opposant et plus coopératif de façon générale.

Je constatais les jours suivants que les animateurs, particulièrement professionnels, avaient trouvé les bonnes méthodes : patience et souplesse. Paul commençait à prendre des distances par rapport au jugement de ses pairs, moins vulnérable aux moqueries et capable de répliquer parfois. Il apprenait à vivre avec ce groupe, en évitant ce qui pouvait lui être nuisible. Il prenait plaisir aux baignades, mais se réfugiait dans le groupe des 4-7 ans lorsque la pression des 8-13 ans, plus forts ou plus habiles, devenait trop forte. Cette capacité de choisir ce qui lui convenait le mieux, passant d'un groupe à l'autre en fonction des activités me paraissait bon signe. Une façon de se préserver plutôt qu'une fuite, puisqu'il décidait quand même d'aller au club, alors que nous lui laissions le choix.

À la fin du mois, il n'était plus question pour lui de laisser Laure y aller seule pour nous accompagner dans nos visites du pays : il y a des cadeaux à gagner et il n'avait pas l'intention de laisser sa part aux autres. Je ne peux pas dire qu'il ait acquis le sens d'appartenance à un groupe ou la capacité d'apprécier le sentiment de triomphe d'une équipe qui gagne. Il était encore trop individualiste pour cela. Mais surmonter ses frustrations, sa peur de perdre, connaître ses limites, endurer quarante enfants plus ou moins déchaînés, c'était un bilan positif et encore un grand pas vers les autres.

Exercices de mémoire

La fin des vacances fut plus calme et plus studieuse : cahiers de vacances pour s'entraîner au calcul, exercices de dénombrement, mais aussi bricolage, jardinage, jeux dans le jardin. Heures tranquilles de lecture ou de longs bavardages prétextes à se remémorer des souvenirs, à structurer sa mémoire ou à poser des jalons sur le temps qui passe. Besoin aussi de se rassurer : ces événements qui me reviennent tout à coup ont-ils bien existé ? Les autres les ont-ils vécus comme moi ? Vivons-nous dans la même réalité ? Toujours très observateur, retenant les détails des situations ou des objets, il restituait des souvenirs, même très anciens, avec une grande clarté. Par exemple, il se rappellerait bien plus tard comment, après une profonde coupure au tibia qu'il s'était faite sur un rocher, je l'avais soigné. Regardant la cicatrice de sa jambe, il me dit :

« Tu te rappelles quand je me suis fait ça ?

– Oh ! C'était il y a longtemps, deux ans ou trois ans...

– C'était à la plage, je m'étais coupé sur un rocher, tu m'as porté à la maison et ça saignait beaucoup. Tu m'as mis un pansement.

– Un pansotte ?

– Un pan-se-ment !

– C'est toi qui disais pansotte avant ! »

Dubitatif, amusé parfois quand je lui rappelais les pirottes (poissons), les podates (tomates) et autres guedouilles (grenouilles), il reprenait sans se laisser distraire :

« Tu m'as mis un pansement et tu m'as donné le petit batteur électrique qui avait deux moulinets en plastique blanc.

– Ah oui ! C'était presque un jouet, il était tout petit, cela fait longtemps que je ne l'ai pas vu... qu'est-ce qu'il est devenu ?

– Il n'est plus dans le tiroir de la cuisine, je l'ai cherché et il n'y était pas.

– Quelqu'un a dû le jeter, on avait peut-être perdu les moulinets. »

Plus il me donnait de preuves de cette mémoire exceptionnelle, plus je m'inquiétais de la mienne. J'avais constaté depuis un certain temps déjà des vides béants lorsqu'on me posait des questions ou que j'essayais de me remémorer des situations. J'avais pendant longtemps concentré toutes mes facultés sur l'objectif que je m'étais fixé et acquis la faculté d'évacuer tout ce qui ne me paraissait pas essentiel. Mon attention se détournait aussitôt de l'inutile comme pour ne pas encombrer mon esprit. Les paroles et les actes de tous les jours ne s'imprimaient pas. Combien de fois m'était-il arrivé, vers 18 h 30, quand j'avais fini de m'occuper de Paul, de réaliser que Laure n'était pas à la maison : elle était allée chez une camarade d'école, mais qui ? Je ne m'en souvenais plus. Elle m'avait certainement dit : « Au fait, à la sortie de l'école, c'est la maman de... qui vient me chercher et j'irai jouer chez elle. » Mais la maman de qui ? Vide béant ! Comment ai-je pu oublier cela... ? Pis, j'étais incapable de me souvenir du dîner que nous avions fait quelques jours avant avec tels amis. Ces pertes de mémoire m'inquiétaient. Étais-je à ce point obnubilée par le travail avec Paul que mon esprit triait au fur et à mesure ce qui était important et n'enregistrait plus les « détails » ?

Il fallait en sortir, de cette obsession, et recommencer à vivre normalement. Faire le point. Où en étions-nous ? Que restait-il de ses handicaps, de ses comportements déviants, des anomalies ? J'avais du mal à les distinguer à présent. Ces particularités faisaient-elles partie du domaine du normal ? Qui pouvait en juger à présent ? Pas moi, qui guettais les moindres signes d'anormalité et les exagérais probablement. Je n'avais pas toujours les moyens de comparer les faits et gestes de Paul à ceux d'enfants du même âge. Cependant, je me fiais à mon intuition. Ce n'était pas même raisonné mais quelque chose au fond de moi me signalait le défaut ou la faille. Dès que j'entendais ou voyais une bizarrerie, le *blong* familier me résonnait au creux de l'estomac. Ce *blong* qui vous surprend quand vous réalisez après une heure dans le train que vous avez laissé une valise sur le quai.

Quand Paul disait tout à coup : « Le premier janvier de l'année dernière était un mardi et mon anniversaire, il y a deux ans tombait un jeudi » *Blong*... on s'en fiche du jour de la semaine, c'est la date qui compte, non ? Pourquoi il dit ça, d'où ça sort ? Il ne va pas remonter aux calendes grecques et me dire que Diogène s'est enfermé dans son tonneau un samedi ? Le souci du détail sans intérêt. Faut-il le corriger ? Intuitivement, je réagissais aux bizarreries des paroles ou du comportement.

Chapitre XI

UN GARÇON COMME UN AUTRE ?

Pour me convaincre de cette formidable évolution, je faisais régulièrement le bilan. Mais était-ce possible dans une situation qui n'avait peut-être pas de fin ? Il y aurait toujours des choses à modifier, des corrections à apporter. Pouvait-on dire : « C'est fini, tout est rentré dans l'ordre, ce qui reste est du domaine du *normal* ? Et puis nous vivons tous avec des handicaps, des défauts, des particularités. Qu'il vive sa vie maintenant, sans béquille et sans gourou. »

Le temps des insomnies passé à analyser les handicaps et à dresser des listes de choses à faire pour l'en sortir était révolu. Tout cela était devenu automatique, faisait partie de ma façon de vivre, le poids de l'angoisse s'était transformé en inquiétude plus générale puis en soucis plus habituels, ceux que partagent toutes les mères. Quelle meilleure preuve d'ailleurs ! Partager des soucis de même ordre, pas de ceux qui oblitèrent l'avenir d'une famille entière : « Pierre ne mange pas bien à la cantine » (C'est très bien, Paul non plus !)

« Mathieu se fait gronder parce qu'il n'écoute pas » (Parfait, Paul aussi). « Il est surexcité en classe l'après-midi quand il a déjeuné avec un copain » (Allons, pas si dramatique). Je ne me réjouissais pas du malheur des autres, simplement je réalisais la futilité de beaucoup de nos sujets de conversation : « Il attrape tout ce qui traîne. » Dieu merci, les troubles envahissants du développement ne s'attrapent pas dans les écoles, mais je remarque toujours les rares cas, à l'école ou dans les squares. Un sixième sens. Les attitudes bizarres, les gestes flous, les regards opaques. Mais non, tu te fais des idées... Alors, j'observe les autres enfants : les mouvements décidés, les paroles qui fusent, les regards clairs, directs, échangés et compris, les actions pleines de sens, la détermination dans les gestes et le comportement. Et là, un je-ne-sais-quoi qui cloche, l'incertitude d'un être dans un environnement difficile à appréhender, impossible à maîtriser. Encore un petit martien, poignant dans son inexistence aux yeux des autres, dans sa détresse ravalée quotidiennement. Le besoin confus de lui venir en aide, des idées qui surgissent involontairement, des solutions intuitives. Le processus est si long, si compliqué, il y faut tant d'énergie et d'endurance, serais-je capable de le faire pour un autre enfant que le mien ? Chaque parent doit comprendre, apprendre et agir. Personne ne peut le faire à sa place. Observer et analyser, sérier les problèmes, essayer des méthodes, renouveler les essais, évaluer les progrès.

Aujourd'hui, je constate que le tempérament de Paul est celui d'un petit garçon sociable, gai, ouvert, curieux de tout. Paul ne s'isole plus, n'éprouve plus le besoin de disparaître aux yeux des autres. Le contact visuel est normal et il n'est pas particulièrement timide. Il accepte le monde sans craintes, se projette dans l'avenir avec optimisme et ses rapports avec les autres sont confiants. Il s'exprime clairement, quoique avec parfois un peu d'hésitation comme pour rassembler ses idées, emploie le vocabulaire à bon escient avec une certaine recherche de précision. Il joue bien avec les autres, mais s'occupe très bien seul aussi, sans s'attacher de façon obsessionnelle aux objets. Il accepte les règles et les comprend, obéit aux ordres et se montre parfois très serviable et attentionné. Il n'a plus de comportement répétitif ou d'attachement à des routines particulières. Rien ne déclenche des crises d'angoisse ou de pleurs incompréhensibles. Il se lave et s'habille seul, trouve et range ses affaires à leur place.

Alors, aujourd'hui, quelles sont les difficultés restantes ? Qu'en est-il de son hypersensibilité aux bruits, à la foule, de ses angoisses dans certains endroits ? Elles ont disparu pour la plupart. Récemment, Paul a assisté à un feu d'artifice sans être dérangé par ces craquements qui nous résonnent dans les tripes. Son premier feu d'artifice avait été un cauchemar, Paul n'avait supporté ni les lumières vives, ni les éclats soudains, encore moins le bruit. Aujourd'hui, il réclame des pétards et crève des ballons avec un plaisir non dissimulé. Il traverse les magasins bondés stoïquement, serein dans les bus comme dans le métro. Les bruits des machines ou des appareils électriques ne lui font ni chaud ni froid. Je l'entends fermer posément sa fenêtre lorsque la sirène du premier mercredi de chaque mois retentit : fini les hurlements. Il n'y a probablement jamais eu de véritable hypersensibilité visuelle. Il est gêné en arrivant sur les plages aveuglantes, mais comme beaucoup.

Des troubles de l'attention ?

Il semble que, du point de vue de l'audition, tout fonctionne normalement, sauf peut-être, dans des circonstances particulières. Il est vrai que nous avons à lui répéter des mots ou des phrases qu'il a mal saisies, quand on lui parle le dos tourné par exemple. Ou veut-il s'assurer qu'il a bien entendu ? Il est probable qu'il entende parfois plutôt un bourdonnement de voix sans capter les mots aussi précisément qu'un autre. Les difficultés d'attention que l'institutrice m'a signalées récemment sont probablement dues à cette difficulté à trier les sons. Il a parfois du mal à suivre une conversation dans le brouhaha. J'imagine qu'en classe son audition peut être perturbée par une conversation derrière lui, des mouvements de chaises, ou le bruit de travaux dans la cour. Ces différents sons qu'il a du mal à évacuer brouillent le discours de la maîtresse. Ils sont probablement inévitables dans une classe de 31 élèves. La maîtresse doit souvent lui répéter les consignes qu'il a mal entendues. Mais quand il travaille en petit groupe, il suit sans difficulté et elle n'a pas à répéter. Y a-t-il vraiment, comme elle l'a suggéré, des difficultés d'attention ou de concentration ? Il « décroche » facilement lorsqu'il s'agit de conjugaison ou d'orthographe, je l'ai bien constaté à la maison mais je pense que ce n'est pas le premier petit garçon de 8 ans que la grammaire rebute. Car lorsqu'il s'agit par exemple d'inventer des bandes dessinées – il en a des cahiers entiers – ou de coller des photos découpées dans les journaux autour desquelles il invente une histoire, il peut y passer des heures, assis à son bureau, et il ne veut pas qu'on le dérange.

Les troubles déficitaires de l'attention avec ou sans hyperactivité sont parfois liés aux troubles autistiques ou au syndrome d'Asperger. Paul n'est pas hyperactif, mais ces difficultés en classe signent-elles vraiment un problème d'attention ? Des tests de cognition pratiqués n'ont pu être interprétés par le médecin : les nombreuses électrodes qui couvraient sa tête et son front l'ont perturbé au point de ne pouvoir émettre les signaux au moment où il entendait les bruits dans le casque. Le neurologue a demandé que soient pratiqués un nouveau bilan psychologique et des tests de cognition par une psychologue clinicienne de l'hôpital. J'attends qu'il prenne un peu d'assurance, car ces tests le troublent et ses capacités sont très réduites dans ce contexte. D'autre part, je ne veux pas qu'il prenne conscience d'une quelconque différence entre lui et les autres. Multiplier les examens le conforteraient dans l'idée d'une maladie car il sait que sa sœur ne va jamais à l'hôpital, ni pour des tests, ni pour des analyses, contrairement à lui qui est suivi dans plusieurs services. Il me paraît très important de ne pas le mettre sur la piste de ses différences ou de ses difficultés constamment, comme le font certains parents que j'ai pu voir dans les émissions de télévision consacrées à l'autisme ou au syndrome d'Asperger. J'ai l'impression que l'on a tellement rabâché à ces enfants et adolescents leur différence qu'ils sont persuadés que leurs handicaps sont insurmontables, qui deviennent à leurs yeux des empêchements rédhibitoires. Cela me paraît plutôt le prétexte à refuser tout ce qu'ils ne se sentent pas capables de faire ou ne veulent pas faire. C'est à nous, parents, de convaincre nos enfants que tout un chacun, atteint de ces troubles ou non, a des difficultés et des handicaps plus ou moins importants dans des domaines divers. Si

l'on a la volonté, et pourquoi pas l'aide appropriée, on peut y remédier. Paul a certainement entendu le mot « autiste » dans nos conversations, mais il ne l'a jamais relié à lui-même et ne sait pas ce qu'il signifie. Il sait qu'il a été « malade quand il était petit », qu'« il n'a pas grandi tout à fait comme les autres mais que cela rentre dans l'ordre ». Et quand il me dit, vexé par un échec : « De toute façon, je suis débile, je ne comprends rien !
– Ah oui ? Eh bien c'est gentil pour nous ! Si toi tu es débile, tes parents aussi et là, je ne suis pas vraiment d'accord, ton père et ta mère sont intelligents, je ne te parle même pas de tes grands-parents qui sont des gens brillants, alors je ne vois pas comment tu pourrais être débile. Personne ne réussit du premier coup, il faut simplement s'entraîner davantage. Tu crois que Laure a su tout de suite faire des multiplications et des divisions sans faute ? Pas du tout ! Elle s'est entraînée et c'est comme cela pour tout le monde. Tu peux tout comprendre si tu fais l'effort et que tu ne te décourages pas au premier échec. » Bien entendu, j'ai moi-même toujours un doute sur ses capacités, mais il n'est pas question de lui transmettre et je me force à croire qu'une rémission totale soit possible. Et puis, comment distinguer ce qui provient de son atteinte autistique de ce qui est le lot de beaucoup d'enfants aujourd'hui : dispersion, manque de concentration ou indiscipline ? Je questionne institutrices et parents pour savoir s'il reste des handicaps flagrants chez Paul, mais rien ne le laisse à penser. Il n'est pas le seul à être « dans la lune » quand la leçon ne le passionne pas. Ces difficultés de concentration peuvent aussi provenir d'un sommeil insuffisant – Paul est un petit dormeur depuis toujours – ou de mauvaise qualité. Paul a toujours peur de dormir seul dans sa chambre, il se lève sans cesse si on l'y force,

quitte à rester assis dans le couloir derrière nos portes fermées. Pour qu'il s'endorme plus rapidement, nous le gardons entre nous avant de l'emporter dans son lit. Il revient systématiquement dans la nuit ou au petit matin dans le lit de sa sœur ou dans le nôtre, où il dort comme une bûche, collé contre la présence rassurante d'un corps chaud. Alors, un chien, peut-être ? Un gros, car la chatte ne suffit pas et d'ailleurs, comme Paul s'agite, parle et rêve beaucoup, cela la dérange. Le raisonner n'a pas encore donné de résultats évidents. Le phénomène du sommeil l'intrigue, cette perte de conscience programmée et la crainte de « tout ce qui pourrait lui arriver » pendant qu'il dort l'empêchent d'envisager de dormir toute une nuit seul dans sa chambre. Cette idée aussi fera son chemin, la maturité nécessaire lui viendra. Nous sommes patients.

Le travail à la maison

Je n'avais pas suivi de très près son programme de CP, les travaux personnalisés se faisaient à l'école sans que je puisse voir au jour le jour précisément les notions abordées. Je lui faisais confiance car sa grande section avait été une réussite et je n'étais pas mécontente de relâcher la pression. Le fait que des difficultés aient surgi en CE1, classe plutôt difficile au programme chargé, n'aurait pas dû m'étonner. Ce défaut d'attention m'inquiétait : était-ce un handicap découlant de sa maladie ou lié aux changements : classe nombreuse et programme difficile ? Il est nécessaire cette année de reprendre le travail fait dans la journée pour vérifier qu'il l'ait assimilé. J'utilise des cahiers d'exercices correspondant à son programme et nous révisons de cette manière les points abordés en classe, car certains lui sont passés complètement au-dessus de la tête. Les cahiers Retz (diffusion Nathan), sont parmi les meilleurs : *J'apprends les maths*, CP et CE1 ; *Cahier du jour, Cahier du soir* chez Magnard sont bons pour la grammaire. Je suis presque sûre que dans une classe à effectif réduit, nous n'aurions pas ce travail de révision à faire ; il comprendrait et retiendrait pendant la classe et les quelques devoirs à la maison donnés en classe suffiraient. J'essaie tant bien que mal de ne pas laisser filtrer cette nouvelle inquiétude, faudra-t-il l'aider ainsi jusqu'au bac ? Ou trouver une école avec des classes moins nombreuses, une école « spécialisée » donc.

Ce mot m'effraie toujours autant. « Pour son bien » ? Où est son « bien » ? Devrai-je me rendre à l'évidence que son « bien » ne correspond pas au mien : ai-je tort de vouloir persévérer dans la normalité à tout prix ? Mon exigence est-elle mauvaise pour lui ? Je vois bien tous les jours qu'on lui en demande beaucoup, beaucoup plus qu'à tout autre petit garçon de son âge. Son anxiété et sa nervosité en sont la preuve. Je crois en lui envers et contre tout. Et ses efforts sont immenses. Je prends soin de monter en épingle la moindre réussite et de diluer les échecs dans des réflexions apaisantes.

Lorsque nous travaillons le soir après l'école, il a beaucoup de mal à maintenir son attention, et c'est bien normal après une journée d'école. Je fais en sorte que les apprentissages soient visuels et ludiques. Pour apprendre sa fable de La Fontaine, il me la dicte sur ordinateur et nous allons chercher les dessins correspondants sur Internet. Il est très fier d'imprimer sa belle page illustrée d'une énorme fourmi noire et d'une cigale qu'il a dessinée lui-même. Pour le calcul, nous prenons un stock de pièces, de billets et de petits objets usuels et nous jouons à la marchande :

« Bonjour monsieur, je voudrais acheter un cadeau, mon fils est invité à un anniversaire...

– Ah bon ! cela tombe bien, j'ai plein de jouets, qu'est-ce que vous voulez ?

– Oh ! Ce minijeu d'échecs est parfait, et puis tenez, donnez-moi donc cet ouvre-boîtes, j'ai perdu le mien. Et puis ce bouchon, là, mon chat adore tuer des bouchons. Combien vous dois-je ?

(Suivent de laborieux calculs.)

– Quoi ! 72 euros et 30 centimes ! Ce n'est pas donné chez vous, monsieur... »

Quand pour la énième fois, il interrompt sa récitation d'une table de multiplication pour ramasser son crayon ou me raconter une histoire, je lui dis : « Laisse ton ordinateur enregistrer tranquillement. Comment veux-tu qu'il y arrive si tu l'arrêtes sans arrêt pour raconter des bêtises ? » Les additions passent mieux quand il fait le robot avec force bruitage et mouvements mécaniques :

« Alors, qu'est-ce qui se passe ? Tu ne finis pas ?

– Il faut mettre de l'huile là, dans mon coude...

– Ah bon, voilà, c'est réparé. »

Récemment, alors que je lui demandais de finir son exercice de conjugaison, il me répondit :

« Non, mon ordinateur est planté, il me faut une disquette de restauration. »

Conversations fructueuses

Nous discutons aussi des réflexions de la maîtresse. Je lui raconte ce qu'elle a dit de son manque d'attention. J'explique mon inquiétude aussi, pour l'amener à parler de ses difficultés. Et, tous les jours, je lui répète : « N'oublie pas, la maîtresse ne doit pas avoir à répéter pour toi », ou : « Si tu entends mal, mets tes mains autour de tes oreilles comme des capteurs, comme dans ton pistolet à écouter les sons avec une parabole. » (le « *sound explorer* » est un instrument qui amplifie les sons de façon surprenante. C'est un excellent exercice pour la concentration auditive. Vous le trouvez dans les magasins Nature et découvertes.) Sans minimiser les difficultés, j'essaie de lui donner des solutions et des conseils, en affichant une confiance que je n'ai pas toujours. Peu de temps après, il me dit en sortant de l'école :

« Je me suis appliqué aujourd'hui, j'étais bien concentré !

– Alors tu as réussi, je suis sûre...

– La maîtresse a dit que c'était bien.

– Et elle n'a pas eu à répéter pour toi ?

– Non, j'ai tout entendu et j'ai fait tout comme elle a dit.

– Bravo, j'étais sûre que tu en étais capable. Tu es tellement intelligent. Je sais bien que si tu écoutes tu comprends tout.

– Oui mais quelquefois j'écoute et je ne sais pas quand même !

– Bien sûr, cela arrive à tout le monde. Dans ce cas-là, tu lui dis : "Marine, j'ai pas bien compris : est-ce que tu peux m'expliquer ?"

– Quelquefois, elle ne veut pas redire.

– C'est qu'elle l'a déjà dit et que vous n'avez pas écouté. C'est sûrement très fatigant de répéter dix fois la même chose à des enfants qui n'écoutent pas. Mais toi, maintenant, tu sais faire attention quand elle parle, même s'il y a des bruits autour de toi, il faut essayer de ne pas les entendre mais de te concentrer sur ce qu'elle dit. Et ne pas interrompre ton ordinateur qui enregistre en faisant des bêtises avec Pierre.

– Quelquefois, elle parle trop doucement, je ne l'entends pas.

– Tu peux lui demander de parler plus fort, mais moi, j'ai eu une maîtresse qui parlait trop bas exprès pour que tout le monde se taise. Et, si on n'avait pas entendu et qu'on demandait à son voisin, elle nous grondait ou nous donnait des punitions.

– J'espère que j'aurai jamais une maîtresse comme ça.

– Moi aussi, mais l'important c'est d'écouter, cela demande un effort pendant la classe, mais après, en rentrant à la maison, on n'a pas besoin de travailler beaucoup parce qu'on a déjà compris. Alors, demain, tu n'oublies pas, Marine ne doit pas avoir à répéter pour toi, promis ? Encore un gros effort demain ?

– Promis, mais seulement demain !

– D'accord, mais ne t'inquiète pas, cela deviendra une habitude et bientôt tu n'auras plus à faire d'effort. Tout cela va s'arranger parce que tu es très intelligent. Le CE1, c'est difficile, Laure aussi travaillait beaucoup, cela ira mieux l'année prochaine.

– Je serai avec Pierre l'année prochaine ?

– Sûrement, il n'y a qu'une classe de CE2. Et comme vous serez plus grands, on l'invitera à la campagne et peut-être même à la mer. »

Paul reparti dans d'agréables rêveries, je songeais avec satisfaction qu'il était capable d'écouter les consignes et de les suivre. C'était l'essentiel même s'il ne le faisait pas tout le temps. Quelques jours plus tard, l'institutrice confirmait, étonnée et ravie, ce regain d'attention et d'efforts. Mes « conversations » avec Paul tenaient un peu du lavage de cerveau, mais elles étaient toujours suivies de résultats pas tout à fait inespérés...

Des manies qui disparaissent

Qu'en est-il aujourd'hui de ses manies ou de ses comportements bizarres ? Nous en constatons tous de moins en moins et le profane ne verra rien d'étrange chez lui, ou peut-être qu'il est plus rapidement contrarié, plus facilement vexé qu'un autre enfant qui se montrerait plus placide dans la même situation. Il y a des petites musiques qu'il ressasse pendant des heures, les quelques notes d'une publicité ou d'un CD-Rom. Je l'interromps parfois : « Bon, stop avec ça, cela fait deux heures que tu chantonnes les cinq mêmes notes, change de disque ! » Perplexe ou inquiet, il a des manies comme nous tous. Quand je le peux, je supprime l'objet de ses manies. Par exemple je le menace de lui donner un sirop pour la toux qu'il n'aime pas pour lui faire passer ces toussotements continuels ou ces raclements de gorge qui ne correspondent à aucun rhume mais à un malaise, à une contrariété. Il se passe parfois des journées entières avant qu'il se sente à nouveau mieux pour oublier de tousser. Que s'est-il passé à l'école ou dans la cour ? Lui a-t-on fait des reproches en classe ? Je mène l'enquête et nous en parlons pour qu'il arrive à comprendre l'origine de son malaise et qu'il arrête de toussoter ainsi sans s'en rendre compte. Lorsque les devoirs à la maison portent sur un point qu'il ne maîtrise pas, il tousse ainsi toutes les trois secondes pendant une heure. Les jours suivants, lorsque la difficulté est surmontée, il ne tousse plus du tout.

Quand il m'exaspère, ce qui est beaucoup plus rare aujourd'hui, je me force toujours à la patience, me retenant d'élever la voix pour corriger des comportements incorrects. Mon père, élevé dans la sévérité de l'ancienne génération me trouve beaucoup trop tolérante. Les gifles et les remontrances tombaient facilement à son époque. L'état d'esprit ne se perd pas si facilement. Moi-même, bien qu'élevée avec beaucoup plus de souplesse et pas ou peu de gifles (je ne me souviens que de celle, magistrale, de mon grand-père, agacé par les fous rires inextinguibles de gamins, que nous avions avec mon frère), je suis imprégnée de cette éducation aux principes stricts, venant non pas de mes parents mais à travers eux. Je balance ainsi constamment : sévir ou laisser passer ? Question que je ne me pose guère avec Laure, pour qui les choses coulent naturellement dans un sens ou dans l'autre. Mon intuition dicte les règles sans que j'aie à y réfléchir vraiment. Elles me paraissent équilibrées, justifiées, conformes à la norme. Mais, pour Paul, je suis souvent dans l'incertitude : le couloir de navigation n'est pas clairement limité. Il faut lâcher du lest dans certaines occasions, parfois beaucoup ; resserrer les boulons dans d'autres, à quel degré, sous quelle forme ? Ne pas le briser, ça aussi, j'y pense : qu'il ait toujours une conscience claire que nous, ses parents, sommes toujours de son côté, *avec* lui, que nous le porterons sans cesse, malgré nos exigences, et que ses difficultés ne changeront rien à cet amour inconditionnel.

Se faire des amis

Nous lisons beaucoup ensemble car la lecture lui fournit des sujets de discussion avec ses amis. Plus il a de connaissances, plus il pourra inventer des histoires pour jouer avec ses camarades sans leur imposer toujours les mêmes idées qui le fascinent lui à ce moment-là mais qui pourraient lasser les autres. Les livres de la collection « La vie privée des hommes » chez Hachette jeunesse avec leurs images à l'ancienne, souvent plus attirantes que des photos, et leurs textes que l'on peut résumer facilement m'aident à lui donner une culture générale. Je choisis non pas chronologiquement mais en fonction de son intérêt du moment (Préhistoire, Premières civilisations, Égypte et Grèce anciennes, Gaulois et Romains, en passant par Astérix, le Moyen Âge en passant par *Les Visiteurs*, Les grandes découvertes, la Révolution, Napoléon, Les chemins de fer, La conquête de l'Ouest, La Grande Guerre, etc.). Les mots croisés lui plaisent : la série *Découvrons... par les mots croisés* aux éditions Retz lui font acquérir des notions diverses en s'amusant (*Découvrons l'histoire, la géographie et les sciences par les mots croisés*, par exemple). Ces différents sujets lui permettent de dialoguer avec les autres et de trouver de nouvelles façons de jouer.

Tout cela a permis de grands progrès dans le domaine de l'interaction sociale. Paul n'a plus peur de « s'ennuyer » aux anniversaires, il sait que les initiatives des autres font généralement écho à quelque chose de connu. Il ne craint pratiquement plus les situations nouvelles, beaucoup plus souple et plus à même de s'adapter grâce à une communication meilleure. Il a aujourd'hui de vrais amis, dont il parle souvent. Il écrit des cartes postales à son « meilleur ami » pendant les vacances et passe beaucoup de temps à lui faire des dessins ou de belles invitations pour son anniversaire. Il ne se formalise plus que ses attentions délicates ne soient pas toujours réciproques. Il est sensible et les déceptions le font parfois pleurer. Il y a peu encore, il était complètement indifférent à ce concept d'amitié. Il en est venu à vouloir inviter ses copains chez lui, même pour dormir. Merci Laure ! (Elle invite si souvent à dîner, à dormir, pour le week-end ou les vacances que j'ai l'impression d'avoir non pas une mais deux filles.) Suivant l'exemple de sa sœur, Paul va volontiers chez des copains pour déjeuner et se rend aux invitations avec plaisir. Aujourd'hui, il dresse la liste des invités pour fêter son anniversaire, réfléchit aux activités qui leur plairaient et en organise le déroulement dans les détails ; il prévoit les difficultés et cherche des solutions. Il se met à leur place pour être sûr qu'ils vont s'amuser et tient à choisir pour chacun, en fonction de ses goûts, les petits cadeaux qu'il découvre dans la chasse au trésor. Il lui vient peu à peu le souci de l'autre, un peu plus instinctivement qu'auparavant. Si son comportement aujourd'hui n'est pas toujours très policé (« Quand est-ce qu'on s'en va, je m'ennuie », dit à haute voix chez nos amis), il est à mon sens tout à fait normal et il faut le regard d'un professionnel pour y déceler des anomalies. Qu'en sera-t-il à la période troublée de l'adolescence ? J'ose espérer que sa vivacité, son intelligence et son bon cœur feront passer ses bizarreries, s'il en reste (et je compte aussi sur sa beauté), auprès des filles…

Il reste un domaine où les progrès ne sont pas évidents. Est-il toujours gêné par cette hypersensibilité aux goûts et aux consistances ? Est-ce un caprice ? Va-t-il manger toute sa vie les mêmes pâtes, frites, steak haché ou poisson pané ? Il se méfie de la nouveauté et fuit toujours certaines odeurs, de fromage notamment. Je lui propose régulièrement de goûter des choses nouvelles mais il se braque facilement.

Je compte un peu sur la pression de ses pairs pour lui donner envie de diversifier son alimentation ; à la cantine, à la maison ou en colonie de vacances, ils lui feront remarquer qu'il ne se nourrit pas comme tout le monde et il est déjà assez sensible aux différences.

Le succès reconnu

J'avais traqué pendant si longtemps ces anomalies ou ces particularités que j'étais consciente de ne pas avoir un regard objectif sur mon fils. Qui mieux qu'une pédiatre réputée pour sa compétence, que nous n'avions jamais consultée, pouvait m'apporter un avis véritablement objectif. Au cours de l'année dernière, Laure se mit à mal dormir, à manger sans appétit et à travailler sans entrain. Elle était découragée par la montagne de devoirs donnés tous les soirs par une institutrice exigeante, qui multipliait interrogations et contrôles. Démotivée également par les punitions à l'encontre de la classe tout entière. Ma belle-mère, inquiète, nous prit un rendez-vous chez une pédiatre de renom. Celle-ci examina aussi bien Laure que Paul, nous rassura sur l'état de Laure après lui avoir posé quelques questions. « Quel beau petit homme ! » dit-elle à Paul en lui palpant la colonne vertébrale. « Quand même, tu devrais lui dire », me souffla ma belle-mère fort peu discrètement. La pédiatre leva un regard interrogatif. Je m'exécutai un peu à contrecœur. Tâchant de réduire à l'essentiel l'histoire de Paul maintes fois répétée, baissant la voix si nécessaire, pour que Paul occupé plus loin n'entende pas, je vis qu'elle l'observait tout en m'écoutant. « Je ne l'aurais jamais deviné si vous ne me l'aviez pas dit. Qu'avez-vous fait ? » Je racontai brièvement, une fois de plus, les recherches, la rééducation, les séances, l'exclusion de l'école, mon refus de l'hôpital de jour, l'inscription dans une école privée, les progrès, le succès de la méthode. Ma belle-mère intervint pour expliquer la chance que nous avions eue de trouver cette école.

« C'est l'école qui l'a sauvé, dit-elle.

– Non, madame, ce n'est pas l'école qui les sauve. Si c'était le cas, cela se saurait », répondit la pédiatre.

Sa réponse me fit un bien immense. Autour de moi, j'entendais dire de plus en plus souvent : « Finalement, il s'en sort bien. J'étais sûr qu'il évoluerait dans le bon sens. » Ah oui ? Eh bien pas moi ! avais-je envie de répondre. Ou encore : « Tu vois, ce n'était qu'un blocage, il l'a surmonté. » Et le pire : « Il s'en serait peut-être sorti sans tout ce travail, tu sais... » Non, je ne savais pas et, surtout, j'étais bien convaincue du contraire. L'ignorance et l'incompréhension venaient me donner des leçons ! Enfin quelqu'un mesurait mon travail. Quelle satisfaction de voir mes efforts reconnus... et par un professionnel. (Il est vrai que je parlais assez peu de ce que je faisais avec Paul, doutant du succès à chaque instant et trop engagée pour en discuter avec ceux qui ne croyaient en rien : ni à la maladie ni à la méthode.)

Ayant deviné ce que Laure avait dû subir ces dernières années, la pédiatre la prit à part pour lui raconter une histoire :

« Quand mes enfants étaient petits, nous avions un petit chien et un petit chat. Un jour, le petit chat a été blessé par une voiture. Il avait l'arrière-train paralysé. Mes enfants ont eu beaucoup de chagrin quand je leur ai dit qu'il ne pourrait plus remarcher. Mais c'était compter sans notre petit chien. Tous deux avaient l'habitude de courir partout ensemble et de jouer à se poursuivre. Mais le petit chat ne pouvait plus et le petit chien avait l'air de lui dire : « Alors, qu'est-ce que tu fais, tu viens oui ? » et il le poussait de son museau pour le forcer à avancer. Et le petit chat faisait des efforts pour suivre son ami, il se donnait du mal pour jouer avec lui. Le petit chien l'attendait toujours et le petit chat ne renonçait jamais. Petit à petit, il se mit à marcher de nouveau, avec peine d'abord, puis de mieux en mieux. Le petit chien le poussait toujours plus, et le petit chat avançait toujours mieux. Jusqu'au jour où on a vu le petit chat courir derrière le chien, ou peut-être était-ce le chien qui courait après le chat. » Laure, comme fascinée, paraissait attendre une suite. « C'est une belle histoire, non ? » Laure, émue, fit oui de la tête.

À la fin de l'entrevue, la pédiatre me demanda si j'accepterais de lui faxer une liste de toutes les ressources qui m'avaient servi pour comprendre la maladie de Paul et organiser mon travail avec lui : « Je vois tant de parents dans la même situation et je ne sais pas comment les aider. » Dans les jours qui suivirent, j'établis cette liste. Énumération de livres, d'articles scientifiques, d'expériences racontées, de programmes pour enfants, pour parents, de sites Internet... Qui allait lire cette somme de documents, pour la plupart en anglais ? En ressortir une approche cohérente, adapter des méthodes de rééducation, mettre au point des programmes ? J'avais déjà fait tout ce travail, je devais leur en fournir l'aboutissement pour qu'ils gagnent un temps précieux. Je résolus d'en faire un petit rapport de quelques pages expliquant la démarche, le déroulement et les buts intermédiaires à atteindre. Mais je me heurtai vite à une impossibilité de plus en plus flagrante : tout cela ne pouvait tenir en quelques pages. D'autre part, mon expérience pouvait être utile, mettre sur la voie de nombreux parents déroutés, leur montrer qu'il ne faut pas perdre espoir et leur apporter, peut-être, une aide concrète si difficile à trouver. Ce livre était né.

Toute une famille transformée

Six ans ont passé depuis les premiers troubles, cette patience a été récompensée mais aussi notre endurance et nos efforts. L'état d'esprit que nous avons dû acquérir nous a tous transformés : on ne sort pas indemne d'une telle expérience. Cette aventure nous a enrichis, nous a donné la capacité de nous échapper dans une autre dimension. Entre autres, elle nous a donné une sagesse dont nous savourons les fruits tous les jours. La souffrance donne du recul par rapport à toutes ces petites choses qui peuvent facilement gâcher notre vie. Cette distance est précieuse. Face aux ennuis, on se dit : « Il y a infiniment plus grave » et on donne à ces déboires l'importance qu'ils méritent, pas plus. Mais à accorder si peu d'importance à des choses qui absorbent les autres, on se coupe. Je suis désormais aliénée et, si je trouve des complices sur cette nouvelle planète, c'est parce qu'ils ont traversé des épreuves semblables. Je ne peux plus partager les faux-semblants, les conversations sans objet, « de salon » comme je les appelle. J'évite le jeu des apparences, les dîners où pas un mot de vérité ne se dit de toute la soirée, les opinions à la mode, l'obsession des biens matériels... Je me rapproche au contraire de ceux qui savent se découvrir, ceux qui osent dire leurs opinions et leurs sentiments, sans honte, sachant qu'ils seront compris ou en tout cas, jamais jugés. Ceux qui osent la vérité dans leurs paroles et dans leurs actions. Le cercle s'est restreint, mais chaque rencontre, chaque échange m'enrichit. Quelle liberté j'ai gagnée à me détacher de ces entraves sociales, intellectuelles et financières.

Grâce à Paul aussi, dans une moindre mesure peut-être car je n'ai jamais été très conformiste, je suis indifférente à la critique, au qu'en-dira-t-on, à ce que l'on peut penser de moi, de mes attitudes ou de mes jugements. Quelle liberté gagnée là aussi : être soi-même.

Je me souviens d'une scène, improbable, si toute la famille n'avait pas été mêlée de près ou de loin à cette épreuve. Nous étions tous réunis à l'église pour le baptême du dixième petit-enfant lorsque, en pleine cérémonie, des rires fusèrent du fond. Je n'eus pas de mal à reconnaître celui de Paul suivi de celui de sa petite cousine. Je ne fus pas la seule à me retourner sourcils froncés un doigt sur les lèvres, ni la seule à me détourner promptement pour qu'ils ne voient pas le sourire irrépressible qui venait à la vue de ces petits visages hilares d'un bonheur contagieux. Cette gaieté se propagea aux voisins proches, aux cousins plus âgés que j'entendis pouffer, incapables de résister. J'appréhendais d'entendre le rire en cascade, si communicatif de Laure, qui aurait entraîné les autres de plus belle. L'hilarité contamina les bancs devant eux, saisissant pères et mères, oncles et tantes qui sortaient des mouchoirs pour essuyer lunettes ou mascara. Bientôt, personne n'osa regarder son voisin, secoué par le rire, ou regarder le dos qui tressautait devant lui. Parrain et marraine s'en mêlèrent. Ceux du premier rang, en pleine vue, cherchaient à garder une contenance digne et n'osaient plus se retourner pour adresser des regards de reproche au petit coupable dix rangs derrière, totalement inconscient du raz-de-marée qu'il avait déclenché. De l'autre côté de l'allée, les amis et les connaissances jetaient des regards étonnés : « Ils sont tout de même curieux dans cette famille », ou réprobateurs : « Mais enfin, personne ne va le faire sortir ? »

Non, personne ne l'a fait sortir parce que ce rire-là était sacré et parce que la même joie coulait dans toutes les veines.

À 16 mois, pour des raisons inconnues, mon fils perdit la capacité de comprendre d'instinct le monde qui l'entourait et qu'il devait percevoir comme incohérent, bruyant, terrifiant. Il m'a fallu le lui expliquer pour qu'il cesse de le rejeter malgré la tentation si forte de s'enfermer dans sa tour d'ivoire. Ainsi, je lui ai raconté l'histoire de ce monde « plein de bruit et de fureur ». Aujourd'hui, il a accepté d'en faire partie et commence à en percevoir la beauté. Peut-être même qu'un jour cet instinct, si durement acquis, lui permettra de ressentir l'émotion, la puissance des allitérations de ce vers : « *It was a tale told by an idiot, full of sound and fury*[1]. » Ce serait là une victoire inespérée. J'aurais ainsi la preuve que, contre toute attente, il aura pu s'ouvrir à la beauté, à la poésie, à la musique de ce monde que sa maladie lui aurait fermé à jamais. Aujourd'hui, mon bien le plus précieux est fait de ces images qu'il peut aujourd'hui ressentir, de dialogues sans queue ni tête, d'éclats de

1. « C'était une histoire racontée par un idiot, pleine de bruit et de fureur... » Shakespeare, *Macbeth*, acte V, scène 5.

rire, de sourires complices et de mots d'enfants... car je sais que tout cela aurait pu ne pas exister.

Il est 23 heures, Paul est dans le jardin. Il aime la lune, les étoiles et la nuit. J'entends son pas décidé, il ouvre et referme la porte de ses gestes précis et ordonnés.

« Maman... appelle-t-il dans un souffle, craignant de réveiller sa sœur. »

Il entre, le regard encore empli des étoiles de cette nuit d'été.

« Maman, tu sais, la lune, c'est le soleil de la nuit. »

BIBLIOGRAPHIE

Asperger H., *Les Psychopathes autistiques pendant l'enfance*, Paris, éditions Les empêcheurs de penser en rond, 1944.

Attwood T., *Le Syndrome d'Asperger et l'autisme de haut niveau*, Paris, Dunod, 2003.

Aussilloux C., Françoise Livoir-Peterson M., *L'Autisme, 50 ans après Kanner*, Paris, Érès, 1999.

« Autisme : l'option biologique. 1. Recherche », *Psychologie française*, tome 43, n° 2, Grenoble, Presses Universitaires de Grenoble, p. 111-195.

« Autisme : l'option biologique. 2. Prise en charge », *Psychologie française*, tome 43, n° 3, Grenoble, Presses Universitaire de Grenoble, p. 199-273.

Baron-Cohen S., *La Cécité mentale*, Grenoble, Presses Universitaires de Grenoble, 1998.

Frances A., Ross R., *DSM IV : cas cliniques*, Paris, Masson, 1997.

Fritch U., *L'Énigme de l'autisme*, Paris, Odile Jacob,1992.

Hameury L., Lelord G., *L'Autisme de l'enfant : la thérapie d'échange et de développement*, coll. C. Barthélemy, Expansion scientifique française, 1995.

Jordan R., Powell S., *Les Enfants autistes, les comprendre, les intégrer à l'école*, Paris, Masson, 2001.

Lelord G., *L'Exploration de l'autisme*, Paris, Grasset, 1998.

Milcent C., *L'Autisme au quotidien*, Paris, Odile Jacob, 1991.

Peeters Th., *L'Autisme, de la compréhension à l'intervention*, Paris, Dunod, 1996.

Schopler E., Reichler R.J., Lansing M., *Stratégies éducatives de l'autisme*, Paris, Masson, 2003.

Sigman M., Capps L., *L'Enfant autiste et son développement*, Paris, Retz, 2001.

Témoignages de personnes atteintes d'autisme de haut niveau ou du syndrome d'Asperger

Barron J. et S., *Moi, l'enfant autiste*, Paris, J'ai Lu, 2001.

Bouissac J., *Qui j'aurai été. Journal d'un adolescent autiste*, Sermersheim-Colmar, Autisme Alsace, 2003.

Grandin T., *Ma vie d'autiste*, Paris, Odile Jacob, 1994.

Grandin T., *Penser en images*, Paris, Odile Jacob, 1997.

Maurice C., *Let me Hear your Voice : a Family's Triumph over Autism*, New York, Fawcett Columbine, Ballantine Books, 1994.

Segar M., *Faire face*, Sermersheim-Colmar, Autisme Alsace, 1997.

Williams D., *Si on me touche, je n'existe plus*, Paris, J'ai Lu, 1994.

Williams D., *Quelqu'un, quelque part*, Paris, J'ai Lu, 1996.

Williams D., *Autism : an Inside out Approach*, Londres, Jessica Kingley Publishers Ltd, 1996.

Méthodes d'apprentissage

Gray C., *Apprivoiser la jungle de la cour de récréation*, Jenison (Michigan), Jenison Public School, 1993.

Gray C., *Conversations en bandes dessinées*, Jenison (Michigan), Jenison Public School, 1994.

Gray C., *Livres de scénarios sociaux*, Jenison (Michigan), Jenison Public School, 1994.

Gray C., *Nouveau livre de scénarios sociaux*, Jenison (Michigan), Jenison Public School, 1994.

Maurice C., *Behavioral Intervention for Young Children with Autism*, Austin (Texas), Pro-Ed, 1996.

Méthode ABA (Applied Behavior Analysis), *Different Roads to Learning* (catalogue de jeux et de matériel). E-mail : ctfeat@ctfeat.org.

Monfort M., Monfort Juarez I., *L'Esprit des autres*, Madrid, Entha editiones, 2001.

Leaf R. et McEachin J. (éds.), *A Work in Progress : Behavior Management Strategies and a Curriculum for Intensive Behavioral Treatment of Autism*, New York, DRL Books. (Méthodes d'apprentissage et d'amélioration du comportement et *Discrete Trial Teaching*.)

Lovaas O.I., *Teaching Individuals with Developmental Delays : Basic Intervention Techniques*, Austin, Pro-Ed., 2002.

Lovaas O.I. et Leaf R., *Five Videotapes for Teaching Developmentally Disabled Children*, Baltimore, University Park Press, 1981. Cassettes vidéo d'accompagnement du livre *The Me Book*.

Sabrina Freeman Ph. D., Lorelei Dake B.A., *Apprends-moi le langage*, Canada, SKF Books 2000.

Schopler E., Lansing M., Waters, *Activités d'enseignement pour enfants autistes*, Paris, Masson, 2000.

Études et documents

Lovaas O.I., Smith T. et McEachin J.J., « Clarifying comments on the young autism study : Reply to Schopler », Short et Mesibov, *Journal of Consulting and Clinical Psychology*, 1989, 57, 165-167. Réponses de Lovaas et de ses collègues aux critiques du rapport, publié en 1993, sur le suivi des élèves mentionnés dans l'article de 1987.

McCeachin J.J., Smith T. et Lovaas O.I., « Long-term outcome for children with autism who received early intensive behavioral treatment », *American Journal on Mental Retardation*, 1993, 97, 359-372. Rapport de suivi, par O.I. Lovaas et ses collègues, des sujets de l'étude de 1987 qui indiquait que les personnes ayant suivi les programmes d'intervention précoce conservaient leurs acquis à l'adolescence. Joints à ce rapport, six commentaires à propos de cette étude, par des chercheurs réputés.

Perry R., Cohen I. et DeCarlo R., « Case Study : deterioration, autism, and recovery in two siblings », *Journal of the American Academy of Child and Adolescent Psychiatry*, 1995, 34(2), February. Une étude de cas sur les enfants Maurice par les psychiatres qui ont diagnostiqué les premiers leur autisme.

Schopler E., Short A. et Mesibov G., « Relation of behavioral treatment to normal educational functioning : Comment on Lovaas », *Journal of Consulting and Clinical Psychology*, 1989, 57, 162-164. Critique par Schopler et ses collègues de l'étude de Lovaas publiée en 1987.

« Autisme et traitements », Zwack P. (président de la Société québécoise de l'autisme), avril 1996 www.sca.uquam.ca.

Bulletin scientifique de l'ARAPI (Association pour la recherche sur l'autisme et la prévention des inadaptations), ARAPI, BP 1603, 37016 Tours cedex 1.

« L'autisme de la biologie à la clinique », Abstracts du colloque des 7 et 8 avril 1995.

« Rapport du réseau INSERM 49-20-06 », Pr Pierre Ferrari, coordinateur du réseau, et Michel Botbol, secrétaire du réseau (http://psydoc-fr.broca.inserm.fr./autismplan).

« Avis du Comité consultatif national d'éthique », rapport du CCNE, saisi par l'association Autisme France, sur l'étude du groupe de travail « neurosciences » (http://arachiosa.univ-lille2./autisme/docs/avis-cnce.html).

Les causes et traitements de l'autisme à la 3e conférence du DAN en septembre 1997 à San Diego. Le DAN (Defeat Autism Now) est une association de chercheurs, de médecins et de parents fondée par l'Autism Research Institute de San Diego, dirigé par Bernard Rimland, Ph. D. (www.odyssee.net).

Auditory brainstem responses in autism : brainstem dysfunction or peripheral hearing loss ?, New Haven (Connecticut), Yale Child Center, Yale University Shool of Medicine.

« Prolonged brainstem transmission time in autism : Brainstem Auditory Evoked Potential », *Psychiatry Res.*, mai 1980, 2 (2), 157-66.

Gaze behaviour of children with pervasive developmental disorders towards human faces : a fixation time study ; absence of a face orientation effect in autism or reflection of a lack of holistic processing of human face, Rotterdam, Erasmus University, Department of physiology.

Escape behaviour in tasks situations, Pittsburgh (Pennsylvania), Western Psychiatric Institute and Clinic.

A normed study of face recognition in Autism and related disorders, New Haven (Connecticut), Yale Child Study Center.

Symptoms of pervasive developmental disorders as observed in pre-diagnostic home videos of infants and toddlers, University of Medicine and Dentistry of New Jersey, Robert Wood Medical School, New Brunswick.

An assessment of food acceptance in children with autism or pervasive developmental disorders, The New England Center for children Southboro, M.

Lack of cognitive impairments in first degree relatives of children with pervasive developmental disorders, Hamilton (Ontario), Department of Psychiatry, McMaster University.

Difficulties in the understanding of false beliefs : specific to autism and other pervasive developmental disorders ?, Maastricht (Hollande), University of Maastricht, Department of Psychology.

Jane Shields, Rosemary Varley, Paul Broks, Adrian Simpson, « Hemispheric function in developmental langage desorders and high-level autism », *Developmental Medicine and Child Neurology*, 38,473-486, MacKeith Press, 1996 (http://www.jaymuggs.demon.co.ul/shields2.htm).

An inside look at the neurobiology, etiology and future research of autism (Advocate : July-august 2000).

From impasse to insight in autism research : from behavioral symptoms to biological explanations. Rachel Yeung-Courchesne and Eric Courchesne (University of California, San Diego). *Development and psychopathology*, 389-419, Cambridge, Cambridge University Press, 1997.

Courchesne E. Ph. D. *et all.*, « Hypoplasia of cerebellar vermal lobules VI and VII in autism », *New England Journal of Medicine*, 318, 1349-1354, 26 mai, 1988.

Courchesne E. Ph. D., Townsend J., Akshoomoff N.A., Saitoh O., « Impairment in Shifting Attention in Autistic and Cerebellar Patients », *Behavioral Neuroscience*, vol. 108, n° 5, 848-865, 1994.

Courchesne E. Ph. D., « Infantile Autism. Part 2 : A New Developmental Model », Department of Neurosciences, School of Medecine, University of California at San Diego and the Neuropsychology Research Laboratory, Children's Hospital Research Center, San Diego (Californie), *International Pediatrics*, 1995, vol. 10, n° 2, 155.

Sites Internet et adresses

Les programmes de thérapies comportementales sont disponibles aux adresses suivantes :

Ivar Lovaas
Director Clinic for the Behavioral Treatment of Children
UCLA Department of Psychology
405 Hilgard Avenue, Los Angeles, CA 90024-1563
Phone: 310-825-2319 Fax: 310-206-6380

John J. McEachin Ph.D., Ronald B. Leaf Ph.D.
Services for Autistic Children
3346 Olive St., Signal Hill, CA 90807
(310) 424-9293 ext. 314 or 306

Bancroft Young Autism Project
Hopkins, Haddonfield, Nex Jersey 08033
Phone: 609-429-0010

De nombreuses ressources sur www.autismefrance.org, notamment les articles écrits par des médecins pour une meilleure compréhension des déficiences.

Groupe de support Asperger France. Café de l'école des parents : 162, bd Voltaire - 75011 Paris et sur @asperweb France : http://perso.wanadoo.fr/asperweb

De nombreuses informations notamment sur les traitements, www.filariane.org
Autisme Europe : www.autismeeurope.org/
Organisation mondiale de l'autisme : www.worldautism.org/
Société québécoise de l'autisme : www.autisme.qc.ca/
Explorer l'autisme : www.exploringautism.org/french/
Opleidingsentrum Autisme : www.ocautisme.be/
The Autism Research Unit (Université de Sunderland, Grande-Bretagne) www.osiris.sunderland.ac.uk/autism/index.html

Programmes d'éducation spéciale pour enfants et adolescents de 2 à 22 ans atteints de troubles autistiques : San Diego Schools Special Education Programs Division. Resources for students with autism 3401 Clairemont Dr. Rm B-28 San Diego, CA. 92117. Contact : Mary Lou Evans mevans1@mail.sandi.net.
Programme d'intervention intensive *UCLA Young Autism Project* (1970-1984) et le nouveau programme thérapeutique appliqué à l'UCLA par Lovaas (1987) www.autism.net/lovas.html. Voir aussi les article sur l'analyse de comportement, la psychologie éducative, les services éducatifs et l'éducation spéciale.
The Early Childhood Intervention Center : 2124 Broadway, #338 ; New York, NY 10023 fournit des programmes et des formations : www.ecicnyc.com.
De nombreuses rubriques et articles sur le site de l'Association aide à l'enfant autiste : www.autisme.net.
ARI : *Autism Research Institute* dirigé par Bernard Rimland Ph. D (4182 Adams Avenue, San Diego, California 92116) et les articles du DAN (Defeat Autism Now). Lire les comptes rendus des conférences abordant les résultats des recherches actuelles sur les diverses thérapies et traitements. Résultats des expériences conduites dans différents domaines par l'ARI ; malabsorption vitaminique et alimentaire : traitement à la vitamine B6 et magnésium (publication de l'ARI n° 19 principalement et n°s 21, 34, 35, 81, 85) ; à la DMG (n° 110) ; article sur l'opportunité de la psychothérapie (n°s 3, 14, 34, 50) sur www.autism.com, source d'information et de ressources non négligeable.
Consulter les programmes de rééducation : Doman (*Institute for the Achievement of Human Potential*) ; Tomatis ; TEACCH (*Treatment and education of Autistic and related Communication Handicapped Children : Division TEACCH*) (Description du programme par Nathalie Poirier, Ph. D, consultante en psychologie, concernant entre autres, le développement du système linguistique : le langage et la parole, la morphologie, les aspects sémantiques et pragmatiques) ; méthode ABA : http://www.ctfeat.org/ABA.html.

Autisme 75 : « Le coin des chercheurs » présente les nouveautés dans les domaines de la recherche, des thérapies et des traitements. De nombreux articles à consulter www.autisme75.

Cambridge Center for behavioral studies : www.autisweb.com. Explication du programme ABA (analyse appliquée du comportement) *ABA Resources for Recovery from Autism/PDD/Hyperlexia*.

Consulter les publications de Future Horizons, Inc. (720 N. Fielder Road, Arlington, TX 76012) www.onramp.net/autism.

LISTE DES RESSOURCES

Jeux

- Formes à encastrer
- Topologie I
- Cubes, puzzles
- Dalles de sol, cerceaux, balles, quilles
- Instruments de musique : harmonica, maracas, tambourin...
- Loto des animaux, des voitures, des objets...
- Loto des sons
- Loto tactile
- Loto des odeurs
- Atelier Séquence photos
- Repérage logique
- Crayon vole
- Je découvre l'heure et le temps, les saisons
- Je découvre la lecture
- La maison des mots
- Apprendre à lire
- J'écris sans faute
- Ardoise *Megasketcher*
- Ordi-Baby
- Structuro

Etc.

Livres

- Série *Petit Ours Brun.*
- Collection des « histoires du Père Castor ».
- Série *Oui-Oui.*
- Série *Bob le bricoleur.*
- Collection *Bonhomme*, Hachette Jeunesse.
- Albums des films de Walt Disney.
- Collection « kid pocket », *Les grandes histoires de la vie* (*L'enfance de Ketchup*, par exemple, en collection jaune, dès 5 ans et collection rouge, dès 7 ans).
- Collection « Les belles histoires », Bayard poche.
- Collection « Benjamin », Castor poche Flammarion (*Le coup de pied*, par exemple).
- Collection « L'Imagerie » chez Fleurus : *L'Imagerie de l'éveil, l'Imagerie de la lecture* (avec les cartons d'images et de syllabes correspondants), *l'Imagerie pour la grande école* peuvent être utilisées pour les séances de travail, les autres *Imageries* pour la lecture et les ateliers « découverte du monde ».
- Collection « Méga », encyclopédie vivante, Nathan : Méga poussin, Méga benjamin, etc.
- Collection *Mes premières découvertes*, Gallimard.

Etc.

Cassettes audio

- *À tire d'aile*, Enfance et Musique.
- *75 chansons, comptines et jeux de doigts*, Enfance et Musique.
- *Vivre le son.*
- *Avec ton corps.*
- *À l'écoute du monde sonore.*
- *Les chansons des animaux,* Gens de Lorraine.
- *Chansons de mes 3 ans*, Nathan.
- *Chansons pour nos tout-petits.*
- *Apprendre en chantant l'alphabet*, Le ballon Belgique, 1996.
- *Chansons et comptines de France*, 1-2.
- *Baby music*, Laurent Meliz.
- *Le Chat botté, Cendrillon, Le Petit Chaperon rouge, La Belle au bois dormant*, etc.
- *J'écoute mes contes préférés*, Hemma.

Etc.

LISTE DES RESSOURCES

De nombreuses ressources sont disponibles chez AFD (Autisme France diffusion) mais également chez Nathan, Petite Enfance, *Boulevard Saint-Germain, 75005 Paris.*

REMERCIEMENTS

Nous tenons à remercier particulièrement les familles Dalmais, De Gale, Donville, Grosjean, Mahieu, Mathonnet, Meyer, Parienti, Siry, Rajkowski, Témélis et Zaveri pour le soutien et l'amitié constante qu'elles nous ont manifesté ainsi qu'Élisabeth G., Jérôme et Françoise F., Alice P., Amine B. et Renée F. pour leurs encouragements.

All our gratitude to Michael Aminoff, MD, DSc, FRCP (Department of Neurology, University of California, San Francisco. Editor of Muscle and Nerve) for counselling us and supervising our research.

Special thanks to Beverly Cramb for her constant support and help by providing us with all the American resources necessary to our son's therapy.

I wish to graciously thank Dr. Eric Courchesne, Ph.D., Director of the Center for Autism Research, La Jolla, California, for the many research articles published by the Center that came to my attention.

He can be contacted by e-mail at Ecourchesne @UCSD.edu

The mailing adress is : Center for Autism Research
8110 La Jolla Shores Drive, #201
La Jolla, California 92037 USA
Telephone (858) 551-7929 Fax (858) 551-7931.

Special thanks to Mary Lou Evans, M.A, National Board Teacher and Bobbie Kohrt, M.A, Senior Psychologist District from the Schools Special Education Programs Division (Resources for Students with Autism), San Diego Unified School District, 3401 Clairemont Dr., Rm B-28, San Diego CA 92117 USA (mevans@mail. sandi.net).

TABLE

Ouvrage proposé par Aldo Naouri.

CET OUVRAGE A ÉTÉ COMPOSÉ
ET MIS EN PAGE PAR FACOMPO (LISIEUX)
ET ACHEVÉ D'IMPRIMER SUR ROTO-PAGE
PAR L'IMPRIMERIE FLOCH À MAYENNE
EN FÉVRIER 2004

N° d'impression : 59307.
N° d'édition : 7381-1377-1.
Dépôt légal : décembre 2003.

Imprimé en France